Also by Mark Henshaw

The Fall of Moscow Station

Cold Shot

Red Cell

THE
LAST MAN
IN
TEHRAN

A Novel

MARK HENSHAW

TOUCHSTONE

NEW YORK LONDON TORONTO SYDNEY NEW DELHI

Touchstone
An Imprint of Simon & Schuster, Inc.
1230 Avenue of the Americas
New York, NY 10020

First Touchstone hardcover edition December 2017

TOUCHSTONE and colophon are registered trademarks of Simon & Schuster, Inc.

For information about special discounts for bulk purchases, please contact Simon & Schuster Special Sales at 1-866-506-1949 or business@simonandschuster.com.

The Simon & Schuster Speakers Bureau can bring authors to your live event. For more information or to book an event, contact the Simon & Schuster Speakers Bureau at 1-866-248-3049 or visit our website at www.simonspeakers.com.

Manufactured in the United States of America

10 9 8 7 6 5 4 3 2 1

Library of Congress Cataloging-in-Publication Data

Names: Henshaw, Mark, 1970– author.
Title: The last man in Tehran : a novel / Mark Henshaw.
Description: First Touchstone hardcover edition. | New York : Touchstone, 2017.
Identifiers: LCCN 2017038255 (print) | LCCN 2017042979 (ebook) |
    ISBN 9781501161285 (Ebook) | ISBN 9781501161261 (hardback)
Subjects: LCSH: United States. Central Intelligence Agency--Fiction. |
BISAC: FICTION / Espionage. | FICTION / Suspense. | FICTION / Thrillers. |
GSAFD: Suspense fiction.
Classification: LCC PS3608.E586 (ebook) | LCC PS3608.E586 L37 2017 (print)
    DDC 813/.6—dc23
LC record available at https://lccn.loc.gov/2017038255

ISBN 978-1-5011-6126-1
ISBN 978-1-5011-6128-5 (ebook)

To every American ever held hostage by a foreign power,
and to those who worked to bring them home.

THE
LAST MAN
IN
TEHRAN

PROLOGUE

The students were dancing on the security wall, shooting guns into the night sky, muzzle flashes mingling with the stars just above the horizon. There was nothing Gavi Ronen could do about it now. The US embassy had stood for just twenty-eight years, a little longer than he had been alive. Its former residents were prisoners in the basement, and he doubted they would ever walk out again.

And so the world changes in a single day, the Mossad officer thought.

No, that was not right. It was true that these people would not have dared try this even a few months ago. The shah, Mohammad Reza Pahlavi, would not have allowed anyone to threaten his American patrons, and those who tried to climb the embassy wall would have earned the wrath of the SAVAK, the secret police. Now those men were in hiding, as the dissidents had been. Their positions were now exchanged.

The rot of Pahlavi's regime had been on full display for years now. He had only assumed the Peacock Throne with the Americans' help, and Mossad had done its share to keep him there. The Islamic Republic had never recognized Ronen's country, but Israel and Iran had reached an entente, a friendship as close as Ronen imagined there ever could be between the Jewish state and any of the Islamic countries. The shah, the CIA, and Mossad might as well have been trying to hold back a flood with their arms and no diplomatic words or covert operations would save Pahlavi's throne now.

The young Mossad officer had sat in Honarmandan Park many times before, sketchbook and pencil in hand. The sculptures there, crafted by generations of Iranian artists, made fascinating subjects for his own art. This was the first time in a week Ronen had been able to sit on his favorite bench, and, listening to the screams of joy coming from the fallen embassy, he was sure that it would be the last.

He heard the crunch of gravel behind him and he looked back. Hasan, his Iranian counterpart, shuffled across the grounds toward him. The young SAVAK officer wore a long gray coat, threadbare at the collar, a gloved hand in one pocket and the other clutching a lit cigarette. His eyes were dark, surrounded by more red than white that Ronen could see in the light of the streetlamps.

He came to a stop just behind the Israeli, inhaled the tobacco, and then sniffed the air. "I smell no brandy on you tonight, Gavi," Ebtekar said. That surprised the Iranian. This was a night to get drunk if ever there had been one.

"I thought it unwise to be out drinking on the streets tonight," Ronen said. "Those men are zealots. I didn't want to give these crowds any more reason to look at me than they already have."

"A smart choice," Ebtekar admitted. "Sharia law has come to my country. I volunteered to work for you because I hated Pahlavi. For that, I came to work for you, but these animals are worse." He sat down on the bench next to the Israeli. The men looked out toward the embassy and listened to the cheers and occasional screams that sounded from that quarter.

"I am surprised to see you here, drunk or not," Gavi admitted.

"I wanted to say my good-byes. Our friendship has meant at least that much to me."

"And to me. How many, do you think?" Ronen asked, nodding to the embassy.

"How many hostages?" Hasan lifted the cigarette to his lips.

"How many hostage *takers*?" Ronen corrected him. "Five hundred?"

Hasan considered the question, studied the dancing silhouette of bodies on the wall. The streets were full, a writhing mass of people in every direction. "Five hundred? At least. Ten times that on the streets," he replied, exhaling smoke. "There will be that many again here by morning."

"And the SAVAK will do nothing?" Ronen asked.

"If there was anything the SAVAK could do, we would have done it already." Hasan shook his head and spoke slowly. "Only guns could stop this and Pahlavi isn't here to give such orders."

"Even if he was here, I do not know if the military would follow him," the Israeli replied. "They can see where this is going as well as anyone."

Hasan nodded. "It was a mistake for the Americans to help Pahlavi hold the throne." Another wave of the cigarette, another long drag. He was speaking to the air now, as though Ronen was no more than a ghost. "He tried to hide his brutality, but such secrets cannot be hidden, and he made you and the Americans into butchers by association."

Ronen had never heard an Iranian speak like this. "Do you say this out of honesty or fear?"

Hasan looked over at his friend. He threw his cigarette into the trees behind the bench, not caring whether it started a fire. A blaze would hardly be noticed on a night like this. "You think I'm crazy to speak my mind?"

"I think that any former SAVAK officer will have to choose his words carefully from this day on," Ronen advised.

Hasan smiled. "So true." He pointed a gloved finger at the embassy. "Do you see those cameras down there? The world is watching this and they know what it means. The shah will not see his country again."

"Maybe his generals will organize a coup—"

"There will be no coup," Hasan assured his friend. "Iran is lost to the West."

"If that is true, what comes after?" Ronen asked.

"I heard a Latin phrase once that I think is appropriate. *Horror vacui.*"

Ronen frowned, squinted at him in the darkness. The lights from the embassy drew hard shadows on his face. "I don't understand."

"It's an ancient saying that physicists love. Aristotle penned it, I think. 'Nature abhors a vacuum.'" He put a hand on his friend's shoulder. "When one government falls, something must take its place and rule the masses. The shah has fallen and someone must take his place . . . Khomenei, no doubt. But the shah kept order through fear. It is what these people know."

Hasan paused to stare at the glow of the embassy lights in the distance, then continued. "To keep them from turning on him as they have on the shah, Khomenei will need to give them something they fear more. What he will give them is America and Israel. Iran will become your eternal enemy. Khomenei will call for Israel's destruction and his followers will never stop trying to fulfill his wish. Your neighbors have learned not to attack your country directly, but my country is far enough from Israel that we cannot attack you directly in force. So we will do so in other ways. There will be bombings in your streets, kidnappings, hijackings of your planes. Israel will survive, that I do not doubt, but she will never know peace."

"My people have not known peace in more than two thousand years," Ronen told his friend. He let that fact hang in the air before turning to the more immediate problem. "I have destroyed our records of you, all the papers shredded and burned. No one will know that you were an informant for Israel."

"I thank you." Ebtekar lit another cigarette, inhaled the smoke, blew it out slow into the dark. "You need to leave Iran and go home.

Tonight. Things are going to move very quickly now. Come the morning, this confusion will end and Khomenei's people will get organized. They will begin looking for any Americans and Israelis still inside our borders, and especially those working for the CIA or Mossad. It will not be safe here for you or any of your people, and the CIA will not be able to help you." He pointed to the captured embassy. "Even if they do come, they will try to rescue their own people first. The SAVAK certainly will not risk themselves for you. We are scattered and our leaders will be lucky if prison is all they receive once our files are opened."

"And you?"

"I will be fine. I destroyed my own service records this afternoon. These mobs will sack SAVAK headquarters, so my records will not be missed. With your papers and mine destroyed, I will be able to reinvent myself as a new man. The line officers will disappear into the crowds until the worst is over, but the high leadership will be executed if they don't escape the country. Those of us left will go to work for whatever intelligence service Khomenei and his people establish after. They will need a secret police as much as the shah, perhaps more. Revolutionaries are a paranoid lot. They imagine there are counterrevolutionaries everywhere. A few months from now, it will be business as usual for me, a new man doing an old job in the service of a new master."

"And they will not recognize you?"

"I think not." Hasan ran his open hand over his clean-shaven cheeks. "If nothing else, I will have a beard. These zealots will require that much." He sighed. "But Gavi—"

"Yes?"

The Muslim didn't answer his Jewish friend immediately. He took a long drag on his cigarette, never looking away from the students dancing on the embassy walls. "I told you that I volunteered to work for you because I hated Pahlavi. That was only half of the truth. The other half is that I came to hope that our countries could become true friends. I have come to see through you what most of our people have never considered and do not believe . . . that the Jews only want a safe home. I don't know where Mossad will send you after this . . . but wherever you go, always keep your eyes here on Tehran. Khomenei and those who come after him will call for Israel to be pushed into the sea, but they have seen you defeat the Arab armies and how you deal with terrorists. That will leave them only one option. Do not ever let them lay hands on it."

Ronen digested the man's words. What was the term he had heard the Americans use? *The Islamic Bomb.* "That would be the most difficult mission Mossad ever takes," he said, his voice depressed. "And the most vicious."

"I know. That is why men like you should lead it. It is as your boss, Meir Dagan, has often said: 'The dirtiest actions should be carried out by the most honest men.' You are the most honest man I know," Hasan told the Israeli. He looked to his friend. "I do not think you and I will see each other again after tonight. To survive, I will have to become one of *them* and I will have to do some very ugly things." He waved his hand toward the yells of the revolutionaries in the distance. "I will have to hurt your country. Please trust that I will take no pleasure in it, no matter what you may ever hear of me. And I will try to curb the worst of it. I will do what I can to stop my people from getting their hands on the bomb, because I know what they would do with it. I do not want to see a small group of men turn us all into monsters."

Ronen nodded slowly. Hasan's words were sour, like bile in his chest. "I suppose we will never share that dinner in Jerusalem that I promised you."

"I should like to have seen the Dome of the Rock," Hasan said, regret in his voice.

"I will miss your company," Ronen said. He meant it as much as anything he'd ever said.

"*Bedrood*, my friend."

"*Tzeth'a leshalom*, Hasan." *Go in peace.*

"I think peace will have to wait for the next life." Hasan took off his coat and laid it on the bench. He tossed his spent cigarette onto the ground, reached into the pocket and pulled out his cigarette case and lighter, ready to feed his addiction again. He started to extract another cigarette from the metal case, then stopped and stared at the box. "I think I've lost my taste for them," he said. Then he smiled. "The first step to becoming a new man." The SAVAK officer set the case and the lighter on the bench next to the young Israeli. He turned his back on the American embassy and his friend and walked back to the park entrance, slower than he had come.

CHAPTER ONE

The Port of Haifa
Israel

He had never traveled on the sea before, and it was a very strange experience, motion but no mechanical sound. Fu'ad had never realized how the mind associates movement with the sound of motors and engines, but there was none of that on this vessel. Instead, he could hear the gulls in the air, the wash of the waves breaking under the bow, even the noise of the cranes and dockworkers still a nautical mile distant. The ship was moving slowly now as she moved to take her place in Israel's largest port beside fifty-six other vessels. Only five were cargo ships like the *River Thames*, which surprised him. The rest were pleasure craft, fishing boats, trawlers, and tugs. There was no need to have dozens of large craft coming in daily, he supposed. Israel was a small nation, after all. Haifa itself was the third-largest city but only a quarter million people lived there. The air was clean, scoured of any pollution by the Mediterranean winds, and he could see the city rising behind the docks. It was large to his eyes, so open and uncrowded compared to the Gaza slums. The injustice of it was maddening.

A quarter million, he thought. After today, this city would be left desolate; every person here would leave on their own, running like rats, and he hoped it would be a hundred years before anyone could return. Allah's obedient children would not be able to live here either, but better no one should have this city than the Jews, who would not be here in a hundred years to reclaim Haifa, he was sure. Today would be hailed by his children as the day when the Arabs finally began to push the Zionists into the sea. It occurred to him that it was a fitting irony that he would start that very campaign by riding into Israel on the sea itself.

He had never felt such liberty in all his life, another irony, that he would only feel this so near the end. He had spent so many years in the Gaza Strip, then in the West Bank, always behind walls and never free to really go where he wished. Hopeful, he had escaped to Lebanon and then a job working on the docks in Beirut for slave wages. He watched the ships come and go every day and felt the pull that all mariners had felt since before Abraham's own time. He had tried to become a sailor but no ship's captain hired him, even for menial work. There were a hundred men vying for even the lowest of jobs on the cargo ships. The sea was the easiest way to leave the Middle East. A man could simply disappear in a Mediterranean port town and make his way north into Europe, where he could make a life away from the Jews and their endless security walls and checkpoints. Fu'ad had watched as man after man, chosen almost at random by the captains, had disappeared from the docks, sailing west or south while he ran his forklift day after day. He had no woman to lift his spirit, just the prostitutes; no home but for the dirty flat he shared with three others he disliked; no wealth as he had to spend his money as fast as he could earn it just to eat and drink and pay the rent on his shelter.

Finally, his anger at Israel and life itself was more than he could bear and he had joined in the bitterness of the men around him. Though they never talked openly of it, some of his friends on the docks were Hezbollah and he asked to join them. They took him in and he found meaning there for a time . . . but the jobs they gave him were tedious, moving more cargo, driving a truck now and again. It put a little more money in his pocket, just enough to buy better food and cleaner women.

He'd been ready to abandon the docks and Hezbollah when the Iranians had come and made him the offer. How they came to choose him he wasn't sure and never asked, but he had no future here or back in Israel, so he accepted his one chance to give his life some meaning. They'd flown him to some African country, kept him in some safe house, and given him the expensive food and other pleasures that he'd lusted after but rarely known. Then, after a month's wait, they'd brought him to the ship and given him his instructions. He'd boarded and taken up the mop, feeling more like the captain of the ship than the low deckhand he was.

He was outside the walls and off the docks, a free man at last. This was how Allah meant for his chosen children to live, and that divine feeling was his sure sign that his mission was the right course, a small taste of what would surely be his for all eternity after his death. From this moment on, he would feel no more pain, even at the end.

The Haifa dock approached. Workers began moving cranes and forklifts into position. Then he saw the crowd assembled on the portside dock. Israeli police were enforcing a cordon. A forklift was on its side, a wrecked container on the ground nearby. However it happened, several people had been hurt in the accident, judging by the number of emergency vehicles. Fu'ad could hardly believe the blessing. All of them would be within a few feet of the *River Thames*. More casualties now and fewer police and paramedics to come after them to help the wounded.

The cargo ship crawled to a stop.

Fu'ad looked skyward and enjoyed the last feeling of cool air gliding over his cheeks. He said his prayer, a benediction on his whole life, pleading for the divine being he would see in a few seconds to accept him and grant him every promised blessing.

He finished speaking to God. He walked over to the one container that he'd kept watch over for the weeklong journey. It was forty feet long, eight feet wide and tall, a standard ISO container in every respect except for the addition of an electronic lock mounted on the front. Type in one code and the door would open.

Fu'ad began typing a different code.

Inside the container, wires ran out of the electronic lock, down to a black box on the floor. The detonators connecting the dozens of barrels of fuel-air explosives that filled the more than two thousand cubic feet were all tied together in a long braid from the explosive blocks to the box. A dozen Semtex bricks were affixed to the walls and ceiling, equally spaced at carefully chosen points. In the center of the barrels sat a series of warm metal canisters filled with a fine powder.

Sure of his course, Fu'ad inhaled his last breath of clean sea air, his last taste of the unhappy world as he pressed the last button.

The Semtex bricks lining the walls of the container detonated first, breaching the container immediately. Fu'ad died as his body was hurled into the air and ripped to pieces by the container walls, which in turn were shredded into metal shards by the expanding pressure wave that was pushing vapor outward in all directions.

The second set of explosives was far less powerful. They fired a fraction of a second after the first, breaching the pressurized barrels of vaporized explosive. Powdered aluminum and magnesium mixed with an oxidizer rushed outward at a frightening rate, smothering the ship's deck and the docks on both sides.

It was the third explosive, the smallest of all, that did the real work. It was a single scatter charge weighing only a few pounds. It fired straight up—

—and the floating cloud ignited.

The pressure wave from the thermobaric bomb was fearsome, a fireball of burning metal particulates that expanded outward in all directions. Wherever the floating gas reached, the fire followed, a million burning tendrils snaking out in a million directions, into every crack and crevice within reach, aboard the ship and on the dry ground below . . . and into the lungs of those who had started to inhale the flammable gas in the fraction of a second before the pressure wave had struck them.

Fu'ad's body was vaporized a moment after it became a corpse, nothing left to identify. The crew of the *River Thames* farther aft died a moment later as the explosion reached them, a wall of flames compressed to the density of steel, burning them alive, shattering their bones, and pulverizing their flesh all at once.

The dockworkers and first responders on the dock died in the same moment. The few bits of their bodies that survived the pounding and immolation were either tossed into the Mediterranean Sea or burned into the side of the vessel next to the *River Thames*.

Cargo containers from the vessel's deck were hurled hundreds of yards in every direction, most in pieces, a few largely intact. Those people in the direct line of sight were dissected by shrapnel flying almost at a bullet's speed. A few were crushed to death by the larger pieces falling like meteors flung down from the stars above their heads.

Unlucky men and women farther from the blast were burned alive, hurled into metal walls, their bones shattering and organs crushed. They died quickly, but not immediately, and in great agony. Some died from the shock wave and flying debris, others were shredded to death by the shrapnel, and a few of the unlucky ones who burned to death lasted just long enough to realize through the agony of their burning skin how they were dying.

The hull of the *River Thames* cracked open, the vessel splitting wide. Seawater poured inside, and the men who had been protected by layers of steel between them and Fu'ad's cargo were thrown into the bulkheads. In half a minute the water had reached both ends of the ship, which began tilting at unnatural angles.

The shock wave also rose straight up, pulling the superheated air along in its wake as it reached for the sky. Mixed in the air was dirt and burning soot, bits of bodies and pulverized metal, and the powder from the warm metal canisters that had sat in the middle of the container—strontium 90, thirty pounds of pulverized dust. The cans, heated from the inside by radiation, disintegrated instantly in the explosion, freeing the strontium to fly into the air. Much of it spread out along the docks. More than half the dust flew skyward, straight up, until the winds overpowered it and began to carry it outward.

The physicist advising the men who had planned the operation had told them that this particular isotope would be perfect for their purposes. Strontium was a "bone seeker" that acted like calcium inside the human body, where it would deposit itself in the bone and marrow and become impossible to remove. Those few unlucky souls who ingested enough would develop bone and blood cancers, Ewing's sarcoma, and leukemia. Their deaths would be horrifying.

The winds were moving eastward at five meters per second. Within two minutes, the strontium traveled over two kilometers and started to descend.

Fearing that Hamas or Hezbollah would someday try to smuggle a nuclear device into their country, Israel's security services had been installing radiation detectors in their ports for years. Inside the port's operations center, computer screens began to scream at their users—beta particles detected in unnatural amounts, gamma photons elevated far above normal. The operators, seeing the explosion on their monitors, hoped at first it was a faulty sensor, an instrumentation fault. Then a second sensor was triggered, then a third, the rate increasing. They were still alive to see the report, so they knew that a nuclear weapon had not been used, which left only a single possibility.

Someone had finally used a radiological dispersion device on Israeli soil, a dirty bomb that would render the Port of Haifa uninhabitable until Israel could find a way to reclaim it from the radioactive dust that would settle on every surface, every roof, and every road along the air current's path. Every building would have to be scrubbed clean, the streets washed down, and the radioactive wash collected for disposal. Every square inch of topsoil would have to be excavated and hauled away to some northern desert, probably the Golan. Let the Syrians have it, they would say. They were still fighting their civil war and in no position to object.

There was no way to warn the people before some would ingest the particulates. In a few minutes, the strontium would reach ground level and children and their parents, and certainly hundreds, probably thousands, were breathing in the strontium. Dispersed as it was over so wide an area, most would not absorb enough to significantly increase their chances of dying in a cancer ward, but that hardly mattered. The fear of it would be enough.

Terrorists had attacked Israel for years, so frequently that most of the population had become numb to it. A bomb went off and within a few hours life returned to normal, the living mourning the dead but taking solace in the fact that they had escaped themselves. But this time would be different. This time, Israel would be frightened like it had not been frightened in decades, since the Yom Kippur War, when its leaders had come so very close to deploying nuclear weapons. Now there would finally be panic, and it would never end because the people who had breathed in the strontium would not know, and could not be sure, whether the bomber of the Port of Haifa really had killed them or not.

Beit Aghion (residence of the prime minister)
9 Smolenskin Street
Rehavia, Jerusalem, Israel

The prime minister's new residence was not yet finished, delayed again by endless complaints in the Knesset about the cost, so the war would start here, in the old one. The PM was an old man, as Israel's head of state usually was, almost by tradition, since Golda Meir had held the office. He was white-haired with a soldier's build, age starting to put a curve in his military posture, but it had done nothing to temper the hard edge of his private manners. His charm in public was practiced enough to convince his people that he could tell a bawdy joke or appreciate one told over a bottle of the Maccabee pilsner that he was known to favor. But when the door closed, he smiled very little, even less when he had to meet with Gavi Ronen, and he drank American Scotch for the same reason. He only called the head of Mossad, the *ramsad*, when there was a problem to be solved in some way that even former soldiers like the PM didn't care to know.

The two men were not friends, but Ronen had no political ambitions, so neither were they enemies. Ronen was merely useful to the old man who lived here, and that was a suitable arrangement for them both. Any *ramsad* had to be a vicious man to be useful, but it always made him unwelcome company to those who had to keep their distance from Mossad's work, lest some unsavory mission stain their images either abroad or at home. The public knew about Mossad of course and generally knew about the kinds of operations Mossad occasionally undertook. But knowing the specifics was another matter. As the Americans said, no one wanted to see how that particular sausage was made. They were content just to know it was being done, and so long as no operation went awry, bringing unpleasant details to light, no one asked questions because no one wanted to know answers.

But tonight the prime minister had called him to the official residence, which was not surprising after the bombing of Haifa. What *was* surprising was that the old man had waited almost two days to issue the summons. Ronen had decided he would go anyway in the early morning had the old man waited that much longer. More surprising was that the politician did not immediately address the subject for which the *ramsad* most certainly was here. Instead, he asked

Ronen to recount for him the night the Iranians had taken the American embassy in Tehran. Ronen had granted the request.

The prime minister set a small glass of Scotch, Glenfiddich single malt, twenty years old, on the desk for the Mossad officer. "You prefer brandy, I believe."

"I gave it up years ago," Ronen said. "That very night, in fact."

I should like to have been there," the prime minister said.

"I should like *not* to have been there," Ronen replied.

"I was in the IDF at the time, standing watch along the Golan," the old man said. He leaned back in his chair and looked out the window. "Revolutions do not spring up full-grown overnight, do they? We should have stayed out of Iran when Pahlavi ruled. It was a mistake, I think."

"You are not the first to think so. I do not think Iran would like us any more now had we not done our part," Ronen countered.

"Surely not," the prime minister said. "The radioactive material in the bomb almost certainly came from Tehran."

"A very strong possibility, but not the only one," Ronen replied.

"And you have no sources in Iran to tell you for certain?"

"I regret not," Ronen confirmed. "Not anymore."

"I had heard that you had an asset there."

Ronen allowed a rueful smile to split his face. "No. When the Revolution took hold, one of my assets chose to stay. He told me that he would become a new man, but I do not know whether he managed to build his new life. I've not heard of him nor from him for forty years. He may have been killed within days after we last talked. He was a good friend, but I have assumed him to be long dead now."

The prime minister nodded. "Regrettable. He would be very useful to us now," he said. "I have ordered the IDF to deploy artillery on the border with Lebanon. If the Iranians did order this, Hezbollah was surely the agent that carried it out. They could have some other operations in motion."

"I agree, but we have seen no movement along the border as yet. Hezbollah has moved neither men nor missiles, before the bombing or after."

The prime minister frowned into his glass. "Have you identified the dust?"

"The preliminary tests suggest strontium 90, a radioactive isotope produced by nuclear fission, but we can't say yet if it's reprocessed nuclear fuel. If so, it could be carrying Pu-240 in the mix, and probably some minor actinides like americium and curium."

"Iran has reactors."

"Yes, but strontium has some industrial applications, so it is possible that our attackers acquired it on the black market from some other country, even one of our allies," Ronen said. He saw the disapproving look on the old man's face and decided that this was not an argument worth having. "Still, in the absence of any other evidence, we must always consider Tehran to be the primary suspect for any such crime," he conceded.

"Indeed." The old man leaned back in his chair. He offered the *ramsad* more Scotch, which Ronen declined. He wanted his mind clear for what would come next. "I regret having to call you here at this hour, Gavi," the prime minister said.

Ronen knew there were several reasons why this was true. "We all knew this night would come eventually."

"Yes," the old man agreed. "Tell me of the investigation."

"*Shin Bet* reports that the port database was hacked. The ship's manifest was erased, so tracing the container carrying the explosives will be troublesome, assuming there's enough left of the container to identify it. The blast yield and the eyewitnesses' descriptions suggest that it was a thermobaric weapon, and such bombs generate blast waves and destruction second only to nuclear weapons. If you have seen footage of the Americans' Mother-of-All-Bombs or their daisy cutters, you have seen one."

"An airburst weapon."

"Yes, but in this case, recovered footage shows it exploded at the level of the ship's deck . . . a cargo ship registered as the *River Thames*. So we know the ship that delivered it but not the specific container. If anything useful did survive intact, it will take weeks to recover, perhaps months, and much of the evidence will have suffered contamination from the seawater, if not corrosion."

"Gavi . . . how long can we keep this quiet? That it was a dirty bomb and not just a conventional explosive."

"Another day at best, I think. *Shin Bet* and the local police have already sealed off the docks, but the media are already asking why we are evacuating so many so far from the immediate blast area. Someone will leak the truth to some reporter and then the story will be on the Internet and broadcast news. If our people do not find out the truth from us, the backlash will be tremendous. It would be the end of your government." It was a bold statement, but it had the virtue of being the truth.

"I know." The prime minister sighed. "We truly cannot control information anymore, can we?" he asked, the question entirely rhetorical. "I will share the truth in a statement tonight and give an order to evacuate the affected areas of Haifa. At least fifty thousand people will have to leave, likely more."

"You may wish to note that the wind is blowing to the northeast, so the cloud isn't moving over Tel Aviv. Some of it will end up in Lebanon, and may even reach Syria, but the particulates will be dispersed enough by then that they shouldn't present a danger to anyone there."

The leader of the Jewish state nodded. "A shift in the winds and we would be evacuating parts of our capital."

"I know. Where will you send the residents of Haifa?"

"We have contingency plans for this," the old man said. "We worked them out years ago, but operation never matches the plan, does it? Those who have families elsewhere have been asked to stay with them. I am told we can shelter the rest in schools and military facilities around Tel Aviv and Jerusalem. The economic disruption will be severe. Haifa's airport is closed indefinitely, and no one can tell me when the port will reopen. Even then, getting the dockworkers to return will be difficult. They will want safety assurances, which we cannot possibly give. We cannot inspect every container on every ship *before* allowing it to dock. We would have ships backed up to Cyprus." The prime minister sipped his Scotch.

"How is the public mood?" Ronen asked.

"Shaken, but more calm than it will be once I admit the truth," the prime minister said. "We cannot abide a sustained campaign using these bombs. We do not have the resources to relocate whole neighborhoods. Haifa alone will stretch us. If the winds had been stronger and blowing toward the lower city . . . ?" He shook his head. "If our enemies have more of these ready to use, they could overwhelm us, forcing us to clear out entire cities faster than we could clean them up. Our people would become refugees in their own country. Many would have to leave for America or Europe, perhaps Russia for those with close ties there."

"I know," Ronen agreed. "Mossad is ready to serve."

The elder statesman put the stopper in the glass bottle and set it back on the bar. "President Rostow will take advantage of the moment. He will call for immediate talks with Tehran."

"You are sure?"

The PM nodded. "He is in danger of losing his election, so he will seize on this. He will suspect Tehran as we do, but he will not want to appear too close to us. So he will offer us a few words of sympathy while calling for a summit with the obvious suspects. And the Iranians will attend because they cannot refuse. If they sent the bomb, they will agree so the Americans will press us to delay any military response while they prepare for war. If they did not send it, they will agree to delay a military response and buy time to convince the world of their innocence. Either way, they will send a delegation."

"Where will they meet? Surely not Washington or New York."

The prime minister shook his head. "London, I would think, given the British relationship with both countries. Or perhaps Riyadh, but I think that unlikely. Does it matter?"

"No," Ronen agreed. "Diplomacy has never been the real path to Israel's security."

"You speak the truth. There has never been a day in our history when we have not been at war," the minister said. He did not try to hide the clear note of sadness in his voice. "I do not want to imperil our relations with the Americans, but we certainly cannot expect their cooperation on intelligence matters much longer."

"That problem may already be solved," Ronen said. "We seem to have a new friend inside the CIA."

"Oh?"

"He, or she, approached us by mail . . . sent a letter addressed to our senior officer in Washington."

"May I see this letter?"

"Of course." The *ramsad* had known that his country's leader would make this request, and so he had brought the letter with him. He lifted his briefcase from the floor, placed it on the table, and pulled out a folded sheet of paper. He offered it to the prime minister, who read it carefully twice.

This document is taken from one of the most sensitive and highly compartmented projects of the Central Intelligence Agency. Please recognize that very few people have access to this compartment. I trust that you will handle this information appropriately. I believe it will suffice as my bona fides.

I have included details for an initial meeting, if you wish to establish a relationship. To help ensure my safety, I will not share my

identity or position with you. In the event that we proceed to work
together, I do not want any specialized equipment or tradecraft.

There are others here who believe as I do. If our relationship
proves beneficial, I will connect you with them.

Your friend

"What intelligence did this man provide?" the prime minister asked.

The *ramsad* reached into his briefcase again, pulled out a manila folder, and offered it to the politician. "The name of the new director of Iran's nuclear program."

The minister's eyes widened. "Our own sources have not discovered that."

The *ramsad* nodded. "The supreme leader has been keeping it private for the man's protection. The last one came to a violent end . . . that business in Venezuela, you might recall."

"I do. But the timing of this is convenient, do you not think?"

"Not convenient," Ronen said. "I suspect the bombing spurred our new friend to act. If so, this could be monumental. He would be an ideological spy, not driven by money or any of the baser motives that drive most traitors. Such men, driven by their principles, are the most valuable."

"And you are certain this man is not a dangle?" the minister asked.

"I considered the possibility, but the Americans do not usually try such games with us. If they were doing so now, it would be cynical beyond imagination in the wake of Haifa," Ronen assured him. "Even so, I would have let the matter die a week ago rather than risk an operation that could offend our allies, but the bombing has changed matters. So I told our Washington chief to respond. We may need such friends in the coming months."

The prime minister read the entire report slowly, taking five minutes to digest the words. Ronen sat in his chair, motionless. Finally, he looked up. "If we act on this, the Americans will know they have a mole."

"They will certainly suspect it, but they will not be able to rule out the possibility that we acquired the information through our own sources," Ronen replied. "I think that alone will protect us. But there is always the risk of discovery."

The prime minister thought about that for a minute. "I do not want to disturb our relations with Washington," he said. "But Israel will not leave its own security in any hands but its own. It has ever been so. Do you see some other choice that I do not?"

"None that I think will guarantee our country's existence," Ronen admitted.

"Then do whatever you think is right."

Reston Town Center
Reston, Virginia

The Israelis would call him Shiloh.

It was surreal, he thought, how an act as simple as sending a letter could be a crime as serious as treason. Most of his choices made so little difference in his life that once he made them, he never thought of them again. Other choices presented themselves and he knew before he made them that they would turn his life in hard, painful directions. Those choices were rare, but the letter he'd mailed out a few days before clearly had been one of them. He'd surprised himself to see how little he hesitated to do it when the moment came, and once he had dropped it in the box, he thought he would regret it, that the weight of that decision would settle in on him. But he felt no different after. In a strange act of self-examination, he'd tried to convince himself that he should have been horrified at what he'd done. He failed. There had been no calling the letter back and he was as unfeeling as he had been before it had slipped from his hand. Then it was lost to him among the millions of letters moving through the system every day, and his course was set.

It was so clear what would happen after. The Israeli embassy on International Drive in Washington would receive the letter the following morning. The bombing of Haifa would have thrown the building into chaos, so the letter would sit on some desk unopened until the late evening. There were only two things inside—his letter and a sheaf of folded pages photocopied from a CIA file usually kept in a locked cabinet in a locked vault.

The staffer who opened the letter would rush to the desk of the Mossad's equivalent of a CIA station chief, whose irritation at the younger man's intrusion would vanish as he read the pages. Being a veteran soldier and spy, the man would be disciplined enough that he would not fumble for the telephone, but it would take considerable focus as he called Tel Aviv for guidance despite the hour, late in Washington and early in Israel. The information's value would not be in question. Whether Mossad could contact the man who had sent the documents to them would be the issue.

America was an ally, after all, and Mossad had suffered the anger of the United States when the FBI found the nation's allies running spies on its soil once before. Jonathan Pollard had been an intelligence analyst for the US Navy. He had also been a pathological liar, a narcissist, a prolific drug user in his youth, and a man with grandiose dreams of becoming a major player in the fate of nations. Pollard made amateurish attempts to broker arms deals with South Africa, Pakistan, and Taiwan before finally contacting an Israeli airforce officer, who put everything in motion. Pollard was deluded and reckless, unstable, and his careless tradecraft aroused a coworker's attention in less than a year. His explanations as to why he was taking sensitive papers out of the secure vault where he worked were pathetic, easily disproved, and eventually the portly American and his wife fled to the Israeli embassy, where they begged for asylum. The guards turned them back and the FBI arrested them both the moment Pollard stepped off the grounds. The operation had been handled in a pathetic fashion and the Israelis responsible had fled the country, leaving their asset behind for the American courts. Pollard's conviction for espionage had strained the ties between Israel and her largest patron ever since.

Now Mossad had another American volunteering to work for them. Was the information he had passed worth another three decades of diplomatic pain if the operation failed? A week ago, the answer would have been no . . . but Haifa surely must have changed whatever calculus Israel's leaders used to judge which assets to recruit and which to leave fallow. Now, surely, there could be no boundaries at all, and they would accept Shiloh's offer.

Reston's heart was the Town Center, an overdeveloped mass of highrise offices and apartments sitting above street-level shops of every kind. The parking was insufficient and the sidewalks overcrowded more often than not, but the restaurants were first rate. Neyla was his favorite,· and only too late did it occur to him that he shouldn't come here again after meeting with a Mossad officer for the first time. It was a mistake, but he couldn't do anything about it now.

He did not know the name of the Israeli woman sitting across from him and would not ask, but Adina Salem was a beautiful woman, petite, her body in fine shape. She had raven hair, shoulder length, and pulled back from her face, and blue eyes that bordered on ethereal. He supposed that Mossad and she both found her appearance to be very useful for recruiting assets, especially lonely men. He wondered how far she was prepared to play on her appearance to convince a man to turn on his country. The oldest profession in the world had always been put to work in the service of the second oldest, for the simple reason that it worked and worked well against the right targets. There never seemed to be a shortage of those. It was amazing how much a man's hormones could twist his thinking.

She was wearing a blue oxford shirt and carrying the current issue of *Wired*, which he had suggested the Mossad contact bring to confirm her identity. He'd watched her present herself to the wait-ress at the desk and give the false name under which he had made the reservation. The waitress had led her to the table, and Salem knew him by the beaten leather jacket and identical *Wired* magazine he had promised would confirm his own identity. Salem had seated herself in the chair across from the man she had never seen before.

She smiled at him and leaned forward. "You may call me—" she began.

He held up a hand. "We both know how this is done. And you can signal your friend in the far booth to relax and enjoy his food. I'm not armed and I'm friendly anyway."

Salem wondered for a moment how he had identified her escort. Mossad had learned to send an armed man to such meetings dis-creetly, even the public ones, and the one who'd drawn the assign-ment today was particularly good at hiding in an American crowd. "We are very grateful for your assistance," she said after a moment. She'd recovered smoothly from the surprise. Her English was fluent, but her accent betrayed her Israeli origins. Many of Israel's citizens were expatriates of other countries, but she was native-born.

"It's my pleasure."

"I will not insult you by asking your name," she said. "Without knowing what to call you, some of our people have named you 'Shi-loh.' I hope you do not mind."

"'His Gift'?" he asked.

"You speak Hebrew?"

"No, but I attended Bible school when I was young. I paid atten-tion."

"It has several meanings. That is one," she said. "And not inappropriate. Your letter came like a blessing from heaven after what happened. I was raised in Haifa."

Shiloh studied the woman, trying to discern whether she was telling him the truth. He supposed she was. She had little reason to lie about that particular fact, and there was a bitterness in her voice that he thought would be difficult to fake, even with her accent. And if his new code name was a true insight into Mossad's collective mind, then perhaps he had guessed correctly that the Haifa bomb had wiped away the old lines Israel had once drawn for itself. Fear had a way of softening morals and Israel's, of necessity, had always been more pliable than most.

The waiter stopped at their table to deliver drinks and bread, then retreated to the kitchen. The woman held her silence until the server had left the table. "Israel could not survive without her friends," she said. "And we have very few, so the friends we do have are precious to us. I hope you understand that."

"I do." Shiloh sipped at his water before continuing. "I'm not the only one in my building who wants to be your friend," he said. "But the others were somewhat anxious about taking this step. I'm sure you understand. I volunteered to make contact with your people, so I'm the test case. If we make this work, I think they'll come along."

Salem stared at her new asset, unsure whether she had understood him correctly. "There is a *group* of people there prepared to help us?"

"A small group," he said.

"May I ask how many?"

"I won't answer that," he said in his kindest tone. He leaned forward and lowered his voice. "I don't doubt that you're a professional, and so I'm sure you know this business. Even small mistakes can be disastrous and I don't think I want anyone to know precisely how many people to look for. I probably shouldn't have mentioned the others, but I wanted you and your people to know that you have more friends than you realize."

"For which I thank you," Salem replied, leaning forward herself.

"That said, we know better than you how our security services do their work. I'm sure you're accustomed to setting the ground rules for your assets, but if you want my help, we must do it my way. *My* friends insist on it."

"I will have to get approval for that."

He repressed a smile. That she hadn't refused that particular demand outright suggested her superiors had correctly assessed the value of the intelligence he could provide. "I'm sure," he said. He picked up the envelope lying beside him on the leather cushion and handed it to the woman. "Inside is a list of sites where we will deliver reports to you. We will signal which one we are using according to the protocol inside."

"How will we know it is from you?"

The man thought for a moment, and then smiled at her. "I'll post it under the name 'Shiloh.' Unless you object."

Salem smiled back at him, warm and approving. "I don't," she assured him.

"We will not send any other information electronically. I'm sure you understand my country's detection capabilities in that regard. And this will be the last time we meet."

"I would regret that very much." Salem took the thin package but made no move to open it, instead packing it away in her shoulder bag. "We will consider all of this very carefully. I do hope we can work together. I want you to trust that we will be concerned for your safety." She reached out and rested her hand on his. "We are happy to pay for your help, and would continue to do so as long as you help us, no matter your reasons. You are taking very serious risks and we want to prove our appreciation." She was surprised that he hadn't raised the issue of money, either in his letter or here in person. Some assets were driven purely by greed or a need to escape personal debts. Others were committing treason precisely because they felt like their own country didn't value them and they wanted payment as proof that their new friends thought more highly of their worth. No matter the reason, money almost always entered the equation sooner rather than later.

"I appreciate that. We can discuss my reasons another time," he said. Salem stared at the man, unsure how to respond to his lack of concern. Assets driven by principle were the most valuable in this business. They were the ones willing to take the largest risks, deliver the most valuable information, and perform the longest. Perhaps Shiloh truly was one of those . . . and if the others he had mentioned were the same? Blessings from heaven indeed.

"Whenever you are ready," Salem assured him. She did not want to pressure the man, not before he'd taken money anyway. Once money had changed hands, the assets always realized, if too late, that blackmail was then a real possibility.

Shiloh nodded. "We have time," he said.

CHAPTER TWO

The first day of nuclear talks had been all preliminaries that dragged on, and for that, Kathryn Cooke was happy not to have a seat at the table. Sitting along the wall by the door, she could at least pretend to be studying some dry document while reading the copy of the *Economist* she kept hidden in her portfolio like a schoolboy hiding his comics in a math book. The retired CIA director understood the minute tactics of diplomacy—who spoke in what order, the tortured language written and rewritten to avoid specifics, the endless repetition as they inched closer to whatever mutual ground there was to be found—but she had never enjoyed them. Cooke had scrounged up the patience for such rituals in her younger years, when the discipline that the US Navy had drummed into her head at Annapolis was still new. She'd been forced to stay in practice during her tenure at Langley, which job had turned out to be as much about diplomacy as espionage, if not more.

Now retired she usually had the freedom to delegate such boring tasks to subordinates at the consulting company she had founded, and Cooke refused to bring such work home. Her husband of nine months had no understanding of or patience for diplomatic subtleties, and she found it liberating to finally be able to speak her mind without having to parse her thoughts for offending words or classified information. Then the State Department had called on her to assist with the nuclear talks. To her frustration, the contract was dependent on her personal involvement and now she was having to exercise old mental muscles that were protesting the work.

A spy's boredom is a diplomat's party, she told herself. She could hardly criticize. Espionage was a game of boredom most days, just one far less comfortable. Even in the finest cities, intelligence officers spent their nights out in bad weather, meeting in decrepit safe houses and hunting through Dumpsters and alleys for hidden packages while the diplomats slept at home or met in gaudy embassies. It was rare for a case officer to find herself in a building like this one until she'd reached the senior levels. Cooke supposed that was so the spies wouldn't spend much time early in their careers rethinking their career choices.

She had done that during the early minutes of this meeting, which she'd spent taking in the details of the Lancaster House. The neoclassical home was almost two centuries old, a palace literally built for a prince, the "grand old" Duke of York, and likely the second finest government building in the United Kingdom. She was quite sure that the White House itself was the only US government building that might be its equal.

Maybe diplomats are the smart ones after all.

She looked down at her watch. Thirty-five minutes until the planned break. They hadn't managed to keep to the schedule thus far, and she wondered why diplomats spent so much time negotiating agendas only to abandon them first thing. She had no hope they would improve on that habit today—

The senior event manager touched Cooke on the shoulder from the doorway, a sudden distraction from the tedious repetition of the Iranian lead's trivial demands about the seating. "Forgive me, ma'am," she said, her voice low, her words framed by a tight Midlands accent. "Sir Ewan is asking to speak with you in one of the drawing rooms. He says that it's quite important."

Kathy frowned, then stood to follow. Given her mood, any reason to leave was a sound one, but the British hostess surely knew which messages could wait until the breaks, which couldn't, and which never needed to be delivered at all. The woman had hosted more than a few diplomatic meetings without an embarrassment in her career in order to earn her current position, a level never reached by those lacking an exquisite sense of discernment between the important and the trivial.

Kathy followed her out into the hall and past a pair of security guards, unmistakable in any country, to another doorway where a man stood waiting. The director of the UK's Secret Intelligence Service, Sir Ewan Lambert, offered Cooke a slight bow and his hand. "Kathryn! Wonderful to see you again." The event manager stepped away, leaving them to talk in private. Lambert waited until the door closed before speaking again. "I am very sorry to draw you out of the room," he said.

"I'm not," Kathy told her former counterpart, known informally as C, the head of MI6. "You know how these meetings go."

"Indeed," Sir Ewan agreed. "I managed to talk my way out of this one. I'm sorry you had less success at it."

"I tried, but it required more diplomatic skill than I could muster."

"It is ironic that diplomatic skill is ever needed to escape diplomatic affairs. It means the ones left in the room to save the peace are always those possessed of lesser skill," Lambert replied, hiding a small laugh where an American would have set one loose. "You may need some now." He nodded his head toward the door.

"Why?" Kathy asked.

"Two bits of interest. First, I was advised by MI-5 in the last hour that a certain gentleman who might prove troublesome has arrived in London," Lambert said. "Gavi Ronen passed through Customs at Heathrow earlier this morning."

Cooke stared at the British officer as she tried to process that bit of news. She'd met the director of Mossad on several occasions when she'd been the CIA director. "Gavi's here?"

"Indeed. He landed in a government plane a few hours ago. It shared no passenger list in advance, but MI-5 got the alert when his passport was scanned. The CCTV footage shows the local Mossad chief met him outside Customs and drove him to the embassy. No sign that he's come out since," Lambert said. "I've asked our people to keep a watch for him and other known Mossad officers in the city. We don't plan on telling the Iranians, but you might wish to let the head of your own delegation know ever so quietly."

"Thank you, Ewan," Kathy said. "I can't believe it's a coincidence he's here on the first day of the talks."

"My conclusion as well. The head of Mossad doesn't tend to travel abroad on short notice unless there's an operation under way . . . the Israeli tradition that a leader should share in the dangers of the front line with his men. But I could hardly imagine they would try anything unusual on our soil. We are allies after all," Lambert offered.

"They may not have to do anything than let it be known he's in town."

"True enough," Lambert agreed. "Every Iranian in the building must know him on sight. Seeing the *ramsad* of Israel on the street would probably have the entire Iranian delegation wondering whether a Mossad kill team wasn't waiting for them in the Hyde Park barracks. They're hardly comfortable with a female spy nearby, much less an Israeli."

"I do my best to hide it."

"If you can manage that, you are a far better spy than I," Sir Ewan said.

"I'm retired."

"You may not be in the service, Kathryn, but you know very well that once in, never out," he said. "The secret world always seems to pull us back despite our best efforts."

"And here we are," she admitted. "What was the other bit of interest?"

"A member of the Iranian delegation asked for a side meeting with you. Majid Salehi."

"With me? Not our head of delegation?" she asked. Kathy searched her mental picture of the room and found the man . . . younger than the rest of his countrymen, quiet; the man held a doctorate in physics from a German university. She couldn't remember which. He'd hardly said a word that she could recall. He'd kept his place along the back wall, nearly opposite herself, sitting next to Iran's Minister of Intelligence and Security, Eshaq Ebtekar, who she had never met.

"No, with you. He asked for you specifically," Sir Ewan assured her. "He's in the next room."

"Does his delegation know about this?"

"I honestly have no idea, though I would assume so. Unless he's a defector, which I would doubt, but stranger things have happened in our business."

"I've seen some of it myself," Kathy agreed. "Let's go see him."

Majid Salehi was a very short man by Western standards and Kathy was a tall woman, so she supposed it was a blow to his ego that he barely came up to her chin. She hadn't planned on offering her hand to shake his, but he had done so after shaking Sir Ewan's first, though not with a smile. "Ms. Cooke," he said.

"Dr. Salehi," Kathy said. "I was very surprised to hear you wanted to meet."

"Yes, I understand." His accent was heavy, suggesting he'd learned English in Tehran, with no native speakers to imitate or with whom to practice. "You must forgive me. I am not accustomed to meeting with women in such a manner," he said, confirming Sir Ewan's speculation. "But in this instance, my personal comforts are not important."

"I appreciate your dedication, sir," Kathy said.

He nodded. "Ms. Cooke, I am talking to you at my own behest and that of certain elements within my government. You were the leader of your country's CIA, so you understand that this is a risk for me. I must ask for your discretion."

"You have it, sir," Kathy said.

"Very good. I asked for this meeting to tell you that Iran played no part in the bombing of Haifa one month ago," Salehi said.

Kathy rocked back slightly, her mind racing. *Back-channel.* "You realize, sir, that I'm not an official representative of the United States government at these meetings. I'm only here to advise our delegates—"

"Yes, and it is for *that* reason I have asked to see you," the Iranian replied. "The hostility between our countries makes it impossible for anyone in my government officially to speak to anyone in yours. We could pass the message to you through another country . . . Switzerland, or the British." He looked toward Sir Ewan and nodded. "But I think you would not believe us if we did so. There is no trust between us. I hoped that by telling you directly, here, that such a step might convince you that it is the truth."

"And because you need us to tell Israel," Kathy said.

Salehi pursed his lips and tightened his fists. Kathy could see that such an admission was very nearly a step too far for the man to make. "The Zionists certainly believe that we were responsible," he said, skipping past her observation. "They will send Mossad after our scientists, perhaps our leaders, but we do not deserve it. We did not do this and we did not help anyone else do this."

They're afraid, Kathy realized. Mossad had a long history of assassinating Iranian nuclear scientists and that had been before someone used a radiological device on Israeli soil. "Dr. Salehi, I can pass your assurances to President Rostow, but unless you have some evidence—"

"I am sure that your NSA has detected no communications between my country and Hezbollah or any of our allies in the region regarding the bombing," Salehi said, cutting her off.

"An absence of evidence is not evidence of absence, sir. Your silence might be nothing more than a demonstration of good communications security," Kathy countered.

"Then there is no evidence I can give you," Salehi concluded. "There is a saying among scientists that you cannot prove a negative. We cannot prove that we are not responsible, and even if we tried to tell Mossad, the Zionists would not believe us. We have no credibility with them—"

"Or they with you," Sir Ewan pointed out.

Salehi nodded. "It is true. We would not believe them if our positions were reversed. But it is the truth." He turned back to Kathy. "Perhaps there is one secret I can offer you that will persuade you that I am sincere."

"And what is that, sir?" Kathy asked.

"My government has not announced this and will not do so, in order to protect my personal security, but six weeks ago, the supreme leader appointed me to lead my country's nuclear program," Salehi said. "In the conference room with your ambassador, I am the most important man on our side of the table. Only Minister Ebtekar is my equal in rank, but like you, he is a minder." Kathy did not doubt that was true. Iran's minister of Intelligence and Security was *Hojjat ol-Eslam*, an "authority on Islam," a learned scholar of the faith and close to the Supreme Leader himself. Ebtekar almost certainly was the Ayatollah's man in the room, and Salehi likely was kidding himself if he thought the other man was just his equal.

"I do not act the role so my position will remain unknown," Salehi continued. "Our chief delegates answer to me when we are behind closed doors. If you tell Israel, Mossad will target me after what has happened. So I offer you my life so you might believe that we played no part in the attack on Haifa."

"Does Minister Ebtekar know you're meeting with me?" Kathy asked.

"I cannot share our internal deliberations with you."

Kathy exhaled and looked at Sir Ewan. The man's eyes had widened, but he otherwise showed no emotion at the revelations. "And you know nothing about the bombing?"

Salehi shook his head. "I do not know who carried it out. Perhaps others in my government do, but if so, they have not told me." He took his own deep breath and let it out, then continued. "Ms. Cooke, only the United States can restrain the Israelis . . . and you must restrain them or many innocents will be killed."

He was probably right, Kathy thought. The question was whether Israel could be restrained at all. "Sir, I will convey your message to the president of the United States. But I cannot commit him to any course of action. He will proceed as he deems best."

Salehi nodded. "I can ask no more than that. But if he does not hold the Zionists back . . . if they refuse to be held back, many Iranians will die, and I cannot promise that Iran will not respond in kind. And that would be a terror for us all."

The British Museum
London, England

Jonathan Burke stared at the massive slab of dark granite, not moving for ten minutes and ignoring the rude looks of tourists wishing the man would leave his prime spot in front of the rock so they could take their selfies. The American studied the hieroglyphs and demotic and Greek script, each character chiseled into its surface with some tool long rusted away into red dust. Two centuries before Christ, an Egyptian stonecutter had spent days carving each small symbol onto the Rosetta Stone to record Ptolemy V's decree in three languages, no doubt aware that a single mistake, one wrong tap of the hammer on the chisel, would force him to start over, assuming the king didn't have him killed first. It was, Jon supposed, one of the original pieces of bureaucratic art and he was amazed that such things existed. The twenty years he'd worked for his own government before his retirement had never shown him any sign that bureaucracies were capable of producing anything beautiful. Like almost everything else these days, the CIA outsourced its artwork.

Jon shifted his weight and put more of it on the cane to relieve some of the stress on his knee. The metal joint was the result of having spent several weeks enjoying the tender mercies of the Russian GRU the year before, and he was still adjusting to the artificial bone. He found the occasional popping noises to be particularly unnerving, but these were subsiding with time. He did wonder whether he would ever be able to walk normally again. The doctors had assured him that he would, for the most part, but as with most things in life, he was skeptical.

The museum was more empty than he'd imagined, given the impressive collections inside, but he supposed most of the locals rarely visited. It was the same for the residents of Washington. Once they'd been to the Smithsonian and the monuments a time or two, fighting the traffic and tourists, there was little incentive to go back. None of the voices around him were speaking English with a British accent, obviously branding them as visitors to the city and the building.

Then one spoke with an accent he could not place. "You are Mr. Jonathan Burke, no?"

Jon turned his head slightly toward the voice, hiding his surprise. The man standing next to him was at least six inches shorter than himself, but far stockier across the chest and shoulders. He wore glasses with thick lenses and he seemed fit, no stomach hanging over his belt despite having passed middle age. He was balding and clean-shaven, and wore a light brown dress shirt under a longer brown jacket that reached down halfway to his knees. Jon tried to process the man's accent, but could not identify it.

The shorter man looked down at the Rosetta Stone and smiled. "Quite a treasure. A cryptographer's dream. So many secrets coming from the sand," he said. Then he looked at Jon's cane. "How is your rehabilitation? I am told the Russians were very hard on your knee."

"Actually, they were very fond of it. They kept pieces of it as souvenirs of our time together," Jon said. "You'll forgive me, sir, but if this is a pitch to work for your country, whichever one it is, my answer is no. You know who I am, so I'm sure you know I'm retired anyway."

"No, this is not a pitch, Mr. Burke. But I have been rude, and I apologize for it. My name is Gavi Ronen. Perhaps your new wife has mentioned me?"

Jon turned his head slowly toward his visitor. "No, but I know who you are."

"That is good. It will save me the trouble of trying to explain myself in vague terms in this setting. One never knows who is milling about. If you would not mind, perhaps we could walk a bit, somewhere we can speak more freely?" Ronen asked.

Jon considered turning the man down, but decided the request didn't qualify as a pitch and so started to hobble down the hall after the Israeli. The other tourists filled the new hole behind him like water in a sinkhole and smartphones began to flash as the pent-up demand for self-portraits was finally released. Ronen waited until they had put several meters between themselves and the oblivious crowd behind them. "I met your wife on occasion when she was the director of your CIA. I visited your Langley several times, but I regret that Kathryn never found the time to visit Tel Aviv. I would like to have talked with her earlier today, but I doubted that her British hosts would admit me to the building."

"A wise decision on their part, given who else was there," Jon said.

Ronen let out a quiet laugh. "Probably so," he said. "It is a shame you are not Jewish. I like your manner. You would do well in my government. When one is surrounded by enemies, one tends to value blunt talk and dark humor more than courtesies," he explained.

"I thought you said this wasn't a pitch."

"That has not changed," Ronen assured him. "You want to talk about something more serious, as do I."

"Actually, I don't really want to talk about anything," Jon corrected him. "You started this conversation."

"Yes." In a few moments, they passed into the gallery of Assyrian sculpture, which was almost empty. The other tourists didn't seem to have much interest in the Balawat Gates today. Ronen sighed and stopped walking. "Your president's decision to call for talks in the face of Iran's attack on my country presents me with certain problems that I must resolve. We were not even invited to attend as observers, much less as equals."

"Mr. Ronen, my wife doesn't speak for the president and I certainly don't. But I think you know perfectly well that Iran wouldn't come if Israel was at the table. As for the rest of it, I'd guess he's concerned about Israel doing something rash that would start another intifada," Jon advised.

"We would count ourselves fortunate if an *intifada* was all we faced now. Someone set off a radiological device inside my country. I think that your wife and others have spent the last week negotiating nuclear proliferation with the country that has been most vocal about calling for Israel's extermination, and which likely provided the nuclear material for the bomb. I also think that your country has decided to withhold information from us at the time when we need it the most. So please forgive my desire to help your president keep these matters in perspective. The United States is making a mistake and my country will bear the consequences. That is not the way to treat one's allies." Jon noted that the man had not used the word *friends*. Ronen sighed. "You do not understand us, I think."

"I'm not sure anyone understands you," Jon assured him.

The *ramsad* looked up at the American. "That is likely true. What other people have been so persecuted for two thousand years? Who could understand what that does to a nation? But I assure you that we are a very rational people. Israel is two hundred sixty miles long. At our most narrow point, we are nine miles wide. A single dirty bomb explodes and we have to relocate tens of thousands of people for months at a time. A nuclear explosion in Tel Aviv would kill five percent of our people outright, perhaps more," the man said, his voice emphatic. "We have been warning the world for decades of this and now we have seen the smallest bit of that prophecy come to pass. So you will understand when I say that my leaders are motivated to address this problem. There is finally hard proof of the Iranians' intentions and your country has chosen to play a game of defense with men determined to cheat. That is a poor decision. Defense is merely the art of losing slowly."

Jon nodded. "You're in a tough spot, I'll give you that."

"Understatement if I ever heard it," Ronen remarked. "Please have Kathryn tell your president this: Israel will not leave its survival in the hands of other countries. We have been at the mercy of others for centuries and it led to the Reich's Final Solution. Never again. I ask your president to remember who is your country's ally and who is not, but whether he chooses to help us or not, there are some issues on which we must be stubborn."

The Israeli finally stopped speaking. Jon looked down at him. Ronen looked back, unblinking. "I'll tell her," Jon said. "But even if she tells someone at the White House, I don't think it will help you."

Ronen shrugged, started to button his coat, then stopped himself short. "If your president chooses to be uncooperative, I hope that Kathryn at least will recognize that whatever we do from this point forward does not mean that I am not her friend," Ronen finished. "It was a pleasure to make your acquaintance, Mr. Burke. Perhaps another time we can speak of friendlier things."

"Perhaps."

Ronen tried to smile and failed, then walked away into the crowd.

Jon moved back to the Rosetta Stone and stood there, looking but not seeing, for another ten minutes until he felt a pair of arms reach around him from behind. Kathryn Cooke rested her head on his shoulder. As tall as her husband, she had short black hair and a fit body that make her look ten years younger. He had spent the day wandering through the museum staring at ancient works of art, but she was, by far, the most beautiful work that he'd seen all day.

"How's the museum?" she asked, her voice quiet.

"Enormous . . . bigger when you have one of these." He tapped his metal knee with the cane.

"When you owned most of the world for a few decades, you need a big place to keep it all," Kathy observed.

"No doubt. I'm pretty sure the Greeks would like to have their temples back," he said, pointing down the hall. He took her hand and led her away from the Rosetta stone, and the crowd again filled the space he vacated. There were more people behind him now than had been there when Ronen had first announced himself. Kathy must have had to fight her way through to reach him.

"I'd love to see it all. I've been to London a dozen times, but I never had time to see much outside of Vauxhall Cross or Thames House. Downing Street once. Now I'm stuck in a room all day with grandstanding Iranians."

"What's the point of being a spy if you can't actually see the world?" Jon asked, keeping his voice low.

Kathy's laugh was short and quiet. Jonathan's sense of humor had improved since they'd married earlier in the year, largely because he now had one. "The Russians must've worked your head over more than your knee if you think the CIA director is an actual spy. But I'm a free woman for the first time in years and I'm going to enjoy it, for a while anyway," she assured him. "As for the talks, I'm an observer, happy to be sitting along the wall and not at the table. Leaves my evenings free, mostly."

"Mostly?"

She smiled. "The Iranians overheard me telling one of the British delegates that I was coming here to meet you, and they wanted to accompany me. They want to 'see the cultural treasures the imperial British stole from their homeland during their occupation after the First World War.'"

"I'm sure Downing Street will appreciate your role in whatever diplomatic scandal comes out of that," Jon mused.

"I'll be persona non grata, I'm sure," Kathy replied. She looked around. They were alone, but she stepped in close to him anyway and spoke, keeping her voice low. "I was pulled into a side meeting before I left . . . one of the Iranian delegation, Majid Salehi."

"What did he want?"

"For me to pass a back-channel message to the White House," she told her husband. She recounted the Lancaster House conversation with him.

"That's interesting," Jon observed. "I had my own visitor here, just before you arrived."

"Who?"

"Gavi Ronen."

Kathy frowned. "Ewan told me he was in the city. What did he want?"

"The same as Salehi, to deliver a back-channel message. Israel's not happy about the talks, especially about not being invited, and they're not going to take Haifa lying down, whether the US helps them smack Iran down or not."

Kathy cursed quietly. "I'll need to swing by the embassy in the morning and pass this along."

"You don't want to do it tonight?"

"No. I don't think Iran and Israel will go to war tonight, and I'm going to have a night out with my husband," she said. Her years as a Navy officer had left her with a fine command voice that she rarely used, and then only when she was refusing to be dissuaded. "We've been married for nine months now and this is as close as we've come to a proper honeymoon, so I'm not going to let anyone sour the trip."

"Yes, ma'am," Jon said, a weak imitation of a soldier taking an order from a senior officer.

"Where are we going for dinner?"

"Wagamama at Leicester Square. I picked up some theater tickets for after," he told her. "I hope you approve."

"Very much so. But even if I didn't, anything would be better than an evening listening to the Iranians accuse our hosts of cultural robbery," she said. "Lead on."

Jon led her to the exit. Kathy saw that her husband was leaning more heavily on the cane than usual. He'd likely been on his feet too long wandering around the museum, leaving his knee sore, but she said nothing. He wasn't one to complain. Kathy still reached into her bag, pulled out a small tube of ibuprofen, and discreetly used a brush pass to put it into his hand. He smiled and held the exit door for his wife, and she stepped out.

They had watched Ian McKellen and Patrick Stewart perform *No Man's Land* at the Wyndham after dinner, which Jon had found depressing despite the impressive performances from the knighted actors. The streets were mostly empty as they walked back to their hotel. Kathy had suggested they hail one of London's black cabs, but

Jon chose to stay on foot. He was as stubborn about his leg as every-thing else, but the West End was one of London's safer neighbor-hoods and a quiet walk with him was a happy thought. The hotel was only eight blocks south and they would pass Trafalgar Square and the Old War Office Building before ending at the Conrad London St. James near Westminster Abbey. The US delegation was quar-tered there, as were the Iranians. Jon had wondered which British officer had thought himself clever by putting them up in the same building.

A long line of cars had formed in front of the hotel. The vehicle at the front was stopped and suffering from a dead engine. Two of the cars in the line, waiting their turns to pull forward and unload their human cargo, were black sedans, both flying a pair of Iranian flags off the hoods—the delegation Kathy had escaped a few hours before. "I guess some of your friends went out for a show, too," Jon observed. "Or they've been pub-crawling."

"I'm not sure they have friends, and I think they like it that way," Kathy said.

Several other cars blocked the Iranians' way, black cabs and rent-als both, hotel patrons also returning for the night. Another line of taxis sat parked on the far side of the road, the drivers hoping that some foreigners might decide the night really was still young. Diplo-matic immunity saved the Iranians from parking fines and congestion charges, but they still had to creep through London's endless crawl of traffic like the locals. The cars rolled forward, slower than Jon moved with his cane. Judging by the length of the "queue," as the Brits called it, they must have been waiting for a half hour at least to reach the front.

The sedans pulled forward, still four car lengths from the hotel entryway. Jon and Kathy were a block from the front door. They crossed the street and Jon stepped up onto the sidewalk, pushing down on the cane to support his weight as he stepped onto the curb.

Kathy saw one of the Iranians open a front passenger door and step out. The man was built heavy for an Iranian, with short hair and a trimmed beard, and a wire running to his ear. "Diplomatic security," Kathy observed.

"I guess he got tired of sitting," Jon added.

"Or afraid to be sitting still in traffic," his wife corrected him.

The bodyguard walked over to the hotel doorman who was directing traffic and began to gesture wildly. The doorman spoke to him, shaking his head, refusing to open up a special path for the Iranian delegation. Diplomatic credentials clearly carried no weight with the hotel staff or the stranded car at the head of the queue. "He'd have more luck slipping him some cash," Jon observed.

"The doorman couldn't move the line faster if the queen herself was asking," Kathy replied.

The Iranian's pleas were accompanied with exaggerated waves of his arms, and Jon could almost hear the argument half a block away. "He's giving it the college try anyway," he said. "I wonder how they would like it if you told them they had chutzpah?"

"You're terrible," Kathy chided him.

"And you wonder why I never became a diplomat."

"No, not really."

The Iranian tried to argue with the doorman for another ten seconds, then gave up making demands. He turned back to the car and made more gestures at his comrades, some Iranian sign language showing disgust for Westerners. He spoke into the transmitter in his hand. Another of the Iranians, a second bodyguard, apparently, began to crawl out of the rear seat to abandon the line of cars.

Four cars behind them in line, a van door opened and two people stepped out, a man and a woman, both young and fit, dressed in jeans and hoodies. "Looks like the rest of the line has the same idea," Kathy said.

Jon looked at the new pedestrians, trying to discern their nationalities. The blue van they had stepped from closed its side door and began to pull out of the line. The couple started to walk up the line of cars.

The Iranians were all exiting their cars now, eight men total. One of the men lit up a cigarette while the bodyguard turned back to the doorman and resumed his argument. His comrades laughed, enjoying the show of their friend still trying to bully a concierge, who was having none of it. He directed the foreigner to lead his gaggle off the street so the other cars could move up now that the Iranian fleet was pulling out.

"Jon, that's Ebtekar, the Intelligence Minister . . . and that's Salehi," Kathy said. The Iranian chief of delegation was the last man out of the car. He took a lit cigarette from another of the men, put it in his mouth, and drew in a deep breath, the end of the tobacco roll flaring in the darkness.

Jon didn't answer. His attention was fixed on the young couple less than twenty feet away from the group and closing the gap. The blue van passed its former passengers, then slowed to a stop three cars down, now blocking an active lane of traffic. The car behind it sounded its horn.

The man and woman both moved their hands to their waistbands, grabbing their windbreakers and pulling them up.

Jon saw it and grabbed his wife by the arm. "Kathy, get down!"

"What is—" she started, then gasped as he pulled her down behind a parked truck, the weight of his body covering hers.

The Mossad officers pulled their weapons from hiding, .22lr pistols, with suppressors threaded onto the barrels. They never broke stride as they raised their side arms. Ebtekar saw it, then dove for cover behind another car. The woman fired twice, putting two shots into Salehi's head. The suppressors swallowed most of the report of the shots, turning the usually loud crack of the small-caliber weapons into popping noises that were almost inaudible over the cars' engines. The Iranian collapsed in a sprawl, his cigarette snuffed on the concrete by the blood spurting from two small holes in his head.

The other Israeli fired his weapon into another Iranian's face from a distance of six inches, putting a pair of small bullets through the bodyguard's left eye. The bullets smashed through the thin bone behind the man's ocular cavity and ripped through his brain, coming to rest at the back of his head, flattening out against the inside of his skull. The dead man dropped, hitting the black street a second after his countryman.

The crack of the weapons, four shots, hung in the night air, and the other Iranians turned in shock, their minds unable to process the murders that were in motion among them. The Israeli woman fired again, the second Iranian bodyguard taking two bullets above his ear. He fell against the hood of a waiting car, his corpse then sliding to the ground.

Her companion pulled the trigger on another target, one of the diplomats, before his partner's dead target reached the pavement. This one fielded the first round with his forehead. The man had been turning, trying to grasp what had happened to his colleague and security escorts as the first bullet struck his skull. His head still turning, the second bullet also punched through him, this round striking his temple, going through thin bone, and pulverizing his brain as the hollow-point round expanded inside his cerebrum. The man's legs buckled and he went down on his knees, then his face.

Someone screamed, the people milling around realized that four murders had just occurred on the open street. The crowd finally understood that the young couple were carrying guns, and the bystanders clustered in groups near the hotel doors exploded into reaction, yells and cries everywhere, people running. The concierge, a veteran of the British army himself, ran for the front of the hotel and held the door for the panicked crowd trying to escape for the cover of the building. The four living Iranians abandoned their dead on the street, three running for the hotel, the last sprinting down the street toward Jon and Kathy, ducking low before turning into the hotel garage.

The Israelis showed no interest in making a clean sweep of the diplomats. They kept walking, their pace a little faster now, returning the guns to their waistbands under their jackets. The blue van's door opened for them, they clambered inside, and the van pulled away, slow and deliberate, then accelerated into traffic. The screams and yells of the bystanders were loud enough to mask the sound of the van's engine as it pulled away.

The Mossad officers had been on the street for thirty seconds; the murders had taken less than five.

Jon pushed himself up, scanning the street for signs of anyone left who might threaten his wife. Kathy stood up beside him. Even with her husband covering her, she had gotten a clean view of the executions. "Jon . . . the Iranians—"

"It's over. Four down," he told her. "Four of them ran." Jon hobbled forward as quickly as his knee allowed, not using the cane. He reached the first body. Salehi's face was scraped open by the asphalt, his eyes unfocused, going dull in color as the blood drained out. His head was surrounded by an expanding red pool.

Jon moved on to the next, then to the third and fourth man. Two shots to the head in each, the aim precise except for the last corpse, where the entry wounds were spaced more than an inch apart, the only sign that one of the victims hadn't been taken by complete surprise.

"Jon?" Kathy asked.

He looked up and shook his head. "They're gone," he said.

Kathy looked around. Bystanders were starting to come back out of the hotel, cries and curses getting louder as the crowd grew. She looked for the blue van, but it was lost in the dark.

Gavi, she thought.

CIA Headquarters
Langley, Virginia

"You think it was Mossad?" Clark Barron hoped that his former superior would not take the disbelief in his voice for a lack of trust in her. The Ops Center had called him two hours before with the news of the London murders, ending a meeting with his senior staff prematurely. Among all of the Agency's sources, public and covert, there had been nothing to identify the guilty party, but Barron hadn't expected any such clues for at least several hours. So the call from Kathy Cooke had been a blessing, albeit a mixed one—a plus that she had been a witness to the event and a terrifying minus that his friend and her husband had been so close to four men executed with precision on an otherwise safe London street.

The acting CIA director touched the volume control on the speakerphone, turning it up so he could hear the woman's voice more clearly. "Gavi shows up in London and twelve hours later half the Iranian delegation is taken out in a professional hit," Kathy said, her voice a bit scratchy from the digital decryption. "It would have to be one impressive coincidence if Mossad didn't do it, but I still hope it wasn't Gavi's people. I'd hate to think they see London as fair game for hunting. The UK is an ally."

"That'll be an open question after tonight. You told Sir Ewan what you saw?"

"I called him before I called you. Sorry, but I figured that would be a professional courtesy given that we're standing on their soil," Kathy advised. "He's probably at Downing Street right now. You might want to warn the White House. I'm sure the president will be getting a call."

"If he hasn't gotten one already. How are the Brits taking it?"

"They're freaked out," Kathy assured him. "They don't have mass shootings over here. They're trying to be stoic about it. Ewan would say they've been 'gobsmacked,' but that's understating it. They're in shock. He was the one who told me that Gavi was in town. At the time, he discounted the idea that Mossad would do anything so ugly in downtown London, so this most definitely caught him off guard."

"He'll bounce back. Ewan's father grew up in London when Hitler was trying to turn it into a smoking crater. The Brits are a tough bunch once you get past the tea and crumpets fetish," Clark said. "But I guess that's one way to call off the nuke talks. The Iranians will recall everyone who survived."

"Yeah," she agreed. "The intelligence minister survived, but I'm sure they'll bring him home."

"Ebtekar? Well, that's something. Who did they take out?"

"A pair of bodyguards, a backbencher, and Majid Salehi. I talked to him one-on-one earlier today, but I need to talk to you about that up close and personal."

She heard Barron grunt into his phone across the Atlantic. "Okay. Can you write up the shootings for us?"

"I'll sit down here with one of your people and draft a cable," she said.

"Great. I'll tell the Ops Center to wake up the right people. Are you and Jon coming home?"

"Tomorrow—well, today I guess," Kathy confirmed. Barron looked at the wall clock and added five hours. It was a little after two o'clock in the morning in London. "Lunchtime, if Scotland Yard is done taking our statements by then. If not, it'll probably be the day after before we can get out of here. Jon is working on the flights."

"You want to do me a favor and let some of our people debrief you after you two get back and catch some sleep?"

"Sure," Kathy agreed.

"Tell Jon we're glad you two are safe. I'll see you both when you get home."

He heard the line disconnect from the other end. Barron reached out, touched a button to switch to a different line, and made two calls of his own. The first was to the Ops Center, which confirmed that the officers there were in a panic mode, gathering all of the intelligence there was to be had on the shootings. The second was to a town house in Leesburg, thirty miles to the west. It was only nine o'clock, so he doubted he would be disturbing anyone's sleep.

The phone rang three times before the owner picked up, just a second before the voice mail threatened to do it for her. "Hello."

"This is the acting director," Barron announced. "Something just went down in London and Jon was in the middle of it. I need you back in the building in one hour."

US Embassy
London, England

Kathy disconnected the call, cradled the phone, and looked up at her husband.

"They killed Salehi, not the head of the delegation and not the intelligence minister," Jon said, thinking out loud.

Kathy stared at him a moment, then realized that his surprise was understandable. He didn't know the players. He hadn't spent one minute at the closed conference, and was happier for it. She shook her head. "I saw Ebtekar and the head delegate run for the hotel. They made it," she said.

Jon pulled a notepad and a pen over and sketched out the street where they had just watched men die—the hotel, the line of cars, the doorman. Then he drew eight stick figures in a circle, the formation in which the Iranians had gathered before Mossad had executed half of them. "Identify them for me."

Kathy took the pen from her husband. "You think Salehi was the target."

"Mossad doesn't kill people randomly, not that I've ever heard, and those shooters had all the time in the world to pick their first target," Jon continued. "If Salehi was the first man down, he was the one they wanted. The rest were just a smoke screen, or someone racking up bonus points."

"It might've just been bad luck on his part," Kathy said.

"I wish. If it was bad luck, it would mean that my vacation didn't just end." Jon sighed.

"You think Mossad knew he was the head of Iran's nuclear program?"

"Yeah."

The White House
Washington, DC

Daniel Rostow had cursed the Twenty-Second Amendment every day since he'd taken the oath of office that first time on the Capitol steps. It was an ugly injustice in his mind that he held the only office in Washington subject to term limits, though a few thousand bootlicker jobs technically depended on him staying in power, not that he worried about them near so much as himself. And even if he won the election, two months off now, his days in the Oval Office would still be numbered, albeit fourteen hundred or so more than before. Each president of the United States had one chance to reset that clock, after which it would begin to count down again if he managed the feat. And once the date of his departure was set on that 20 January, whether in four months or four years, he would grow a little more impotent every day, watching his party's loyalty rot away at a creeping pace as his allies looked more and more to their own political survival.

For the moment they wanted his help, but he'd been surprised to find the campaign was sour. He'd always enjoyed these political wars fought on the stump before, the marathons of sleep deprivation, fast food, and endless lies told in small towns and big cities, all relieved only by the joy of humiliating some opponent every day the polls told him that he was on top. Now he looked at those numbers each morning like a cancer patient reading his own chart to see whether some treatment would buy him a few more years of life. It was cruel, he thought, to chase this office since his youth, with every decision weighed against whether it brought him closer, and then to find the ecstasy of winning it turning a little more bitter every day.

He pushed the thought aside as often as his mind allowed, but it was usually there, leering at him every moment—

The Oval Office door opened, the sound cutting off his meditation. The people who felt free to enter unannounced numbered less than five and only one was in Washington at the moment. Gerald Feldman, the national security adviser, walked in carrying several file folders. "Make it fast, Gerry. I'm on the way out."

"Andrews?"

"Quick hop down to Charleston. Turns out that one of the Haifa dockworkers has a mother down there. Had? He's dead, she's not, you figure out the grammar. The campaign managed to set up a photo op. Should dominate the news cycle tomorrow."

"They'll wait for you." He offered the folders to the president. Rostow made no move to take them and the national security adviser set them on the desk.

"Those the latest numbers?" Rostow asked.

"Among other things," Feldman replied. "Rasmussen has you four points down, CNN by three, the usual margins of error. Trend lines look flat. We've got eight weeks to boost you up, if you believe any of these," Feldman said, touching the papers.

"I stopped believing any of them back when Trump got elected," Rostow lied. "Haifa didn't give us a bump?" His new terrorism speech was all Churchill and Reagan, wrapped in high school words, but an attack on Israel was no 9/11, not here. Terrorists had attacked the Jewish state too many times for another assault to turn enough voters' heads here, even if it had been a dirty bomb. The fascination with that development had faded within days as the masses tired of hearing about radioactivity and dispersal patterns that sounded like science lectures and weather reports.

"If it did, it's within the margin of error."

"That doesn't help," Rostov grumbled. "We need to shake up the race."

"Ask and ye shall receive." Rostow glared at the religious reference. He was a private atheist and a public Methodist. Feldman ignored the look as he pushed the second folder in the stack toward his commander in chief, this one labeled with classification markings. "Someone fired on the Iranian reps to the nuclear talks in the middle of a street in London."

Rostow looked up to his national security adviser, the news seeming to take its time registering in his mind. The president opened the folder on the Resolute desk and stared at the AP photo inside. It was a full-color image, sharp resolution, dead bodies still uncovered, with blood visible under the streetlights. "When?"

"A few hours ago," Feldman said. "Four dead."

"Has anyone claimed responsibility yet?" Rostow asked.

"No, but you know who it is."

Rostow said nothing for a minute, riffling through the photographs and staring at Salehi's dead eyes. "Has this hit Iran?"

"I'm sure the rest of the delegation has called home by now, so the mullahs must know. We've probably got an hour before the masses hit the streets over there. I don't speak Arabic, but I know 'death to Israel, death to America' when I hear it."

"No response from Iran? Nothing from Hezbollah?"

"NSA reports some chatter in Tehran and Beirut, but nothing between them. Hezbollah hasn't moved any assets toward the border. It's strange."

"Yeah. You'd think they'd be shooting Katyusha rockets into Tel Aviv by now," Rostow observed. "I want updates on this hourly from the Situation Room . . . and call the DNI. From this point forward, no one shares intel on this with Israel. If Mossad's willing to do something like this in the middle of London, then it must be Operation Wrath of God all over again. They're looking for a bloodbath."

"Half the public is going to want you to be in the middle of that bloodbath," Feldman observed. "It's a bad time to look weak on terrorism."

"That half was never going to vote for me no matter what," Rostow countered, waving away the argument. "Look, we'll support the Israelis in public. In private, I don't want anyone giving them so much as a *National Geographic* map until they've settled down. We're not going to be accomplices to a massacre. Besides, if I start sending out Delta Force operators to shoot terrorists on Israel's behalf, the other side is going to accuse me of killing people to earn votes. The public gets a whiff of that kind of desperation and I'm done. I'm not *that* far behind in the polls, so that's not how we're going to play this. Understood?"

"Tel Aviv won't like it," Feldman noted.

"Tel Aviv doesn't like me anyway," Rostow said. "As for the race, let's see if we can get Iran to come back to the table. We take the calm approach and tell Iran to do the same, but with a lot more security. The more Israel gets rowdy, the more my opponent calls for military action, the more we'll look like the grown-ups in the room . . . and maybe Israel will want to look like grown-ups, too, so they stand down on their own," he continued. "Not exactly a Nobel achievement, but I get free coverage doing something only the president can do, while my opponent sits back and snipes. Then we tell the voters that hotheads can't be peacemakers." He put his finger on the photographs. "It's not much, but maybe it'll shore up the numbers until we can figure out another way to play it. So let's see if the mullahs are willing to talk."

Beit Aghion (residence of the prime minister)
Jerusalem

The prime minister offered Ronen no Scotch this evening and was drinking none himself. The alcohol and small talk had eased their way into the ugly discussion they'd endured when the Mossad chief had visited last. Now the operation had begun, blood had been shed, and there was no room for clouded judgments and Dutch courage. "I am told that your operation in London turned out well," the old man offered.

"I hate to say such operations 'turn out well.' The target was killed and we suffered no casualties or arrests. By that standard, it was successful."

"The Iranian delegation was recalled to Tehran and those foolish talks are over. We offended an ally, but we will heal that in time. It is worth the price to sow confusion and panic among the mullahs of Tehran."

"Not too much, I hope," Ronen said, his voice quiet and flat. The prime minister looked up at Ronen, surprised at the man's expression of apparent sympathy for the enemy. "It is a difficult thing, to instill enough fear in an enemy that he retreats instead of lashing out," he explained. "It would not take much to push them into war."

"When have we not been at war?" the senior official asked.

Ronen nodded at the remark. "That is true, but there are levels and infinite varieties of war. Not all of them can be controlled or managed. Few of them, in fact."

"Yes. But in all of them, uncertainty is our friend. I assume the British have not traced your operation back to you?"

"They saw me at Heathrow, no doubt, but I could not have stayed home, not for an operation such as this one. It is our tradition that the man who gives the order shares the risk on such dangerous assignments. I could not lead my people if I did not do that," Ronen said. "And given the little time we had to plan, we could not hide the nature of the operation, but we left no physical evidence they can tie to us. So they will have their suspicions but no proof. When their foreign minister calls to demarche you, I suggest you deny everything."

The older man nodded. "I would not do otherwise, but I will not enjoy it. Where will your next operation be?"

Ronen considered the question. There was only one answer he could give. "Tehran. Where else could we go? The real threat is there, so we must attack it there."

"You have another name?"

"Several. I have four teams in the field now casing targets and people," Ronen said. "But Shiloh gave us a true prize already, one that our own assets had not given up. So I think we would do well to prioritize the targets he identifies for us. We may do more damage to Tehran's nuclear program and it will protect our own assets from discovery. That alone would make it a wise course."

"He has given us more information?"

"No, but he will very soon," Ronen said. "Ideological spies are usually the most eager to share, to the point that they often must be restrained for their own safety. I hope that Shiloh has more discipline . . . and we must be cautious. He has promised to connect us with others who may be sympathetic to us. After Haifa, I think it unwise to depend on a single source, no matter the quality of his information. We need to build our networks, even in our allies' countries, so I intend to give our people my approval to approach the candidates Shiloh names, but with care. Any of them could suffer the same weakness of eagerness."

The prime minister nodded. "They have my approval as well, for what it is worth. I trust your judgment, Gavi. Do your duty."

"Always." Ronen bowed his head slightly toward the Israeli chief of state and then made his way out of the office, not wanting to prolong the conversation more than was truly useful. Almost one hundred of his officers were in the field, engaged in the most danger-ous operations they could perform for Israel, and there was work for him to do tonight.

He would not enjoy it. *Tehran*, he thought. He had run opera-tions there before, but he had never sent one of Mossad's teams to kill a man there. His predecessors had, but not him.

He thought of Hasan. It had been forty years since they had last spoken, the night the revolution began. *If you are still there, still work-ing for your people, then I am sorry to make life hard on you, but you understand what I must do.* Ronen knew the other man would do the same. They would not have been the first friends to find themselves facing each other across a battlefield. History was cruel that way. *Do what you must, old friend. I expect nothing less of you. But we will win. I will pray that you will not suffer for it too much.*

CHAPTER THREE

There was little sun today, but it was still a bit warm for the season. Virginia summers usually broke in late September, which was still a few weeks away. Kyra Stryker was a native but had never really been comfortable with the wet summertime. She had heard that some foreign countries gave tropical hardship pay to their Embassy Row workers in the District to make the midyear suffocation a little easier to bear. She supposed that was more than the CIA would ever be willing to do.

The glass door to the courtyard closed behind her and she ignored the smell of tobacco and the muttered conversation of two colleagues. The yard usually was empty at this hour and the smokers could come here to punish their lungs out of sight of their coworkers. Only a raft of ducks searching through the colored leaves on the lawn took notice of them before returning to their business.

Her target was no challenge to find. Jonathan Burke was sitting at one of the round tables along the semicircular path that connected the east and west doors to the open yard. She hadn't seen the man for months. He had been gone for almost a year, courtesy of the Russians and medical rehabilitation. Learning to walk again had been slow agony for him, made only marginally easier by the help of his new wife. His wedding to Kathryn Cooke, the former CIA director, had taken place in the hospital chapel and he had managed to stand out of his wheelchair long enough to exchange the vows, with Kyra holding him up on one side and Clark Barron on the other. Nine months later, he was still using a cane, no doubt as much for appearance as necessity. She was certain that he liked giving the impression that he could beat someone's brains in if they dared to say something stupid in his presence.

Jon was hunched over, head down over an open notebook, pen in hand. The sleeves of his blue oxford shirt were rolled up, his only concession to the stickiness filling the air.

She sat down next to the former chief of the CIA Red Cell at the table. "I would have thought that spending a year in rehab would have cured you of masochism."

Jon recognized her voice, his eyes flicking sideways toward her for a moment, but he didn't look at her. "On the contrary, it taught me patience in pain." He scrawled something in the notebook with a pen. His block-letter handwriting was disgustingly precise, like some font on a computer.

Kyra looked up at Jon's opponent. *Kryptos* rose above them, four tall, curved sheets of aging green and gray copper connected to a pillar of petrified wood. James Sanborn, the artist, had carved hundreds of nonsensical letters into the metal of his masterwork. Half were arranged into a Vigenère cipher table, the other half into an encrypted message in four parts. The fourth of these, a string of ninety-seven characters, had never been solved. "Even the NSA doesn't tilt at that windmill anymore," she told him. "They tried to crack part four once. They worked on it for a whole day and decided they couldn't break it without diverting resources from actual operations."

"I'm aware."

"So why are you still on it? Chasing fame and glory?" Kyra asked him.

"Just a good night's sleep. I took up cryptography to kill time in the hospital. Funny how it gets under your skin."

"We have an employee assistance program to help people with addictions," she said.

"I doubt the Office of Security would have an issue with code breaking as a hobby. There are some vices the Agency encourages. But, as I am retired, it's moot." He finally looked up at her as he tapped the "Visitor: No Escort Required" badge clipped to his shirt pocket. "I'm just here for the day. Kathy and I saw the London murders go down and Barron wanted some analysts to debrief us. They took me first while Kathy spent time making parish calls to some old friends. She's getting grilled up there now."

"I know. I ran into her this morning while you were sitting under the bright lights. She told me to hunt you down here if you didn't come to the vault after your interview. It's good to see you again, Jon." She walked around behind him, put her arms around him and held him tight, longer than was professional. He returned the embrace, his hand on her arms, to her surprise.

"And you," he said.

"Actual manners," she noted. "That's new."

"Marriage has a civilizing effect on men, or so I'm told."

"She's too good for you."

"Yes, she is," Jon said. "So . . . chief of the Red Cell?" Kyra was quite young for the job, still in her late twenties, but the only people who criticized her selection either didn't know about the Distinguished Intelligence Medals being held under her name in a locked cabinet on the Seventh Floor or simply disliked the unit on general grounds and took every excuse to denigrate it regardless of who was sitting in the chair. He'd faced the same for years.

"You're welcome to have the job back."

"No, thank you. *Retired.* I don't take orders from anyone now, a state of being I've found to be remarkably peaceful."

"Do you take them from Kathy?"

"No—" Jon's eyes narrowed as he realized that she was asking a deeper question than he'd first thought. "You didn't."

"I did. She's already talked to the director. Think of yourself as a consultant, if it makes you feel better."

Jon sighed, closed his notebook, and stood. "Collusion between women never ends well for the man caught in between," he said, reaching for his cane.

"There's the real Jon," Kyra declared in triumph. "Cynical and pessimistic."

"Just had to knock the rust off," he said.

CIA Director's Office
Seventh Floor, Old Headquarters Building

Before today, Kyra had only heard stories and rumors about what went on in the director's conference room. She lacked the seniority, and the desire, to get invited into meetings here despite her accomplishments. She was the chief of the Red Cell, but her ride to that position had been quick enough to create enemies in the building, none of whom really knew her or whether she had truly earned the job, not that they actually cared. The more ambitious bootlickers simply resented anyone rising faster than themselves, no matter from where or how they were climbing the ladder to the Seventh Floor. There was no one path to the top and they were more worried about the speed of the climb than any particular way there. Someone moving up fast would draw attention away from them and that was enough to provoke snide looks in the halls. Whether or not one got invited to talk with the director in private was one of the many ways the ambitious climbers gauged progress and Kyra had now been invited.

She pulled the door open and drew the immediate attention of both the front staff and the hidden security officers watching her through a remote monitor. "You are . . . ?" The assistant to the director was the same woman who had been sitting in that chair four years ago when Kyra had first come through the door, and the question she posed was offered in the same words and tone she'd used then. The gray-haired woman was, still, ruthless in guarding access to the director, at least as much as the hidden security guards were, but pleasant so long as visitors followed her instructions.

"Kyra Stryker. This is Jonathan Burke," she announced, gesturing to her companion, who had hobbled in behind her. "Director Barron asked us to come up."

Kyra's name was in the computer, which saved her from an escort out of the vault. "I'll tell him you're here," the assistant said, reaching for her phone.

"Thank you," Kyra said, afraid to say anything else. She moved away from the desk and saw the security guards inside the post staring at her.

"Don't bother." Jon walked over to the director's door, his cane thumping on the carpet as he went. He used it to tap on the metal frame, then opened the door before the assistant's protest really started.

"Jon!" Clark Barron pulled himself out from behind his desk to shake the analyst's hand as he came through the door. "Get yourself in here." The director was taller than Kyra by only a few inches, his hair shot through with gray more from stress than advancing age. His suit was a Joseph Bank off-the-rack, neat but not expensive. The second man in the Agency's history to rise through the ranks to the top post, he had never been one to put on airs. His appearance mattered only insofar as it didn't detract from his ability to command respect from others in the room.

"Good to see you, Clark," Jon replied, limping over to the couch. Kyra closed the door, hiding the sour looks of the assistant and armed guards, then joined her mentor.

"I hope you didn't have to park too far out. I imagine it takes a while to walk in here with that," Barron said, nodding at the cane.

"A perk of marrying your predecessor is that I now get the rock-star parking I was so unjustly denied before," Jon said.

Barron laughed. "Your wife tells me you're coming back."

"I really have no idea where she got that notion."

"I might have an idea," Barron told him. He turned to Kyra before Jon could ask him another question. "Thanks for coming," he said.

"Was it optional?" Kyra asked.

"No, but those who've been under fire with me get a little extra hospitality," the director told her. "Congratulations on the promotion, by the way."

"Thank you, sir. I presume it was your doing."

Barron smiled, a look of pure mischief on his weathered face. "I might have recommended you for it. It helped that there weren't many candidates for the position."

"I suppose not," Kyra replied. "Thank you, all the same, but I'll give it up if Jon wants it back."

"Under no circumstances," Jon told her.

"Coward," Kyra said.

"Hardly. I prefer to think of myself as a man who enjoys the simple life," Jon countered.

"If that were true, you wouldn't have gotten married," Barron observed.

"Why Kathy asked me to marry her is one puzzle I am quite happy to leave unsolved," Jon said. "Murdered diplomats, not so much, even if they are Iranians."

"Yes," Barron agreed. "Have the Brits ID'd the shooters yet?"

"They hadn't by the time we left," Jon replied. "Scotland Yard found the van in a warehouse in Folkestone, down the coast from Dover. It had been sanitized. The shooters are probably out of the country and on their way home." Jon didn't say "to Israel," as there was no hard evidence of that fact, but it was an unspoken assumption that they all understood. "They recovered the shell casings from the crime scene, but without the guns that fired them, that won't tell them much beyond the caliber and maybe the brand. They're trying to trace the seller, but I doubt they'll have much luck there."

The CIA director shook his head. "Probably not. Anyone willing to execute diplomats in the middle of London is going to be thorough."

"They have been so far," Jon agreed. "There's something else. One of the Iranians met with Kathy in private—"

"Majid Salehi," Barron told him.

Jon nodded. "He asked her to pass a back-channel message to the president. He said that Iran had nothing to do with Haifa. They're hoping that we can get Israel to not retaliate. Or they were hoping. It's a bit late now."

"Kathy believes him?" Kyra asked, skeptical.

"He outed himself as the new head of Iran's nuclear program to make his point. That new title is probably why he's dead right now," Jon replied. "But with Iran, who knows? Salehi didn't say whether he was acting on orders or on his own. But if he was under orders, it would be extraordinary. Iran must be terrified of how Israel is going to respond to approach us like that with their coat open."

"After forty years of calling for Israel's extermination, they should be. So Salehi will have to forgive us if we don't just take his word for it. Not that he's in a position to complain now," Barron replied. "Mossad's our first guess for the killers. Who's your second?"

"The Russians, but even they try to be a little more subtle than this when they're offing people," Jon answered. "There are two intelligence services I'd prefer not to screw with—the Russians' and the Israelis', and not necessarily in that order."

"If they were Mossad, I'm sure they were out of the UK before the sun rose," Barron added. "They're probably back in Tel Aviv by now. Mission accomplished."

"Probably right," Jon agreed. "But there was something odd about the shooting." He pulled out the paper that he and Kathy had sketched out in the embassy two days before and pointed to the Iranian stick figures, now with names written alongside them in Kathy's handwriting. "This is where the players were standing. Kathy pointed out that the shooters didn't kill the head of the Iranian delegation," he said, pointing at one of the figures. "That one ran inside the hotel . . . left his people outside to die. But the shooters could've taken him out. They had plenty of time to line him up for the first shot or the second."

"Who did they kill first?" Kyra asked.

Jon pointed at another figure. "Salehi."

"We learned about his new job from the Brits a few weeks back," Barron admitted. "They've got an asset who's connected with Iran's nuclear program at a deep level. If someone here leaked that to Mossad, I'll have to take a very unpleasant trip to London to apologize to Sir Ewan. That report was in a code-word compartment. If we can't protect something like that, we'll be lucky if MI6 doesn't stop sharing intel on Iran with us altogether."

"The Israelis could've found out about Salehi through their own sources," Kyra observed.

"That's my hope," Barron said. "It's also possible that the Brits have a mole in MI-6. I talked to Sir Ewan and he's already got an investigation under way. But we can't assume the leak didn't come from us." The director frowned, his mental gears turning a bit before speaking again. "If Salehi was telling the truth, how would we prove that to Israel?"

"Find out who did it," Jon concluded. "But he didn't give us any idea where to start."

"The Iranians would have to be conducting their own investigation," Kyra observed.

"Yeah, just like O.J. wasn't going to rest until he found the real killer," Barron scoffed. "Don't worry about it. We've got a lot of people who can look into that. What I want you to do is look into this mole problem. If we have one and he's feeding Mossad information about Iran's nuclear program, then he's pouring gas on a fire."

"Isn't that the FBI's bailiwick? Or at least the Counterintelligence Center," Kyra pointed out.

The CIA director leaned forward, arms on the desk, his hands clenched together. "We've had one mole or defector after another show up over the last twenty years, and the damage they do gets worse each time. Everything Aldrich Ames gave the Russians, he photocopied. Thousands of pages of material. Then Robert Hanssen started giving them thumb drives. Tens of thousands of pages. Ten years later, Bradley Manning burned CDs and passed three-quarters of a million documents to Wikileaks in a matter of months. Then Edward Snowden left the country with an entire hard drive. We still don't know how many files he took, but the last estimate is that he took almost two *million* reports in a single shot." Barron put his forefinger on the table to make his point. "It took us eight years to catch Ames and it took the Bureau twenty to catch Hanssen. We can't afford to take that long anymore. These moles are stealing larger amounts of classified material in shorter amounts of time, doing more and more damage faster and faster. We need to start finding them and shutting them down within *weeks*, not years."

"I'm not a counterintelligence officer," Kyra noted.

"I know. Just work with our people to see if you can come up with some creative tactics to flush this guy out in a hurry," Barron ordered. "I'll call down and plow the field for you. Then I'm going to have to call the FBI director and warn him that we might have a breach. He'll want to send someone over to join the investigation, and heaven knows where this will go after. So I'd like to have our hooks into this for leverage before the Bureau comes in."

Kyra looked over to Jon. "Glad you're staying for the fun, for a few days at least."

"It's all fun until someone loses a kneecap," Jon said.

**1H12 Old Headquarters Building
CIA Headquarters**

"If you're going to conscript me, the least you can do is give me my old office—" Jon stepped out of the elevator and stopped short when the rubber tip of his cane caught on the carpet. He had expected to see the old second floor, with its dim lights and a floor that looked as unclean as ever, as though the black and white tiles had soaked up the sins of the staff as well as the dirt on their shoes. "Wrong floor."

"No, it's not," Kyra told him. She directed him down the hall.

"They moved us."

He found the door in less than a minute, marked to the side with a formal placard, the plain kind designed by some committee that considered humor a waste of the taxpayer's dime. It had only two words in generic white letters stamped on a black background, no display of color though the name demanded it—*Red Cell*.

"Barron gave it to us as a reward." Kyra swiped her blue badge. "He thought we deserved an upgrade."

The lock switched open and Jon pushed the door and marched in, then stopped, suddenly unsure which way to go. The space had actual cubicles instead of the bullpen he'd set up with its half-height dividers. The maps and unframed posters he had hung on the old walls were absent, and generic art stared back at him. The place was as sterile as any other analytical office in the building. "He did us no favors," he said.

"He meant well," Kyra said.

"Good intentions count for nothing. It's what you actually do that matters. I suppose we'll manage." He set his cane against a desk and sat himself down in a chair. He stared at the wall, but there was nothing unusual for his mind to grab on to. He found it disturbing and turned to look out the window instead. "Mossad kills four Iranians in London. I'm surprised that Hezbollah isn't launching rockets into Tel Aviv by now."

"Maybe our first bit of proof that Salehi was telling the truth," Kyra observed. "Iran wouldn't have to ask Hezbollah twice to attack, and after Haifa, if one rocket came down on Tel Aviv, it would be an open war. Tehran might be giving us time to talk Israel down."

"It's a possibility," Jon agreed. "And it's been two weeks since the bombing. If you're Israel, that's enough time to receive stolen intel from a Langley mole and put together a covert op if you're motivated. It would be tight, but you could do it. So our first question is how long our insider has been operating."

"The timeline doesn't rule out a mole volunteering to work for Israel *because* of the bombing," Kyra suggested. "Assume he makes contact in the first few days after. He has to prove he's not a dangle, so he has to give them something serious up front, and Salehi's name and new job title would qualify. If that's the first thing he gave up, that would maximize the time Mossad had to put together an op and get a team in place."

"That would make him an ideological mole," Jon thought aloud, his eyes still staring off at some distant point in space. "If our hypothetical turncoat wants Iran's nuclear program destroyed, maybe he can't access all of the intel Mossad needs, so he's pointing them at people who can."

"It might also mean our mole probably hasn't passed much intel to Mossad yet. If he's only been operating for a couple of weeks, they might not even have their ops plan worked out."

"Good news for Barron," Jon replied. "For us, not so much. No other data to work with."

"If he's ideological, he'll be pushing to give them a lot more intel, and soon. The ideological ones are always motivated to the point of being reckless. Penkovsky sure was. He dumped photo rolls by the dozen on his handler back in the early sixties. Scared his handlers to death," Kyra added. "Our mole might make some mistakes and give us some freebies."

"Since when has our luck ever been that good?" he asked.

CIA Headquarters

Matthew Hadfield shuffled down the corridor, staring at his own feet as any self-respecting analyst would. He was an introvert of the first order and preferred to spend the time walking between offices inside his own head, not looking up. Case officers were the socialites who wasted those walking moments talking about frivolities. Even on his happier days, it was a habit he found grating to hear, much less to take part in it, and he was in a dark mood this morning. So he plodded along, ignoring the people he passed moving in either direction and hoping that none of them knew him, lest someone try to engage him.

He was lanky without being thin, tall, with dark hair just starting to gray at his ears and two days' growth on his face. His clothes were rumpled, tactical pants fraying at the hems and a polo shirt he kept tucked in. He had dark circles under his eyes, giving the impression that he was perpetually deprived of sleep and rarely amused by anything, but he'd earned those black bags this time. He'd slept not at all the night before, but adrenaline and a caffeine pill washed down with a Diet Coke had combined to keep his mind working, if not clear. They did nothing to suppress the anxiety in his chest. He could have taken some Xanax for that, he supposed. He had a full bottle at home, but he'd forgotten to take any this morning. That happened often when his mind was focused on some unpleasant problem, which seemed to be more or less constantly of late.

On any given morning, he would have passed through entrance security and gone straight to his office—an emptied storage closet with a network connection and makeshift furniture. Space was nonexistent at headquarters these days. Twenty years of federal service deserved something better, he believed, but there was no arguing with the office chiefs of staff who doled out the seating assignments. They told him that he was fortunate to have a door and privacy. He could've been given a cubicle like all of the other analysts in his group. Hadfield had been amazed and disgusted at the fanciful arguments they could create to convince themselves of their own competence.

Another right turn, then another, and the vault was ahead on his left. He held his badge against the reader, but the door refused to open. He pressed the doorbell, waited for a response that didn't come, then pressed it again. Finally, he heard the door buzz as some receptionist touched her desk switch, and he made his way inside. Hadfield asked the woman where the area security officer's desk was located and she pointed him to the hallway on his left. He thanked her and made his way along the cubicles until he reached a set of real offices. He walked past four more doors, scanned the plastic nameplates until he found the man and the title he was looking for.

The door was open. The man was writing something and didn't look up until the analyst knocked on the metal door frame. "What can I do for you?" the area security officer asked. He did not look up.

Hadfield frowned. "I was pitched last night."

The man stopped writing and raised his head. "You're sure about that?"

"She wasn't very subtle."

The man stopped writing and raised his head. "What's your name?"

"Matthew Hadfield."

"Who pitched you?"

"Israel. Mossad."

The man's eyes opened wide. He'd been asking for a name or a personal description, not a country and certainly not an organization. "How do you know that?"

"The woman who pitched me said so."

The security officer set his pen down and pointed his hand toward the empty chair by his desk. "Let's talk."

The Red Cell Vault

Special Agent Jesse Rhodes was only medium height and not especially handsome, in Kyra's opinion. He was dressed in a white button-down shirt, navy-blue pants, and matching jacket cut large to accommodate the Glock 22 that he carried in a belt holster. He looked to be in his late thirties, likely a decade older than Kyra, and wore an intelligence community blue badge and a mood she decided was only lightly suppressed condescension. He had entered the vault with a confident march that impressed neither of the analysts who met him inside.

Kyra made the appropriate introductions. Rhodes stated his name like he was under interrogation himself and didn't offer his hand. "I'm the Bureau liaison to the Counterintelligence Mission Center. I run counterespionage over there. You were the ones who brought Alden Maines back from Russia last year," he observed. Kyra nodded. "We were getting all geared up for a manhunt we figured was going to take years. Anyone who managed to get him out of Moscow and into a US courtroom was going to have their career made. Then you dragged him back in a couple of weeks. Disappointed a lot of glory hounds at the Bureau."

"All her," Jon said. He pulled a chair away from the table and let himself fall into it.

"You're the one the Russians grabbed in Berlin," Rhodes observed. "I thought you were a staff officer."

"Was, past tense, and technically, they caught us both," Jon corrected him. "They just got her later, when she decided it was time to let them."

"Things worked out well. It wasn't a given that they would," Kyra said, choosing her words with care.

"I read the file," Rhodes said. He shifted gears in mind, if not in attitude. "Let's be clear right now. Traitors are not nice people, so playing nice is not how we catch them, not with you and not with anyone who might be connected to the case. You will cooperate as I require it, or I will cut you out."

Kyra stared at him and read his face, looking to see whether he was truly arrogant or simply a man filled with more bluster than real confidence. Jon punctuated the seconds tapping his cane against his artificial knee. "You want this mole caught and we want this mole caught," Kyra said, her tone cold. "You're working out of the Counterintelligence Center, but you're still in our house and the Bureau's not in the same league with the GRU when it comes to intimidation. So let's not play games comparing bits of anatomy I don't even have. You're welcome to the credit when it's all done," she assured the man. "We're used to our successes being private. Just don't think I'll let you hang the Agency out to dry if you screw it all up."

"We understand each other, then," Rhodes said, cautious.

"Yes, I think we do." Kyra offered a piece of paper to Rhodes, who eyed her with suspicion before taking it. "Last chance for a peace offering," she announced.

Rhodes fell silent as he read the cable Jon and Kathy had written up days before. "Did Mossad get Salehi's name from us?"

"We can't rule out the possibility," Jon told the man. "It was in one of our compartments."

"Well, good for me," Rhodes said. "The more Iranians they smoke, the more data points we get and the faster I get to arrest someone."

"Never mind that shooting Iranians in the open like this tends to start wars," Kyra said.

"Not my problem," Rhodes argued. "The Israelis' neighbors all want them dead. Scare the mullahs into backing off and the Israelis get to live a few more years without rockets coming down on their heads like Hitler's V-2s came down on London. Israel doesn't get invited to many state dinners, but if that's the price of survival, I say it's cheap."

"Easy for Americans to say. *We* get invited to state dinners," Kyra said. She sat down on the table behind her next to Jon and folded her arms. "Trying to kill your way to peace is self-defeating."

"Say that again after an Iranian dirty bomb has given cancer to your kid," Rhodes retorted. He waved his hand dismissively in the air. He looked at Jon. "You like watching her fight the battles in here?"

"She needs no help from me to win a fight," Jon said. "And I find it useful to observe how people respond while she takes them apart. In this case, I've learned that you're one of *those*."

"One of those what?"

"One of those people who mistakes cynicism for insight," Jon told the man.

Kyra's secure phone rang. She answered it. "Red Cell." She listened to a voice that neither Jon nor Rhodes could make out, then replaced the handset. "The director's office," she explained. "They want us upstairs. Someone got pitched last night."

Rhodes's mouth stretched into a smile, as though he had to remember how it was done.

CIA Director's Conference Room

Kyra had expected to be a backbencher, one person of dozens sitting along the wall, expected to listen and not talk, but it was apparent that she and Jon would be at the table. Barron was standing in the hall outside, reviewing a file. He stopped them at the door and offered them copies. Looking past the director, Kyra saw one other person was in the room, a man at the table who she'd never met.

The docket Barron had provided was an Agency personnel file, the first one she'd ever personally handled. Such files were usually stored encrypted on secured servers and often classified as highly as any information the Agency held. To see one printed out was surreal.

She looked at the photograph inside and recognized a man sitting across that table and down two chairs. Matthew Hadfield had been more than a decade younger when the picture had been taken, likely the same photo security had taken for his staff badge when he'd entered on duty.

The papers inside revealed far more.

```
Personal Information
```
Matthew Egan Hadfield

```
GS and Step:          14-8
Time in grade:        5 years, 3 months, 14
                      days
Entry on Duty (EOD):  29 Oct 1999
Military Service:     none
```

Awards and Commendations
```
18 Exceptional Performance Awards
DNI Galileo Award
```

Current Employee Data
```
Assigned Office:     Operations Center
Career Service:      Directorate of Analysis (DA)
Occupational Title:  Military Analyst
```

Education
```
BA History, 1995, Duke University
MA History, 1999, Oxford University
Graduate, Advanced Analyst Program (AAP),
2006, Sherman Kent School for Intelligence
Analysis, CIA University
MA National Security and Strategic Studies,
2009, US Naval War College
```

She scanned the training record, which was extensive but restricted to analytical course work except for the occasional personal security classes offered to anyone preparing for an overseas trip. The list of his past assignments was surprisingly short. Hadfield appeared to be the type of analyst who preferred to stay in one place, becoming a deep expert on one subject rather than jumping around every two or three years in the pattern of an ambitious climber. There was a two-year gap that had started seven years previous, which Kyra found curious—medical leave, with no further explanation given. That information would be in a separate file in the Office of Medical Services, releasable only by the order of the directors of the Agency and the Office of Medical Services itself, who must not have thought it critical for the present meeting.

The director waited until she'd had a moment to scan the front page before speaking. "Mr. Hadfield visited his area security officer this morning and reported that a Mossad officer pitched him last night," Barron told them, his voice quiet.

"Mossad?" Kyra asked. It was not especially rare to hear that a foreign country had pitched a CIA operative to commit espionage. It was far more rare for such countries to be allies. "He's certain?"

"Yes. We knew that Haifa gave Mossad a reason to toss out their usual playbook regarding Iran, but I didn't think they'd toss out the one they use for dealing with us. They haven't recruited an American since Pollard, so if they're getting into that game again, we need to shut it down before the *Washington Post* finds out. Relations with Israel are knotty even when we're trying to be friends."

"Has he talked to anyone else about it?" Rhodes asked.

"A couple of our counterintelligence people who needed to open the file on this," Barron assured him. "But Security kept him sequestered, so it's still a small circle."

"I want copies of the video of their interview," Rhodes demanded.

"We'll get them to you."

Rhodes nodded. "Nobody else talks to him about it without clearing it with me first." He walked past the analysts and took a seat next to Hadfield.

"Sir, why are we here?" Kyra asked, her voice very quiet. "A counterintelligence investigation isn't in our usual lane."

"I'll explain after," Barron replied. "For now, just listen." He led his subordinates into the room.

Kyra looked at Hadfield. He was sitting forward, hunched over, his chest collapsed in a rounded slouch, his head sticking forward on his neck. His tension was too obvious to miss, and Kyra thought it justified. An interview with the Agency's security services was never a relaxing experience. CIA Security projected an unsympathetic spirit toward any visitor. *Pity the soul called here to answer questions.* The message was clear though unspoken. And now the FBI was ready to pile on.

The CIA officers took their seats at the end of the table opposite Rhodes and his subject. Rhodes opened a leather portfolio and unscrewed a fountain pen, an expensive Visconti. He looked at his watch. "It is ten o'clock a.m. Thursday, October eight. I am Special Agent Jesse Rhodes, FBI liaison to the Counterintelligence Mission Center. You know Director Barron. This is Kyra Stryker and Jonathan Burke, both assigned to the Red Cell. Please state your name for the record."

Hadfield shifted in his seat and rested his arms on the table. "Matthew Egan Hadfield."

"And what is your current assignment?"

"CIA Operations Center."

"That's the watch office?"

"Yes."

"Please tell me what you told your area security officer this morning," Rhodes ordered.

Hadfield shifted in his seat again. "I, uh . . . I was eating out last night, at a restaurant, the Blue Ridge Grill in Leesburg. I was by myself. A woman joined me in my booth. She said her name was Sarah—"

"And you'd never met this woman?" Rhodes interrupted.

Hadfield shook his head. "I don't get out much. I'm divorced and I've never been much of a draw to women. They don't just start flirting with me in public," he explained. "So I figured she wasn't there to hit on me. I was hoping, I guess . . . maybe I'd get lucky once in my life. But someone who looks like that coming on to me would've been a triumph of hope over experience."

"Describe her, please?" Rhodes asked. The man's questions were really orders and Hadfield saw it.

"She was really pretty, tall, maybe five ten? Black hair past her shoulders, skinny . . . like model skinny. She spoke with an accent. I couldn't place it, so I couldn't figure out where she was from until she told me."

"Which was where?" Rhodes asked.

"Well . . . she tried to make some small talk for a minute, like she was coming on to me, but I think she saw it wasn't working. Then she said, 'I've come to convey an offer from the State of Israel.'"

"A straight-up cold pitch?" Kyra asked, her voice quiet.

"Not usually Mossad's style," Jon agreed.

"No kidding," Barron muttered. "Straight up and ham-fisted doesn't work unless you already know your mark. So they were gambling."

"Also not Mossad's style," Jon said.

"She said, 'We know who you work for,'" Hadfield continued. "And she said they knew I was having financial problems and they would help me if I would help them in return."

"*Are* you having financial troubles, Mr. Hadfield?" Rhodes asked.

Hadfield looked away from the man toward his fellow officers, then to the floor. "Yes. My son, Aric, developed cancer a few years ago when he was eighteen months old . . . acute myelogenous leukemia. Six months of chemo put him in remission, but he relapsed the next year. He went through two more rounds of chemo, but during the third he, um . . . his liver failed. That was it. He died a week later."

He was not lying. Kyra could see it. There was very real pain behind his words and his face, the kind of wound that healed only very slowly if at all.

"My wife developed depression—"

"And your wife's name?" Rhodes asked, cutting him off.

"Elizabeth."

"Thank you. Continue."

"She developed depression. I was afraid she was going to kill herself, but she wouldn't see a counselor. I kept trying to help her, but she divorced me instead. So now I've got alimony and debt from Aric's medical bills. Cancer is really expensive even when you've got decent insurance. So, yeah. I've got some financial issues."

Rhodes scribbled in silence, then looked up. "Did the woman at the restaurant give any details about her offer?" he asked. His voice was devoid of sympathy, his tone unchanged.

"Just that they would give me money to pay the medical bills, and a stipend, in return for information."

"Did she say specifically what information they wanted?"

"No." Hadfield shook his head. "It took me a minute to realize she was trying to pitch me . . . I locked up. It was unreal, you know? It was like I couldn't process what she was saying. I couldn't even think, to be honest. I should've told her no, but I told her that I'd have to think about it."

"How did she respond?" Rhodes's fountain pen was earning its keep now, the man writing as fast as he could move his hand.

"She said, 'That's all we can ask' and that she'd get in touch with me in a few days."

"She didn't say how or where?"

"No," Hadfield said. "But if she knew I was Agency, she must know where I live. I don't know how. Maybe she was watching my house. She knew I was at the restaurant and I didn't decide to go out until an hour before."

"Could you identify this woman from a photograph?" Rhodes asked.

"Yes. I'd know her if I saw her."

"Good." Rhodes nodded, continued scribbling for almost a minute. "Are you happy with your career?"

"What does that matter?"

"Disgruntled employees are prime targets for recruitment, and we need to explore all of the possible reasons why this woman might have targeted you. Now please answer the question," Rhodes urged. "Are you happy with your career?"

"Not really."

"Why not?"

"I was doing really well before Aric got sick," Hadfield said. "But I had to leave for two years. When I came back to work, I knew something was wrong with me, inside. I couldn't focus on anything. I couldn't control my temper. I couldn't sleep. I checked myself into the Employee Assistance Program. They said I had depression and PTSD." He gritted his teeth, his face twisting as painful memories entered his mind. "When you're living in a hospital, trying to save your child, there's this fear that digs into you, all the time. You stop thinking about the future. Your whole life becomes about surviving one more day, one more hour. Just make it until nighttime and maybe you can escape everything for a little bit while you sleep. After we got out, I couldn't think a day ahead, much less a week or a month. I was paralyzed. I still am, to be honest. I don't know how to shake it off."

Rhodes didn't respond immediately. He kept his pen moving across the page for a half minute, and then he looked up again. "Mr. Hadfield, what would—"

"I have no loyalty to Israel," Hadfield said. The lanky analyst didn't look up from the floor.

"Why do you think I was going to ask you that?"

"You're asking me about the four reasons that people commit treason, right? Money, ego, ideology, and revenge. I've got money problems. I had a good career going until Aric got sick and people treated me like crap after I got back . . . still do, honestly. So there's your ego and your revenge. That's three of the four boxes you can check off. Sympathy for Israel is the only reason left."

"How do you feel about what happened in Haifa?" Rhodes asked.

"The bombing?" Hadfield asked. A look of disgust crossed his face. "I spent two years watching them pump poison into my boy to kill his leukemia, so I can imagine what Israeli kids will look like in a hospital, dying of who-knows-what kinds of cancer because a bunch of radioactive dust fell out of the sky like snowflakes. So, sure, you can check off my ideology box, too, I guess. I can see why a foreign intel service would think I'm a good target."

"Would you be willing to take a polygraph about this?"

Hadfield shrugged. "I have to do that every five years anyway. Not a big deal."

Rhodes nodded. "We'll set one up."

"Whatever. Am I excused?" Hadfield asked, sarcasm edging into his tone.

"I have nothing more right now, but I'll have some follow-up questions for you later." The implied order was obvious. Hadfield stood and trudged out of the room, clearly anxious to end the interrogation.

Rhodes waited until the door closed behind the analyst before speaking. "I want him to go through our mug books of suspected foreign intelligence officers—" he started to tell Barron.

The CIA director pushed a folder across the table to Rhodes and gave Kyra and Jon their own copies. "Our Counterintelligence Center already had him do that after our security officers interviewed him. He identified the woman as Adina Salem. She's a legal adviser at the Israeli embassy," Barron said. "Our mole must've passed Hadfield's name to her as a possible recruit."

"How many people know about Hadfield's personal situation?" Rhodes asked.

"No idea," Barron said. "Probably everyone working in his group when his son got sick. Anyone in the Directorate of Administration who touched paperwork related to his leave of absence. Dozens, easy, maybe more than a hundred."

"We'll put Salem under surveillance," Rhodes told him.

"If you see her engage in an operational act, you might consider arresting her," Jon said.

"That would burn our one good lead—"

"In the entire history of the FBI, no spy has ever been uncovered only through surveillance. Watching her, sure, but it'll take years to find the mole and you'll still need another break to make it happen," Jon observed. "Salem straight pitched Hadfield, so Mossad has changed tactics. You might want to do the same. Arresting her would force Mossad to change up their operation and that might lead to mistakes that we can detect. Just a suggestion."

"A gamble you mean, and a fat one," Rhodes said.

"No question. But counterintelligence is usually a slow business. Do things the usual way and you could be hunting this guy for twenty years," Kyra advised.

Rhodes had no answer for that. "I need the names of everyone who's worked with Hadfield since his son got sick. Give me those and I'll cross-check them with the names of everyone who has access to the Salehi compartment."

Barron frowned as he pondered the request. "I'll talk to Security to see whose files we need to release."

"Thank you," Rhodes offered. "If you'll excuse me, sir. I need to check in with my people." He closed his portfolio, screwed his pen shut, and left the room.

"That man is ambitious," Barron observed.

"He's not wrong about digging into Hadfield's history to see if anyone there might have access to the compartments," Kyra admitted. "That could end this search in a hurry."

"It won't be that easy," Barron said, disbelieving. "It's never been that easy."

"Probably not," Kyra agreed. "But I wouldn't have believed that Mossad would try a cold pitch, either."

"Good point," Barron said. "I need you to do something."

"Whatever we can, sir," she offered.

Kyra saw a flash of anger on his face, just for a moment. "The Bureau has hunted moles in our ranks before. Back when they were hunting Robert Hanssen in the late nineties, the Bureau refused to believe that one of their own could've been the traitor, so they latched on to one of ours. They persecuted the man for years but they couldn't find anything on him. The problem was that the longer they went without finding anything, the more convinced they became that he was some kind of superspy. Absence of evidence was evidence of guilt."

"That's a really bad mind-set when you're mole hunting," Jon observed. "It plays out like a conspiracy theory."

"Yes." Barron paused, breathing deep to calm himself. "Rhodes is jumping on the first suspect he's got. After everything Hadfield's already been through with his son, I worry about what this could do to him. So I want you to watch out for him. Keep me in the loop so I can deal with the FBI director if Rhodes starts crossing lines."

"Are you sure you want to get involved?" Kyra asked.

Barron smiled at the young woman, a futile attempt to lift the dark pall filling the room. "Always happy to have a good brawl with the Bureau."

• • •

Rhodes walked into the security room lobby and displayed his badge to the security protective officer sitting at the station. "Do you have a secure phone I can borrow for a minute?"

The SPO pointed at an office behind the front desk. "He's out today. Keep the door open. Don't touch anything in the desk."

"Thanks." Rhodes stepped across the hall, lifted the handset, and dialed a number from memory. "It's Rhodes, over here at Langley. I've got a live one and I want a couple of surveillance units. The first subject's name is Adina Salem. She's a legal adviser at the Israeli embassy. I want eyes on her by close of business." He waited for the woman on the other end to speak before continuing. "The second subject's name is Matthew Hadfield. Yeah, he's a US citizen. Salem tried to pitch him and she might try to contact him again. We need eyes on him in case she does." He paused and listened to the reply. "I'll get you his particulars by the end of business."

The agent on the other end confirmed the names. "Yeah," Rhodes confirmed. "Get it set up and I'll check back later." He replaced the handset.

CHAPTER FOUR

Dulles Toll Road West
Herndon, Virginia

Hadfield steered his truck into the exit lane for Route 28 North without bothering to use his signal. The detour would add at least a half hour to the drive, but he could not afford to pay the Greenway fee. The foreign extortionists who owned the next sixteen miles of asphalt would charge him another six dollars if he continued on and his cash flow could not withstand that expense very often.

He shifted gears, slowing as he passed through the tollbooth and watched the green light tell him that his account had been charged. He shifted again, sped up, and merged with the mass of cars going north.

The FBI was mole hunting. He wondered how many other people in the building knew—not many, he thought, but that would change in a hurry. Director Barron had taken the humiliating step of inviting FBI special agents into the building, they had marched in like Hannibal crossing the Alps and started interrogations, and heaven alone knew where and when they would stop. That kind of news got around.

Quis custodiet ipsos custodes? Who watches the watchers? he thought. *The FBI.*

Like most analysts, he'd studied the great counterintelligence cases—Aldrich Ames, Lee Howard, Robert Hanssen, John Walker, and a dozen others. The glaring commonality among them was how long it had taken to determine their identities. In almost every case, the Agency and the Bureau had needed years, even when the men had been reckless, driven by no mission beyond padding their savings accounts and salving their egos. A life in prison seemed never to have entered their minds.

Could he endure prison? He considered the question. No one really knew that until they went, did they? He had to assume that the answer was no. Would suicide be a choice? He'd considered that after Aric had died and his marriage had fallen apart. So many people had come to that point and turned back when they finally faced oblivion . . . and the decision must be doubly hard for a traitor. When to do it? The Bureau would give no warning before making the arrest, and they would stop him from killing himself if they could. Try to enjoy life a little too long and they would catch him and he would end up forever in prison. Move too quickly and he would rob himself of days or months, maybe even years, of life that he could have enjoyed. What would be the right moment?

He didn't know that either.

He walked into his apartment, a rented basement under the home of a young couple who were parents to three adopted children. It was a small studio, a thousand square feet. Rent in the District was in the same league with Manhattan and San Francisco, so he'd been forced out to the far suburbs. He could have roomed with some other analysts, split the rent on a larger place, but that was for younger people than himself and he needed his solitude. He had a private bath and a bedroom, but his kitchen was a hot plate, a bookshelf that he used as a pantry, and a small refrigerator that sat by his bed. He had no television, preferring to stream shows off the Internet connection that his landlords offered. It was all he could afford for a thousand dollars a month. The studio sat below ground level, so a dehumidifier sat in the corner, running constantly in order to kill the moldy smell that would otherwise have flooded the room.

Hadfield sat down on the edge of the bed and stared at the worn carpet on the floor. The Ops Center night shifts were interminable and he was sure they were growing longer as winter approached. He rarely saw daylight now, sleeping in this basement for the few hours when the sun was up. It was dark when he awoke in the evening and the sun had barely risen in the morning when he arrived home. Today the clouds and rain had hidden it, rendering the sky a gunmetal gray from one horizon to the other.

He stood up and walked into the bathroom. The pill bottle was sitting on the sink, still open, and he doled out two of the blue pills and swallowed them without water. They held the worst of the depression back, but he could feel it still there, waiting for him to miss a dose so it could seize his mind and flood him with paranoia and anger and all of the other emotions that had tried so very, very hard to drive him mad. Even with the drugs, he couldn't really control his thoughts. It was both curious and ugly, he thought, how one could remain obsessed with memories that were so agonizing. They were pain itself, but he would rather die than let them go. They hurt him like nothing else he had ever known, but they were his most valuable possessions, and he wondered if those two facts together didn't mean that he was insane.

Headquarters had been off-limits. The doctors hadn't allowed it. Aric's chemotherapy had compromised the boy's immune system and any exposure to a contagious disease might have killed him. So even during the few days every month they let him and his wife take the two-year-old boy home after his white blood cells had regenerated, they'd been forbidden to live their lives. They could not eat out at restaurants or see movies. Going to church, with the pews filled with sniffling children, was unthinkable. They did their grocery shopping at midnight to minimize contact with others. And work? If a single colleague decided to fight through a cold at the office and Hadfield picked it up, it might have been too late for Aric by the time they realized he was ill. The family had been under a kind of house arrest, enforced by the merciless laws of biology, the doctor's orders, and their desire to keep their son alive.

Aric spent months in the hospital room as the nurses pumped poison into his little body, hoping it would kill the leukemia a little faster than it was killing him. Matthew patiently cleaned up Aric's vomit day after day when three antinausea drugs failed to hold down what little dinner he'd had managed to eat. Matthew and Elizabeth had slept in shifts with the boy, two nights on, two nights off. They'd stolen a second hospital bed from an empty room and stationed it next to Aric's, giving them a queen-size bed to share, but a full night's sleep in a hospital was a rare event.

The doctors finally declared Aric in remission after six months. They brought the boy home, but they still had to live as shut-ins. Aric's hair grew back and his weight soared from the steroids they kept him on until he was obese. The chemo had changed the color of his eyes. The dentist was concerned that his adult teeth would be permanently damaged by the harsh drugs and never grow. He probably would be sterile.

Aric relapsed nine months later. Elizabeth had wept for hours, her body shaking in his arms.

"The chemo isn't going to cure him, so we have to go for a bone-marrow transplant," the doctor said. "We'll check the national registry for compatible donors. After we find one, we'll give Aric two rounds of chemo to get him back in remission. Then we'll give him an intense round that will destroy his bone marrow. After that, we'll transfer you to Children's National downtown for the transplant."

One week into the second round, Aric's liver failed. The overworked organ had given up trying to filter the poison out of the boy's system. The doctors had to stop the chemo. There would be no transplant. Aric had a week to live.

A month after, the funeral behind him, he'd thought work might heal him. The first morning, he returned to his old schedule, waking at five, in his car by five thirty, and he entered the Langley compound a half hour later. The guards waved him through and he found the top floor of the garage almost empty as usual.

His badge still worked. He passed through the turnstiles and the wave guides and walked the few steps further to the vault door. It was locked and he could not remember the combination. He waited a half hour until another person arrived to open it. Hadfield stepped inside and walked to his office. His nameplate was not on the wall. A new one had been inserted in the holder with a name he didn't recognize cut into the plastic in white block letters.

The group chief's office was just at the end of the short hall. The man was sitting at his desk, his hands on the keyboard. Hadfield knocked on the door frame.

The chief turned around and saw him. His head pulled back in surprise. "Oh, hey, haven't seen you in a while."

"Yeah. I came to report in . . . tell you I'm back."

The chief nodded, his mind clearly trying to work out some puzzle. "Okay . . . um . . . where've you been?"

Hadfield's mouth opened slightly, his own mind frozen in surprise. "I've been in the hospital with my son. He had leukemia." How could you forget that? The thought exploded in his head, driving every rational thought off the stage of his mind.

"Oh, oh yeah," the chief said. "How's he doing?"

"He died," Hadfield replied. He felt a warm heat in his chest, his heart starting to pound faster.

"Oh, I, uh . . . I'm really sorry to hear that. When did it happen?"

"Two weeks ago." The heat in Hadfield's chest was expanding, creeping up toward his head now, and he felt a fever starting to rise. "Someone else is sitting at my desk."

"Yeah, yeah. We were short on space and so we had to find a place for one of the new analysts to sit. You were in the hospital"—he said the word as though he'd remembered where Hadfield had been all along—"so we gave it away."

"I need a place to sit," Hadfield said.

"We don't have anything here in the vault. We're full up. We managed to find some space for some of our people over on the fifth floor of Old Headquarters. Head over there. They might have an empty desk."

Hadfield was breathing heavily. "What about my account?"

"I don't know. I mean, what account were you working before you left?"

You don't remember that either. *That thought erupted in his head with more force than the earlier one.* You forgot about me! *It was like someone was yelling in his ears, pure rage and hot anger being carried directly into his head. "Iran's nuclear program."*

"Yeah, that's right. That's a pretty hot account, so we couldn't just leave it open, so we reassigned it."

He felt his anger surge again, this time faster and more intense than any he'd ever felt in his life. Hadfield's eyes began to scan the room. An office chair was within reach. The urge to grab it, throw it at the callous man . . . it swelled inside, like it was coursing through every cell.

Another thought entered. This is not you.

The anger was so fierce, so strong now, it overcame him, binding his tongue. He felt darkness rising around him, smothering his every thought.

For the first time in his life, Matthew Hadfield had murder in his heart.

And then another emotion, this one calm, and he knew, more than he knew anything else in the world, that if he gave himself up to the anger, he would hurt the chief, maybe kill him. He would follow the chair across the desk and beat the man with anything he could find until his skull cracked . . . or he would wrap his hands around his throat and squeeze until the man's larynx was crushed . . . or he would stab him with whatever sharp object he could find—

Hadfield sucked in a deep breath. Another thought. This is wrong.

The world froze around him. He clenched his teeth, squeezed his eyes shut, tried to take control of himself again.

"You okay?" the chief asked.

Hadfield looked up. He forced the rage down, put on a calm face, as straight an expression as he could manage. "No. No, I'm not."

He turned and walked out. The anger screamed in his ears to go back. He focused on moving ahead, one foot, then the next, then the next.

After a few days, the chief said he'd found a desk for him in another vault, this one in the Old Headquarters Building, accessible only by a corner stairwell. It was a small room, holding fewer than a dozen analysts, each with a cubicle smaller than the norm. It was dark despite the windows at the far end and quiet despite being overcrowded for its size.

"We actually don't have a desk," the senior analyst in the room said. "The only space we have is in there." She pointed toward a door.

The room behind was filled with half-full boxes with names hand-lettered on the sides. Cables and surplus computer hardware were stacked in one corner, the cables in tangles. A single computer sat on a folding table against the wall by the door. "This used to be an office for someone, so that computer is connected to the network. Sorry there are no phones. No Internet connection either. I was going to clean the place out and use it for my office, but we didn't have anywhere to put the boxes," she explained.

Hadfield stared at the room. "This will be fine," he said, his voice entirely dead.

"Okay." She turned and left him.

Hadfield stepped inside and closed the door.

For three months he sat in the storage closet, the door closed. He came out only for bathroom breaks and to buy lunch, which he always carried back inside. He knew almost none of the people in the vault outside and had no desire to meet them. Every day, he sat in the room, watching his Agency e-mail in-box, hoping that some message, some tasking would come. He put in a form to have an Internet connection installed. The group chief denied it, citing a lack of money.

He asked his other superiors for an account, a portfolio he could work. He needed something to focus his mind on. They promised him they would find him one. He stopped asking after the first month.

He came home one day and Elizabeth was gone. The divorce papers were on the table. She had applied for a new position at work that would take her away. He realized that in the days since Aric had died, she had hardly talked at all. He had tried to talk to her, but her answers, when she had answered at all, had been flat, without emotion of any kind. His wife, he decided, had died with their son.

Divorce laws in Virginia were heavily skewed in favor of the mother and Elizabeth got everything she wanted. She hadn't asked for the house, so he sold it. They had bought it together, had their child together in it, and fought cancer in it. On the last day he lived in it, he looked at the empty rooms. The only memories he could bring forth were painful, drowning the happy ones. Their empty bedroom felt like a battlefield the day after the killing had ended and the ghosts of the dead were still wandering the spots where they had died.

January passed. He still had no account, no assignments. He found himself going to the Agency library and checking out books to read to pass the days as he sat in his closet with the door closed. He burned through one a day for weeks, tomes on cryptography and foreign intelligence services, histories of espionage cases and covert operations. He read about Ames, Howard, Hanssen, and Walker. After a month he thought his mind would vomit if he ingested another sentence. He put in for a transfer to another group.

The group chief rejected that too. The man was up for promotion in a month and it would reflect badly on his application if senior analysts were fleeing the group. Hadfield has been away for almost two years, *the chief had written on the rejection, without mentioning why the analyst had been gone. Hadfield wondered if the man even remembered why as he'd typed.*

Mr. Hadfield's accumulated expertise is a valuable asset, and he owes his home office some time in place before going on rotation again.

Hadfield finished reading the rejection, deleted it from his classified in-box, and then had picked up his chair and hurled it against the far wall with a scream that carried every bit of his anger and hate for life and death itself.

No one knocked on the door to see what had happened.

He put a pot of water on to boil, then fetched an iPad from under the bed. It was four years old, and the battery barely held a charge anymore, forcing him to keep it plugged into the wall constantly.

He logged onto Facebook, scanned a few posts by people he knew, distant family and high school friends. He checked a few groups to which he'd subscribed and made a few posts. Then he turned the iPad off, lay back on the bed, and stared at the ceiling, thinking of prisons and oblivion until the pot boiled and he set about making breakfast.

CHAPTER FIVE

Adina Salem was a woman of discipline, but not of habit. Habits were dangerous things. An intelligence officer who commuted by the same routes at the same times, who frequented the same stores and restaurants and theaters, made life easy for her enemies. Being Israeli was reason enough for many of those enemies to want her dead. Being Mossad was enough for all the rest, and thus she wanted to make them all work very hard to realize that desire.

This particular morning, she took the Metro to work, leaving the train at the Cleveland Park stop, then making the near-mile fifteen-minute walk to the embassy. That this saved her from driving through the Washington traffic would have been enough incentive even had she not been a spy, but her job gave her another, more immediate excuse. Some of the real diplomats said it was too dangerous to walk and so drove every day. She was sure they were justifying their laziness, but she was forgiving about that. They had all been soldiers—Israel's military conscription requirement was universal for both men and women—but none had been members of the *Sayeret Matkal*, Israel's special forces counterterrorism unit. Serving in that unit had a tendency to redefine one's definition of danger.

She made her way through Hazen Park, then walked north along Reno Road. The sidewalk under her feet was laid in a brick parquet pattern and she could only see a few dozen yards to either side because of the trees that joined with a metal fence and low stone walls to hide the embassies of Ethiopia and Bangladesh. There were more trees along this road, she was sure, than grew in all of Israel. The amount of greenery in this part of the country amazed her to no end. No other area in which she'd ever served had ever seemed so alive, even if all of the trees did make the humidity oppressive in the summer. Washington enjoyed none of the cool coastal breezes that washed over Israel from the Mediterranean Sea. She missed that, more so now. She'd been raised in Haifa and seeing the images and reading the reports of the attack there had left her homesick in a way she'd never felt before. But Salem stayed at her post. In Haifa, she would have been only one more laborer among thousands. Here, she could be the cutting edge of Israel's sword. To prevent another such attack was a service as important as helping her country heal from the last one, perhaps more. The next dirty bomb could kill more, lay waste to more city blocks, or perhaps it might be a nuclear bomb of another kind altogether.

She reached the gates of her own embassy and displayed her badge. The guards let her pass and she made her way inside, walking with the small crowd arriving with her until she reached an intersection past the lobby. The real diplomats turned in one direction, she in the other. She was listed as a legal attaché, but her office was one of the rooms set off for Mossad.

Salem logged onto her computer, checked her e-mails, and responded to several, two of which were actual legal questions posed by her supposed counterparts at the State Department in Foggy Bottom. She drafted responses to both, asked a true lawyer to review her answers, and then sent them on their way. Then she joined staff meetings with US trade representatives and a British diplomat who wanted to discuss the London shootings. She sat along the backbench for both of these and said nothing for almost three hours.

It was lunchtime before she was able to start working on her real cases.

Her superiors had approved Shiloh's proposed communications plan. The man insisted on physical dead drops, to minimize the chance for NSA or some other intelligence service to intercept truly valuable reports that could point to him; but he preferred to signal those dead drops electronically. Mossad was comfortable with both preferences. Salem launched her web browser and visited a Facebook site, a *Doctor Who* fan page recently established and which approved very few new member requests. At the moment, there were only a dozen people in the group, and the moderator, Salem herself, was ensuring that the number stayed in the low double digits.

She scrolled through the discussion thread until she found a new post made that morning by "Shiloh Litzman." The Jewish surname was unnecessary but Salem assumed her asset was trying to show solidarity with her people.

```
Just binge-watched Series 6.
```

"Binge-watched" was Shiloh's term for loading a dead drop. His comms plan had listed ten possible drop sights, each corresponding one of the "series" numbers.

Series 6. She unlocked her safe, pulled out a hard-copy binder and checked Shiloh's list, then replaced it and walked over to a colleague's desk. "I need to make a run tonight."

"Where?"

"Loudoun County. Forty miles west. I'll need clean transportation."

The man looked at her over his bifocals, not sure he had heard her correctly. "Loudoun County? So far out?" he asked. "What cover for action will you have for that?"

"No good one," Salem admitted. "I'll work up something."

The man frowned. He knew Salem did not make trivial requests. "Better you not get stopped. I'll need a few hours to make the arrangements. What time will you go out?"

"Late. After dinner," Salem replied. The dark would give her an added measure of security. She would need it without a more solid explanation for such a long trip.

The man nodded. "I'll let you know when everything is ready."

International Drive NW
Washington, DC

Rhodes left his car parked on the street and made the three-block walk to his new surveillance post on one of the side streets near the embassy. It was a two-story cookie-cutter home built in the 1970s with a faint smell of mold that rose up from the basement. There were other Bureau vehicles positioned around the Israeli embassy on the other streets where there were no good residential homes owned by patriotic citizens ready to let the FBI commandeer them for an operation. The special agent had staked out the locations himself, to make sure the visual coverage of Israel's territory in the capital city was total. Adina Salem might find a way in and out of the embassy without being spotted, but it would not be because the Bureau had left her a blind spot to use.

He entered the residence by a side door, passed through the mud-room and kitchen, and hiked the stairs to the master bedroom, where the surveillance team had set up. Two men were working the cam-era and spotter scope, and another was sitting by a radio to handle comms. His deputy, Special Agent Raleigh Fuller, saw Rhodes pass through the door. "Sir," he said, acknowledging the SAC's arrival.

"She inside?" Rhodes asked.

"Arrived on foot at nine this morning, didn't leave for lunch," Fuller said. There was always the possibility that the Mossad agent had left using some covert means, but there was no good reason to question the surveillance team's competence. One of the junior men made room for Rhodes to look through the eyepiece of the spotter scope, which was directed to the front of the Israeli compound. The building was smaller than many of the more ostentatious embassies in Washington, beige, with half-circle windows running around the top level and a black metal gate surrounding the perimeter. The compact footprint made it easier to secure, though the Israelis probably thought it uncomfortably close to the street. The Jewish state's enemies were fond of car bombs and the best defense against those was sheer distance. The embassy of Pakistan sat directly across the street and Rhodes imagined that the security staffs of both buildings probably spent their days staring at each other through darkened windows if not from the rooftops.

"You bored?"

"Things get exciting for about thirty seconds when she shows up at breakfast. Target's a lady, if you hadn't noticed. Since then, not so much."

"Thank me that you're not on the other detail. They're sitting in a van out west of the city watching that Agency analyst. You get Hadfield's records?"

"Pulled them from the Office of Personnel and Management this afternoon," Fuller assured him. Fuller extracted a file from a brown leather briefcase and set it on the table. "Nothing inconsistent with what he told you. Started working for the Agency straight out of graduate school in late '99, strong career until a few years ago. Divorced from one Elizabeth Hadfield, one son Aric, deceased of leukemia at age two years. Deposits seven percent of his salary into the Thrift Savings Plan and pays his alimony on the first of every month, direct deposit from his paycheck into an account at Middleburg Bank. No criminal record, no arrests or outstanding warrants, a couple of moving violations."

"We need to talk to the ex-wife."

"We'll track her down."

"No hurry. They split a couple of years ago, so she probably doesn't know anything but we'll cover that base," Rhodes said. "Any good bets on when Salem shows?"

"She never leaves at the same time, but she's never left before seven or later than eight thirty, so she'll come out in the next hour if she sticks to that routine. She did spend one night in there, so she might not come out at all."

"Office affair?" Rhodes suggested, still looking through the scope.

"My official explanation so far is 'reasons unknown.' We don't have a lot of data points yet." They had been watching Adina Salem for a week now, long enough to learn that the woman did not keep to a strict schedule. Six days out of seven she had arrived and departed on foot. "Gotta say, nice to be watching from a house for once. Can make a decent pot of coffee when you're sleepy and go pump your bilge like a normal human being."

"Enjoy it while it lasts," Rhodes said.

"We've got this lady covered," Fuller advised. "If she runs out for a meet, we'll pick things up from this end."

"They'll meet up," Rhodes assured the man. "Hadfield's dirty. Go read his file when you've got a chance. The guy's a mess."

"If he's the mole, seems kind of dumb that he'd report a pitch," Fuller observed.

"Or kind of smart in some way we haven't figured out," Rhodes said. "We're gonna crack him open and we're gonna do it fast."

They sat in the room for another half hour before their patience was finally rewarded. Salem emerged from the building at eight forty. The sun had disappeared more than an hour before and the Mossad officer was a dark shadow except when she passed through the light escaping the embassy windows.

"There she is," Fuller called out.

Rhodes picked up the radio mic. "Rabbit's out of the cage," he said.

"Five minutes late," Fuller noted. "She's on foot, proceeding east on Van Ness. Probably heading for the Metro station."

"Metro team is in position?" Rhodes asked.

"Yes, sir."

Rhodes nodded. He leaned forward and looked through the spotter scope again. "Where are you going tonight?" he asked the Mossad officer as she walked into the dark. He stood up again. "Let's hit the road."

Leesburg, Virginia

Leesburg was forty miles outside of the District and she'd never driven out so far in this direction. It was beautiful country past Dulles Airport, rivers as wide as the Jordan, and wild undergrowth that the residents restrained only through constant effort. The foothills of the Blue Ridge Mountains filled the low horizon to the west, covered to the summits with more trees and brush. Salem appreciated that she was allowed to see it all. The State Department's Office of Foreign Missions required some nations' diplomats to stay within a twenty-five-mile circle of their embassies precisely to restrict their ability to conduct espionage. That order usually applied only to those whose home governments were openly hostile to the US or guilty of behaviors abroad offensive to their American hosts. Israel was not on that list, though more than a few politicians here thought it should be.

I would be fuel for their fire, Salem admitted to herself. She was making this drive to perform a task "inconsistent with her diplomatic status," as the FBI would call it if they knew what she was about tonight.

She could have driven here directly from the Israeli embassy in less than an hour, traffic permitting, but she'd taken three times that long to be as certain as she could be that she was operating in the black. She'd made the walk from the embassy on Van Ness Street back to the Cleveland Park Metro station, switched trains twice, then picked up a clean rental car, a black Ford Fusion, at the Reston Metro station left for her by another officer. She'd taken side roads to Leesburg to avoid the toll-road stations and their cameras, and made her way here following a map that she'd committed to memory. Her surveillance detection skills were as good as anyone's in the Mossad, but that really meant very little. If the Bureau knew about her, they could surround her with so many cars that she'd never see the same one twice, and then it wouldn't matter how good her training had been. Her instructors had drilled her and the rest of her class like whipped mules to beat the skills into them, but there were limits to how many license plates and combinations of makes, models, colors, and brands the human mind could hold. There could be cars all about her, and perhaps even an aircraft above her, made impossible to detect by the constant traffic coming and going from both the Dulles and Leesburg airports not twenty miles apart.

Salem turned onto Evergreen Mills Road and stared in the mirror. There were no lights behind her. The Woods Road came up on her right at the end of a pine forest and she took the turn, no signal light. The road was wide and newly paved, running behind the local landfill, with no tree cover to hide her from a plane. After a half mile, the road bent to the right and began to wind through a section of woods where the trees grew tall. Salem killed the headlights and opened up on the gas. The road ran without a curve for a bit and she pushed the car up to sixty miles an hour. She navigated by what little moonlight made it down through the trees.

The Banshee Reeks Nature Preserve was another quarter mile beyond, deep into forest. Salem pulled the Ford into the preserve on the left, where a winding dirt road lay beyond, blocked off by a cattle gate. She stared at the path beyond, disturbed. This was not a good place for a dead drop. There was no possible cover for action here, no good excuse that an Israeli diplomat could give for being inside a locked park after hours this far outside the District. Ten years fighting terrorists as part of the *Sayeret Matkal* had beaten most of that nervousness out of her, but this went against every lesson Mossad had ever taught her.

She reached into her pocket and felt for her diplomatic passport. It would save her from an espionage charge if the Bureau caught her, but suddenly it seemed like a very thin thread on which to hang her freedom.

There was nothing for it. She stopped the car and left it running while she picked the padlock. It was a Schlage, but she'd practiced on the same model and it came open with little effort. Salem pulled the chain out and swung the gate wide enough for the car to pass through. Once inside, she returned and replaced the gate and the chain. She considered the lock. Not many people would drive this back road at this late hour, and the few that did probably wouldn't see far enough past the tree line to notice an open lock hanging loose on the gate. Still, it was always the little details that broke the big investigations open, so Salem spared two seconds to lock the Schlage again and hide that small bit of evidence of her passing.

"Target has entered Banshee Reeks," Rhodes heard, holding the radio up. The surveillance plane was passing overhead, less than a thousand feet up, which had given the surveillance team the freedom to drop back once Salem had passed into the countryside where the traffic was sparse. One of the men in the tech van was watching the Israeli on a thermal camera image sent down from the plane and overlaid on a map of the area, while his partner called out the woman's location turn by turn.

"This is either a dead drop or she's meeting an asset," Rhodes said.

"Operational act all the way." They'd known that from the moment she'd switched to the second Metro train. A search on her license plate and her convoluted route off the toll roads had just served to confirm her intentions.

"This is a bad place for it, for her, and for us," Fuller said. "She's got no cover for action to be this far out or to be breaking into the place. And the map says it's one way in and out. We go in after her, she'll make us for sure. You want to grab her?"

"Any chance we can keep up with her on foot?"

"Running through the woods if she drives more than a hundred yards or more, and she'd heard us stomping on the leaves at least that far away."

Rhodes considered the answer. "How long to make a dead drop in there, do you think?"

"Depends on the place, but if I were her, I wouldn't want to be in there long. Ten minutes?"

Rhodes nodded. "That's our mark. If she's on her way out in less than ten, it was a dead drop and we maintain surveillance. If she takes longer than that, then she's meeting with asset."

Rhodes picked up his iPad and stared at the map. "Send two units back out to the main road to pick up surveillance again when she comes back out. Other units deploy off the road here by the entrance, lights out. Six men on foot in the trees in case she makes us on the way out and tries to run on foot."

Fuller nodded, pressed his own mic, and began to issue orders. Black cars and SUVs on four different roads behind began moving in different directions.

Salem drove, lights off, until the moon reflected off a metal grain silo behind the trees on the right. The woods on that side ended abruptly a little way down, and she turned onto a small dirt trail that bent north off the road.

A fine bit of navigating in the dark, she told herself, with only the fat slice of a waxing gibbous moon to brighten up the swales and ridges that she'd had to cross.

There was a small house just behind the wood line where the paved road met the trail. She stopped the Ford and killed the motor.

Salem exited the car and looked back across the long field. There were no lights she could see, no sound of cars off on the Woods Road now several hundred yards behind her. An aircraft sounded in the distance, but it was very quiet; she couldn't make out distance or bearing. It was likely that the plane was either coming or going from the municipal airport that the map in her memory said was a few miles to the northeast.

She started walking toward a small building that she could see in the moonlight. A white-tailed deer, a twelve-point buck, was grazing in the field to the south. It saw the woman in the moonlight and ran, its doe and three fawns following behind. She took that as a good sign that she was alone. Other unwanted guests passing through recently would have frightened the animals away as she had done.

The building was small, not old enough yet for the brick to be deeply weathered. The fallen tree that Shiloh had described in his communication plan was a few dozen yards behind, easily found even in the low light. The earth around it was damp enough for her shoes to begin sinking down even though there had been no rain for days. She made her way to the larger end of the downed tree and knelt, stopping short of putting her knees into the moist earth. She could not see inside and finally had to resort to a microlight. The red beam revealed Shiloh's package inside, an envelope wrapped in a ziplock bag and sealed with duct tape.

Salem pulled it out, killed the light, and listened as the world around her sharpened up again—the plane was still there somewhere, but she heard nothing else.

She made her way back to the car, holding the package against her body, trying to fox-walk in silence, but in the dark she could not see all of the leaves and branches underfoot and a few snapped and crunched as she moved—another reason this was a bad place. Stealth was impossible in these woods, too much underbrush and leaves.

She passed the house, half expecting the FBI to come rushing out, rifles drawn. No one emerged as she walked past, the little building looking as dark as before. Salem kept moving and reached the car. She looked around again and listened. All was as it had been for the last ten minutes. She mounted up.

"She picked something up," Fuller noted. The infrared image from the drone circling above couldn't reveal what she'd taken from the tree, but Salem's movements were not difficult to discern. "No meeting with an asset."

Rhodes swore. "I'd love to know what's in the package."

In her seat, Salem stared at the envelope. Was it against some protocol to open it in the field? She could remember no rule forbidding it, and she had found herself wondering for most of the drive out what secrets Shiloh had left for her here in these woods.

She pulled out her folding knife, cut through the duct tape, and pulled the plastic bag open. The envelope was sealed and she sliced it along the short end. Inside were several folded sheets of bond paper and a thumb drive. She opened the documents and riffled through the pages. Most looked like regular intelligence reports with headers full of impenetrable crypts and code words, classification markings and lists of recipients. But the sheet on top looked like a common letter. Thinking Shiloh perhaps had written it to her, she read it through twice.

British Senior Intelligence Service (SIS) liaison has identified the buyer as Asqar Amiri, a British expatriate working from Kish Island for the Iranian government to arrange the clandestine acquisition of arms and sanctioned nuclear materials . . .

No, this was not for her, Salem realized, and it was no typical intelligence report. There was no author or recipient listed, no crypts or code words, nothing to reveal the provenance of the letter.

There was no time for such questions now. She folded the papers and returned them to the envelope, which went back into the plastic bag. She closed her knife and stuffed it and the papers into her satchel on the passenger seat, then started the car.

Rhodes looked out into the woods. His eyes had adjusted to the dark and he knew roughly where the units and men were in the trees, but could make none of them out. That left him satisfied. If he couldn't find them, neither would Salem.

Fuller checked his watch, a military analog whose hands glowed a dim tritium green. "Ten minutes."

Rhodes looked into the back of the van to the junior officer watching the drone feed. "What's her status?"

The younger man waited a few seconds to answer. "Rabbit is in her vehicle."

"It was a dead drop," Rhodes said.

Fuller lifted his radio. "Subject is outbound, approaching main gate in two minutes. All units stand by"

Salem drove slowly back out, looking into the woods ahead every time a curve approached. The moon lit her path, but she could not see far into the trees. She considered turning on the headlights, but decided against it. The chances that anyone would see them from the road were small, but *small* was not *zero*.

She reached the gate and stopped. She had seen nothing for the length of the road, not an animal or bird anywhere. She supposed that the sound of her engine, however quiet, had been enough to frighten them away from the road.

Perhaps.

Salem rolled down the driver's-side window a few centimeters so she could listen to the woods as well as see them. She tuned out the noise of the engine and heard only silence at first, then insects. No birds, no sound of any other car coming up the Woods Road.

The plane was still there . . . no louder, no quieter.

Where was the airport? Five miles? She had been on her errand more than ten minutes now, far more than enough time for the plane to cover that distance or fly out of earshot if moving in some other direction. Was it another plane? She didn't think so . . . the engine noise was pitched no higher or lower than before.

The plane must have been circling, she realized, and pulling a very tight circle very near her position to sound so close for so long.

It was a fine place for an ambush. The Mossad officer had seen it on the map hours before. The Woods Road had no way off except the openings only at the ends, a mile apart, with no other intersections and trees walling it in on both sides for its full length. If anyone—the police, the FBI—blocked off the ends, escape by car would be impossible. It would be easy for her to lose a human running through the woods at night, but dogs would be another matter. She knew there was a subdivision to the northwest of her position, the county landfill to the east. She could jump that fence, but she could not possibly make it to the main highway on foot by any route before any pursuers did in a car.

Had Shiloh set her up? No, she decided. There was real intelligence inside the package, something valuable. But that did not mean she had not been followed. Where they could have acquired her tail, she didn't know. There would be time to analyze that later.

Salem's options were limited. Nothing moved in the dark ahead, but that did not mean that the black woods were empty.

If the Americans were here, when and where would they move?

You cannot pull a subject from a moving car, her instructors had taught her years before.

She had been a fool to lock the gate behind her, she realized. She would have to get out of the vehicle to open it again. She would be in the open, on foot, a half-dozen meters from the vehicle. She could run the gate, but if the Bureau was here, it would set them off and she doubted she would get ten meters onto the road before they cut her off.

Salem scanned the tree line again. If the Americans were here, they were well hidden. If she opened the door, the interior lights of her car would destroy her night vision, blinding her for a few crucial seconds.

She closed her eyes and tried to recall the map she had studied on the table at the embassy that morning, struggling to remember all of the possible routes, the locations of the roads, the developments.

She opened her eyes. There was one possibility.

In years past, she would not have tried it, but Shiloh was important, perhaps vital to her country's survival now. Whatever the full contents of Shiloh's package were, they would be a clue that could lead the FBI to Israel's friend. Salem had a duty to deny them that if she could.

"What is she waiting for?" Rhodes muttered. Salem had stopped her car, the engine still running, but the Mossad officer hadn't gotten out for almost a minute.

"She made us," Fuller said. It was a guess, but one that seemed more likely the longer the woman sat in her car. He took Fuller's radio and lifted it, holding it close to his face.

If it was a trap, there was one way to test it.

Salem put the car in reverse. The Ford's lights came on.

"She's running!" Rhodes yelled. He cursed then yelled into the radio. "All units, move!"

The headlights seemed to come on from every direction at once, engines suddenly roaring to life. Large SUVs moved forward, sealing off the Woods Road at either side of the nature preserve entrance in both directions, their doors opening, men and women pushing out, automatic weapons raised. Salem heard rustling behind her and turned. Men erupted from the underbrush behind her, carrying rifles.

Salem spun in her seat, looking out the rear window, and fed gas to the engine, running the vehicle backward until it was moving at eighty kilometers per hour. The headlights shone past her, brightening the woods. Salem pushed hard on the brakes and cranked the wheel hard, and the car spun on the asphalt. The wheels hit dirt and grass as the Ford rotated. Salem was switching the gear and pushing down on the accelerator long before the car had finished the turn, and it shot forward, never having stopped.

"Where's she going?" Rhodes yelled.

"No idea," Fuller muttered.

The junior officer in the back stared at the electronic map on one of his monitors. He didn't wait for authorization before calling out to the other cars on his own headset. "All units, subject has a possible escape route through the subdivision to the northwest."

"Units Alpha, Bravo, Delta, Go! Go! Go! Echo, you're on us!" Rhodes yelled. The SUVS in the formation pulled back, arced into short turns, then leaped forward, engines screaming into the darkness. Rhodes pointed at Salem's car, lights receding fast. "Stay on her so she doesn't backtrack."

Fuller stomped the accelerator.

Two FBI chase cars had smashed down the gate, the lock breaking open and the chain shattering. The leader was closing the distance only a few dozen meters behind her now, a black van with a black sedan behind. That was helpful. She'd thought the SUVs would come in, but the Americans were coming after her in cars no more built for off-road runs than her own. She had the small advantage of having driven the road once now and knowing how sharp the curves were. She drifted to the outside, slowed a little, and suddenly accelerated through the turn. The van behind her tried to follow, but it was top-heavy. Its tires slid on the asphalt and the vehicle sailed off into the woods, its headlights going dark as it smashed sideways against a tree.

"I thought you could drive this thing!" Rhodes watched as Echo, the sedan that had been trailing behind them roar past, not slowing as the driver heard his superior's yell and decided no one in the van needed medical attention.

Fuller grimaced. "She's not built for this," he grumbled. He pressed the accelerator again and the van grabbed the dirt and gravel under its tires and moved toward the road.

The small house where she'd stopped before was getting closer. Salem killed the car's lights and spun the wheel hard right, pushing hard on the brakes to dump some speed.

The car immediately began to shake, the wheels grinding on dirt and then bouncing on gravel as it jumped off the blacktop onto the narrow trail. Not expecting the turn, the Bureau sedan behind her sailed past, wheels locked and white smoke erupting from underneath as the driver tried desperately to slow enough not to roll the vehicle when he turned it. The car sailed off into the open field, the occupants saved from being thrown around only by their restraints. The special agents would be yelling into their radios, calling for reinforcements to deploy . . . where?

Salem pushed the car as fast as she dared on the uneven trail, afraid that some large rock would emerge from the dark and break an axle or rip out the gas tank. She was moving over unknown ground now. She heard debris hitting the undercarriage at a furious rate, like gunfire.

The trail curved to the left. She took the turn, then saw the break in the trees through the right. She spun in that direction, plowed forward, and the trees fell away. She was in an open field now, sloping down to the east. There was a building ahead, a large maintenance structure at the end of a paved road, lit by streetlamps. The dirt trail ended at the building's entrance and the car smoothed out again as the wheels rose up onto the asphalt. She floored the accelerator and smashed through the chain-link gate closing it off.

The road curved twice in a large backward S, and then she was in the subdivision she had seen on the map in her head. All of the streetlamps were on, the houses dark except for porch lights, and she hoped that no one would be walking on the road at this late hour. Salem got the car up to speed, a hundred kilometers per hour. The road was almost straight here and she would reach the four-way stop where the Woods Road came arcing around from the east in less than a minute. If the FBI had not cut off that intersection, she would have a chance.

There were no cars ahead, no blue lights, and she pushed the Ford faster, its engine screaming now.

She saw headlights from the east—one of the Bureau's SUVs coming down the Woods Road, running at least as fast as she was. It would be a race for the intersection, and there was no room to swerve around at the speed she was driving. She would run up dirt embankments on the other side.

If she won the race, the SUV would not be able to stop before passing through the cross in the road and shooting onto the gravel road on the other side of the intersection to the west. It would take several seconds for it to stop if it didn't spin out—

She sped up, judged the distance—

She wouldn't make it first.

Salem exhaled and pressed down on the brake.

She could not dump speed fast enough to stop. She would still overshoot the intersection . . . and the FBI's driver in the other car saw it. Thinking she was still going to run, he pulled to the left side of the road, putting the SUV in a position to turn right as wide as possible to stay with the target.

He realized too late that she was dumping speed and pushed hard on his own brake. The wheels locked, tires screaming and melting on the asphalt from the friction, white smoke spewing into the dark.

The FBI vehicle's headlights filled Salem's own car with blinding white beams. The special agents saw the Israeli woman raise her hands, an instinct that did nothing to protect her.

The SUV hit the Ford broadside behind the front wheel at just under fifty miles per hour. Salem's passenger-side doors crumpled as the metal frame was crushed inward, all of the airbags firing at once. Salem was thrown against her seat belt, forward and sideways at the same time, her head smashing into the side post. Her tires were now sliding on asphalt, then on white gravel, spinning to her left. The Ford hit wet grass and slid over the edge of the embankment, down the slope into a fallen tree, where it stopped short, metal crunching close outside.

The FBI driver and his passengers flew forward at the impact, their own belts stopping their momentum, their body armor saving them from long linear bruises along their chests as inertia tried for several seconds to throw them through the front window. The SUV died with a shriek as the metal frame surrounding the motor collapsed, plastic and glass shards from windows and mirrors blowing outward. The front axle crumpled and the forward part of the engine tried to retreat into the engine block, fluids and steam erupting as its hoses breached. The tail of the SUV left the ground as the front end stopped faster than the frame could absorb. The vehicle bent in the middle as the armored car arced upward, and they saw Salem's car spin away from them onto the grass and then down the short hill into the trees. Then gravity pulled the machine back to the ground just as the SUV behind struck them, unable to stop.

Salem opened her eyes. The world was blurred and tilting around her. She raised her head and the world spun.

Some instinct inside told her to run. Her car was dead, but she could still lose the Americans in the trees, couldn't she? She didn't know these woods. Would the men somewhere nearby shoot her? Were they dead? She couldn't think.

She tried to open the door. It wouldn't move. She looked out the window and saw the car resting against a dead tree. So the world really was tilting, or at least the car was.

The FBI team recovered, all suffering whiplash and strained muscles, but every one of them in better shape than Salem thanks to the armor they wore and the lightly armored car carrying them. They were able to open all of the doors save one, the forward passenger door, which was bent in its frame. The four men emerged from the utility vehicle, and the special agents from the two trailing vehicles joined them. Bravo's vehicle was spewing steam; Delta had managed to avoid the pileup by swerving onto the dirt shoulder of the road at the last second, the embankment alone keeping the SUV upright.

They all wore tactical pants, dark jackets with the FBI letters reflecting in the lights, and thigh rigs for their side arms. They raised the carbines they were carrying and moved toward the wrecked car down the embankment.

The team leader reached the vehicle. The passenger window was missing. "Ma'am! Can you hear me?" The passenger door was smashed shut. He couldn't reach the woman without crawling through the window.

Salem turned her head toward the voice. Her eyes would not focus properly. "I . . . *ken*." Had she spoken Hebrew or English? She couldn't tell.

"FBI. Please don't move." The FBI agent fumbled for his flashlight and shined it into the car. The Israeli woman barely winced as the light hit her eyes. There was blood on her forehead, starting to run down over her cheek. "Emergency services are on the way. Don't move. We'll get you out."

Salem disobeyed the man and fumbled for the seat-belt release. It popped and her body slid down on the seat against the door. She turned back and looked around the interior, but could not find what she wanted. Her mind was not cooperating, her thoughts jumbled and foggy. She felt around the floor and her fingers finally touched the envelope. She pulled it out, then turned back to the broken window.

"She's trying to get out," the team lead realized. He shouldered his rifle and moved around the car, tried to move down the embankment, slid on the grass, and managed to push himself back onto his feet. He heard engines in the distance. Rhodes and the rest of the surveillance units were closing on their position.

He pulled himself along the front of the Ford and reached Salem as she pushed herself out of the window. Her balance still compromised, she fell, landing on the ground. The special agent grabbed her, as much to help her as to restrain her. His teammates moved in from both sides. Groggy, Salem took a swing at the man holding her arm, a strike at his nose. She missed, hitting his shoulder, not enough to hurt. She couldn't orient her body or control her muscles.

Two of the agents raised their 9mm H&K MP5 rifles at her head. Their leader waved them off, then directed the others to help him get her up to the road. Someone pulled the package she was holding from her hands and rough hands lifted her by her armpits. She staggered, her legs refusing to cooperate. They reached the top of the embankment as the first of the other vehicles arrived. Someone pulled her arms behind her and cuffed her wrists.

"Do you have anything in your pockets I should know about?" someone asked.

"No." That came out in English, she was sure.

"Do you have a weapon on you?"

It took her several seconds to process that question before she could answer. "No." There was no point lying.

They did not take her at her word and patted her down, two men still holding her up while another ran his hands over her body, looking for the gun or knife that she wasn't carrying. They emptied her pockets of the detritus they found, keys and her passport. Salem couldn't resist any of it. More vehicles came rolling up, lights and sirens breaking through the silent night. There were seven men around her, all wanting a piece of the arrest.

Rhodes stepped out of the tech van and saw the crash site for the first time. Alpha's SUV was wrecked beyond repair. Bravo, probably also a total loss. His own van would need bodywork to repair the damage from the tree and the Echo sedan had a bent axle courtesy of the rock it had landed on when it left the pavement for the open field. Only Delta's vehicle was in good shape.

He cursed under his breath. "I told them to stop her, not try to kill her."

"No keeping this one quiet," Fuller said. "The whole neighborhood's gonna come looking."

Rhodes nodded. He saw his men holding the suspect up and he walked over, holding out his credentials. "Ma'am, I'm Special Agent Jesse Rhodes. Are you Adina Salem?"

"I . . . I can't . . ."

One of the agents gave Rhodes her passport. He glanced at it.

"Ms. Salem, we're going to sit you down in one of our cars until medical help arrives," Rhodes told her. "Where's the ambulance?" he asked.

"En route, still ten minutes out," someone advised. The Delta driver had radioed the local paramedics before he'd even gotten out of his SUV. "We're out in the boonies here."

Salem felt her handlers direct her to one of the cars. The passenger door opened and they lowered her onto the seat, pushing her down as she sat so her head wouldn't strike the roof. One of the Special Agents began to check her for injuries. He began flashing a small light across her eyes, checking for cranial damage. "I am a legal adviser . . . at the Israeli embassy." Her brain was finally starting to work again, but her vision still did not want to focus. "You must . . . contact my ambassador immediately."

"We'll contact your ambassador after we process you at FBI Headquarters."

"I have diplomatic immunity," Salem said. She suddenly coughed, a violent racking in her chest, and it was a half minute before she could speak again. "I am an Israeli diplomat—"

"That's not all you are," Rhodes said. "Ma'am, I need to know—"

"I will not answer questions."

The sound of a siren cut through the dark after ten minutes and Salem saw the ambulance reach the top of the rise in the road to the north and begin to descend toward the crash site. They would cuff her to the gurney while the paramedics examined her, then take her to a hospital for tests. Assuming she had nothing worse than blurry vision and aching muscles, she would find herself in an interrogation room by morning.

None of that mattered. Salem looked around at the armed men and finally saw the one holding the brown envelope. *I'm sorry, Shiloh*, she thought. Whatever report Shiloh had tried to share, she prayed that it wasn't enough to lead this person, Special Agent Rhodes, to the man that Salem was sure she had just failed.

CHAPTER SIX

Hadfield dropped his bag by the desk and typed his name and password into the terminal before bothering to sit down. Logging onto the Agency's internal network was no fast process and he always let the computer run as he settled in for his shift.

The room was quiet. It was always quiet until some horrid thing killed people in large numbers somewhere in the world, but most nights here were full of tedium and coffee, whispered conversations among bored analysts looking to pass the time. So this was no desirable posting. Hadfield had not wanted to take it, but his managers had needed to check a box on their to-do list to satisfy their Seventh Floor masters. They were using him to fill a breach, a living, breathing plug in the dike of management requests flooding in from on high.

"Welcome to another glorious night in the service of your country," the man next to him muttered. The FBI liaison to the CIA Operations Center was a kindred spirit in his attitude toward this particular job. He was a junior man in the Bureau, had signed on to be a special agent, but his managers had sworn that his computer forensics skills were too valuable to let him out into the field. Then they assigned him to duty such as this, using none of his talents and putting the lie to their claim that they needed him for more than checking those same boxes on their own version of the to-do list.

"How much longer before you rotate back?" Hadfield asked.

"Six weeks. You?"

"Three months and change. Counting the days."

"You and me both," the FBI officer said. "You hear anything about a mole hunt going on over here?"

"Yeah, I heard something like that was going on," Hadfield replied, his voice low.

"I told the bosses that as long as I'm here, I could help out. No joy, I don't get to play. I'm not one of the director's stars like the guy running the investigation."

"Who's that?"

"A guy named Rhodes. He thinks this is the case that's going to move him up at the Bureau, so he's tearing up the world. I heard he arrested someone a few hours ago."

"Yeah?" Hadfield asked.

"Yeah," the Bureau officer said, bitterness in his tone. "The grapevine back at the Hoover Building says that it was some diplomat trying to retrieve a dead drop out in Loudoun County somewhere. A woman, I heard, but no idea which country she's from. Rhodes will probably make sure we'll all read about it in the *Washington Post* tomorrow or Monday."

Hadfield shrugged. "One more spy off the streets of DC."

FBI Headquarters
J. Edgar Hoover Building
Washington, DC

The doctors finally cleared Salem's release from the hospital midmorning. She had a concussion with the expected headaches and nausea, for which she was given Percocet and Kytrel. The special agents doled out the drugs on a schedule, lest the woman decide that suicide by overdose was an honorable way to serve her country. Jon had thought the precaution moronic. Salem's diplomatic immunity guaranteed her quick release, so killing herself would've been a truly stupid tactic. They could only hold her long enough to confirm her credentials.

Now the Israeli sat alone in the interrogation room where Rhodes had left her an hour before. Jon and Kyra had watched the special agent question her all morning. It had been a futile display. Salem hadn't uttered a word other than to repeat her demand that someone contact her embassy. The CIA analysts were sitting in the observation room, off to the side because the six other special agents in the room had refused to make room in front of the window. Neither analyst cared about the professional slight. They'd seen what they needed to see. Jon had quietly predicted that thirty seconds into the interrogation the FBI officer would come up empty and he'd been correct.

Rhodes had spent the last hour with his team trying to settle on some new tactic that might force their suspect to talk before the deadline. Kyra had listened to the useless discussion as patiently as she could manage, but Jon's intolerance for stupidity had rubbed off on her over the years and it was finally more than she could bear. "This is a waste of time," she finally said when the circle of officers reached a silent slump in their conversation.

The entire group turned in her direction. "If you have some magic CIA way to crack her open that doesn't, you know, violate the Geneva Conventions, then share, by all means," Rhodes told her.

"These days, the 'magic CIA way' is to recognize a lost cause when we see it and spend our time thinking about what we do know, not trying to pressure a suspect who knows we've got no leverage," Jon advised, his tone even.

"She's got immunity and Tel Aviv isn't going to wave it, so all she has to do is wait and she'll get to walk out of here without saying jack," Kyra said, piling on. "I think we'd do better to focus on what you did gain from the raid while you've got the time, because once she goes back to Israel, the mole is going to know that you're looking for him and life is going to get a lot harder."

"And just what else do you think we got, *Miss* Stryker?" Rhodes demanded. "You and your partner there were the ones saying we should bring her in. Fine, there she is and we can't get her to talk. The intel in the package she was carrying is compartmented, so we can't do anything with it until CIA reads us in. We traced the rental car and it led to a disposable credit card and a fake driver's license—"

"Have you asked why the dead drop went down in Banshee Reeks?" Kyra asked, cutting him off.

"It was a remote location—"

"No!" she said, her temper finally starting to rise. "Who do you think picked the drop site?"

"She did," one of the men said, nodding over his shoulder toward the interrogation room window at Salem.

"No, she didn't," John corrected him. "Are you really that dense?"

"Hey, you're here as a courtesy," Fuller told him. "So you listen—"

"We've done nothing but listen for the last hour. I can't speak for Kyra," Jon said, "but I'm stupider for it. The fog of war, we can deal with. The fog of stupidity, to which you are adding every minute, not so much."

"All right, Jon, that's enough," Kyra told him, her voice soft. The man frowned and went silent. She turned back to Rhodes. "Mossad is one of the most professional intel services in the world. So unless she and all of her colleagues have gone insane in the last month, there is no possible way she would have picked Banshee Reeks for a dead-drop site. It's forty miles outside of Washington, which put her at least an hour away from her embassy, assuming she didn't run into traffic and was willing to run the toll roads, which would leave an electronic and video trail. If she drove the side roads, it would take her twice that long. She had no cover for action going in to a locked site after hours and had to commit an illegal act just to get in there, so any sheriff's deputy wandering by would've had grounds to detain her, much less the Bureau. And that road leading into the site was a mile long and open only at the ends. It was a trap waiting to happen."

Rhodes considered Kyra's argument. "You think the mole picked the site."

Kyra nodded. "Of course he did. The only question is why they let him."

"Not a chance!" Fuller insisted. "Letting the mole run the op runs counter to every rule—"

"The Israelis just watched a dirty bomb contaminate a very large chunk of one of their largest cities," Jon interrupted, his voice even. "You might consider whether Mossad's rules have changed. Desperate people are willing to consider desperate options. So if our mole has already passed them valuable intel and promised them more, they might be willing to take serious risks to get it."

"Like letting the mole pick his drop sites," Kyra added. "The question is why he would pick that site."

"Because he would be familiar with it," Rhodes said.

"That's obvious," Jon replied. "*Why* is he familiar with it?"

"Because he lives in Loudoun County," Fuller said, trying to follow the trail that the analysts were laying down.

"Not exactly a quantum leap in deductive reasoning, but yes," Jon conceded.

Kyra stood long enough to take an iPad from one of the men, who gave it up only on a silent order from Rhodes. She launched a mapping application and talked as she typed. "You *have* seen a case where the mole dictated the drop sites."

"Robert Hanssen," Rhodes said after a moment's thought.

Kyra nodded at him. "In most HUMINT ops, the handler approves the sites. That makes it easier for him to spot surveillance and create a logical cover for action if he's confronted, but it's more dangerous for the mole. Hanssen knew that, so he refused to play by those rules. He controlled the times and places, and the Russians went along because his information was valuable enough to justify the risk. You know where Hanssen left most of his dead drops?"

"Nottoway Park, Vienna, Virginia," Fuller told her.

"Three miles from his house. And where was the dead drop he had just serviced when he was finally arrested?"

"Foxstone Park," Rhodes replied.

"One mile away from his house. He could get there on foot in fifteen minutes even if he wasn't in a hurry," Kyra replied. "The simplest cover for action is the best, so Hanssen picked locations where he could say he was just out taking a walk. Maybe the same principle applies here. Salem was the one taking all the risks in using Banshee Reeks. So how could the mole have cover for action there when he made the drop?" She held up the iPad, showing the group a map of the area that Rhodes's team had raided the night before. There was the subdivision, a half mile away through the trees, through which Salem had fled.

Rhodes took the computer and scrolled around the map. There were only a handful of houses beyond the neighborhood within walking distance for miles in any direction. "You want us to investigate some random intel officer who might live in a subdivision because it happens to be a half mile through the trees from a drop site? Forget it," he said. "Given how many of you people live in Northern Virginia, random chance alone says you've got some people living in that development. I'm not going to waste my people's time checking into someone just based on their geography."

"Your choice . . . a bad choice, but yours to make," Jon said. He pushed himself to his feet.

Kyra shrugged and handed the iPad back to Rhodes. She followed

Jon through the door into the hall, leaving the other men behind. "I'll get the names of all of our people living in that neighborhood."

"I'm sure the Bureau will appreciate your efforts on their behalf," Jon replied, his tone dry.

"They'll never say so."

"It's amazing what you can accomplish when you're not interested in who gets the credit."

Rhodes exhaled, a long slow breath designed to release the anger that had been rising inside him like a swollen river. "I don't want him back in the building," he ordered.

"What about her?" Fuller asked.

"Only with my approval," Rhodes decided. "She's halfway civil at least. Are the forensics back on the package?"

"The crime lab is still working on it, but preliminary results came back clean," Fuller reported. "No fingerprints, no sample suitable for any kind of DNA analysis. The envelope and pages were all generic stock, probably came out of some supply closet at Langley. We imaged the thumb drive and gave a copy to Langley. I've got people interviewing the rangers out at Banshee Reeks, but I guarantee they won't have seen anyone leave the package."

"Yeah, we weren't going to have it that easy," Rhodes admitted. "Where does Hadfield live? Anywhere near Banshee Reeks?"

"In Ashburn, ten miles from there as the crow flies."

"And he didn't go anywhere near it yesterday?" Rhodes asked.

"No," Fuller replied. "I checked with the surveillance team this morning. He follows the same routine every day. Gets up, spends the day at Langley, goes home. Maybe stops at the grocery store or goes to some drive-through to pick up dinner. Last night he didn't even do that. Stayed in all night."

Rhodes frowned.

"Okay. Stay on him."

Kyra's habit had always been to reach her desk by 0600. Jon had always done the same until the Russians had crippled him, but she'd seen the wisdom of keeping the schedule of rising early and getting work done in the solitude of the morning. This month of the year, it was still dark outside at that hour, and only a few lights were on in the New Head- quarters Building across the loading dock. Kyra did not bother to turn on the vault lights, instead letting the monitor do that work until the sun would come up in an hour or so and reveal the rest of the world.

She had put in a request to the Seventh Floor the night before to release the names of any CIA officers who lived in the subdivision that backed up against Banshee Reeks. There was only one, and it had taken a second request, this one made directly to Barron, to pry the man's personnel file loose.

```
Personal Information
William Fallon

GS and Step:          Senior Intelligence
                      Service (SIS)-1
Time in grade:        10 years, 7 months, 22 days
Entry on Duty (EOD):  13 April 1993
Military Service:     none

Awards and Commendations
12 Exceptional Performance Awards

Current Employee Data
Assigned Office:      Center for Cyber
                      Intelligence (CCI)
Career Service:       Directorate of Operations
                      (DO)
Occupational Title:   Manager
```

Education
BA Mechanical Engineering, 1988, Stanford University

She was mildly surprised to find the promised files were in her in-box. She had sent the request to Barron's late the night before and she hadn't been sure his staff would even pass it to the director at all. The time stamps showed the files had arrived only four hours after she had asked for them. Barron, it seemed, had laid down the law with his staff on Kyra's messages. For an Agency that normally ran at the speed of government, the request had been filled with astonishing speed and Kyra wondered what threats Barron had leveled to push those particular file requests to the head of the queue.

Kyra extracted the attachments from the e-mail and opened them, then decided to attack the files recovered from the Banshee Reeks drop site first. There were five of them, each a Microsoft Word document recovered from the brown envelope pulled away from Salem. Four of them clearly were Agency reports, with all of the usual marking, crypts, and file numbers. She searched for them in the Agency's classified holdings and the system blocked her accessing any of them online. *They're all compartmented,* she saw. *That's bad news.*

One document differed from the other four. It was short and straightforward, bare of all formatting, a detail that told Kyra it was not a CIA report. It looked like someone simply typed it out on a word processor.

British Senior Intelligence Service (SIS) liaison has identified the buyer as Asqar Amiri, a British expatriate working from Kish Island for the Iranian government to arrange the clandestine acquisition of arms and sanctioned nuclear materials. British sources

with indirect access to his department claim
that Amiri is negotiating to buy radioisotope
thermoelectric generators (RTGs) from a
dealer operating near Kandalaksha Bay,
Murmansk.

SIS is trying to recruit Amiri with a
repatriation offer as the incentive. Amiri
has not been vetted, but liaison has agreed
to arrange a clandestine meeting for one case
officer with Amiri in Basrah. Procedures will
be onerous, but this might be a chance to
get some detailed and specific information
about his reported objectives for the Iranian
government.

She read the report through twice, then brought up the interface
to the Agency's databases. She typed *Asqar Amiri* and ran a search.

The computer reported no results.

Kyra stared and began typing in other keywords and search terms,
checking the report as she went for other unique keywords she could
try. There were plenty of hits on Kandalaksha Gulf and RTGs, but
nothing on Asqar Amiri.

She began typing again, this time an e-mail to the CIA director.

TO: Clark Barron
FROM: Kyra Stryker
SUBJECT: Recovered intel

The intel reports recovered from Banshee
Reeks appear to be compartmented. I will need
the access lists to those compartments.

    One document references an Iranian
    operative acquiring illegal nuclear material
    from Russia—our mole problem and hunt for the
    strontium in the Haifa bomb might converge.
    The problem is that this report does not
    appear in any Agency database I can access. I
    need to know whether it's being held in some
    compartment outside of the main system.
        Kyra

She sent the e-mail, sat back in her chair, and stared at the icon on the monitor that represented the second file Barron had sent her. She clicked on the icon.

William Fallon's record was lengthy, which she'd expected. The man had been in the Agency's employ for more than twenty years. He had started as a case officer, but had applied for a position in management only five years after entering on duty. He had never stayed in any one assignment more than three years and in most for two, jumping from office to office, with no commonalities between the portfolios each assignment covered. *More interested in moving up than learning anything,* Kyra decided. *He took whatever job was open as long as it was a promotion.*

Reading the man's annual performance evaluations took her an hour. His scores were high, but the comments entered by Fallon's superiors were drafted in the diplomatic language of bureaucrats who wanted to avoid protests and appeals. None had any issue with Fallon's operational skills, but a half hour's reading revealed a common criticism and another half hour confirmed it. The words were carefully chosen, but anyone who'd read enough reviews could see the message. Fallon was a narcissist and quite possibly a sociopath.

She turned to the other file that Barron had sent her, but got no farther than the first page when Barron's reply arrived.

TO: Kyra Stryker
FROM: Clark Barron
SUBJECT: Re: Recovered intel

Access lists attached. Had my minions do some research on the Banshee Reeks reports. Can't find the one you're looking for or the Iranian's name in any compartment. Who wrote the report?
    Barron

That's a fine question. Kyra brought the Banshee Reeks files up again and read them through one more time, looking for evidence pointing to their author, but finished with nothing.

There was another possibility. She leaned over, took the mouse and keyboard, and navigated to the metadata window, showing the hidden information attached to every Microsoft Word file that stored its author's name. The Agency had security tools that could strip the data out, but many officers forgot to use it on occasion.

She picked the first report, clicked the last few buttons, and the window came up.

Title: Iranian arms dealer trying to acquire uranium enrichment centrifuges
Subject: Nuclear proliferation
Author: Samantha Todd

Todd.

She looked at the other file Barron had sent her connected to William Fallon and reread the cover page. It was a file from the inspector general, only a few dozen pages long. Kyra stopped and stared at the screen.

REPORT OF INVESTIGATION
Disappearance of Samantha Todd(2016-0068-IG)
June 24, 2016

She picked up the black phone and dialed an outside line.

"Hello." Jon's voice was alert.

"It's me," Kyra said. "I need you to come in."

"Lunchtime?" he asked.

"Bring your boss, if she's available." Kyra hung up the phone and began to read.

Agency Dining Room 2 was a restaurant maintained so the director's chef could stay busy on days when there were no visiting guests. It had once been reserved for senior personnel only, but an egalitarian director had decided he didn't like the elitism and had opened it to all comers, which kept it busy. One usually needed a reservation, but occasional exceptions were made for special guests such as former Agency directors.

A server seated the trio by the windows that overlooked the north Langley woods and the George Washington Parkway. The Potomac River was just a few hundred feet beyond. Kathy looked out at the sight, almost identical to the one she had seen from her office years before.

The server took their drink order and left for the kitchen. Kathy waited until he was a safe distance away, then looked to Kyra. "What's up?"

"I've been going through the stuff that the FBI recovered at Banshee Reeks. I found something that I wanted to run by you two before I took it to Barron. What can you tell me about William Fallon?" she asked.

Kathy's face darkened, a look Jon had seen only rarely and knew that she reserved for the few people she truly disliked. Kyra could feel the anger reaching out from the woman in waves through the air. "You've never met him?" the older woman asked.

"No."

"He was our deputy station chief in Iraq when I was here," Kathy explained. "He was the bureaucratic version of Genghis Khan. People either loved him or hated him, nothing in between. He played bureaucratic turf games the way prison gangs try to carve out new territory inside a jail. What's the connection with him and this case?"

"Some of the intel recovered at Banshee Reeks was written by an officer named Samantha Todd." Kyra saw Cooke's face twist again at the mention of that name. "Director Barron sent me the Inspector General's report on her disappearance and Fallon's personnel file. The IG's file was pretty thin."

Kathy cocked her head. "I guess you wouldn't know that story, would you?"

"Should I?" Kyra asked.

"No. The investigation was compartmentalized," Kathy told the other woman. "Sam Todd was a case officer . . . She did a couple of tours, one in Pakistan, another in Argentina, a headquarters rotation. Then she volunteered for war zone duty. They assigned her to work Iranian nuclear proliferation and she landed in Fallon's unit. He sent her to Iraq. A lot of Iranian expats live in the southern part of the country, where the Shi'ites dominate, and she went down there looking to develop assets, and she didn't come back. The DO ran a manhunt in Iraq, but no one found anything. Fallon and several of his team were interviewed, but the investigation never went anywhere for lack of evidence. If ISIS or some other insurgent group grabbed her, they never went public. We were always afraid she would show up in one of those execution videos, but nothing like that ever came out. No propaganda movies, no nothing."

"The Iranians have a habit of grabbing Americans who wander too close to the border," Kyra noted.

"We considered that, but they usually try to squeeze us when they do that, at least for an apology, if not some kind of diplomatic concession. That never happened with Todd." Kathy picked up her water glass and sipped at it, staring at her husband. Kyra could see that this was a painful subject for her.

"Eventually, we had to tell the family. They didn't know she worked here and they didn't take it well," she said, looking at Jon.

"Do you think Fallon was responsible?" Kyra asked.

Kathy turned back away from the window. "Fallon was ambitious, he had an ego fit for a politician, and he liked to get creative with the rules and never took responsibility when things didn't work out," she recalled. "Todd wrote some of the intel that the Bureau recovered?"

Kyra nodded. "A report that the Brits were trying to recruit one of their expats who was trying to buy some radioactive generators for Tehran. He was unvetted, but SIS apparently agreed to put Todd in the same room with him anyway. But the report wasn't formatted like an Agency cable. It looked like an e-mail, and it isn't in any of our databases or compartments. So the mole had a report from Todd that was never entered into the system."

"A fabrication?" Jon asked.

"Maybe, but I don't think so," Kyra said. "I can't prove it though."

Kathy cursed. "I wish we'd had that during the investigation," she said. "I can't say for sure, but my guess is that Fallon was running some kind of unapproved op. If he sent Todd to that kind of meeting and it went south, his career would be dead."

"That would explain why they were sharing e-mails outside the regular systems," Jon observed. "He could've sold it to her as some kind of covert communications protocol set up just for that operation. She might not have even realized what Fallon was doing."

"What about the other reports the Bureau recovered?" Kathy asked.

"All compartmented. Barron gave me the access lists. Fallon and some members of his old team appear on them."

"Sounds like the list of candidates for the mole just got very short," Jon offered.

"Maybe," Kyra agreed. "But I don't know how to confirm the Todd report. Todd's not here to do it. The mole could confirm it, if we knew who he was. But if we knew who he was, we wouldn't need to confirm it. Catch-22."

"There is someone else who could do it," Kathy observed.

Kyra furrowed her brow, thinking. "I don't—"

Jon smiled at his wife. "The expat arms dealer, if he actually met with Todd. Of course, you'd have to find the dealer, and he's probably in Iran, which is denied territory. But I'm sure the director could clear the decks for that kind of operation." He looked at his wife with new admiration. "I love the way you think."

"I have my moments," Kathy replied as she lifted her water glass, a serene look on her face.

CIA Director's Office

"She's not wrong," Kyra observed. She set the hard copy of the Todd e-mail on Barron's desk. "Finding the arms dealer and confirming the report would certainly narrow down the suspect list. And those Russian RTGs that Todd talks about in her report could be the source of the strontium used in the Haifa dirty bomb."

"Maybe. The bigger questions are whether we can find Amiri and if he'll talk to us," Barron countered. "MI6 might be able to arrange a meeting if he's still one of their assets. Anything else?"

Kyra frowned. The director's body language betrayed a higher level of stress than she had seen in him before. "Something new?" he asked.

"Yes, sir. The IG investigated Fallon and several members of his team when Todd disappeared. Some of them appear on different access lists for the intel recovered at Banshee Reeks, but none of them appears on all of the lists. So either one mole has figured out how to breach one or more compartments, or we have several moles and they're working together."

"Our own Cambridge Five?" Barron asked. "The *Washington Post* will label them the Langley Five or whatever number we end up dealing with."

"Sir, with Salem burned, the only lead we've got now is this Todd cable. Let me go to Iran—"

"No," Barron said. "The mullahs would arrest you for breathing while American."

"Sir, you're the one who's been saying we need to find this mole quickly. This is the only way I see to do that . . . and it might give us an opportunity to accomplish something else."

"And that is?"

"Find Sam Todd. I think she was trying to meet with Amiri when she disappeared. Amiri might know what happened to her. In fact, he might be the only one who knows what happened to her."

"So, find the mole, find the strontium source, and find Sam Todd, all in one stroke? Sounds like a pipe dream."

"We won't know if we don't go."

Barron hesitated, a worried look on his worn face. "There are rules to the spy game, and the Iranians don't play by them."

"I know, sir, but the reward is worth the risk. I don't know if she's alive or dead, but neither does her family and that's not right. If she's still out there, we should do everything to bring her home. If she's not, we should find out so someone can tell her loved ones. Even if that's all we found out, it would be worth it."

Barron frowned at her. "Why does it matter to you?"

"Sir, you know I've been caught in denied territory. Jon pulled me out of Venezuela, you pulled me out of Russia. Todd deserves the same, but right now all I see is a cold case that no one else is working on. I think we owe her better."

Barron sighed and considered the woman for a minute. "I'll call Sir Ewan and see if they'll help us out. If they're willing to provide cover for you over there, you'll have a bit of a safety net. How's your British accent?"

"Nonexistent."

"It'll take me a day or two to set things up, assuming Sir Ewan cooperates. Learn fast."

The Red Cell Vault

Kyra punched Rhodes's number into her secure phone.

"Rhodes."

"This is Stryker. We've got a possible connection between one of our people and your case."

"Who?"

"William Fallon. I'll show you the file when you get here," Kyra promised.

"Did you dredge his name up just because he lives in that subdivision?"

"Yes, but there's more to him. He was investigated a few years ago."

"So he's got motive," Rhodes observed. "What did he do to earn time under the bright lights in a dark room with some of your people?"

"You'll need to come to Langley and sign some forms before we can talk about it. But if Hadfield knows Fallon, it might explain how Mossad got Hadfield's name for a pitch."

"I'll be there in an hour."

Kyra cradled the phone and stared at her computer, not seeing anything on the monitor. Then she picked up the phone again and dialed another number.

"This is Hadfield."

"This is Kyra Stryker from the Red Cell. Do you have a few minutes to talk?"

The Red Cell Vault

"Have you ever met Bill Fallon?" Kyra asked. Hadfield sat across from her and had protested having to answer questions while Rhodes was in the room. Kyra, in a taxing fit of diplomacy, had convinced the analyst to stay.

"I've heard the name. Nothing good," Hadfield replied.

"What've you heard?"

"That he was involved in something in Iraq that maybe got someone killed," Hadfield admitted. "Stuff like that, you hear about the big picture, but they don't share the details around the building. If it gets out into the open, it makes the Agency look bad. Why are you asking?"

"We can't tell you that," Rhodes cut in. "Just answer the questions, please."

"Did he pass my name to Mossad?" Hadfield asked.

"What makes you ask that?" The FBI officer shifted in his seat.

"Mossad thought I was worth pitching, so someone told them my story," Hadfield offered.

"Did you hear anything else about Mr. Fallon?"

Hadfield grimaced at some hidden memory. "That he would have lied to the pope's face during confession?"

"Don't get cute," Rhodes ordered.

"You're picking my brain about a guy I've never met," Hadfield retorted. "What am I supposed to say? Anything I can tell you wouldn't even qualify as hearsay."

"Who else knew about your son?" Rhodes asked. "Would Fallon know?"

"Plenty of people knew, after the fact. I don't know how many. That kind of story gets around the building, too. Maybe Fallon heard it from someone."

"That's a weak answer," Rhodes told him.

"It's the only one I've got."

"Where's your ex-wife?"

Hadfield rocked back at the question. "I don't know. I haven't talked to her in a long time. Why do you care?"

"Maybe she's got a better answer."

"And maybe you're an idiot."

"How about I charge you with obstruction? How about that?"

"How about I show you the finger and then show myself the door?" Hadfield asked.

"I think that would be a mistake—" Rhodes started.

"I know what you think," Hadfield said, cutting him off. "I don't care. I've seen people like you, playing games when real people are the pieces on the board and everyone's life gets torn up no matter how things play out. You want people like me to be afraid of you or just not have the spine to push back when you give an order you don't really have the authority to give, so you can control the situation. The fact is, after a doctor tells you that your child has one of the nastiest forms of cancer around, you suddenly see just how stupid most people and their little games really are. Then you watch that little boy go through more pain in a year than most people go through in their whole lives and it makes you see things right. Five years ago, I would've jumped at the chance to hit the street and be a pawn on your board . . . play in the big game, have a little excitement, and boost my own career. But frankly, *sir*, now I'm just tired. I've lost my wife and my boy. So it'll take more than threats from you to make me dance because the idea of losing my job and going bankrupt just doesn't raise my blood pressure anymore."

Kyra stood, walked to the vault door, and threw it open. Surprised, the men in the room looked up. "Special Agent Rhodes, would you step outside a moment, please?"

"No. Now close that door or—"

"If you don't step outside right now, the next person who will come through that door will be Director Barron. Once I tell him how you've treated this man without cause, I have no doubt he'll be on the phone to your director before our security officers get you out the front door," Kyra said.

Rhodes frowned, then stood up and walked out, and Kyra began to close the door behind him. Confused, Rhodes put his hand on the door to stop her. "You said you wanted to step outside."

"I said I wanted *you* to step outside. I didn't say I was going with you." Kyra shut the door on him, then returned to the table.

"He's not coming back in?" Hadfield asked.

"His badge isn't on the access list," Kyra told him. "He's not coming back in until I let him." The door buzzed to make the point. Kyra ignored it.

"So you're the good cop?"

"I'm not a cop at all. I'm Agency, just like you, so I couldn't arrest you if I wanted to," Kyra told him. "Now let's talk, just us."

"I already told you, I've never met Bill Fallon."

"I believe you," Kyra assured him. "That's not the only reason I asked you to come. The Bureau arrested Adina Salem who pitched you. You won't be seeing her again. Rhodes caught her trying to recover a dead drop. One of the docs inside the package was a cable written by one of our officers, a woman named Sam Todd."

Hadfield exhaled, long and slow, before speaking again. "She's the one who went missing in Iraq."

"Yes. Bill Fallon was her boss at the time. That's why we asked if you knew him. If you did, he would've become, shall we say, a person of interest."

"Do you know what happened to Todd?"

"No," Kyra said. "I'm just trying to piece together what happened, and I appreciate your cooperation." She sighed and leaned back. "Go on back to your office. I'll call you if I need to ask you anything else."

"What about Agent Douche out in the hall?"

"I'll handle him."

Hadfield ran a hand through his hair, his frustration obvious. "Fine," he said. "But if you guys do need me for anything else, you ask the questions." He pointed at the door. "I don't want to talk to that guy again."

"I can't promise that," Kyra admitted.

Hadfield stomped out past Rhodes when Kyra opened the door. The FBI officer was tempted to detain the fuming analyst but Kyra motioned him back into the vault. "You do that again—" he began.

"Why don't you stop with the threats? They haven't gotten anyone to work with you so far. I can't imagine why you think it'll start working now," Kyra advised.

Rhodes fought down his temper, trying to control the surging anger. He succeeded, but just barely. "I'm getting tired of you people not cooperating with me."

"Agent Rhodes, you're ambitious. I get that. You want to break this case because it'll make your career. I get that, too. But you'll get a lot further a lot faster if you'll stop trying to beat everyone around you into submission. You came in here expecting us to throw up the barricades—"

"Which you did."

"Only because you didn't come in peace. You came looking for us to give you trouble and you treated us accordingly before we'd done anything. So all this grief you're catching is your own karma coming back on you. Anytime you're ready to actually work with me, I'll work with you," Kyra finished.

Rhodes stared at the woman, trying to come up with some sexist name he could level at her. After a moment, he finally decided against tossing out any insult at all. "What did he tell you?" he asked.

"You heard the good stuff. After I left you in the hall, I spent the time trying to calm him down, a job for which I have little patience or skill."

"You'd better keep me in the loop on anything you find," Rhodes demanded.

"Contrary to your paranoia, we are professionals and haven't withheld anything from you that you're cleared to receive. You'll know something as soon as we do," Kyra said.

CHAPTER SEVEN

Beit Aghion (residence of the prime minister)
Jerusalem, Israel

The prime minister's call had not been unexpected. The American news services had broken the story of Adina Salem's arrest, leaked by some glory hound at the FBI, and Ronen had known the prime minister would want to hear the facts that no journalist could have known. So the *ramsad* had called the embassy in Washington to gather what details he could, committed them only to memory, and waited in his office for the summons.

The old man had been surprisingly cordial about it, offering Ronen the usual drinks and engaging in conversation about trivial matters for a few minutes before finally attacking the subject at hand. "You know that the American ambassador demarched me earlier today."

"The arrest of our officer in Virginia."

"Yes."

Ronen nodded. "I am surprised President Rostow did not call you to perform the deed personally."

"He despises me, deeply enough, I suppose, that it overcame any desire he had to humiliate me himself. How is your officer?"

"*Geveret* Salem? The FBI released her per Article Nine of the Vienna Convention on Diplomatic Relations and the State Department has declared her persona non grata, as expected. She is on her way home," Ronen told him. It was normal for a foreign national to be given a few days to leave the country they had offended, so they could close their affairs, though the deadline could be shortened in unusual cases. Salem was a single woman and had not been in Washington long enough to acquire much that would need to be shipped back to Tel Aviv. Arranging her departure had been straightforward. "In any case, you have my apology for the embarrassment this has caused Israel. I will offer my resignation, if you wish." He had a letter for that purpose in his coat pocket.

The prime minister waved away the suggestion. "We should not try to change horses in the middle of the river, as one of the American presidents liked to say. But it appears your new friend at the CIA was a dangle after all," the old man observed.

"No, I think not," Ronen replied.

The prime minister raised an eyebrow. "Then how did the FBI know that she was one of yours?"

"I am uncertain," the *ramsad* admitted. "But the information that Shiloh gave us on Salehi was accurate and far too sensitive for him to have been a dangle. No, something else breached Salem's cover. She reported that Shiloh was ready to give her the names of several other officers prepared to help our cause. She may have pitched one who reported the encounter. She would not have given her name, but perhaps he was able to identify her for the FBI. That is the only theory I have, unless she committed some other error that she failed to report."

The prime minister hid his frown behind his glass of alcohol, which he drained before speaking again. "She was inexperienced?" he asked.

"She is young, but not raw," Ronen said. "She performed very well for us in several operations in Egypt and the Muslim communities in France, so we thought she was ready to try Washington. But the United States is a very different culture. Salem has a bias toward action that did not serve her well there. It put her at great risk with little hope for any reward. So she will come home and we will reassign her to another field."

"You will not terminate her position within Mossad?" Israel's senior leader had little patience for failure.

Ronen shook his head. "In these times, we need every officer and she is a good one. Her failure was as much my fault as her own. We simply need to find the right place and the right targets for her, a team where that instinct for action will be an asset instead of a disadvantage. We have no shortage of those now."

The old man nodded. "It is your decision, of course. Has this endangered your 'Shiloh'?"

Ronen didn't answer his superior for a moment. The truth was that he had spent little time thinking about anything else since he had learned of Salem's detention, and he was still unsure of the answer. "I cannot answer that. The FBI recovered Shiloh's package, so we do not know everything it contained and cannot guess whether they can identify him through it. But the Americans are not stupid. They know for certain now that they have a mole, but I have too little information to say whether this affair has left him in any immediate danger . . ." Ronen trailed off, his mind still working on the problem. He shook his head. "We cannot calculate the risks without knowing all of the variables and we know less than I would like about our asset."

"Then he is dangerous," the prime minister observed.

"Yes," Ronen agreed. "I am told that he contacted us and offered to deliver the information to us at another site. I approved the operation—"

"And you trust that he is not setting up your people?"

"How could one ever trust a person who betrays his own country? Such men are useful, yes. To be trusted? Never. But I believe he still wants to help us." The Mossad director stood and began to button his suit jacket. "If you will excuse me, sir, I must get back. Our Washington office will be calling back on whether we have Shiloh's package."

"Of course," the older man said. "But you must be careful, Gavi.

This affair with Salem will pass. I think that Haifa has earned us enough sympathy in the United States that we might be forgiven once, but a second offense of this kind could cost us more goodwill than we can spare."

"I understand," Ronen replied. "And if my instincts about Shiloh are wrong, you must accept my resignation in the morning."

"I will regret it very much if that becomes necessary," the prime minister told him.

Ben's Chili Bowl
Washington, DC

The Mossad agent finished the half smoke and wiped his face with a napkin. It was impossible to eat the hot dog in any kind of dignified fashion, slathered as it was in the chili that Americans loved so much, along with a ridiculous amount of mustard and chopped onions that had caused his mouth to burn and surely would do the same to his stomach later. Even the wildly misnamed "healthy options" on the menu were buried under ladles of the meat stew, and the turkey burgers did nothing for the patron's health when they were paired with an enormous basket of chili cheese fries. This eatery was a landmark in the district, over seventy years old, but the Israeli man thought it a miracle that it had any repeat customers. They should all have dropped dead of a clogged artery after a single outing.

It had taken him much of the day to get here by the indirect route he had chosen. He had started at the Jefferson Memorial, then worked his way north through the Air and Space Museum, then the National Archives, where the darkness had depressed him. He had decided against taking a tour of the International Spy Museum, thinking that particular destination would be a cause of considerable mockery by the FBI if he was caught later.

He had considered a stop at the Holocaust Museum but that holy place deserved better than to be a stop on his surveillance detection route. He had promised himself that he would go there, but it was going to be on the final day of his tour in Washington, DC. He knew that he would only be able to bear a visit to the museum once and that he would weep by the end of it. The man had lost his great-grandparents to Hitler's camp at Sobibór and to see their story told in all its details would make the day one of the most important and disturbing of his life. It infuriated him that anyone in this world could be so sick in spirit as to deny the Nazis' attempt at genocide.

He had finally arrived at this little greasy spoon that, for some reason that eluded him, drew celebrities and political leaders in a kind of culinary pilgrimage, a bizarre American hajj. He had ordered what the woman ahead of him had ordered and, to his surprise, found it disturbingly delicious. He tried not to think of all the ways it likely violated the *kashrut,* the Jewish dietary laws. He was not one to keep kosher—a virtually impossible task when one was engaged in covert operations abroad—but this meal violated the laws of good sense at least as much as it did the laws of God. Perhaps that explained his guilt at having enjoyed it as much as he had.

He pushed the empty tray away and made his way to the small bathroom. He closed the door, locked it behind him, then set about taking care of the reason he'd spent the day outside.

Shiloh had signaled that there was a package waiting via a single message.

```
I dug up the Blu-ray set for you the other
night, but I heard you had some car trouble
on the way over. Really sorry to hear it.
If you want to come by tonight, it's still
waiting. I'll throw in Series 3 for you, too.
```

The Mossad chief of station had checked the list and cursed when he saw the location data. The unknown mole was a bold one to leave a dead-drop package here and the station chief had considered refusing his approval to retrieve it. As with the Banshee Reeks site, where Adina Salem had been detained, it was not a sound operational choice. It was apparent that Shiloh was not a field officer, but it seemed the *ramsad* was prepared to forgive that failing given the times, and Shiloh was giving them a second chance to receive the intel that Salem had tried to recover. That suggested it was especially valuable, which would justify some added risk. Still, they needed to find a way to convince Shiloh to let them pick the sites, or at least reject the ones that were overly risky, like this one. Too many patrons came through here, though he supposed none of them would be motivated to look inside the toilet tank. The Mossad officer lifted the ceramic top off and looked inside. The package was there, a simple letter inside a sealed ziplock bag attached to the inside wall with duct tape. He flushed the toilet, letting the water drain, and pulled the letter out. It had been submerged and he used a paper towel to wipe it off before tucking it away in the inside pocket of his jacket. He replaced the top of the tank, then washed his hands, unlocked the door, and stepped out.

Another man was waiting by the door, tall, African American, a powerful build covered by a fine tailored suit. Their eyes met.

The Israeli smiled and stepped aside. "All yours."

"Thanks," the American muttered. He stepped into the bathroom and closed the door.

The Mossad officer made his way outside and began his walk back to the embassy, another surveillance detection route that would, mercifully, be shorter than the one that had led him to the restaurant. He began to walk west along U Street.

It took him two more hours to reach the embassy, where he handed over the envelope and his duties for the day came to an end.

But he took a few minutes to rest his sore feet and to draft his report. That task done, he added the appropriate names to the distribution list, and then one more. Salem had championed Shiloh's value as an asset to her less courageous colleagues, and he knew it wounded her to be sent home, leaving him to another handler. She would be relieved to know that Shiloh's information again was in their hands.

Israeli Institute for Intelligence and
Special Operations (Mossad) Headquarters
Tel Aviv, Israel

The building's location was a state secret. It had guards and barriers and all the usual security, but anonymity was the real wall protecting it, and that defense was tissue thin. That this place had remained hidden so long was a miracle of sorts. Ronen had only two real fears left. The first was that Iran would someday set off a nuclear device inside his country, not just a dirty bomb but a true warhead that would erase one of Israel's cities from the landscape. The second was that the site of Mossad's home would someday be revealed to the world. If that fact ever escaped into the world, children across the Middle East would begin to dream of becoming the suicide bomber who set off the truck bomb that wrecked the headquarters of the *HaMossad leModi'in uleTafkidim Meyuhadim*. The man who succeeded in that operation would become a martyr venerated by endless generations of future killers.

The building itself was one of the more modern facilities in Israel. The grounds were meticulous and clean, adorned with sculptures created by some of the country's more famous artists. Ronen's single regret these days was that he did not get to spend more time outside the building, walking in the gardens and enjoying the greenery that was too rare in the countryside outside the walls.

It was very early when he entered the building, the sun only start-ing to rise over the horizon. The short meeting with the prime min-ister had convened late in the night and then he had returned home to sleep for a few hours, which was becoming a rarity. He thought it a fortunate thing that his wife had left him years before. Ronen still loved the woman and it had always hurt that his country had claimed more of his life than she had. Now, in the midst of these events, she would hardly have seen him at all. She deserved better and had found it with another man. He was saddened but not angry. Her new husband was a good man who had served well in the Israel Defense Forces and was as devoted to her now as Ronen always wished he could have been.

The walk to his office was less than five minutes. He said nothing to anyone on the way until he reached the outer door. Sitting next to it on a plain wooden chair was Adina Salem.

"Have you been home?" Ronen asked the woman. The lack of sleep was apparent on her young face.

"No, sir. I came here straight from the airport. I have information I wanted to share."

"Come in." Ronen opened his door and turned on the light. The woman followed behind him and closed the door as he sat down behind his desk.

"Sir, I regret the loss of Shiloh's intelligence—"

Ronen waved away her apology. "Do not worry about that. I have no doubt that you did all you were able to do to preserve it. Perhaps more than you should have, from what I read," he chided her gently. "You should not endanger your life to protect such things in countries where your life and freedom are not at risk."

Salem nodded, her expression still depressed. "I understand, sir. But I find it strange that the FBI had a considerable force waiting at the drop site."

"Do you think Shiloh was a provocateur? That he set you up for arrest?" He had his own thoughts on that matter, but he wanted to hear Salem's before deciding her case.

She hesitated before answering. "My instincts tell me otherwise, but perhaps that is wishful thinking. I do not know how the FBI knew to be there, but I do not think it was Shiloh."

Ronen nodded to the young officer. "I trust my people. Your word is enough. Was that all?"

"No, sir," Salem continued. "I admit, I opened Shiloh's package and scanned the contents on the scene. Perhaps that was against protocol, but I was anxious to see what Shiloh had given us. There were several reports inside. One was quite different from the others."

"How so?"

"It was not formatted like a normal intelligence report. It was more of a letter. I do not know who wrote it and it was clearly not intended for us."

"Do you remember what this letter said?" Ronen asked.

"Only part of the first sentence. I kept repeating it in my mind so I would not forget it. I wrote it down after my release from FBI custody." She reached into her pocket and extracted a slip of paper, which she held out for Ronen. He took it and read the words, written in block letters.

> British Senior Intelligence Service (SIS) liaison has identified the buyer as Asqar Amiri, a British expatriate working from Kish Island for the Iranian government to arrange the clandestine acquisition of arms and sanctioned nuclear materials.

Asqar Amiri. Another name for Mossad to extinguish. Ronen studied the paper, reading it several times.

"The author of the letter said that this Amiri was involved in smuggling materials for Iran's nuclear program," Salem added when Ronen looked up. "He also said that Amiri works out of Kish Island

and was involved in a deal to buy radioisotope thermoelectric generators from the Russians."

Ronen's eyebrows went up at that bit of news. "RTGs?"

Salem nodded at him. "Yes, sir. I did a bit of research earlier this morning while I was waiting here for you to return. Some Russian RTGs use strontium 90 as their power source, the same element that was used in the Haifa dirty bomb. Sir, of all the material in the package, I think that was the report that Shiloh most wanted us to have. If Iran acquired those Russian devices, then Shiloh may have given us the source of the nuclear material used to attack Haifa."

"That is quite possible . . . and the name of the man responsible for delivering it to our attackers," Ronen agreed. There was no question, the man named on the page merited an operation, and the *ramsad* found his anger rising. This was the kind of information the Americans should have been passing through official channels. *We should be receiving this . . . but not this way.*

He looked up at the young woman. "Clearly justice must be delivered to such a man. Would you like an opportunity to redeem yourself?"

"Yes, sir!" Salem exclaimed.

"I thought so," he told her. "Go home and clean up. Rest tonight, then report back in the morning. And, Salem?"

"Sir?"

"I received a call shortly before you arrived. Shiloh signaled another drop and one of our officers was successful in retrieving it this time. Your friends in Washington are still going through it, but the officer who secured it wanted you to know. It seems that Shiloh did not set you up after all."

"Yes, sir. Thank you, sir," Salem said. She turned and left his office.

Ronen picked up his telephone and pressed a single button. The call was answered on the second ring. *"Bo-ker tov.* I want to see him in my office within the next hour. *Kol tuv.*" Then he replaced the phone and read the paper a third time. *And* kol tuv *to you, Shiloh*, he thought. *You are doing us a great service.*

Surrounded as their country was by hostile neighbors, Israel's leaders had always been firm believers that one execution, the right person snuffed out at the right moment, could be worth entire divisions of men and armor on the battlefield. Many foreign leaders had thought twice about supporting attacks on Israel out of the simple fear that they might awaken one night to see a Mossad barrel pointed at them, or, more likely, just never awaken at all. The Americans liked to joke that it was God's job to judge terrorists and their marines' job to arrange the meeting. Mossad had arranged many such meetings but not as many as they would have liked.

There were fewer than a hundred members of that particular Mossad unit. All were recruits from Israel's special forces or other groups within Mossad itself. All had trained for two years in the Negev Desert before moving out into the field, where they might reside for years at a time to conduct a single operation. The mullahs in Tehran lived in fear of that Mossad unit. It was not implausible that these few dozen had done more to hold back Iran's nuclear ambitions than the efforts of the rest of the world combined.

The head of the unit sat in Ronen's office. His hair was peppered with white, the only real sign that he was growing old. The rest of his body was in excellent shape, not overly muscular, but there was clear strength visible through his shirt. He was not entirely morose, but it took either a very funny joke or a considerable amount of alcohol to make him laugh.

He was as sober as Moses today. The man read the paper carefully, then folded it and placed it back on the table. "Asqar Amiri," he said. "We have heard his name before, but we were not able to learn from where he operates until now."

"It is never a simple thing to find men who don't want to be found . . . harder when one's allies withhold useful information. Now we know," Ronen observed. "How long to send a team?"

"I will have to redeploy one of my teams already in Iran. I can have a small unit on Kish Island by tomorrow night. A larger one would take a few more days, possibly a week."

"Very good," Ronen said. "I would like to hear that this man, Amiri, has been extinguished within the week."

"If he is there now, that should be possible. If he is not, the team will find his base of operations and watch for him. I will be able to give you an estimate of his life expectancy then, depending on where he is and which assets we have to deploy."

Ronen nodded. "See to it. And if there are any other bits of low-hanging fruit in Shiloh's reports, feel free to pluck them at the earliest moment of opportunity."

"We already have one picked out in Tehran. We will deal with him and then I will redeploy that team to Kish to handle Amiri, assuming they have not already finished him."

"Good," Ronen replied. He valued men who shared the dangers of the front line with their subordinates. It showed commitment, both to the mission and to Israel itself. Soldiers would follow such men into Gehenna itself. "I want Salem assigned to the Kish Island unit. After her failure in Washington, I want her to have an opportunity to redeem herself at the earliest moment. It is important our people know that we do not lose faith in them when a mission fails through no fault of theirs."

"Have her report to my office in the morning and I will arrange it," the subordinate assured him. "I assume we have permission to proceed?"

"You do."

The field officer nodded, stood, and walked out, already calculating options and possibilities in his mind. In the office, Ronen leaned back in his chair, took the Salem report, and filed it in the drawer behind his desk.

Jamaran District
Tehran, Iran

The target in Tehran was Dr. Qolam Rouhani.

Mossad had many of its own sources in Tehran and had been using the intelligence to assemble a list of nuclear scientists who would be executed if and when their deaths were needed to ensure Israel's survival. But this particular name had escaped them. The Iranians had been keeping the identities of their nuclear scientists hidden for the same reason they had not announced the now-dead nuclear program director's appointment. That had not saved him, and thanks to Shiloh's first tranche of information, it would not save the scientists who had likewise labored in anonymity.

The *ramsad* had approved a team of fifteen to remove Rouhani from the world, an unusually large group for this kind of operation. There were twelve men and three women, all veterans of the *Sayeret Matkal*, Israel's finest commando unit. They entered the country on separate days using false British, Russian, French, and Swiss passports, and met at a designated safe house just outside Tehran's limits that Mossad had maintained at great expense since the Iranian revolution. The equipment they needed had been cached in the basement for years, sealed inside metal crates buried under the basement dirt and covered by the concrete floor. It took two hours to crack through it with the small hammers kept in the upstairs closets and dig through with the shovels kept in the garage. The Semtex, ten kilos' worth, and detonators were in separate boxes. They would only need a small fraction of that for this first operation; the rest, later perhaps, depending on whether the *ramsad* named other targets in their area of responsibility.

The team was divided into five units, each named after a letter of the Hebrew alphabet. The Het squad, three men, established cover for the team, renting three cars, buying food, and taking care of the other logistics that would be needed for the next week.

The Ayin unit, six men and one woman, had the tedious job of gathering the bits of data needed to bring Rouhani's life to a violent close. They had little information on the scientist other than his photograph and the address of his residence, but they really needed nothing more to start. Two days' surveillance suggested that he was a man of habit. He arose both mornings at five o'clock and walked out of his house at five forty-five lost in thought, hardly aware of his environment. He drove the same route to his office both days, which was located in an industrial complex ten miles away with no identifying signs. The two Israeli officers who followed him had spent those days in their car parked three blocks away, sitting until their buttocks cramped on the thin padding of the seats in their rental car, a locally manufactured Saipa Tiba, a low-end four-door subcompact that, mercifully, had air conditioning. It was not difficult to follow Rouhani. Tehran's streets were well maintained and Rouhani's early drive to avoid the heavier rush-hour traffic kept things simple for the Ayins.

Rouhani broke for lunch and walked around the building at half-past noon for thirty minutes each day, then returned inside. He left for home at three, drove his morning route in reverse, and arrived at a fixed time. His evenings proved less predictable. The first night he spent at a local pub watching soccer with friends, the second at home with his girlfriend, who was his neighbor's wife judging by the early hour at which she left for her home after spending only two hours on Rouhani's couch. Both nights, the man had retired by ten and was asleep by eleven.

They watched him a third day just to be certain that the first two hadn't been unlikely coincidences of scheduling, but nothing changed. Rouhani's faithful adherence to routine was the only approval they required to proceed. They knew enough about the target to plan the kill, and had gathered enough information to work out the escape routes for the two teams that would perform the act.

The Aleph and Bet squads were one man and one woman each. The Alephs had the honor of being the trigger on the gun, as it were, the pair chosen to execute the man that Israel had decided should die. The Bets were backup, there to shadow the Alephs, perform their mission if something or someone unexpected stopped the first team, and cover them while they were in the act of slaughtering their target.

The murder itself only took an hour to arrange. The Alephs and Bets waited until almost two o'clock to begin. The stars above their heads were washed out by Tehran's lights, but the moon was full and high enough to let them see the path running between the houses. The scientist parked his car in a locked garage attached to his home, which was no obstacle. The female half of Aleph picked the lock to the door in ten seconds, which was more time than she needed to get into the car once she discovered Rouhani kept it locked even in his own home. Her male counterpart took the rest of the hour doing the real work on the car while the Bets kept watch outside in their vehicle fifty yards down the street. It would have been simple enough to walk into Rouhani's bedroom and shoot him in the head. They would have needed only seconds, but Mossad preferred to kill with style when possible. Terrorists were not the only ones who understood that theatrics could send a message, and Mossad wanted Israel's enemies to be forever looking over their shoulders and under their seats.

They closed up the car, and slipped out into the side alley between the buildings.

They spent the rest of the night sitting in their own car three blocks down the street by Bahonar Park. Rouhani would be awake in two hours and dead in three. They were sure of the quality of their work, but the *ramsad* wanted visual confirmation of the execution. So they talked to pass the time, mostly of mundane matters . . . nothing about old operations or predictions of future ones. They spoke of family troubles and politics.

The digital clock in the car's dash reported that it was almost five. The Alephs had learned that Ayatollah Khomenei himself had lived in this neighborhood for most of his life. They thought it fitting that a new campaign to save Israel from the mullahs for another decade would pass through the hometown of the man who had made this country Israel's mortal enemy.

The lights in Rouhani's bedroom came on at the appointed time. Through their shared binoculars, the squad saw the slight movement of shadow in his room behind the curtain. Rouhani took his usual half hour to shave, shower, dress, and swallow a quick cup of sweet tea, slather jam on lavash bread, and eat some feta cheese. His appetite sated, the man entered his garage two minutes later than the average time that the Ayin unit had reported.

He started his car and opened the garage door by hand. Then he opened the driver's-side door, took his seat, fastened the safety belt, and eased the car out onto the street. He parked again, ran back to the house, and closed the entrance to the carport, then walked back. Seated and belted inside the car again, Rouhani put the automobile in gear and began to drive. He noticed two parked cars ahead. He could not recall seeing them on the street the evening before, but he was never particularly observant about his surroundings.

Rouhani approached the first car. There were two people inside, he realized, just sitting there. He turned his head. They were looking at him.

One of them, the woman, raised a hand, holding something. A phone? It was the right size, but she didn't put it to her ear—

The directional charge hidden in the driver's seat headrest exploded, a fraction of a kilo of Semtex firing straight into the back of Rouhani's head. His scalp melted and his hair burned off instantly as his skull came apart like a melon rind hit by a sledgehammer and everything inside was blasted against the front windshield, which spider-webbed from the shock wave and was painted with blood and brains. The car's side windows blew out from the overpressure, fire and smoke rushing out, and the muffled rumble of the explosion escaped out into the morning air. Rouhani's headless corpse was pushed forward by the explosion until it struck the steering column. The man's foot was still pressed on the gas pedal and the car continued to move forward, veering to the left due to a slight misalignment of the front tires, finally striking a tree at just over thirty-five kilometers per hour, the engine still running.

The Alephs pulled forward, following the planned escape route back to the safe house. The Bets had had their own backup detonator in case the other team's unit failed. Had both devices been stubborn and refused to work, the male half of Bet had been cradling an AK-47 in his lap. He hadn't wanted to use it. There was no élan in gunning a man down that way. He started their car and the woman beside him took a photograph of Rouhani's wrecked car and body as they passed by. She looked in the rearview and saw neighbors started to emerge from their homes, wondering about the source of the loud noise that had disturbed their quiet sleep. Groggy and distracted by the sight of Rouhani's automobile crushed against a tree and starting to burn, they failed to notice the make or model or color of the two cars or any other bit of information the Iranian security services could have used to track down the man's killers.

The last squad of the team, Qom, was the smallest, actually a single member, the youngest of the group at just twenty-eight. His job was communications. He had missed out on the more exciting parts of this particular mission, he thought, but he did have the honor of

telling the *ramsad* that another of Israel's enemies had been extermi-
nated. The *ramsad* acknowledged the message personally and offered
his gratitude for their bravery in the defense of Israel, but he gave the
unit no orders to come home. Instead, he told the Qom that it should
be ready to move by nightfall. There was another target. The *ramsad*
provided the broad outlines, but the head of their unit would meet
them personally to share the fine details of their next assignment.

The young man disconnected the call, then looked up at his
teammates. "The *ramsad* expresses his gratitude for our services and
his satisfaction that the operation came off without any complications. He also has new orders for us."

"A new mission?" one of the Alephs asked.

"Yes. We are to deploy to a safe house on Kish Island. I have the
address. We will join an officer there who is coming from home. All
other operations are delayed."

"Any reason given?"

"No," the Qom admitted. "We will receive the particulars in person tomorrow."

"Then let's get moving," the male Bet told his friends. "If everything else is being pushed back, then the *ramsad* must think someone
on Kish Island is in desperate need of some justice. Let's make sure
he gets his share of it." The rest of the team muttered their agreement and then broke up and started packing their gear.

Leesburg, Virginia

"You hear that ruckus the other night?" William Fallon's neighbor
was the talkative sort and had a talent for coming out the door in
the mornings to start his commute whenever Fallon was doing the
same. An overweight refugee from New York City, Walter spoke with
a Queens accent that grated on Fallon's nerves, no matter the subject

of the conversation, and he was either impervious or oblivious to Fallon's body language. Still, the intelligence officer couldn't bring himself to tell the northerner to bugger off. The man's wife was attractive and Fallon didn't want word of his lack of manners getting back to her ears. One needed to keep one's options open, after all.

"No."

"Happened late, real late," the neighbor reported. "After midnight. I was still up, playing games, and heard the crash, even through my headphones. Somebody was driving way fast in the neighborhood, really gunning the engine, and they T-boned another car. I stepped outside, but I couldn't figure out where it came from. After a few minutes, I saw the ambulance lights and ran on over. The wreck was down at the intersection, over by the drainage pond. I'm surprised anyone came out of it. Funny thing was, it wasn't the police who were in charge."

Fallon frowned. The man had his interest for once. "Who was it?"

"A bunch a' guys in FBI jackets."

"The Bureau?"

"Yeah. Loudoun County deputies showed up with the ambulance, but they weren't running the show. It was those federal guys. Two of them rode away with some woman in the ambulance. Looked like they had her cuffed to the gurney. Didn't know the feds would arrest you for reckless driving," Fallon's neighbor recalled. "But she was a hottie. Probably a drunk, though. I'd love to know who she was."

Me too, Fallon thought. "Sounds like I missed something big. If you hear anything else, let me know."

"Yeah, sure thing."

The commute into Langley was miserable, an accident at the intersection of the Dulles Toll Road and the Capital Beltway having backed up traffic for ten miles. Fallon navigated through Dulles Airport so he could get onto the airport access road and avoid both the tolls and the traffic, but it still took longer than an hour to make the drive. His reserved parking space saved him from a long walk to the building, which still did nothing to improve his typically dark mood.

He walked into his vault a half hour later than he preferred, the office secretary already at her desk. "Director Barron's office called early. He wants to see you in his conference room."

"When?"

"He said as soon as you arrived."

"'He said'?" Fallon asked. "He called himself?"

"It was him," the secretary confirmed.

CIA Director's Conference Room

```
FM AMEMBASSY LONDON
TO DCIA WASHDC IMMEDIATE


TEXT
SUBJECT: ASSASSINATION OF IRANIAN SCIENTIST
QOLAM ROUHANI


1. (TS//NF) UK EMBASSY TEHRAN REPORTS VIA
MI6 LIAISON THAT IRANIAN SCIENTIST DR. QOLAM
ROUHANI WAS ASSASSINATED YESTERDAY NEAR HIS
HOME IN JAMARAN, TEHRAN, BY PERSON OR PERSONS
UNKNOWN.


2. (TS//NF) A SHAPED CHARGE WAS HIDDEN INSIDE
THE DRIVER'S SIDE HEADREST OF ROUHANI'S
PERSONAL VEHICLE. PHYSICAL EVIDENCE SUGGESTS
THE CHARGE WAS DETONATED REMOTELY. ROUHANI
WAS DECAPITATED SHORTLY AFTER 0530 WHEN HE
LEFT HIS HOME FOR WORK.
```

3. (TS//NF) FORENSIC ANALYSIS OF THE BLAST
BY IRANIAN POLICE SUGGESTS A SEMTEX CHARGE
SIGNIFICANTLY SMALLER THAN ONE (1) KILOGRAM,
SUFFICIENT TO KILL ROUHANI AND ANYONE ELSE
INSIDE THE VEHICLE BUT NOT DESTROY THE
VEHICLE ITSELF.

4. (TS//NF) INVESTIGATOR POSITIVELY
IDENTIFIED ROUHANI'S IDENTITY VIA
FINGERPRINTING AND FAMILY IDENTIFICATION OF
PHYSICAL TRAITS OBSERVABLE ON THE INTACT PART
OF THE BODY. DENTAL MATCHING WAS IMPOSSIBLE
DUE TO THE STATE OF THE VICTIM'S CRANIUM.

The CIA watch officer on duty in the Situation Room delivered the paper to the Red Cell on Barron's orders. It was the last stop on a tortured route that had started in a restaurant in Tehran where an Iranian turncoat on the MI6 payroll had reported the assassination to his British handler, who had written up the juicy tidbit and sent it off to his own superiors at Vauxhall Hall in London. The British shared the information with their American cousins after sanitizing some of the more sensitive details, and the CIA liaison shortened the report and dispatched it to Langley within an hour after he received it.

Kyra read the cable at a far slower pace than she normally consumed such things and then reread it a second time. The information had clearly passed through several hands before finally reaching hers, which meant details likely had been twisted and obscured. For some reason she couldn't fathom, Agency cables were usually drafted using the universal language of bureaucracy, all passive voice and ambiguities combined to present their message in the least detailed manner possible. But in this particular case, the unknown author in London had been smart enough to know who the audience was for this particular report and he kept the language tight and blunt, especially in the last sentence.

```
5. (TS//NF) IRANIAN AUTHORITIES ATTRIBUTE
ROUHANI'S DEATH TO ISRAEL'S MOSSAD BUT HAVE
NOT ELABORATED.

END OF MESSAGE TOP SECRET
```

"I assume that Rouhani was another one of your code-word compartments?" Rhodes asked.

"You assume correctly," Barron confirmed. "And we didn't learn about him from the Brits either. We developed that bit of intelligence on our own."

"So this tells us nothing."

"It tells us that somebody finally passed the Banshee Reeks intel to Mossad," Kyra said. "If true, the good news is that we have at least a partial copy of their kill list."

"The bad news is that arresting Salem pinched off a solid lead—" Rhodes started.

"You wouldn't be sitting down to interview William Fallon if you hadn't," Kyra observed, shutting him down. "And the Israelis would've gotten Rouhani's name a few days sooner. Same result."

The phone on the table buzzed. Barron leaned forward and pressed a button. "Sir, William Fallon is here to see you," the secretary announced.

"Thank you." Barron looked up at Kyra. "When are you heading out?"

"As soon as we finish talking to Fallon."

"I'll ask Jon to come in for a few days to work with Mr. Rhodes here until you get back."

"I'm sure you'll earn his undying love if you do," Kyra offered.

"I don't care about his undying love. He owes me," Barron said. "And Agent Rhodes . . . Sam Todd's case is also a code word compartment, and we've got plenty of those getting spilled open these days. So, unless you can make a very strong case why I should change my mind, the rest of your team doesn't get read-in. They know he's a person of interest and that's plenty for now. We'll keep you in the loop on any developments there and you can argue for more access then."

Rhodes frowned but decided not to argue for once. "Yes, sir."

Barron didn't rise when Fallon entered the room. "Director Barron—" Fallon started. His voice was quite friendly, which seemed out of line with the details Kyra had gleaned from his personnel file.

"I'm not staying," Barron announced. "I'm just here to make the introductions. This is Special Agent Jesse Rhodes of the FBI, and this is Kyra Stryker, chief of the Red Cell. She's working with the Bureau for this investigation. I expect your full cooperation with them both."

"Investigation?" Fallon asked, surprised.

"They'll explain it." The director nodded at Kyra. "Have a good flight."

"Thank you, sir," she said.

Barron walked out, closing the door behind himself and not being quiet about it. Rhodes pulled out a set of credentials, which he held out toward Fallon. "Have a seat, please."

"I . . . okay." Fallon took the nearest seat. Rhodes uncapped his pen, and scribbled a date and time on a legal notepad. "Mr. Fallon, are you aware that the FBI arrested a spy in your subdivision a few nights ago?" Rhodes asked.

Awareness dawned on Fallon's face. "One of my neighbors told me this morning that there had been some kind of incident. He told me that he saw some Bureau officers ride away with a woman in an ambulance," Fallon replied. "What was she doing there?"

"She was retrieving a dead drop at Banshee Reeks."

"Seriously?"

"Do you think I'm playing with you?" Rhodes set a copy of Adina Salem's photograph down on the table. "Do you know this woman?"

Fallon looked at the picture and shook his head. "No. Should I?"

"This is Adina Salem. Until her arrest, she was listed as a legal adviser to the Israeli embassy here in Washington. We reviewed the information in the package she was trying to retrieve and found a report written by a Samantha Todd several years ago, but which was never entered into any CIA database."

Fallon rolled his eyes and his head slumped down. He took a deep breath and laid his hands flat on the tabletop. "That again."

"So you know Miss Todd?"

"Of course I know her. C'mon, the inspector general went over all of that with me!" Fallon protested.

"We know," Kyra replied. "You pleaded ignorance."

Fallon shrugged. "I don't know what happened to her."

"But you sent her out on the assignment where she disappeared," Rhodes observed.

"Yes."

"You didn't file an ops cable proposing the meeting," Kyra observed. "I tried to look it up. It doesn't exist."

"It was an oversight at the time," Fallon explained.

"Here's the problem, Mr. Fallon," Rhodes announced. "Mossad is out there tearing up Iran right now. Then we find a Mossad agent trying to recover intel written by Sam Todd and not in any database, and the drop site for that happens to be a half mile from the house of one of the very, very few CIA officers connected to Todd's disappearance. So the only people who could possibly have passed that intel to Mossad are people who were in contact with Todd before she went missing . . . but no one admitted to the IG that Todd was passing them reports. So I'm inclined to think that somebody was lying. In fact, I'm inclined to think that they withheld evidence from the

IG to stay out of trouble, despite the fact that such evidence *might* have helped the Agency find Todd. And it's not going to be hard to convince Director Barron that someone willing to leave a *woman* to rot in an Iranian prison in order to protect themselves might be just the kind of person willing to sell intel to Mossad."

Fallon stared at him, eyes wide. "I wouldn't . . . I wouldn't do that—" he said, tapping the table with his index finger, punctuating his words.

"There aren't that many people to look at, Mr. Fallon, and I don't think it's a coincidence that the dead drop was within spitting distance of your back deck," Rhodes offered. "So either you're lying or someone is setting you up."

"I'd say the latter," Fallon said, grabbing at what he obviously thought was a way out.

"And why would they set you up?" Rhodes asked.

Fallon waved his hands in the air. "I have no idea. Maybe I hurt somebody's feelings, I don't know—"

Kyra shook her head. "No. Someone isn't going to commit treason and set you up for it just because you were rude—"

"It's *not* me!"

Rhodes spoke carefully, trying to contain himself and choosing his words with precision. "Unfortunately for you, I can't just take your word for it. So as of this moment, here's what's going to happen. I'm going to recommend that the director place you on administrative leave. The SPOs outside will escort you from this room out of the building."

"That'll destroy my career—" Fallon protested.

"I'm sure that Sam Todd, sitting in her cell in Tehran somewhere, is just crying over how hard your life is right now," Kyra spit out. "Your other choice is to tell us what really happened with Sam Todd. If you didn't do anything wrong, that'll help clear all this up a lot faster."

Fallon gritted his teeth. "I have nothing more to say about it. I didn't do anything wrong."

"Then I must also ask you to surrender your passport," Rhodes told him. "Please don't leave Virginia and don't leave Loudoun County without telling the Bureau first." He passed the CIA officer a business card. "Please contact my office first if you need to travel."

"And if I don't?"

"We're looking for a mole. I don't think you want to give us more reasons to consider you a suspect," Rhodes told him. "But if I find that you've tried to hide anything from me, I'll have you charged with obstruction of justice."

Fallon let out a snort of derision and took the card. "You're wasting your time looking at me."

"Go home, Mr. Fallon," Rhodes said.

The door closed and Kyra and Rhodes let out a long, slow breath. "A shame that Jon wasn't here," Kyra said. "He would have enjoyed that."

Rhodes nodded. "That man was rattled."

"He was," Kyra confirmed. "I didn't see any signs of deception when you asked him about the dead drop . . . but when we mentioned Todd, his head went down, he hardly blinked when he talked, repeated phrases, pointed a lot," she observed. "I reread the IG's notes on his interview with Fallon a few years ago. He didn't behave that way at all at the time. He probably knew that interview was coming and had time to rehearse himself. Today, you nailed him without any warning."

"So he's lying about Todd but not about the dead drop," Rhodes concluded.

"We know Fallon has always been ambitious. He wants to reach the Seventh Floor and is willing to take risks to get there. So back when he was running the Iran shop, maybe he decided that whatever intel they were dredging up wasn't sexy enough. So Fallon sent Todd out on risky ops, but Fallon didn't enter her reports into the system because people would've come asking where they came from."

Rhodes saw the direction of her thoughts. "Then Todd goes missing, and instead of coming clean, Fallon and his people hid the evidence and lied to the IG to save themselves, despite the fact it meant leaving Todd in Iran. But somebody involved had a conscience."

"Or just really didn't like Fallon," Kyra said.

"I can believe that," Rhodes agreed. "He's very dislikable."

Kyra smirked a bit at that. "Either way, Fallon gets framed for the dead drop using a report supposedly written by Todd. Now the Bureau has a reason to go dig into his life *and* reopen Todd's case. They frame Fallon for a crime he didn't commit so he might get nailed for the one he did, or at least fall under suspicion enough that we fire him. You've got surveillance on him?"

"As of this morning," Rhodes said. "We also have a warrant to tap his phones and his Internet connection."

Kyra nodded. "Who's next on your interview list?" Rhodes handed her an index card, which the CIA officer scanned. She looked up, surprised. "Are you kidding me?"

"Again, do you think I'm playing?"

"The director of analysis. The director of operations. The chief of the Counterintelligence Mission Center. The head of Agency security. *Director Barron*," Kyra read off the card. She stared at Rhodes, her eyes practically boring holes in the special agent's face. "I thought for a minute that you were actually starting to play nice."

"They all have access to the intel that we recovered, and you said yourself that it pays to be thorough," Rhodes told her, smirking. "Have a good flight."

CHAPTER EIGHT

Kyra was not an especially religious woman, but setting foot on Iranian soil was a moment for either prayer or a stiff drink, perhaps both if one's religion allowed. Her grandfather had been a drinking man, a Scot for whom alcohol was an all-purpose solution to any problem. She'd inherited his eager taste for it and so had given it up. She never touched it now, and it was technically illegal in Iran anyway. Her options thus reduced, she tossed off a quick and silent prayer into the ether and hoped that anyone listening wouldn't be too surprised to hear from her. Still, she didn't put all of her faith in the supernatural. Kyra's dirty-blond hair was now dyed black and hidden under a head scarf, and she wore glasses that she didn't need. It was not a total disguise, but her British passport negated the need for more.

There were no direct flights to Iran from the United States, leaving her to fly to London and switch planes at Heathrow, which served to strengthen her cover story when the Iranian customs officer checked her passport and other papers. She had been practicing her British accent, binge-watching the BBC and talking to herself under her breath. More than a few Iranians had graduated from British schools and so could recognize a bad accent when they heard one. So she kept her mouth shut as much as possible, answering the customs officer's questions with as few words as she could. The man stared at her, then at her passport photograph. He snapped his questions at her and she couldn't tell whether his hostility was aimed generally at Westerners or whether he had some more personal reason to focus it on her. After five minutes, he finally stamped her passport and waved her through, and she passed out of the security area.

The embassy driver, really a British Senior Intelligence Service officer, had met her in the baggage reclaim area, as promised. She traveled light, nothing incriminating in her bags, and the man led her to his vehicle. Within an hour after landing, they were on the Tehran-Qom Freeway, driving north. She had expected to see barren terrain here and there were short stretches that matched her imagination, but more often there were cultivated fields and towns that were, by turns, modern and decrepit. She could read none of the signage, of course, all of it in Persian, which looked like children's scribbles to her eye. Her driver was not using a GPS receiver and she wondered whether he could read the signs or had simply memorized the route by landmarks.

Tehran was enormous and dense, holding almost as many people as New York City in less space, and inducing claustrophobia like Kyra had never felt before. The streets were narrow and the alleyways between them seemed to form mazes that even the most experienced native would be hard-pressed to navigate if they strayed too far from home. There were almost no trees, nothing living but the people and animals in the streets.

The driver turned off the Ferdowsi Avenue into the British embassy compound and the world around her changed in an instant. The British government's outpost here was an island of life in the middle of the city's urban desert of buildings and asphalt. Trees taller than the buildings surrounded the complex, blocking out the world, letting Kyra imagine for a moment that she wasn't in the middle of a city and a country that would arrest her just for being an American.

"They took ours over, too, you know," the driver told her.

"Excuse me?"

"The embassy, in 2011," he said. "The Iranians took over our embassy, as they did yours in '79. Disgraceful affair. The mullahs blamed it on excited students, of course, but here you can't do such a thing without the government smiling down on you. They took no hostages, but we were shut down here for four years. The whole place was in a terrible state when we came back . . . 'Death to Israel' and whatnot sprayed on the walls, most of the electronics stolen. It was a right mess. So we've got that in common, your country and ours."

"Not quite." Kyra half smiled at him. "They gave your embassy back."

"Our cousin from the colonies has arrived, I see." Alun Grayling, the SIS station chief, was younger than Kyra had imagined, or at least he appeared to be. Time was being very kind to him if he was older than forty-five and it was only the gray at his temples that made him seem that old. He was medium height, in fit shape, and wore a blue tailored suit that implied he cared about his appearance. All of the British intelligence officers she had met exuded an air of sophistication so uniform that she wondered whether it wasn't standard issue, somehow injected into all their recruits when they entered into the Vauxhall Cross for their first time.

"Kyra Stryker, sir." She did not try her best British accent on the man. She was sure it would have offended his ears.

"A pleasure, Ms. Stryker," Grayling welcomed her. He offered her the guest chair in front of his desk before returning to his own. "You must have some fine friends back home. Sir Ewan called me himself about your visit; it seems he received a call from your CIA director, asking for our assistance."

"For which we're very grateful," she replied.

"It is our pleasure. A good number of us are still unhappy about the tiff we had with the locals here a few years back that shuttered the embassy. So any chance to have a bit of good fun at their expense is welcome."

"I'm impressed at how quickly you got everything arranged."

"Yes, well, normally there would be extensive talks about such an arrangement between our governments, but we tend to approve things rather more quickly when bombs are going off. It puts a bit of pressure on our forgers, though. You are here, so I trust your documents passed muster."

"No problems coming through customs. But I promise not to abuse the Crown's hospitality by waving them around."

"Much appreciated," Grayling said. "In what other way can we assist you?"

"I'm trying to contact an Iranian arms dealer," Kyra told him. "Asqar Amiri."

"Ah."

"You've heard the name," Kyra observed.

"Indeed. Mr. Amiri is not Iranian. He's British by birth," Grayling said. "His real name is Oscar Longstreet. Radicalized while at university back home. No idea why that life appealed to him . . . he came from a wealthy family, had every advantage, but he was a terrible student, expelled from several fine schools. His friends reported that he had no obvious religious leanings of any stripe until the Iraq War broke out in the early part of the century. Fifteen years ago, he assassinated an expatriate imam in Oxfordshire on orders of the Iranians and then fled to Tehran and changed his name. He decided that Iran wasn't for him after a few years. The problem was that he couldn't leave because Interpol had a notice out on him, so the civilized world was off-limits. The Iranians don't trust him very much either. He's useful to them as an intermediary for buying prohibited supplies, as he can pass for one of us, so they keep him. He is free to move about inside Iran so long as he doesn't try to shake off his handlers. He did that once and they made him regret it, so he behaves himself. They only approve his departure from the country for specific missions and even then only when he has a Quds force escort with him."

"And you haven't tried to exfiltrate him?"

"Oh no," Grayling said. "He's both suffering and doing good for us much more here than he would be back home."

The meaning of the man's words was clear. "You did recruit him," she realized.

"I wouldn't say he's an official asset, but he knows that we are the only way he might ever leave Iran, much less stand on British soil again without handcuffs. So it's a long leash we're holding, but I can require the occasional favor of him. What is your interest in him?"

Kyra rehearsed Sam Todd's file for the man. "Amiri's name came up in a report written by one of our officers who went missing a few years ago. I'm here to confirm it's genuine."

"Which means you need to be in a room with him," Grayling noted. "I can arrange that, though the protocol for meeting him is somewhat unorthodox . . . but getting him to discuss anything related to the nuclear program will be another matter. He has helped his Iranian masters retrieve bits of banned nuclear technology from time to time and they take an exceedingly dim view of anyone sharing information regarding those operations. They've come to appreciate life without heavy sanctions and truly do not want them levied again. Amiri knows more than enough details about their past acquisitions to have all of those put in place again."

"Where can I find him now?" Kyra asked.

"He's on Kish Island, so far as I know. It's a more liberal place than the mainland, a vacation spot for foreigners, so Amiri has much more liberty to indulge his vices there. Also, Tehran does not require a visa to visit there, so it's the smuggling and black-market hub for Iran. Any illegal item you want, you can find it there or someone who will procure it for you, and the Khamenei family controls all of it."

The name was familiar. "As in former Iranian supreme leader Ali Khamenei?"

"Yes, the same family," the man confirmed. "His brothers built their wealth in no small part by running Kish like Mafia dons. I would try very hard not to draw the Khameneis' attention or depend on a diplomatic passport to save you if you do. So please take great care. If you find yourself in trouble, there will be very little I can do to help. It would be quite fortunate, in fact, if I could even locate you."

"I've worked some foreign streets before. I know how to be careful."

"Very good. We will arrange the flight and the meeting. But I must ask that you not do anything to burn Mister Amiri," Grayling replied. "We don't use him often, but we do use him."

"I'll do my best."

Grayling nodded. "It was a pleasure to meet you, Ms. Stryker. I do hope that things come out as you would like."

"Thank you, sir, for everything."

"Cheers, madam."

Dariush Grand Hotel
Kish Island, Iran

Kish Island felt like a different world from Tehran, clean, bright, less Persian influence in the buildings. There was real money here. Kyra could feel it as much as she could see it in the architecture and lit signs, and she was sure the river of profit flowing through the island was not rolling downstream to the common people on the mainland. It was a vague impression, one she couldn't articulate in words. She had felt it before, in Moscow, a city where the government and organized crime had become a single entity. Here, too, the modern neighborhoods and fine shops were a facade for something less honest.

Kish seemed contrary to all of the values that the theocrats running Iran claimed to stand for and she imagined that they would have closed it down if they didn't have their own self-serving reasons for letting such a place function.

No doubt money was not all that came through here either. Asqar Amiri operated from Kish, which meant that illegal weapons probably visited the island as often as the tourists. Illegal nuclear cargo almost certainly came here, though less frequently than more conventional black-market goods. There would be information brokers as well. At hubs like these, contacts willing to provide facts were as valuable as anything else and commanded their own market prices. The only question was who the prime dealers in such secrets were and to whom would they sell.

The flight from Tehran to Kish Island had taken a bit less than two hours, too short for Kyra to properly enjoy the business-class seat. *The British like to travel in style, I'll give them that*, she thought. She could hardly criticize. The Directorate of Operations was not tight with a penny when it came to ops. Case officers traveling as businessmen stayed in the nicer suites offered by the nicer hotels, dressed in fine clothing, and carried the other amenities needed to pass as men and women of means. It was almost a universal truth that people contemplating treason felt more comfortable dealing with people who appeared wealthy. Kyra could only suppose it gave the traitors-in-waiting confidence that they would get paid, if nothing else. Some assets were willing to give up their countries for their beliefs, but most were only willing to sell them out.

Now she had arrived at her lodgings and she was unsure whether the hotel was merely magnificent or crossed the line into gaudiness. It was modeled after the ancient palace at Persepolis, one of the capitals of the empire when Persian kings had tangled with the Greeks until Alexander the Great reduced the city to a burned husk. A very long rectangular fountain stretched out in front of the structure, flanked by high pillars, each topped with two stone oxen, horned and facing in opposite directions. The entrance was a hollow square, with yet more pillars on either side, stretching the full length of the building. The inside confirmed the Iranians' love of columns, which reached up from a marble floor covered in places with enormous Persian rugs. Guests coming or going waited in chairs that had intricate motifs carved in the arms and headrests. A long stone relief high on the wall depicted courtiers and foreign emissaries presenting tribute to the ancient kings.

One of the desk clerks spoke passable English and checked Kyra into her room . . . not one of the nicer suites, she noted; Grayling's hospitality had its limits, apparently. She found her way to the room and let herself in, careful to lock the door with the deadbolt once in. The television offered fewer channels than she'd hoped, and most of the programming was in Farsi. The news program showed video clips from which she could discern the subject of the story, but little else. The reporting seemed fixated on the Haifa docks. The same video, weeks old now and cribbed from CNN International, kept repeating every few minutes, showing the black smoke rising from the half-sunken ship resting in pieces dockside.

She was surprised to find that she had an Internet connection. No doubt it was monitored. She launched the Virtual Private Network (VPN) app on her iPad, a utility that set up an encrypted communications tunnel. She tapped out a message to Langley on the keyboard.

```
Arrived. Our cousins promised to make
introductions. Waiting for a call.
```

The portable computer spent a few seconds scrambling the words using a mathematical algorithm that no Iranian supercomputer could crack in less than a few billion years, then tore the entire mass of unreadable numbers into digital packets and fired them off into the ether. That act might raise some suspicions, but she doubted that she was the first foreigner to communicate securely with home using that particular technology. Besides, there were probably cameras and audio bugs in the room anyway. They would watch her no matter what she did. *Just let me have the bathroom to myself*, she implored them silently. They wouldn't, of course.

She closed down the VPN, brought up an e-book, and sat back in the recliner to read.

The telephone rang three hours later. "Salâm," she answered. She spoke no Farsi but had memorized a few of the more useful phrases during the flight across the Atlantic.

"Salâm. This is the front desk," came the answer, the latter bit in English. "There is a message here for you, delivered in the last few minutes. You may retrieve it at your convenience."

"Thank you," Kyra answered. She cradled the phone. *A message?* It would not be from Langley or from Jon. No one from Langley would be so stupid as to try to communicate with her through such an obvious channel when she was in hostile territory. *Grayling?* That made a little more sense, as the British knew more about her plans than her own people at the moment. But she imagined that the SIS wouldn't use a straight call to the hotel to reach her any more than Langley would.

That left one obvious candidate. *Amiri.*

Grayling had already talked to the asset somehow and the man was sending her directions for the meet? Maybe. It still felt wrong, her gut twisting, but she had no other leads to the man's location. There was nothing for it but to take the message.

She set the iPad down and went for the door. She checked the hall, both directions, before stepping out and locking the door behind her. The corridor was as empty as it had been hours before when she'd come up, the dark carpet soaking up the light from the ceiling. There was no one as far as she could see, all the way to the end of the hallway. She made her way back toward the elevator.

A few feet from the small foyer, one of the room doors opened. Kyra shifted to the other side of the hall to put distance between herself and whoever was coming out . . . a man, young and bearded, a nationality she could not determine on sight. He turned his back to her to lock the door as she passed him—

She heard the door on her side of the hall just behind her open. She started to turn, but a Taser touched the back of her neck and she gasped in pain as every muscle in her body locked up in an instant. She heard the crackle of the weapon as it jammed her nervous system with electricity, but she could not think, pain replacing every thought that tried to enter her mind. She toppled forward, saw the floor coming up to meet her face, then hands grabbed her from behind, catching her inches from the carpet. Something stabbed into her neck, small, a needle, and a cold chill flooded into her veins, rushing outward. It reached her heart and she felt it fill her chest. It surged upward, into her head, and then the whole world went as black as space itself. Even the stars went dark.

Adina Salem sipped her ginger ale and stared across the street. She would have preferred something considerably stronger, but the soft drink gave the appearance of an alcoholic beverage without interfering with her ability to think clearly. She had been here for an hour, trying to get a feel for the rhythm of the streets. Kish Island was another world from Washington, DC. She'd barely had time to settle into that city before she'd found herself ejected from the country. She truly lamented that loss. There had been much there that she'd wanted to see, and she liked the Americans she had met during her few months in their homeland. She'd even liked the food. Now she could never return and all she would miss there had made her list of life regrets considerably longer.

Amiri was here, somewhere. It was not a big island and the *ramsad* had thrown an unusually large team at this operation. She'd been surprised to find herself assigned to the unit so soon after her failure in the US, but grateful. It left her no time to brood about her mistakes there and proved that Ronen had not lost faith in her skills or her potential . . . or that he was desperate, but she hoped it was not so. In any case, there were a dozen others like herself on Kish now, searching this little false paradise for Amiri and his known associates. She wanted to be the one to find the man. Shiloh had passed his name and she should have been the one to recover that intelligence. Now she had a chance to put Shiloh's information to its proper use and pay the American spy his due respects.

It would not be easy, she was sure. Amiri had managed to stay active in the world's nuclear market for more than a decade without getting himself killed or detained. To survive so long when Mossad was watching—and Mossad was always watching—was no small accomplishment.

Another ten minutes passed before she saw her mark—one of Amiri's likely associates, a younger man, but one who had previously been connected to another Iranian operation for the nuclear program. That one had been nothing significant, a contract for a few minor parts that Mossad had determined were destined for the uranium centrifuges at the Natanz enrichment plant. But this man had smuggled the parts into Iran through Kish Island. That lone fact was enough now to make him much more interesting than he had been before.

The man went into the Cbon Cafe from the lot behind the building where he had left his car, and Salem made her way to the crosswalk by the bus stop. She watched the street for a break in the traffic. A bus came up and made a clean sweep of the commuters waiting, then pulled away, a bit of smoke spewing from the exhaust. Salem saw her opening and made her way across the street.

The man was standing at the counter, waiting for some order that he'd already placed. Salem walked up and stood near him, just close enough that he could see her. She didn't look back at him. Instead she waited until the server took her order, then she stepped back and turned. She made eye contact with the mark and smiled. He returned it. "Excuse me," she said in Farsi, a language that she knew the man understood. "Do you know how I can get to the Pardis Mall? I'm supposed to meet a friend there in an hour."

"It's not far," he said. "A half kilometer north of here on Khayyam Boulevard." He pointed at the street outside the window.

"Oh, thank you."

"You are a tourist?" he asked.

"No, I'm here on business," she said. "Only for a few days. It was a last-minute trip, so I didn't have much time to buy a map before I left."

"Ah," the man said. "Then perhaps you need a guide."

"Perhaps. Are you offering?" Salem asked. She smiled at him, a very friendly look.

"That depends on the reward, I suppose."

"Perhaps we can start small," Salem suggested. She extracted a pack of cigarettes from her pocket, Cleopatras. "Would you care for one?" she asked. "North African tobacco."

The man shrugged and took one of the smokes from the pack. He lit up and sucked in the nicotine, which sent his synapses firing in a frenzy of satisfaction. He also sucked in the small bit of radioactive dust that Mossad had injected into the tobacco roll and dusted on the paper, not enough to kill him, but enough that Salem and her colleagues would be able to track him using the Geiger counters they'd brought with them. All cigarettes already contained polonium-210, just not in the amounts of these doctored ones. Salem thought it ironic. Russia had assassinated Alexander Litvinenko by poisoning him with the very element that every smoker in the world ingested on a daily basis, just in much smaller quantities. Whether the amount in this man's cigarettes was enough to poison him, Salem didn't know and didn't care. He was a threat to Israel, no matter how minor, so if it killed him, it was justice. She only required the radioactive material to not kill him too quickly. She and the rest of the Mossad officers needed a day so they could put the polonium to a far more constructive use.

He blew out the first breath of smoke. "Very nice," he said, staring at the beautiful woman.

"I'm glad you think so." They chatted for a few minutes until the server called their orders. They picked them up and the man offered to escort her to the mall, but Salem begged off with a story of having other errands to run first. To satisfy his enthusiasm, she made a promise she had no intention of keeping to meet him for dinner, and slipped him a false business card with a number that would connect him with an answering service that she would never bother to check. He watched her go, appreciating the view from behind as she made her way outside.

A sedan was waiting for her behind the café, there as promised, dark windows, engine running. She walked up, opened the rear door, and let herself in. "Any problems?" the Ayin asked.

"None," Salem said. "How long will he stay tagged?" This had been the first time she'd used this particular tool.

"Until he dies," the Ayin said. "If he smokes it down to the nub and we left him alone, a few months at most. But he is one of Amiri's men, so he will not have so long to wait." Polonium was orders of magnitude more deadly than cyanide. A microgram of the element, smaller than a speck of pepper, was more than enough to kill a man within a few weeks. It would be an ugly death, slow and painful, as the radiation emanating from the substance lodged in the bones ate him from the inside out.

The Ayin looked back at the woman in the rear seat. Salem was staring at the open cigarette pack in her hands. "You should give those to one of the Hets when you get back to the safe house. I would not want you to consume one in a forgetful moment."

"I don't smoke," Salem assured him.

She felt a different kind of cold on her face now. Kyra opened her eyes and a stainless-steel field stretched out before her until it met a painted cinderblock horizon. The world was sideways, something hard pressed against her face. She was seated in a chair, her torso leaned forward over a metal table. She pushed herself up, a harder task than she'd imagined. Whatever drug was in her system was not going quietly. The room moved around her in a wobbly circle for a few minutes before she could regain its sense of balance. She was awake now, but her mind was still struggling to think, her reflexes slow and control over her body tenuous.

The room was mostly empty, clean enough to surprise her, and too bright for comfort. The light above was LEDs hidden under a glazed cover that softened any harsh brilliance. The floor under her feet was covered in industrial carpet and she could tell the pad underneath was thin, lying over plain concrete. Those cinderblock walls were painted a monotone yellow color, with windows high up near the ceiling in a row, but little daylight was coming through. She looked at her watch. It was twilight now and the streetlights outside had come on. The sun would be gone within fifteen minutes and the moon was already up.

She tried to stand, her head feeling remarkably heavy, but she was stopped short when her arms refused to come up. She looked down and saw the metal handcuffs chaining her arms to the table. Her arms were numb and spread far enough apart that she couldn't even touch her own fingers together, a precaution to keep her from picking the cuffs, she was sure.

Kyra looked to the door. It was locked, of course, with a heavy dead bolt set above the knob. She had no tools to pick it open, even crude ones. It was metal set in a frame made of the same material, so she wouldn't be kicking it in. The hinges were set on the other side, so she wouldn't be lifting it off them.

The windows were too small to climb through and the ceiling vents were smaller still. There was a fish-eye camera mounted in the ceiling. She supposed she could find a way to smash it if she could free herself. That would bring someone running—

The door opened and a man walked in, bearded, his skin rough and heavily lined, too much exposure to a harsh sun. His Western-looking features suggested he was no more a native than she was, assuming she was still on Kish Island. Kyra realized that she hadn't checked the date on her watch and had no idea how long she'd been asleep.

"Ya look like fresh rubbish," he said, his British accent thick. "It's not the nicest sleepy medicine in the world, but there are worse concoctions they could give ya."

"You're Amiri," Kyra said. Her voice came out hoarse.

"I am," he confirmed. "And you're Grayling's girl."

"Nice way to welcome a woman to your flat," Kyra said. Her words came out slurred. Her mouth felt numb.

"What, Grayling didn't tell you about our little protocol." It clearly wasn't a question. "You are a new one. Nothing he hasn't gone through. I have to keep up appearances, especially with a Westerner. And you're a bleedin' American by your accent, so I did ya a favor when I told 'em to dose you. If you'd given 'em a moment's trouble, they would've killed you and been done with it all, though maybe they'd have decided to have a little fun with you first. These Quds Force boys would cut your throat just for talking . . . or they might pay me to hand you over. They always like to have another hostage to offer back when it's time to sit down and talk sanctions." He tossed his cigarette stub onto the table and didn't bother to stamp it out.

"It'd be safer for me if I just made you go away, ya understand. Everyone on my crew is tied to the Quds Force, given to me by the mullahs, and that's what they're expecting me to do. So when Grayling tells me that someone who's not one of his needs to talk, I have to leave my options open, in case things go all pear-shaped."

"You've given people up to the mullahs?" Her mind was finally thinking more clearly now.

"Not many. A few. I'm sure Grayling told you I'm trying to earn my way back home, but I can't do that if I'm not still free and breathing. He understands how it is, the price of business. He's learned not to send anyone my way who isn't worth the time. Which means you're an interesting one. CIA? FBI?"

Kyra looked at him, then nodded up toward the camera in the ceiling. "Oh, don't worry about that one," Amiri said. "Picture, but no sound. These Quds Force types got tired of listening to people in here yell for help or whatever. And none of them speak English anyway."

"Grayling didn't tell you who I work for?"

"No. It don't really matter. You all answer to the same people. But you do need to get down to the business here before the boys watching start wondering what we're talking about. They send someone in here and I'll have to treat ya just like any other curious type."

"That would be a dangerous thing to do," Kyra advised.

"So what little tidbit of information am I missing, then?"

"Langley's looking for a mole. I got your name from a report we recovered from a dead drop he left. Our traitor was trying to pass your name on to his handler so they could come looking for you," she told him.

"And who was his handler?" Amiri asked.

"Mossad."

"Well, that ain't exactly news. They been looking for me for a long time."

"They're not just looking anymore. Mossad gunned down the last man this mole named in the middle of a London street in front of a hundred people," Kyra said.

"Salehi? That one?"

"That one," Kyra confirmed.

"Smashing. Just smashing," Amiri muttered. "So how does helping you help me? Because you're not Mossad."

"Israel is getting the intel they want from the mole and not from official channels at Langley. You answer some questions, it helps us find him. We find him, we get leverage with Israel again and tell them we won't help them unless Mossad leaves you alone."

"You got that kind of pull back home?"

"I'm here on the director's orders," Kyra assured him. "Another reason you don't want to hand me over to Tehran, by the way. You do that and you'll have Mossad *and* the Agency looking for you."

Amiri frowned. He sat down in the chair across from Kyra and rubbed his beard. "I got no desire to tangle with Mossad, I will say that. No one in their right mind wants the Israelis after 'em. I'm not so worried about CIA, but those Jews, they're a vengeful bunch. I've known a few men they snuffed. They don't just kill you, they do it with style. They like to send a message. You hear how they took out Hamas's best bomb maker?"

"No," Kyra admitted.

"Ho, good one, that story," Amiri said. "I'd done business with him. So had the PLO, Hezbollah, and every other group over there. Mossad went looking for him and found out where his workshop was. They waited until he went out, I don't know, to lunch or whatnot, and they let themselves in. They found his phone, took it apart, packed some plastique into the empty spaces, wired it all up, and then left it like they found it. When he came back, rumor has it that the head of Mossad himself called him up. 'Hello, is this Rafi?' he asks. 'Yes,' Rafi says. And then the phone blows up. Shaped charge took his head right off his shoulders and his hand off his wrist. At least that's how I heard it. Probably not right in all the particulars, but close enough. I know I never heard from Rafi again." He frowned then pulled a pack of cigarettes out of his shirt pocket, extracted one, and lit it up. "Yeah, I'm not too keen on having that bunch after me. A man likes to sit on the loo and know it's not going to blow him through the ceiling. It'll make a man crazy if it goes on too long and those Jews aren't the kind to just up and quit. Long memories they've got, and they hold a grudge."

"I can help you," Kyra said. "You kill me or give me up to the Iranians and you've got no one to help you get off their list."

"They're not gonna take me off their list. Give me a mulligan or two, maybe." Amiri put the cigarette to his mouth and sucked on it, the smoke filling his lungs. He looked away from her, thinking, and then exhaled, the white cloud rolling out of him then wafting toward the window. "All right, you ask me your questions. I might answer 'em, I might not, depending. Some things I just can't tell you because the Iranians would kill me quicker than Mossad and they do know where to find me. So ask and we'll see if I can work your deal."

"Fair enough," Kyra said.

They had waited the hour before the Ayin pulled the car out of the lot onto the street. Salem pulled out her smartphone and launched the controller app on the home screen. It filled the screen and connected to the radio receiver that was tuned to the GPS tracker attached with magnets to the underside of the mark's car. It took them only fifteen minutes to find the vehicle parked outside a dockside building at the Kish port facility on the island's northern end.

They watched the area for ten minutes and saw no one. "The security here is pathetic," the Ayin remarked. "I am amazed this man has ever eluded us."

"It's a large world and we are always stretched thin," Salem told him. "And the security inside the building is probably stronger. Cameras?"

"There and there," the Ayin told her, pointing to them. "You should be able to evade them easily. The one at the door will be the most trouble, but it appears to be looking out, not down. Hug the wall and you should be able to stay out of its field of view."

Salem launched another app on her phone that connected to the radiation detector now in her bag and put a map on the screen, centered on her position and showing the area around her to a radius of ten meters. She dismounted and made her way through the parking lot to their target's car. The device immediately found polonium-210 where Salem's mark had tossed the impregnated cigarette butt onto the sidewalk. She trusted no one would pick it up.

She touched her earpiece, which any passerby would have mistaken for a Bluetooth headphone. "Moving now," she said. Salem made her way toward the largest building, aiming for a corner that she judged was unobserved, then stalked along the perimeter until she reached the locked rear door. It was armored, she saw, and set in a reinforced frame. A numeric keypad was mounted into the wall beside it. Her mark had smoked the doctored cigarette to the nub and polonium had stained his fingers every time he handled the lit paper. Salem leaned close to the door, then pulled the radiation detector out, putting it only inches away from the knob.

The number on the phone jumped. She replaced the Geiger counter in her bag and made her way back to the Ayin. "That's it," she reported after she closed the passenger door. "Amiri could be here."

The Ayin nodded and pulled out his own phone, then looked up at the sky. "If he is not, there will be others there who will know where he is."

"We do not know how many are inside," Salem observed.

"I know," the Ayin admitted. "But what we know of Amiri's

operation suggests that it is small. Fewer men draw less attention. We will keep watch here until the others arrive and try to get a count."

"They are already on their way here. I will search the perimeter and see what I can learn of the floor plan."

"Very good," the man replied. "Be very careful. If this is Amiri's building, then there will be soldiers here, Quds Force most likely. We can take them, but only if we can surprise them. If you are caught, we will lose you. We cannot afford that."

"That will not happen," Salem assured him. She was determined to keep this promise. After her failure in the United States, she had much to prove, to her country and Mossad surely, but more to herself and to Shiloh.

"So what do you want to know?" Amiri asked.

"Did you meet with a CIA officer named Sam Todd in Basra about three years ago?"

"Girl, I've met a lot of people in Iraq. The mullahs are always sending the Quds Force and a lot of other people across the border. Half of 'em are buying and stealing everything that isn't bolted down and sending it back across the border. The other half are bringing explosives over and teaching the insurgents how to blow your boys and the Iraqis into little pieces. So what makes you think I could remember meeting some American?"

"I think you'd remember her."

"*Her?* Oh." Amiri looked away from the woman, frowning at some private memory, and he snorted. "You would ask about that one," he said, a rueful look on his lined face. "No, I didn't meet with her. I was supposed to . . . Grayling asked me to do it, a favor for some CIA friend of his that I'd never met. I'd just started working off my sentence, as Grayling likes to call it, and I thought a few favors might shorten it, if you understand me. So I told my employers that I'd been contacted by some unsavory types who were offering some military kit that a few of the locals had looted from one of Saddam's ware-houses. The story got me to Basra." Amiri stopped, thought again for several seconds, then slapped his hand on the table in anger. "But that stupid girl, Todd, she didn't realize that the insurgents were watching all of the Americans in town. Some of the boys grabbed her when she left her hotel for dinner and beat on her awhile. She finally gave up my name and they dragged her back across the border and then here to Kish. I was able to talk my way out of it . . . told 'em that the deal must've been a CIA setup to grab me and toss me into Abu Ghraib and squeeze me for everything I knew. That got me off, but the mullahs didn't let me travel for a good while after."

The man stopped talking and stared down at the floor, disappear-ing into his thoughts again. Kyra let the silence hang for a minute, to see whether he would start talking again of his own accord. Her patience finally ran out. "Where is she now? Is she still alive?"

"She ended up where the mullahs send all the people they really don't like. They sent her up to Evin Prison in Tehran, but what hap-pened after they marched her inside . . . Alive? That was years ago, so I've got no idea, and I'm not stupid enough to ask."

"Do you know what Todd wanted to talk about?"

Amiri sat up straight and stared at the young woman in amaze-ment. "You don't know?"

"Long story."

"Humph." Amiri shrugged. "I don't know. I assumed she wanted to know about the deal I was brokering for Tehran at the time."

"What deal?"

"With the Russians," Amiri told her, as though speaking to a child. "After their empire fell apart, the Russian army started selling kit on the side to feed themselves . . . guns, vehicles, whatever they could pawn off. That time, they had something the mullahs wanted. The old commies had set up a series of lighthouses on the north coast years before, stuck 'em in places so remote that you couldn't run a

power line to them. So they hooked them up to RTGs . . . radioisotope thermoelectric generators. Know what those are? No? Batteries
full of radioactive junk. The radiation heats up the casing and the
device turns the heat into electricity. Well, a few of those RTGs went
missing. One of them had been at Lishniy Island in the eastern Kara
Sea, and Moscow told those soldiers to go find it. The soldiers came
back and said that it must've washed out with the tide, but they'd
taken it and were offering it and a couple more they'd pilfered to the
mullahs. My employers sent me to make the deal. I figured that's
what your girl Todd wanted to ask about."

"Where are the RTGs now?"

"Here on Kish."

Kyra stared hard at the man's face, trying to read his expressions.
"If they were the source of the radioactive dust in the dirty bomb that
blew up in Haifa, giving the RTGs up might get Mossad off your back
permanently," she suggested.

"Huh," he grunted. "Don't think I'm dumb enough to reach out to
Mossad. They're just as likely to listen to me and then kill me."

"They just want to make sure Tehran doesn't hit Israel again—"

"Girl, you think Tehran did that to Israel? Don't be daft. The mullahs like to make a show of being religious crazies, but when they're
indoors they aren't nuts and they surely ain't suicidal," Amiri said.

"Then who did it?" Kyra asked.

Amiri laughed. "Oh, don't think I'm gonna rat out that bunch," he
said. "Bad enough I've got Mossad wanting to smoke me."

"Then give up the RTGs to the Brits," Kyra implored him. "It
would be your ticket out."

Amiri's smile faded. "You might be right. You might not. If you're
a spook, you know how they think about people like me. They always
want to keep you in place a little longer, keep you feeding 'em the
good stuff no matter how dangerous you tell them it's getting." He
studied Kyra's face, narrowed his eyes as he thought. "They're here

on Kish, but that's all I'm going to tell you, 'cause the SIS won't be the only ones interested. You go back and make Grayling an offer. You tell that bloke that he's got three days to come collect them and me, package deal. He doesn't show up for them, I make the offer to someone else. Might be enough to get Mossad off my back or maybe the CIA would like to score that trophy—"

The crack of guns sounded outside the room, in the distance. Kyra looked past Amiri to the door as the man's head jerked around. He pulled a small radio from his belt and jabbered into it in Farsi, pure gibberish to Kyra. A frantic reply answered him. Amiri cursed, drew a side arm, and ran for the door.

"Hey!" Kyra yelled. She jerked her arms against the shackles. Amiri didn't look back at her as he ran out, turned a corner, and disappeared.

There were sixteen on the team now that Salem had joined them, one more than they had had when they sent Qolam Rouhani off into the next life, and this would be an operation unlike most they had run since joining Mossad. There was no division of labor now, no small group of two or three pulling the trigger on the target while the rest navigated the way in or out. All were former *Sayeret Matkal* and all were carrying weapons. The enemy was Quds Force, trained special forces soldiers like themselves, so it was possible that none of the Mossad team would come out of the warehouse again. But if the dirty bomb that had exploded in Haifa had been born in this building, at least some of the men inside would answer for that crime.

Four of the Israeli men lay prone in sniper blinds, hastily arranged wherever they could find cover, one on each side of the building to seal it off and kill anyone trying to enter or leave. The first shot came from an M24, an American sniper rifle. The first of the men taking a smoke break outside dropped as a bullet split his head open from a distance of four hundred yards. His partner went down a second later as a round from a second rifle punched through his brain stem before his friend's death had registered in his mind.

The other twelve Israelis rushed the building, teams of four, coming in from opposite sides. Each carried a Tavor MTAR-21 assault rifle raised to eye level as they ran in the dark through the parking lot. One sentry taking his own cigarette break by a window on the top floor saw movement below in the moonlight. The Israelis had taken out what few artificial lights there had been, but nature herself was not giving them her full cooperation. The sentry frowned, reached for his radio, and was raising it to his mouth when a sniper's bullet plowed through the "triangle of death" shaped by his eyes and nose and took off the back of his head as the slug came out the other side.

The Israelis reached the doors. Forewarned by Salem that the entryways were armored, the lead men pulled shaped charges from their packs and attached them to the hinges and locks. The teams backed away as their leaders unspooled the detonation cord attached to the explosives. They didn't use their radios to coordinate the blasts. They had agreed that the doors would be blown at the same moment, three minutes after the raid began. The team leaders pressed the switches on the detonators.

The doors blew inward at the same moment, ripped free of their frames, and became flying weapons that killed three men, one each on the north, west, and south. The east sentry survived by chance alone as he was standing just to the side of the door as it was blasted into the building. His luck gained him five seconds of life, but he was stunned and deafened, and unable to use his radio before the Mossad team entered and cut him down, three shots to the head.

There had been two dozen men inside the building and on the roof when the operation had begun. Now there were seventeen and the Israelis faced almost even odds, though they didn't know it yet, and they had finally lost the element of surprise. The sound of the doors being blown off their hinges had done that, but the enemy was not yet organized. The boredom and lack of drills here over the years had left the Quds Force complacent and unprepared. Their response was slow and half of the Iranians were not at their posts.

The north Mossad team encountered their first resistance, two men running for their stations when they turned a corner to see the four unknown intruders who shot them down before either could raise his pistol.

The west team was the next to encounter hostile forces and the first to finally meet a squad larger than themselves. Six Quds Force officers met them at a T-intersection in the hallway. Both the Israelis and the Iranians shot at each other from behind corners at their ends of the corridor, but only one Quds soldier was carrying a weapon larger than his pistol. He emptied his magazine down the hallways while his teammates swapped out theirs. They never got to use them, as a grenade came skittering down over the tile and exploded, killing four men outright and leaving the other four helpless on the ground, stunned and bleeding from their ears and cuts made by the shrapnel. The west team ended their suffering a few seconds later as it closed the distance and put bullets in the head of every man who still had one.

The Iranians were outnumbered now. The enemy, whoever it was, was carrying assault weapons and light explosives, and half of their own were not answering their radios. None of their response plans allowed for losing so many of their men so quickly, and confusion had set in. Their chain of command was broken and they could not figure out who was the senior man left alive.

The south Mossad team was the first to take casualties. A small unit of the Quds Force sentries had finally laid hands on their own assault rifles and were running to the sound of the guns when they saw four people carrying bullpup rifles pass to their front at the end of the corridor. They raised their own and opened fire, hitting three, two men and a woman. The team leader was struck on the shoulder, which spun him around before knocking him to the floor. The man behind was struck in the throat and went down, blood gushing out of the hole below his jaw. The woman was struck in the head and killed outright, most of her skull shattered and its contents sprayed out on the wall. The last man in the line cursed and threw himself back behind the hallway corner. He pushed himself up to kneeling, raised his weapon, and filled the hallways with enough lead to discourage anyone thinking about a forward charge. He looked to his companions. His leader was still alive, he saw, the man trying to push himself across the floor to find some cover. The other two were not moving.

He held his trigger down until the rifle stopped firing, sooner than expected, and a Hebrew curse followed as he checked his weapon. The Tavor had jammed. He wrestled with it, but the rifle was stubborn. He pulled a grenade and sent it down the hall, where it went off, killing one of the hostiles who had shot down his friends. He jumped forward two steps, grabbed his female companion's fallen rifle and returned to cover. He made it just as the Iranians threw their own grenade. It skittered down the hall but hit the body of one of his dead comrades and stopped short before exploding, tearing the corpse into parts. He felt the blast but the shrapnel could not reach him behind the corner, instead tearing holes in the building. He raised his new weapon but held his fire, listening for footsteps in the hallway. The Quds Force soldiers were moving cautiously, guns raised, looking for any movement that would prove their adversaries were not all dead. The Israeli waited, his anger screaming for him to fire.

A few more seconds, and he unleashed it. He turned the corner, kneeling, aiming up as he fired. The first two Iranians went down almost together. The third managed to shoot but every round went into the ceiling as the Tavor's slugs punched through his torso, jerking his body backward. The last Iranian used his extra second to focus on his target before shooting. He pulled the trigger to his own AK-47 an instant before the Mossad officer's shots blew through his head, but it was time enough. Most of the AK rounds missed except for the last, which shattered the Israeli's knee and plunged the young man into a kind of agony he had never imagined possible. He tried not to scream and failed, then gritted his teeth to shut off the cries that he only distantly recognized as his own.

The south Mossad team was down.

Kyra could hear the gunfire more clearly now, the shots coming faster and closer. Her heart was punching her ribs and she could hear the blood rushing in her ears. She strained against the cuffs again, then tried to slip one of her hands out. Amiri or his men had locked the restraints on her wrists so tightly that they hurt even when she wasn't pulling against them. She ignored the pain and pulled hard until the metal cut into her skin and drew blood. She saw it but couldn't feel it, the adrenaline in her system blocking the hurt.

Finally, she stopped. She couldn't rip her hands free.

She heard an explosion in some nearby hallway, surely a grenade or some other small explosive. Men yelled and screamed in pain. One man shouted a panicked stream of Farsi pleas that was cut off in an instant by the repeated cracks of a carbine.

Kyra's chest was heaving now as her breathing accelerated. She fought to control herself as her instincts screamed for fight or flight, but she could do neither.

The door slammed open and Kyra came out of her chair like a small rocket until the metal cuff stopped her.

Amiri rushed inside, a pistol in his hand. He took cover by the door frame, looking at some unseen invaders in the hallways. He reached around, fired at someone, then jerked his hand back inside as his target returned fire.

"Unlock me!" Kyra yelled. The man ignored her, firing again—

—Amiri screamed as a round punched into his gun hand, tearing muscle and breaking bone. His pistol flew off somewhere and he jerked his mangled limb back. His blood was flowing freely out of a hole that Kyra could see ten feet away. The man looked at her, his eyes wide in panic and fear.

"Unlock me!" she yelled again. She jerked against the cuffs.

Amiri said nothing as he gripped his crippled hand, squeezing it at the wrist with the other, as though he could force the pain out of his body along with the blood that was now dripping onto the floor. His eyes jerked around as he searched the room for a way out—

Amiri saw Kyra's focus shift from him to something behind and he turned. The Mossad invaders came in, both men, Tavor rifles raised and aimed at Amiri. A woman followed, her own gun raised as she covered the hallways. Kyra's own eyes went wide as the woman stepped in from the darkened hallway into the light of the room, then turned and faced the wounded man.

Adina Salem.

"No, please!" Amiri yelled in English, then something Kyra didn't understand in Farsi. He held his hands up as though to deflect the bullets that these soldiers would surely fire. "I'm not one of them! I'm working for the British!"

Salem stared at the man for several seconds, no emotion on her face . . . no anger, no pity. Then she spoke. "You brought the RTGs to Iran," she said in English.

Amiri's eyes went wide with fear. "I didn't know—" he started.

"For Haifa."

Salem pulled the trigger, a three-shot burst. Kyra recoiled at the sight and sound of the back of Amiri's head erupting as the bullets passed through it. The image seared itself into her memory as Amiri's head shattered. His body dropped to the ground.

Kyra finally pulled her eyes away from the corpse and looked at the shooter who had just killed Amiri. Salem looked back at her, then raised her rifle again.

• • •

Salem said something in Farsi. Kyra shook her head. "I don't understand," she said, her voice shaking from the shock of what she had just seen.

"He said he was working for the British," Salem told her, switching to English and pointing at the body on the floor with her rifle. "You are British?"

"American."

"CIA?"

"Yes," Kyra replied. She straightened her back. Her heart was still hammering away, but a peaceful calm settled on her. "You're Mossad." She regretted saying the word the moment it came out. It was possible that the shooters might have orders to leave no witnesses who could point the finger at Israel.

Salem ignored the comment, as good as confirming the other woman's assertion. "Was he lying?" she asked, nodding at Amiri's bloodied form.

"No," Kyra said. "He was a Brit, trying to earn his way back home. He didn't want to work for Iran anymore."

"A decision he made years too late." Salem turned to her companions and exchanged words in Hebrew. The men nodded in agreement, turned, and walked back out into the hallway, raising their guns again. More shots sounded in the distance. Neither woman flinched or looked away from the other.

"Why were you talking to him?" Salem asked.

"He had information on one of our officers who went missing a few years ago."

"And why did he capture you?" Salem nodded toward the cuffs still bolting Kyra to the table.

"Appearances." It was only a partial lie.

"A man who helps one of your officers disappear and you think you are chained here for appearances?" Salem scoffed. "I think you are either a liar or naive. It does not matter which. If I leave you chained here, the Iranians will find you when they come and you will disappear, too. So I will help you if you help me."

"What do you want to know?" She had nothing to offer but information.

"You know why we killed him?"

Kyra nodded. She held herself very still, trying not to give this Israeli woman the slightest cause to use her weapons. "The RTGs that he bought from the Russians were the source of the strontium used in the Haifa dirty bomb."

Salem stepped forward and slammed her Tavor against the metal table. "Where are they?"

Kyra raised her hands as far as the cuffs would allow. Salem frowned, then walked over to Amiri's corpse. She searched the body for a minute until she found the handcuff key in his pocket. She turned back and unlocked one of Kyra's handcuffs, then tossed the key on the table. "Where?" she repeated, impatience in her voice.

"Here on Kish. That's all he would tell me. He wanted to barter them for a trip home," Kyra replied, trying to keep the shaking out of her voice. She picked up the key and unlocked the other cuff. It fell onto the tabletop, the clank of metal on metal. "Our officer was investigating the sale of the RTGs when she went missing."

"In another warehouse?" Salem demanded.

"I don't know. But he said the mullahs weren't responsible for Haifa. He didn't tell me who was, but I think he was telling the truth."

Salem checked her rifle, then looked back at Kyra. "I suggest you do not go outside for a few minutes. We have men around the perimeter who will kill anyone who tries to leave. We will be gone in ten minutes. Then it will be safe." The Israeli turned, raised her rifle, and walked through the door, leaving Kyra alone with Amiri's broken corpse.

She found Amiri's gun on the floor, picked it up, and checked the action. The grip was dented where the bullet had struck after passing through his hand, but the weapon appeared functional. It could at least fire the round in the chamber. Kyra walked to the door, closed it, crouched beside it with the pistol raised, and stared at the dead Brit on the floor as she waited for the shooting to stop.

After a few minutes, the building was silent. Kyra stood, inhaled deeply, raised her weapon, and opened the door. She moved out into the hallway, leading with the pistol. Several of the lights were blown and the corridor was dark. Only the emergency light at the end revealed the bodies in her path. An AK-47 lay beside one of the dead men. Kyra lifted it off the floor, keeping her pistol raised to cover the hall. The rifle was still loaded and functional. She slid the pistol into her waistband, then raised the AK and began walking toward the lights.

She hadn't been conscious when these men had brought her in, so she did not know the way out. She reached the intersection and turned left, a random choice. That led to another hall. There was blood on the floor here, but no bodies. Someone had dragged away at least two people, maybe three. The walls were blackened and perforated with holes, evidence that grenades had been thrown. She retrieved a full AK magazine from another man's dead form, then kept stepping quietly forward.

There was no sound but her own light footsteps and the buzz of broken lights. Kyra kept her eyes focused past the end of her rifle barrel, but there was no movement, no other sounds. The smell of the blood was powerful and she could taste iron in the air. She'd smelled death before and seen blood spilled, including her own. She breathed deep, trying to slow her pounding heart and labored breathing. Kyra closed her eyes for a single second to center herself, then looked down the hallway again, focused on the moment, only on the scene ahead of her.

She turned another corner. An Iranian man was propped against the wall, his hands covered in his own blood. His head turned up toward her, lolling on his neck like it was too heavy to hold up. He said something in Farsi and she heard the gurgling of blood mixing with his words. He tried to raise a pistol at her, but his arm refused to bend at the elbow, the tendons in his arm shot away. Then his head fell forward and he didn't move again.

The bile rose in her throat and she pushed it back down. She swapped her damaged pistol for the dead man's sidearm, then raised the AK again. *Keep moving*, she thought. Someone here would have gotten off a distress call. Someone from the outside would be coming and they would not be merciful to anyone they found left inside among their dead brothers.

She moved forward again, more random turns, more of the dead lying in her path. How many had she seen? A dozen now, at least, all Iranians, she was sure. Salem and her Mossad team would not have left any of their own behind. That would be whose blood she'd seen smeared across the floor outside the interrogation room, she realized. Mossad had taken its own casualties.

Another turn and she saw a door at the end of a hallway, metal, a different color from the rest. This corridor was empty. She moved ahead, more quickly now, until she reached the end.

The door was unlocked. She pushed against it slightly, just enough to crack it open. It was night outside, the only light coming from distant streetlights. She moved the door farther. No bullets slammed into it, and she assumed whatever perimeter guards Salem's team had left outside had retreated with their comrades. She pushed the door open and stepped outside, crouching low in case she was wrong. There were no gunshots, only the sound of waves against the docks in the distance.

Kyra kept the rifle raised until she reached the edge of the parking lot, then tossed it under a van. Walking with a machine gun through the streets of Kish would draw too much attention, but she kept the pistol, hidden under her shirt. It was a smaller weapon than she had ever carried and the shape and weight of it felt strange pressing against her abs. She couldn't identify the model and had neither experience shooting it nor spare magazines for it, so it was small comfort, but better than her bare hands.

She looked back at the warehouse, the side door still hanging open where she had left it. There was no movement anywhere in sight.

Kyra finally heard the sound of cars, one at first, then several, a half mile away and getting closer, their engines screaming. She looked for the lights of the city in the distance and then ran into the dark.

Kyra ran behind warehouse buildings to stay out of sight of the approaching cars, then followed the coastline. Navigating by the North Star, she walked east, then south, as the coast bent to her right. She looked back. She could no longer see the warehouse or the docks.

Her hands were shaking and she couldn't steady them. She stopped and dropped to her knees. It was a mistake. For the first time in more than an hour, her mind could finally focus on something other than fight or flight. The memory of the few seconds when Salem had shot Amiri in the head filled her thoughts. Her heart began pounding again. She felt anxiety surge in her stomach as the mental movie replayed itself in her head in all its bloody detail over and over. She'd seen men die before, but only once had she seen one killed so very close. Now, in her mind, Kyra saw Salem point the weapon at her again—

Kyra leaned over, her weight on her arms, and threw up in the sand until she dry-heaved. Then she sat back up, closed her eyes, and tried to calm herself, but her emotions listened to her mind only slowly. *You're alive. It didn't happen.*

Ten minutes she sat there before her heart finally slowed again. *Time to go*. She forced herself to stand and start walking again, still shaky. Putting her focus on the mission was the best way to clear her thoughts. It would give her battered mind something else to think about.

After another hour, she saw a landmark she recognized, a building she'd seen from the window of her hotel room. She turned the mental map in her head until she lined herself up and could set her course. She found the hotel a half hour after.

She came through the front doors. A few patrons sat in the grand foyer, talking quietly. No one looked up. She made her way to the elevators, then up to her room.

Everything was where she had left it, as though she had been out only for dinner. Now she wanted nothing more than to collapse onto the bed and sleep, but there was no time for that. It had taken her hours to find her way back to the Grand Dariush. Doubtless, the Iranians had found Amiri and his team dead some time ago; they would be looking for the killers, and it was a small island. The Quds Force and the rest of Iran's security services would be searching through their holdings, looking for any tidbit that would single out any foreigner on Kish as an intelligence officer. Salem's team likely had their own way off the island, perhaps an Israeli submarine stationed offshore waiting to surface, but Kyra had no such help on her side. She had only one way off and could only hope that the Iranians wouldn't be stopping every foreign tourist on the way out.

One problem at a time. She had to get her intel home. Kyra retrieved her iPad, fired up the encrypted VPN, and began to type.

```
1. Contact made with Amiri. Todd report
confirmed. He agreed to meet with Todd but
meeting didn't take place.
```

```
2. Amiri said that rumors indicated Todd
was taken to Evin Prison shortly after her
detention. Todd's present condition and
location are unknown.
```

```
3. Amiri reported that the source of the
radioactive material used in Haifa was one
of three RTGs sold by the Russian military
to Iran, but that Iranian government was not
responsible for Haifa. Also said that all
RTGs are still on Kish, location unknown.
```

She paused, looked up and stared out the window into the dark, trying to find the best words to recount the rest of the story in the dry language the Agency preferred to use in such messages.

```
4. Amiri assassinated earlier today. Mossad
located his warehouse through methods unknown
and executed him and an unknown number of his
associates.
```

```
5. Officer Stryker interrogated by Mossad
officer Adina Salem. Told Salem about the
RTGs under duress in return for release.
```

Kyra added the GPS coordinates of Amiri's shattered warehouse to the paragraph. She stopped typing and squeezed her eyes shut, then opened them, trying to focus on the blurry screen. *Now what?* Her mind was foggy. She stared at the iPad until the thoughts finally came.

```
6. Unless directed otherwise, Stryker will
return to Tehran to report Amiri's execution
```

to SIS. Would appreciate any help available to
plow the field for that request. Will return
to Langley after, as soon as practical.

She sent the message through the VPN's encrypted tunnel back
to Langley. That task done, she turned the iPad off and fell back onto
the bed. *How to get off Kish?* She ran through the possibilities. There
were always only two ways off any island, by air or sea. Was the first
really denied her? She picked up the phone and called the front desk.

"Mitoonam komaketoon konam."

The words flew by her. She assumed they were some variant
of *may I help you?* She dug through her memory for the few Farsi
phrases she had tried to memorize on the flight over. *"Aya shoma
Engilisi harf mizanid?"*

"I do," the man replied. "May I be of service?"

"I need a shuttle to the airport," Kyra said, trying to affect her
best British accent. She was sure it was as horrid as her Farsi certainly had been a moment before.

"I can arrange a shuttle in one hour. A taxi will be more expensive
but can be here in ten minutes," the clerk said in a British accent
better than her own, she was sure.

She wondered whether choosing the faster option wouldn't raise suspicion. "Thank you, sir, the shuttle will be fine." Kyra hung up the phone
and lay back on the bed. She left the light on to ensure she wouldn't
sleep, but her body disobeyed, the stress finally lifting off her enough to
let the exhaustion take her, and her mind descended into the darkness.

Kish Island

The phone pulled her out of sleep after a half-dozen rings. "Madam,
your shuttle has arrived."

"Thank you. I'll be right down," Kyra said, her words slurred. She put the phone down and sat up, silently cursing herself for succumbing to her exhaustion. The image of Adina Salem shooting Amiri in the head had played in her dreams, robbing her of any rest the nap might have granted. She was sure that would not change for a while.

She looked down at the iPad on the nightstand and saw the notification on the lock screen that Barron's message had come through. It took the device a few moments to decrypt the cable after she entered her password.

    1. Director regrets Amiri's death and will
    inform SIS.

    2. Warehouse located at the coordinates
    provided is owned by Morning Sun Imports,
    which company is controlled by the Khamenei
    family. The company has a second building in
    the dockyard one half mile north of the first
    facility. Technical assets will be deployed
    to monitor the site.

    3. Proceed to Tehran as described. Do not
    meet with SIS. Return home at earliest
    opportunity.

I guess they really don't want me checking out that second warehouse. Fine by me, Kyra thought. It might've been worth a try the day before, but now it would have been stupid in the extreme, what with Iranian security swarming the building. She was under no illusions that her good luck was inexhaustible.

The Khamenei family owns Morning Sun Imports? The thought tumbled around in her mind. *Then Amiri worked for the Khameneis.*

That made sense. He had procured nuclear material for the Iranian government and Ali Khamenei had been the supreme leader.

Did Khamenei order Todd's kidnapping?

Whether he had or not, it was almost certain that the supreme leader of Iran knew of it. She had no doubts that there were very few men in Tehran who could issue the orders to keep that secret.

She looked back down at the iPad. The cable included a map with the second Morning Sun warehouse marked, a half mile distant from the one where Amiri had held her. It was a recent photo, taken no doubt by one of NRO's satellites tasked by Barron to watch the site. There were a number of military vehicles around the building and soldiers standing in the open. *Good luck getting inside that one, Salem.*

She closed the browser, deleted Barron's message, and shut down the computer, then finished packing and left the room. The hallway was empty again. This time she made it to the elevator.

Kyra walked to the front desk and checked out, an unnecessary maneuver, but it allowed her to grab a newspaper from the reception counter. The text was all Farsi and she couldn't read a word, but it was useful for wrapping the pistol and disposing of it in a garbage can after the shuttle left her at the Kish International Airport ten minutes later.

The airport was quite modern, if small, perhaps the size of a large college-town airport back home. The ceiling was glass tile with recessed lighting and a blue neon border at the perimeter that hurt her eyes when she stared at it too long. Kyra navigated the ticket desk, her British passport drawing some extra scrutiny, then security. A small market on the way to her gate offered food and water, and only then did she realize how long it had been since she'd eaten anything, much less a proper meal.

Kyra made her way to the gate. Her watch showed that she had one hour before boarding. She sat down in the chairs by the windows overlooking the tarmac and focused on a point on the airfield's far side, avoiding eye contact with any of her fellow travelers. She imagined that if the Iranians knew that she'd been at Amiri's warehouse, they would have detained her when she produced her passport minutes ago; but there would still be no relaxing here, on the plane, or in Tehran if she made it that far.

If the Iranians came for her now, there would be nothing she could do. A commercial flight was always a trap for a spy and there was, quite literally, nothing in the world she could do but put herself in it and pray that her cover would be enough to keep it from closing around her neck.

CHAPTER NINE

Hadfield walked through the empty halls of the Old Headquarters Building to the elevator by the library, his feet moving slowly. It had been taking ever more willpower to drag himself to work every night and that commodity was becoming harder and harder for him to dredge up. But much as he disliked his present duty, the thought of returning to a normal office during normal hours almost sent him spiraling down into a panic attack.

He reached the center, took his desk, and stared at his monitor until the system finished logging him on and he launched the usual applications. He opened the cable database and stared at the list of communiqués that had come in since the shift change. The one on top caught his attention. He opened it and scanned the headers, all cryptograms and code words. The cable had come in not from an Agency station but some other location. He couldn't even identify the author, but the header information directed that the message be routed . . .

. . . *straight to the director*, he realized. He stared at the first paragraphs.

```
1. Contact made with Amiri. Todd report
confirmed. He agreed to meet with Todd but
meeting didn't take place.
```

```
2. Amiri said that rumors indicated Todd
was taken to Evin Prison shortly after her
detention. Todd's present condition and
location are unknown.
```

He brought up the print window and directed the message to one of the laser printers in the next room. Then he locked his computer and walked over to fetch the hard copy.

He walked south along the corridor and turned right, his feet shuffling along the carpet. The President's Daily Brief Office at the end of that hallway. The men and women who delivered daily briefings to the president of the United States and other senior officials were among the few who kept the same hours as the Operations Center staff. Barron was on that list of people who got briefed, but he was far from the most senior. The briefers spent their nights poring over reports, dry-running their presentations, and dragging analysts in from their beds to answer questions, all to be ready to give their customers the finest intelligence the United States could collect. He actually felt sorry for them on the morning that the president or some other arrogant official canceled their briefing for whatever trivial reason. It was one of the few emotions he felt anymore.

He let himself in. The secretary smiled as he came through the door. She'd seen him before. Hadfield held the cable out to her. "This just came in. I'm sure Director Barron wants to see it first thing in the morning."

"Thank you." She checked the code words. "You need to route a copy of this to the Red Cell, too."

"I'll take care of it as soon as I get back."

"Quiet in the Ops Center tonight?"

He shrugged. "It usually is."

CIA Red Cell

Jon shuffled through the hall, his cane tapping out a third footstep, until he reached the last vault on the left. He reached down to where his new badge was hanging off his shirt pocket and stared at the plastic card for a moment. It was odd to see his own photograph surrounded by a block of green. For twenty years, he had worn the blue badge of a staff officer. Now to see himself carrying the green badge of a contractor seemed very strange. "Should've asked for more money," he muttered.

He waved the badge against the reader mounted in the wall. The vault door made no sound. He frowned and repeated the action, with the same result. Jon stared at the badge, wondering if someone in security hadn't encoded it incorrectly, then let it hang again from the clip on his pocket. He reached for the doorbell, then stopped as his eye fell on the room placard mounted above it.

The Red Cell plaque was gone. In its place, someone had posted a printed card: *Salem Investigation.*

"Oh, you are kidding me," he muttered. Jon pressed the doorbell and heard it sound inside. No one answered and he pressed it repeatedly until the door finally opened.

Rhodes stood in the doorway. "Mr. Burke."

"Bureaucratic petulance becomes you," Jon replied.

"We needed more space. Yours fit the bill and Director Barron signed off," Rhodes countered. "Do you have something for me or are you just here by mistake?"

Jon considered four different responses, two of which were likely to get him arrested and a third that involved words that he'd promised his wife to never repeat. He finally chose to say nothing. He held out a folder. The FBI officer took it and opened the flap. Kyra's report was inside.

Rhodes scanned through it, his eyes growing wide. "Salem is on

Kish Island," he muttered. "That was fast. She must've read through the intel before we arrested her."

"I'm surprised that the package being cut open didn't suggest that to you," Jon noted.

Rhodes glared at him. "You know your partner just became a suspect," he said.

Jon cocked an eyebrow. He hadn't expected that particular threat. "I clearly underestimated the depths of your petulance."

"It's not petty revenge. The mole tries to pass Amiri's name to Mossad. We stop that, but then Stryker travels to Kish, and in less than a day, the guy's dead. That doesn't sound like a coincidence to me."

"Apparently, the implications of Salem reading the mole's intel is still lost on you," Jon observed. "And Rouhani's assassination before Kyra went to Kish, suggesting that the mole found a way to deliver the intel through an alternate channel. I don't suppose the fact that Kyra reported his death in an official cable counts for anything."

"That's actually what I'd expect. It would be suspicious if she didn't."

"You're a purebred conspiracy theorist, you know that?" Jon asked, amazed. "Kyra does her job and it's evidence that she's a mole. If she didn't do her job, you'd see it as evidence she's a mole."

"Not true, and you don't know if things on Kish went down the way she says they did."

"If you're going to simply disregard any statement anyone makes that doesn't fit your theory, why bother with an investigation at all?" Jon asked.

"Oh, please," Rhodes muttered in disgust. "Salehi, Rouhani, and now Amiri. Three names in different compartments and no one had official access to all three except for the director and a few senior officials. So everyone thinks there's more than one mole working together, but it's always more likely that there's just one. Isn't it true that the Red Cell is free to look at anything and everything the Agency studies?"

"Yes, but that doesn't mean we get automatic access to all of the intelligence the Agency has," Jon corrected him. "Only the director and a few others on the Seventh Floor get that."

"Which is why I'm going to interview all of them," Rhodes assured him. "Kyra could always tell people who control the compartments that she's working some special project for the director and needs access."

"Believe me, getting other people to cooperate with us on routine projects can be a serious challenge. Getting them to open up compartments practically requires Seventh Floor intervention. They would have to confirm any such request, which would raise red flags, and if they read her into the compartment, her name would appear on the access list," Jon argued.

"I bet your partner is very good at getting people to do what she wants."

"Something you can't seem to manage, but she is vastly better with people than you are, I'll grant you," Jon told him. "Unless you have something intelligent to offer, I'm done with this conversation." He hefted his cane, hobbled back out to the hall, and closed the door.

"Please state your name," Rhodes ordered.

"Mackie Staunton. Mackensie, if you need my full first name."

"Mr. Staunton, according to your personnel file, you were a case officer under William Fallon in Iraq, correct?"

"Yes. I was his deputy station chief," the man answered. He stared across the small table in the conference room at the notepad sitting in front of the FBI special agent.

"And you served in that position for how long?"

"Four years."

"Did you know Samantha Todd prior to that time?" Rhodes asked.

"Yes. She and I EOD'd together."

"EOD?"

"Enter on Duty. It means we joined the Agency at the same time," Staunton explained.

"How would you describe your personal relationship with Mr. Fallon?"

"Friendly. We don't socialize much outside of work, but, yeah, friendly. What's this about?"

Rhodes ignored the question. "And you were in Iraq when Samantha Todd went missing there?"

"Yeah."

"I've read the investigation report. Do you have anything to add?"

"No. That investigation spiked my career and now I'm stuck behind a desk. Why are you asking me about it now?" Staunton demanded.

"The FBI arrested a spy a few nights ago very near Mr. Fallon's home," Rhodes told him.

"I hadn't heard anything about that."

Rhodes showed him Salem's photo. "Do you know this woman?"

"No."

"You're certain?"

Staunton shook his head. "I don't know her. Who is she?"

"The woman we arrested," Rhodes told him. "We're done for now, Mr. Staunton. Please do not talk to anyone about this conversation. I'll have more questions for you soon."

"Sure." Staunton stood up and walked out of the conference room.

Fuller waited until the CIA officer had left the vault before entering and approaching Rhodes. "He say anything useful?"

"Denied everything. We have the warrant?" Rhodes asked.

"The judge signed off. Got his work phones tapped and we can read his e-mails and texts, both work and home computers. Fallon, too, and the rest of his little cult of personality. If they try to talk to each other, we'll know."

"Nice," Rhodes said, approving. "Who's next up?"

Fuller pulled out a notepad and read off the names. "Sally Ramseur. She worked with Fallon and Staunton and she was on another one of the access lists. I doubt you'll get any more out of her than you got out of Fallon or that guy who just left. I think that group is tight."

Rhodes smiled. "Then we start calling down the bigwigs. Director of ops, director of analysis, Barron. They all had access to the leaked intel, they all get pulled in."

"Talking to 'em is one thing," Fuller cautioned. "Getting a wiretap order on an Agency director is something else . . . and forget surveillance. He's got a security team around him all the time. He couldn't have made the dead drop at Banshee Reeks."

"Doesn't mean he couldn't have ordered someone else to do it, like Stryker," Rhodes offered. "Rostow ordered CIA not to help Israel. Barron wouldn't be the first CIA director to push back against a president he didn't like."

"Careful, man. You start picking on agency heads, you're running with some big dogs. You better make sure our senior people are willing to back you up before you make those moves."

"You don't get to be a big dog yourself by sitting on the porch while the big dogs run," Rhodes advised. "Somebody here is helping Mossad run an illegal war against the direct orders of the president, and if it's Barron, then he's got people helping him do it. He worked under Kathy Cooke, who's married to Burke, who works with Stryker. That's another tight little group there, and there could be others in the mix. So we're going to take this place apart."

"Just don't get bit, boss."

"Don't worry about it. We crack this open, we'll be writing our own tickets back at the Bureau."

"That bad?" Barron asked.

Jon threw himself onto the director's couch and stared out the window. It was dark outside, nearing midnight, practically the only time that was open on Barron's schedule. "He took over the Red Cell vault."

"Yeah, I'm sorry about that," Barron replied. "Rhodes made the request through his own chain of command and I got a call from the FBI director. I know it was a cheap shot, but we're short on space and Kyra's out of the country for a while. Until this is over, you can work up here. There's an empty desk two doors down."

"Not a goal I ever aspired to, but it beats the library, I suppose," Jon replied.

"It'll show we're cooperating."

"For what little that gets us," Jon said. "Rhodes is either starting to take shots randomly or he's trying to provoke us. He's decided that Kyra's a suspect."

"He thinks we're all suspects," Barron admitted. "He hasn't demanded an interview with me yet, but I won't be surprised when it comes. Ambition feeds paranoia."

"It also feeds lousy reasoning. He's twisting facts to suit his theories, and ignoring facts he can't twist." He shook his head in disbelief. "I would suggest calling the FBI director and asking him to pull Rhodes out, except the man would decide you and I were both conspirators trying to protect a mole."

"Speaking of which," the director said. "I read Kyra's report. So Amiri *was* supposed to meet with Todd."

Jon nodded. "Which means that Todd's report was genuine, but it was never entered into our database. That means that the meeting was entirely off the books. Fallon was digging for sources, and he probably ignored the safety protocols for meeting targets in high threat areas.

Todd might not have even realized the danger she was in. Things went off the rails and Fallon covered it up so it wouldn't hurt his career. Probably convinced a few other people to do the same. That would explain why Todd's report was never in our system . . . not because of the intel it contained, but because it exposed an unapproved op."

"Nice theory. How do we prove it?" Barron asked.

"We connect Fallon to Amiri," Jon replied. "Todd's report said that a British officer pointed him toward Amiri. So we find the British contact. We pin the request to have Amiri meet with Todd on him and then confront Fallon and the rest of his old team with it. Do we have anything on that warehouse Kyra marked in the cable?"

"I had some people take a look. It's owned by a company called Morning Sun Imports, controlled by the Khamenei family. They own a second warehouse in the same dockyard, about a half mile north."

"No kidding." Jon frowned and looked away at nothing in particular. "Mossad has killed two Iranian nuclear scientists now and Tehran has said nothing. No accusations, no angry predictions about Israel being wiped off the earth . . . all quiet."

"Interesting, isn't it? I thought maybe they were trying to make a point with the silence . . . add weight to what Salehi told Kathy before he died, trying to prove their innocence by not lashing out. Now I'm wondering if they're just trying not to draw attention to the man behind the curtain."

"Or buying time trying to cover things up. In any case, they can't keep it up forever. If Mossad keeps killing their people, they'll have to push back eventually. Once they do, this whole thing will spiral down and nobody will be able to stop it." Jon checked the time. "I'll work on connecting Fallon and Amiri."

"What do you need me to do?"

"Talk to Sir Ewan at Vauxhall Station. Find out who on his side of the pond knew Fallon well enough to grant favors."

"I've got a better idea," Barron said. "Why don't you and Kathy go finish your vacation in London? She knows him better than I do. I'll let him know you're coming."

"So we can break the news about Amiri to him?"

"Something like that," Barron admitted. "Kathy is a better diplomat than I am, and I could use her help with that right now. If it helps you smooth things over with her, she's getting to go back to London. Finish your vacation."

"Works for me."

"Good," Barron approved. "Rhodes is interviewing Fallon again in the morning. I want you there."

Jon nodded. "Kathy and I will head to London after."

CHAPTER TEN

Ramot Alon
East Jerusalem, Israel

The neighborhood known as Ramot Alon had been a demilitarized zone once, before the '67 War. It was part of Israel now, though no other country accepted this fact. Even Israel's allies called it illegal, a violation of the Geneva Conventions, a "settlement" the Arabs said could not exist if there was ever to be peace. Fifty thousand Jews lived there, more coming in every month, a few at a time, and none willing to leave.

After today, Taleb thought, they would all leave on their own, running like rats, and he hoped it would be a hundred years before any of them could return. Allah's obedient children would soon take it back. How soon he could not say, but he prayed none of the Jews would be left in a hundred years to stake any claim to it.

Taleb gently pushed his foot down on the accelerator and the pickup truck rolled forward another few meters north on Golda Meir Highway. It was a four-lane road, far larger than this settlement needed, but the fact that the Israelis had built such an oversize street was proof that they planned for Ramot to grow, becoming maybe ten times its size. That would not happen, Taleb was certain, but for today the traffic backup would have been more fitting for Tel Aviv than this place. There must have been an accident ahead, a bad one slowing the traffic to a crawl, but he had been patient. He supposed it did not truly matter if he caused an accident and was discovered. He had no real destination, in fact, and could end his mission whenever and wherever he chose, and whose lives he wished to take. He had never felt liberty mixed with power like this. The Israelis had denied him both and now to have them mixed together was a potent drug, heady beyond all reason.

Ha-Rav Elazar Square was a hundred meters ahead, one of the largest intersections in Ramot. Judging by the cars around him and the pedestrians clustered ahead, there were hundreds of people within range, possibly a thousand. He had not thought to end the matter here. He had planned to drive a bit farther north and east. There were two synagogues there, the Sha'agat ha-Arie and the Tiferet Yosef, sitting close together. He was certain that the device in the bed of his truck, covered by a hard shell, could destroy either, and perhaps damage whichever he didn't target beyond repair. But perhaps he had been guided here instead, the crawling traffic giving him time to realize that it was a better place—more people, certainly . . . and more than that. The road here was actually a paved shallow valley between two berms rising east and west. That would contain the explosion, keep it from spreading out in those directions, concentrate the blast.

The cars crept forward again, another few meters, and he saw the Israeli police standing in the intersection, directing the traffic around the accident. Someone had run the light and struck another vehicle. Both cars were destroyed, and surely the drivers and any passengers also from the look of the debris and the number of emergency vehicles in the crossroad. Taleb could hardly believe the blessing. A better spot to fire the device, more casualties. It was a blessing.

It took another ten minutes to reach the front of the lineup. His lane was moving and the policeman was expecting him to rumble through over the shattered glass and plastic in a left turn like the other cars. Instead, Taleb stopped his truck at the stop line. The officer blew his whistle and waved furiously at him to continue.

Taleb said his prayer, a conversation with Allah, pleading for his acceptance of the greatest sacrifice the young Palestinian could offer.

The officer frowned and walked forward to see whether the stopped driver was suffering some mechanical problem. The beater truck certainly looked like one of those old models that rolled around Jerusalem, stalling out at every other stoplight. But if the engine was dead, the driver was not trying to turn it over . . .

Taleb finished speaking to God. He reached down and pulled the cotter pin out of the side of the small black box screwed into the dashboard. Wires ran out of the little black cube down to the floor and under his seat through a PVC pipe that tunneled through a hole from the truck's cab back into the cargo bed, which was filled almost completely with PVV-5A, a plastic explosive. Their detonators were all tied together in a long braid from the explosive blocks to the wires reaching back from the cab.

Sure of his course, Taleb flipped the metal switch on the black box.

The PVV-5A ignited, all five hundred pounds of it, five for every person who died in the explosion, some crushed by the shock wave and flying cars, others shredded to death by the shrapnel, some burning. The bomb dug out a crater more than six meters deep before the earth itself ate enough of the destructive energy to stop its downward blast. The shock wave reached out to the sides, striking the berms as Taleb had foreseen they would, and riding the slopes upward, pulling the superheated air along in its wake as it reached for the sky. Mixed in the air was the dirt and burning soot, bits of bodies and pulverized metal.

The residents of Ramot Alon heard the booming noise of the explosion that spread in a circle from the crater that was Taleb's grave. They knew the sound. Many had previously lived elsewhere in Israel and had heard bombings and falling mortar shells before. *Not again,*

they thought, almost as one. *Not like Haifa.* They hustled their children inside their homes to save them from inhaling the radioactive
dust that surely would start to settle in their yards in a few moments.

Inside the Israel police station in Ramot, technicians held their
breath. The more religious among them prayed, the less devout mut-
tering curses as they all waited for their computers to report that
radiation sensors across the city were being tripped by the falling
dust one after another in a pattern that followed the wind. Most tried
to call their families to warn them to stay inside and all wondered
where they would have to live for the winter months while the Israeli
government reclaimed Ramot Alon from the contamination that was
about to rain from the sky.

The sensors never went off.

The George Washington Parkway
Washington, DC

Barron stared down at the papers in his lap, trying to find the last
sentence he'd read on the page. The pothole in the road had been
deep enough to jostle the armored SUV, heavy as it was, and make
him lose his place. The driver in the front had muttered an apology
for the momentary violence and Barron had gone back to the book,
that day's copy of the President's Daily Brief. He had twenty more
minutes to read it through before he would have to discuss it in the
Oval Office if the traffic patterns held steady—

The secure phone sounded. He lifted the handset and checked
the display on the back, then pressed a button, connecting the call.
"Barron."

"This is the Operations Center," said the senior duty officer. "Sir,
there's been an explosion in Israel in the last five minutes, in Ramot
Alon, eastern Jerusalem. The location and blast radius suggest a car

bomb. Casualties are unknown at this time, but they will be significant."

"Define 'significant,'" Barron said.

"We can only guess, sir, but at least several dozen, possibly a hundred or more."

"Any signs that it was radiological?" Barron asked.

"It's too early to tell. The National Geo-Spatial Intelligence Agency is deploying assets and the State Department is contacting Tel Aviv now. We might know more in the next half hour. We'll forward those reports to the White House Watch Office as soon as they arrive."

"Tell the senior duty officer there to bring them straight to the Oval," Barron told him. "And do the same if Israel starts moving military assets into Lebanon, the West Bank, or Gaza. I'm sure they'll be moving units right up to the line, but I want to know if anything larger than a rifle squad crosses the border." The orders were almost certainly redundant, but the CIA director wanted no misunderstanding. Worse mistakes had been made in the heat of events far less dangerous than these.

"Yes, sir."

Tehran

A crosswind struck the plane as the wheels were inches above the tarmac and Kyra felt the tail yaw. It was a small aircraft and had been subject to every gust of wind on the flight from Kish, leaving a few passengers queasy. The pilot held the altitude, straightened out, then put the plane on the ground. The wheels screeched, smoke erupting as the captain in the cockpit applied the brakes hard enough to throw most of the passengers forward. The passengers around her gasped in surprise and muttered complaints, but Kyra said nothing. She'd landed on an aircraft carrier during a night storm and those sixty seconds of terror had cured her of any fears she'd ever had of flying. If a navy pilot could land on a moving runway on a pitching sea, it would take more than a bit of high wind on a sunny day to excite her.

The plane slowed to a near halt, then rolled slowly off the runway toward the terminal building. Kyra watched the ballet of the ground crew directing the aircraft toward its berth, then looked at the skyline beyond. By appearance alone, it could have been Denver, the Alborz Mountains rising behind like the Rockies sixty-five hundred miles away, or maybe Seattle, the Milad Tower looking for all the world like the Space Needle back home in the west. Tehran was larger than either, eight million souls living here, and she wondered how many of them truly hated Americans.

The loudspeaker came on and the senior flight attendant spoke quickly in Farsi. The aircraft came to a stop, the seat-belt light turned off, and Kyra joined the rest of the passengers in standing and preparing to deplane. The forward door opened and within a minute she was marching forward down the aisle.

She followed the line of people walking up the ramp until they reached the open space of the terminal. The small crowd parted ahead of her and she saw a man she did not know standing at the edge of the thoroughfare holding a card: STRYKER in block hand letters. He was shorter than she, compact build, bearded, with a serious look. She was sure she did not know him.

No thanks, she thought. *Not taking rides from strangers today.*

She walked past him, avoiding eye contact, and made her way into the rush of people moving toward the baggage claim. She waited until she had put some distance between herself and the gate, then cast a glance over her shoulder. The man was gone.

She looked for him, but his appearance had been too common for this part of the world for her to pick him out among the other men. She bumped into a woman ahead of her, apologized in broken Farsi, and walked with the flow, looking forward. It was a crowd as large as any she had seen at any of the airports she had passed through over the years, too many people for her to get any sense of whether someone was following her—

She felt something hard press into her side. "I would have preferred that you accepted our hospitality at the gate, Miss Stryker," the man behind her said in clear English. "It would have made for a more enjoyable ride, but you will come with us. If you try to fight, we will leave your body in the desert and no one will ever know what happened to you."

She looked down at her waist. The man's hand was covered with a jacket and she could not see the pistol he was holding against her ribs. "Who are you?" she asked.

The man did not answer, instead nudging her with his weapon toward a service exit at the near end of the large room. She walked forward. Another man in civilian dress moved toward the door and opened it. "You've got friends," she said.

"Far more than you." He directed her through the exit. She stepped through, heard the door close behind. She started to turn back to look at the man, but the bag came down over her head and the entire world disappeared.

CHAPTER ELEVEN

CIA Red Cell

"Please state your name," Rhodes ordered.

"Sally Ramseur."

"Miss Ramseur, you were William Fallon's chief of staff?"

"That's correct," she replied.

"And you served in that position for how long?"

"Three years."

"Did you know Mr. Fallon prior to that time?" Rhodes asked.

"No. He recruited me for the position. A mutual friend told him that I was doing a good job in the same position for a different group chief and he talked me into transferring," Ramseur replied.

"Which friend told him that?"

"Mackie Staunton."

Rhodes scribbled on a notepad before speaking again. "And you were serving in that position when Samantha Todd went missing in Iraq?"

Ramseur stared down at the floor, a look of depression settling over her face. "Yes."

"You were interviewed by the inspector general regarding Miss Todd's disappearance. I have the report. Do you have anything to add to that?"

Ramseur didn't look at the FBI officer and hesitated to answer. "No," she said.

"You're certain?"

Rhodes held up Salem's photo. "Do you know this woman?"

Ramseur looked at the photograph. "No, I don't."

"Very well," Rhodes told her. "We're done for now, Ms. Ramseur. Please do not talk to anyone about this conversation."

Ramseur nodded without speaking, then stood and left the room. Rhodes followed after her and waited until she left the vault to talk to Fuller. "She was the last one of Fallon's group on the list. She didn't give up anything useful, but I didn't press her hard. I think she might crack open if we push her. I'll give her a few days to think about it and then bring her back. Where are we on getting the senior leaders down here."

"They're not cooperating," Fuller admitted. "Busy people, or so their assistants say."

"You tell their assistants that I'll start charging people with obstruction if they don't make themselves available."

"Happy to do it," Fuller agreed. The man checked his watch. "Close of business."

"Not for us. You get on the phone and hammer those top-floor idiots until someone caves. I want their bosses in that conference room before the weekend," Rhodes told him.

"And what're you going to do?"

"Take a ride."

Ashburn, Virginia

Rhodes opened the van door without waiting for the occupants to do it for him. He'd called ahead and they were expecting him. He checked the camera before opening the door. He climbed inside and pulled the door closed behind him. "Evening, boss," the unit lead offered.

"What's happening?" Rhodes asked, nodding toward the house a hundred yards up the street. The team stuffed inside the vehicle was composed of grunt labor, junior officers whose names he hadn't wasted time learning.

"Nothing," the man replied. It was true, but he worried that Rhodes might come unhinged at the answer. His friend had stopped trying to hide his impatience in recent days. "Hadfield's doing what he does every night. Came home from work this morning, had breakfast, slept most of the day, and now he's sitting in there playing online games and watching movies until it's time to go to work again. Having more fun than we are."

"And you still haven't tracked down his ex-wife?"

"She wasn't living at the address listed in the divorce papers, so we're tracking her down through the bank where Hadfield sends his alimony. He hasn't missed a payment since the divorce. Not one. Even sends a little extra every so often. He may be having financial trouble, but he sure looks like he's trying to be a good guy."

Rhodes let out an exasperated breath. The frustration was rolling off him in waves that no one inside the van could miss. "He's playing us. I don't know how, but he is."

"We haven't seen it."

"Then we're missing *something*."

"Nothing I can think of," the team lead assured his superior. "We've had eyes on him every second he's outside Langley. We've combed over every place he's gone and there's *nothing*. If he's running an op in front of our eyes, then he's the best spy we've ever seen, 'cause he's doing it *flawless*."

"He is *not* better than we are at this," Rhodes said, slapping his open hand against the van wall, not trying to hide his anger. The younger agents kept their eyes focused on the monitor screens and other equipment in front of them, afraid to look at the man lest they become the targets of his wrath.

Rhodes stared at the monitor showing one of the camera feeds pointing at the house where Matthew Hadfield lived. "We've got to take the initiative," he said finally. "Make him react to us instead of us waiting for him to screw up." He looked at the rest of the surveillance team, then pointed at one of the men. "You . . . what's your name?"

"Jackman, sir."

"Time to go undercover, Jackman."

He'd missed *Argo* when it had been in the theaters, courtesy of his son's cancer. Watching it now, he found it driving him to anger unlike any movie he'd ever seen. It wasn't the opening scenes, the embassy in Tehran falling to a mob, the Americans taken prisoner, beaten and humiliated, that affected him. Hadfield felt nothing during that sequence, which didn't surprise him. He'd felt precious little empathy for anyone since Aric had died.

It was the scene where some State Department bureaucrats offered a truly moronic plan to rescue the hostages by giving them bicycles to ride three hundred miles to the border while posing as journalists or teachers or agricultural experts from some NGO. Rage had erupted inside him, the incompetence on display touching some nerve. Langley had its share of such men. He supposed every government agency did—

There was a sudden banging on the door, hard enough to rattle it on the hinges. He tapped the space bar to pause the movie, then left the laptop on the couch and walked to the door. He threw it open.

A young man was standing there, eyes wide, gasping for air. "Mr. Hadfield," he said in some bizarre accent the CIA officer couldn't place. "You must come with me. You have been compromised. They know you work for us . . . that you met with Salem. If you come with me now, we can get you out of the country."

"What? Who are you?" Hadfield asked.

"My name is not important. You must come, now! The FBI is on its way here. We have assets in place, ready to get you to Tel Aviv, but we must go!"

Hadfield reeled back. *"Tel Aviv?"*

"Yes! You know who I work for! Come with me!"

Hadfield stared at the man. "No. Leave *now*."

"Mr. Hadfield, they will arrest you for treason and you will spend your life in prison unless—"

"Leave before I call the FBI." He slammed the door and threw the dead bolt.

Inside the surveillance van, Rhodes hit the monitor with his palm and cursed. "All right, Jackman, come back in," he said into the radio. He waited to curse until after he'd shut off the device and then thrown it against the wall.

"So much for a confession," one of the junior officers muttered.

CIA Director's Office

"What are the chances Mossad knows about the second warehouse?" Barron asked. He stared at the photograph on his desk.

"I'm sure they do. I'm also pretty sure they won't move on it," Jon replied. "Security around it is brutal now, and if the RTGs are there, the Quds Force will move them, probably to the mainland. The question is where they'll end up and whether Mossad will try something there."

"Is that why Stryker went back to Tehran?" Rhodes asked.

"Agent Rhodes, I invited you here as a courtesy to keep you updated on relevant events," Barron said. "But if you're going to just throw around unfounded accusations at my people—"

"They're not unfounded." Rhodes pulled a sealed, double-wrapped envelope from his satchel and handed it to Barron. "Stryker gets taken to a warehouse that Mossad raids a few hours later and she was the only one who walked out. Looks to me like she led them to it. My only question is whether someone here—"

"Like me?" Barron asked. "I'm the one who approved the trip—"

"After she asked you to send her," Rhodes noted. "And you've got Hadfield, who worked for Fallon, getting pitched by Mossad—"

"Speaking of Hadfield, what was that you tried to pull on him last night?" Barron asked, his voice calm.

"Sir?"

"He came to Security this morning and reported that someone posing as a Mossad officer came to his house last night and tried to convince him to exfiltrate to Israel. But it wasn't Mossad, was it? It was your people. FBI Director Menard told me this morning that you've had Hadfield under surveillance since this all started and you didn't report that anyone showed up at his house," Barron explained. "Which means that either you're completely incompetent or you tried to provoke Hadfield and failed."

"Those options aren't mutually exclusive," Jon added.

"Menard isn't going to recall you, but I've got that bug in his ear," Barron said. "Don't ever try anything stupid like that again."

"By the way," Jon added, "Kyra's never even met Fallon."

"So you say. Maybe I haven't found a link yet," Rhodes said.

"And you won't," Jon assured him.

"Don't tell me that you can vouch for her," Rhodes interrupted. "There were people ready to vouch for Aldrich Ames and Lee Howard—"

"And Robert Hanssen," Jon noted. "He was one of yours, or haven't you read about that case?"

"What's your point?" Rhodes demanded.

"My point is that Hanssen got to run rampant for years because the special agents hunting him wouldn't stop to examine their own faulty thinking."

"You can't deny the timing—"

"Timing is a pathetic basis for a conclusion in the absence of other evidence," Jon declared. "You jump from conclusion to conclusion every time something happens, latching on to the first theory that runs through your head each time and ignoring anything that doesn't support your latest idea. It's no wonder you've got so many suspects. You need a conspiracy to make it all work."

"I guess you've never heard of the Cambridge Five," Rhodes observed.

"A single counterexample of a real conspiracy doesn't make a compelling case that one exists now," Jon replied. He turned to Barron. "If you'll excuse me, I have a plane to catch."

"Where are you going?" Rhodes demanded.

"London," Jon told him. "Vauxhall Station, if you must know, to find out something useful instead of thrashing around here."

"See you when you get back," Barron told him.

CHAPTER TWELVE

Tehran

There were men on both sides of her and there had to be a driver in the front. If there was another passenger forward, there would be four men in the car, enough to subdue her even without the gun still pushing into her side, so she sat still and focused on her senses instead. She tried to maintain some sense of direction as the vehicle worked its way through Tehran's streets, but that proved impossible. She heard nothing but the men's occasional voices, the sound of the motor, and her own breathing inside the black hood. Kyra had a decent sense of time and figured they had driven for almost forty-five minutes before they finally came to a stop, but that helped her not at all. The driver could have taken a convoluted route to whatever destination they had just reached simply to throw her off.

The doors opened and one of the men pulled her from the car, not as rough as he could have been. Hands grabbed both of her arms and guided her as they walked. She could tell by the slight echoes that they'd parked inside a building, but she could not get a feel for the space from the sounds alone. She walked through hallways, turned corners, and then her escorts warned her of steps downward. She moved forward carefully and managed to descend a flight of stairs without falling.

The men pushed her into a chair. She was surprised that they did not tie down her arms.

"You may remove your hood." It was a man's voice, calm, speaking in practiced English. She pulled the bag off her head.

The room was small, perhaps eight feet by ten. The floor was covered with thin linoleum, a hideous green color, and the walls were dirty white and covered with messages scratched into the fading paint, some in Farsi, one in English. *No one stays here forever,* she read. There was a small window on one side near the ceiling and Kyra could see daylight through the three layers of metal grating that ensured she would not crawl out. There was no bed, no toilet, no sink. The ceiling was very high, fifteen feet at least, and a light bulb hung from the ceiling with no switch she could discern on the walls to control it. The door was steel, no handle on the inside, with a slot at the bottom to pass trays of food in and out. The space reeked of mold and some pungent cologne that her interrogator was wearing.

"Do you know where you are?" It was the same man who had caught her at the airport. Kyra looked around the room. It was all concrete floor and walls, metal chairs and table, nothing to identify the place. She shook her head. "We call it the Evin House of Detention. You would call it a prison." He smiled. "Did you know the shah built it?" He looked around, appreciation on his features. "His secret police controlled it."

"I request that you contact my embassy immediately and advise the ambassador that you are holding a citizen of the United Kingdom," Kyra said. She prayed the man hadn't discerned her true nationality.

"We will call the British embassy when you and I have finished our conversation, but only because the United States has no embassy here," the man said.

Kyra showed him no reaction. "What am I being charged with?"

"You are not being detained. We have not even restrained you. On the contrary, you are a guest."

"Then Iranian hospitality is less refined than what I'm used to."

"I do hope you'll forgive all of this, but it is necessary to maintain appearances. But I think that I am not the first man to say that to you in recent days."

"Appearances for who?" Kyra demanded.

"That is the insightful question," the man told her, surprised. "For certain elements within our government. I cannot give you names, of course."

"I'll settle for yours."

"I am Eshaq Ebtekar, the director of the Ministry of Intelligence. And you are Kyra Stryker."

"If you will check my passport—" Kyra started.

"The false British passport you are carrying?" he asked her. "You are an American. We knew who you were the moment you landed in Tehran a few days ago. We have good relations with the Russians and you have had dealings with them of late. They shared what information they had on you with us after they sent you home last year," Ebtekar told her.

Kyra kept her own expression fixed. Like so many English speakers here, Ebtekar's accent sounded British, which meant he'd either studied in the UK or had had a British tutor in Iran. Either way, she wondered whether he had dealt with Westerners enough to read her face. "If you believe I'm an American, why didn't you arrest me?" she asked, choosing her words. "That *is* what you do to Americans."

Ebtekar smiled at the woman. "Not always, but often, yes. In your case, we hoped that you might help us," he said.

"Help you," she said. "Why would you imagine that I would do that?"

"You know who Majid Salehi was?"

Kyra took several seconds trying to decide whether to reveal what she knew. If the Russians had shared their intelligence on her with Ebtekar, then pleading ignorance would likely annoy the man. She also doubted that the head of Iran's Intelligence Ministry personally came to see every American detained on his country's soil, so perhaps he was not lying when he was asking for her country's help. Salehi had done the same.

She decided to gamble. "He was the director of your nuclear program. Mossad killed him in London."

"Yes," Ebtekar said. "He tried to pass a back-channel message to your government, but we do not know whether your president received it. If he did, he chose to disregard it, probably because he did not believe it."

"Chanting 'death to America' tends to undermine trust that way."

Ebtekar stared at her, then let out a short laugh, little more than an exaggerated breath. "It surely would, I agree," he admitted. "You do understand that such language is, for the most part, hot rhetoric for the people. It helps to distract them from the failings of their own leaders."

"When you go around chanting, calling for genocide, you shouldn't be surprised when people take you seriously."

"That is why I hope you will listen to me now," Ebtekar told her. "What Salehi told your president was true. Our government did not order the bombing of Haifa and you must tell Mossad to stop these attacks. I have convinced our supreme leader to be patient, but his more conservative advisors are calling for blood. He has decided that we will retaliate if the Israelis attack again. We will strike back and then it will be beyond my power to stop whatever comes after. Already, some lone wolf has bombed Israel again, so I think we have little time before things move far beyond our control. That is why I gave the order to have you brought here . . . though I am grateful you came to Tehran of your own volition. Taking you from your hotel on Kish would have been far less convenient."

Kyra narrowed her eyes as she looked at the man, trying to figure out the game. "Your word carries no weight at all, sir, with us or with

Israel. If you want President Rostow to make a serious effort to stop Mossad, you need to give me some evidence."

"Proof of our good faith?" Ebtekar asked.

"More than that," Kyra said. "You say you didn't bomb Haifa? Then tell me who did."

Ebtekar exhaled, then stared into her eyes. "I told our leader that you would demand that, if you were going to listen at all. It took considerable discussion, but I convinced him it was necessary. He has given me his consent to show you such proof if you demanded it, but only with conditions. Please, come with me."

She followed Ebtekar out into the hall, where several men were waiting. They surrounded her as she fell in behind the man, who led her through the corridor. There were metal doors on both sides and she did not bother trying to count the number. There was total silence except for their own footsteps and Kyra wondered whether the cells were empty or full of occupants simply too frightened to make any sound.

Ebtekar opened a door and descended two flights of stairs, which creaked despite their metal construction. Another door at the bottom opened into a corridor that led off in both directions and ended in intersections. The basement of Evin Prison was a maze, she was sure.

And then Kyra heard the screams, like nothing she had ever heard in her life, cries of agony beyond anything she had ever experienced. She felt rage welling up inside her and she was not sure that she wanted to control it.

"Remain here," Ebtekar ordered the other men. He held his arm out to direct Kyra to the left. "Follow."

She obeyed, anger rising as she walked and heard moans of despair mixing with the wails of pain. The basement was brightly lit, but every door was closed and it would have been very easy to get lost. The entire bottom floor was as close to a literal dungeon as Kyra thought she might ever see in her life. The Iranian led her on a winding route through the network of halls until they reached the dead end of one of the hallways.

"This is Ward 209," the man said, like a professor lecturing a student. "This is where we detain those we deem threats to our national security." Ebtekar stopped at the last door on the right and unlocked the small window, sliding the metal grate to the side. "Look." Kyra looked at the man, her expression a mix of anger and suspicion. She heard the sound of something striking flesh and then a scream of pure agony, a man wishing to die.

"No," Kyra told him. "I don't want to see it."

"Inside is your proof—" Ebtekar started to tell her.

"I will not watch you torture someone!" she said, nearly yelling at the man.

"Do not get self-righteous with me!" Ebtekar hissed back. "Your country has tortured men before when it suited your purposes, and we are not making him suffer for no purpose. That man you hear inside is no dissident or prisoner of conscience. He is not in there because he angered some man of influence by sleeping with his daughter. That man is responsible for the bombing of Haifa and has put us on a path to war and economic desolation for years to come. There were others who followed, and they are here also, but *he* gave the order."

"He could be anyone and I wouldn't know the difference. Just watching you torture a man isn't evidence."

"Do not dismiss what I tell you so quickly," Ebtekar hissed. "He is the supreme leader's own brother."

Kyra reeled back, her mind racing. "Even if that's true, why would he—"

"Why would he order the bombing of Haifa?" Ebtekar asked. "Even the supreme leader did not know of it until the act was done. When I learned that strontium had been detected at the blast site, I convinced the ayatollah that the bombing could drive the Israelis to the edge of madness. I told him that having Salehi pass the message to your president in the hopes it would buy me time to find out who had ordered the attack. Only a few men had authority over the RTGs, so it did not take long."

"That doesn't explain why his brother ordered the attack."

"The Khameneis control Kish Island. Do you understand what that means? The family has enriched itself from smuggling and the other criminal trades that flourish there. But lifting the UN sanctions started to hit their interests hard. So many items once available only through their black market became legal again. Our people became accustomed to a better economy and so had less of a stomach for the hard-line policies of our government." Ebtekar pointed at the closed metal door. "A few years ago, that man had Amiri negotiate a deal with the Russian military to buy those radioactive generators.

"And that man"—Ebtekar hit the door—"had his people remove the strontium core from one of them and fashion a dirty bomb with it. He believed that setting one off on Israel's soil would make Mossad lash out, and he was right. He believed that his brother would respond, attacking Israel through our Hezbollah allies, and the turmoil would restore the black market and thus his income and influence with the hard-liners. He did this for his own gain and power."

"But that would hurt your people—" Kyra started.

"What do our elites care for the people? Do you think our leaders go hungry or worry about money? We do not feel such pain," Ebtekar said. He put his hand flat on the metal door to the torture cell. "They care for power and that comes from money and fear. He was sure that attacking Israel would replenish both. The black market would grow strong again, the hard-liners would have an excuse to start another round of arrests of the dissidents and the moderates, and his brother would approve of the money and control it ceded to their family. But he misjudged his own brother. Our leader is a religious man, pious but not a fanatic. He does hate Israel but not enough to start a war that would destroy all our progress."

Ebtekar held up a thumb drive and pressed it into her hand. "On this you will find recordings of our interrogations. Your CIA can verify that the man in the video is the supreme leader's brother and that his suffering is not staged. You must show this to your president and he must show it to Gavi Ronen. The men who attacked Israel are no longer a threat and Mossad must stop killing our people. The supreme leader has declared that if Mossad kills one more of our people, bombs one more of our facilities, our retaliation will begin and Hezbollah will send rockets down on Israel like rain from Lebanon."

Kyra furrowed her brow, confused. "Why Gavi Ronen? Why not the prime minister?"

Ebtekar smiled, an expression that Kyra found entirely unnerving. "Gavi Ronen," he said again, as though the man's name explained everything. "I am not offering an ultimatum. I know my people. I am offering yours the only path that doesn't lead to war. I cannot ask for your trust, but I must ask for your belief that I am not a liar."

Kyra took the thumb drive, looked at it, and closed her hands around it. She looked up at Ebtekar. "That's not for me to decide," she told him. "And I have a condition of my own."

"What is that?"

"A few years ago, one of our officers went missing—Samantha Todd. Amiri said she ended up in Evin Prison. I want her released."

"I know of her detention. What you are demanding is not possible."

"Why not?"

"I will show you."

Ebtekar led her out of the building, up the winding staircases, and through a cell block. Kyra saw almost no one on the way. The silence was disturbing, more than any nightmare she could ever remember.

Evin Prison was a monument to misery and cruelty and there was a dark spirit about the place that seemed to stain her soul just by standing inside it. She could not imagine how it must feel to be so cold inside, that one could visit such a place and not feel horrified. Just the sounds she had heard were trapped inside her mind and she couldn't get them out.

There was a car waiting for them outside, a black Mercedes, and a driver held the door for Ebtekar and his guest. Kyra crawled inside, Ebtekar followed, and the vehicle pulled away. Kyra looked behind and finally saw Evin from the outside. It was a square concrete blister, dirty and topped with razor wire, guard towers rising like parapets. There was no mistaking it for anything other than what it was, and there was no doubt in her mind that it was the ugliest building she'd ever seen. Knowing, even vaguely, the horrors that were going on inside made it feel more hideous still and she turned away from it, determined not to ever lay eyes on it again.

The Mercedes was joined by two other vehicles, armored SUVs, and the convoy drove south on the Chamran highway. Looking ahead, Kyra saw the Milad Tower approaching on the right. Tehran was like many other cities she'd visited, modern in parts, with amazing constructs and brilliant architecture in one borough, then quickly turning decrepit in another, with ramshackle homes cobbled together from whatever materials the residents could find or steal. Such beauty and misery coexisting so close together. Now, as always, she felt nothing but depression and anger when she saw it. These people were capable of so much more.

The driver exited onto the Hakim Expressway and followed it east for a few miles before turning south again. The roads began to narrow but the convoy stopped for nothing. Finally, they slowed. Kyra looked to the right and saw a brick wall topped by a layer of concrete and a metal fence topped by sharpened spikes pointing outward. The wall had been painted over—an outline of Iran, then red and white stripes leading to a crude drawing of the Statue of Liberty, the face replaced by a skull. They drove on, a bit farther, and she saw other murals, every one an insult to the United States. Kyra was surprised to see they had left the US seal intact on the brick wall by the embassy gate. She thought the concrete design had merely weathered over the years, but realized as they approached that someone had beaten on it with a hammer, smashing out the details, but not enough to obscure the symbol. The brick around it was better maintained than she had imagined it would be, but she supposed Tehran wanted to keep its trophy in some kind of decent shape.

Ebtekar watched Kyra as she saw a building go past. "Do you know where you are?"

She turned away from the scene to look at her host. "Yes."

"The Revolutionary Guard maintains it. The compound is off-limits to both foreigners and our own people."

The car passed through the gate and Ebtekar's driver parked it near the building entrance. Kyra exited the car, then stood, frozen, staring at the compound. The old US embassy building was small compared to others she'd seen. It was only a two-story structure with no particular beauty to its design. It looked like an old high school, like those she'd seen in the poorer counties of central Virginia where she had grown up. She had seen this place in photographs and movies. Fifty-two of her countrymen had been taken captive here for four hundred forty-four days, subjected to beatings, interrogations, and mock executions. They had been marched about and trussed up, held in solitary for weeks at a time, blindfolded and paraded in front of the crowds. The guards had mocked them and used empty guns to fake games of Russian roulette with the prisoners' heads as the targets.

Ebtekar seemed to understand the emotion running through the American woman and said nothing until Kyra came to herself. "We call it the Nest of Spies."

"Says the man who runs Iran's spy agency," Kyra observed.

He glared at the young woman but no useful retort came to his mind. "Are you ready?" he asked. She nodded, and he directed her course with an outstretched arm.

The southeastern end of the embassy compound was heavily wooded, a small nature preserve in the middle of Tehran. Ebtekar walked ahead, Kyra following, the security detail a few paces behind her. Wearing no abayah, she drew looks from a few of the people they encountered, but no one was curious enough to approach them.

They crossed the tree line and the sunlight disappeared above the branches, breaking through to the ground in broken streams. Their feet crushed the leaves underneath as they walked, the sound mixing with the passing of cars just a few dozen feet away behind the compound wall. Ebtekar led her around the small forest, following a trail that was not apparent to her.

Finally, he reached a small clearing, maybe ten feet square by her estimate. Ebtekar held out his arms toward the ground. "She is here," the man said.

Kyra looked down and saw no signs of a grave, which made sense. If Todd had died and been interred here a few years before, the weather would have wiped away any signs of fresh-tilled earth long before. "It's not marked."

"My decision," Ebtekar said. "It was done in secret and I did not want anyone to disturb the site. I could not send her home, so I thought perhaps this might be enough. No one would disturb her rest, and it had been American soil in another time."

"I'm surprised you didn't bury her out in the desert somewhere," Kyra spat.

"I am not without feelings. She was a spy, but it was always a mistake to hold her, and the error grew worse with time," Ebtekar admitted. "As the days passed, all of the ways, the opportune moments to release her that would not have done our country more harm than good, all vanished. Foreign prisoners have a . . . what is the term . . . a 'shelf life'? Yes, that is it. When you arrest a spy who can offer you leverage, you must trade her while there is still value to the transaction. Hold her too long and you are seen only as cruel men keeping her from her family only to cause pain. Who could sympathize with such men?"

"But you never released her," Kyra observed.

Ebtekar nodded. "When the Khameneis took Todd, they only wanted to erase a threat to their smuggling enterprises on Kish. She refused to cooperate with their interrogations and so it took a few weeks for them to realize that she was not the threat they thought she was," he explained. "I suggested that they give her up, but they dithered over the question. That was the great mistake. Had they released her immediately, they could have claimed to have rescued her from unnamed criminal elements. But they spent months trying to determine how to trade her back to your country while claiming to know nothing. Then Todd fell ill. They could not let her die, so she was taken to a hospital . . . a *military* hospital. That was when Todd realized she was in government custody, which created a humiliating problem. If they released her, eventually the truth that the criminals and the government were in cooperation would come out."

"That would have led to the exposure of Khamenei's activities on Kish, his family's criminal ties," Kyra realized.

Ebtekar nodded. "Do you understand? To admit the corruption of our government? We are a theocracy. Our leaders claim that Allah grants them the right to rule. For the world to have hard proof that they are just oligarchs, greedy and corrupt, no better than criminals? Just the shah in a different robe? They fear it would bring on a new revolution. If these men are not Allah's servants, then there is no excuse for the heavy hand they use on the people."

Kyra considered the man's answer. "Let me bring her home. Show the world and your own people—"

"That good men can still rise to the top?" Ebtekar said, finishing her question. "You do not understand how this country works. No man leads here without the corrupt ones behind him. He may pretend to advocate moderation and reform, but he knows where his bounds are and who draws them." Ebtekar sighed.

Kyra needed only a second to see the implication of his words. "When did she die?"

"Last year. When a person loses hope that they will see home again . . . I am afraid we all need hope as much as we need food. A person's soul can starve to death."

"And when she died, Tehran could never admit they'd had her at all," Kyra finished the thought.

Ebtekar shook his head. "To admit that they had held her until she died? Much of the world would think that we had simply executed her at the first or tortured her, left her to the rapists or starved her to death in Evin Prison, and we would never be able to prove otherwise. So she had to disappear. They did not care what happened to her body, so long as there were no pictures. They wanted there to be no proof they had ever held her. It was better for her to forever be a mystery that is never solved."

"Do you know what her family has been through?" Kyra said, trying to suppress her rage. She failed, just a bit, the hostility creeping into her voice.

"Do you know that the mullahs do not care? If the feelings and desires of their own people matter so little to them, surely you can see that the feelings of Western infidels count for nothing."

Kyra knelt down and placed her hand on the dirt, her fingers extended, saying nothing. She stayed there for several minutes, then stood. "You need to let me take her home," she said.

"I cannot," Ebtekar said. "If you do, the world will know what happened to her, and you may bring a revolution down on our heads."

"Give her to me. I can tell my people that it was done as an act of good faith. That and the interrogation movie might be enough for us to approach Israel, if you also give up the RTGs."

Ebtekar shook his head. "I cannot give you the RTGs. If I tried, I would be sent to Evin myself. I am working on another way to resolve that issue, but it cannot involve anyone from the West. That said, if Mossad stops the attacks and this situation quiets down, then in time I might be able to arrange the return of your officer's body," he said, gesturing at the grave. "It would have to be done in secret, of course."

"Of course."

He grimaced, then looked at the American woman standing before him. He nodded toward the old embassy building. "Would you like to go inside? Very few of your people have been here since the revolution. Much of it remains as it was that day."

Kyra followed his gaze and studied the old building. "I don't want to see your trophy," she told him, more anger seeping into her voice than she'd intended. "You already showed me the prison where you torture your own people. I don't need to see one where you tortured mine. Now please take me back to the British embassy. I need to contact my people."

"As you wish."

They drove on for several minutes, the city becoming a blur to her as she disappeared into her own thoughts, until the driver in front slowed the Mercedes to a stop. The British compound was on the other side of the street, and Kyra felt a sense of relief settle on her that cut through the dark atmosphere that had surrounded her for days. She reached for the door handle. "Miss Stryker," Ebtekar said.

"What?"

"The evidence you will see on that thumb drive must not become public. If you or Israel show this to the world, we will claim it is a

Western forgery and then events will go where they will," Ebtekar cautioned. "I truly do not want war. I never have. Please tell your people that."

"Yes, you do," Kyra replied. "You just don't like the way this one started."

"Many others in our government feel that way, but I do not. I have never wanted war with Israel. I want this to end."

"The side that's getting bloodied up usually does."

Ebtekar nodded. "I wish I could disagree," he admitted. "Miss Stryker, if you or someone you trust talks to Gavi, would you pass a message to him for me?"

Kyra stared at him, then looked toward the front of the car. The soundproof window was still up. "You know him," she realized.

Ebtekar looked out the window and smiled. "I knew him, before the Revolution. The very day your embassy was taken, we met for the last time, after dark in Honarmandan Park. Who would have imagined that two men, security officers and close friends, would become the chief spies of their countries, their jobs forcing them to treat each other as the most vicious enemies? Life has been cruel to us."

"What's your message for him?"

"Tell him . . ." Ebtekar paused as he searched the archive of his memories, thinking back to some moment that was long past. "Tell him that if he will call off his people, then perhaps we will not have to wait until the next life for peace. He will know what I mean. On that thumb drive, there are instructions for passing a message to me. I would ask you to make sure he receives them. If the evidence I am passing him is not enough, there may be something else I can do that will convince him that I am sincere."

"What's that?"

"I do not wish to say," Ebtekar told her. "Not now. But he will see it and he will know that it was me."

"I will try, sir." She threw open the door and crawled out of the car. She checked the road to make sure she had an opening, then walked across toward the British embassy and didn't bother to look back.

US Embassy
London

The old embassy had overlooked Grosvenor Square since the days of Eisenhower, its massive gilded eagle with spread wings on the roof recognizable even from the air. Securing the compound had become problematic in recent years. The British had gone the extra mile and a few miles more trying to protect both their capital city and their ally's base of operations from extremists, more than a few turning out to be homegrown, much to the government's frustration. The US president had assured the prime minister that the decision to build a new facility on Nine Elms Lane in Wadsworth was not a lack of American faith that their hosts could keep them safe, but the British leadership knew it had been a serious consideration.

The new embassy was far taller than its predecessor, a high glass cube on the shore of the Thames surrounded by an oval perimeter that kept traffic and car bombs at a safe distance. The building was covered with photovoltaic panels that produced more electricity than the facility used, with the rest shunted to the surrounding neighborhood. There was even a lake on one side—which the State Department had insisted was absolutely *not* a moat—a park on the other, and six gardens inside the building itself, including one on the ambassador's terrace.

The ambassador to the Court of St. James was a post usually reserved for the most generous of political donors or some other notable partisan, but this one had met Kathy a few times when she'd run the Agency. His marriage to a senator's daughter had been no impediment to his attraction to the CIA director at the time, but Kathy had given him no opening on that front. The ambassador's attempt at seduction had been indirect enough that she hadn't felt the need to tell his wife, which chit Kathy had discreetly told the man to cash in now. The cost of settling that debt was letting her use his office for this particular meeting.

"It is very good to see you again, Kathryn," Sir Ewan said. "I'm quite pleased you and your husband were able to come back to our fair city so soon. And it is a true pleasure to finally meet you," he said, turning to Jon. "Having married this lovely woman, you are a gentleman of proven taste."

"Or inexplicable good luck," Jon said. "But thank you."

"Ewan, I'm afraid that this trip is for business as much as the last. We need a favor."

"Whatever we can provide, within the usual bounds of course."

"Of course," Kathy agreed. "We need to know who was the handler for one of your assets a few years ago, an expatriate named Asqar Amiri."

"The soul who Mossad just dispatched," Ewan observed. "Yes, I know him. We do not typically share that kind of information. I assume that you must have an exceptional reason for wanting us to share it."

"We think that a few years ago, one of our people ran an unapproved op in Iraq," Jon explained. "He sent a case officer to Baghdad, a woman. According to his reports, one of your people offered to set up a meeting between her and Amiri. The manager who we think was running the op was William Fallon."

"Whoever it was probably didn't know the op was illegal," Kathy started to assure him.

"I'm rather distressed to hear that, because I was the man," Sir Ewan admitted.

Kathy stared at her old friend. "You?"

"Indeed. I recruited Amiri years ago when I was our senior man in Tehran," the Brit said. "He was not a terribly valuable asset at the time, but he had soured on life in the Islamic Republic and his desire to return home was a strong motivation. I thought he might have potential, so I encouraged him to develop his connections. He had a talent for smuggling which the Khomenei family appreciated and he burrowed himself inside their operations like a tick. He became useful to them and a worthy asset for us, to the point that it requires—well, required—my personal approval to put anyone in a room with him, which I granted to Clark when he asked a few days ago. There are quite a few people at Whitehall who are very unhappy now that I did that, if I may say. If you don't mind, I'd be very grateful if that young lady, Stryker, came through Heathrow on her way home so we could ask her a few questions about Amiri's unfortunate end."

"I'm sure that can be arranged. I'll talk to Clark," Kathy assured him. "How did you know Fallon?"

"We met at one of our liaison meetings at Langley, a year or so after I recruited Amiri. In one of our side meetings he told me that his people were looking into smuggling operations in southern Iraq. He was looking for sources of information beyond what your own assets were providing. We discussed Amiri, but I counseled him against a meeting. Mr. Fallon was insistent that it would be an opportunity to prove Amiri's value to some of my more skeptical superiors, so I did agree to set up a meeting. When Amiri told me that the Agency officer never showed up, I supposed that the logistics simply hadn't worked out . . . happens all the time with covert meetings, you know . . . someone detects hostile surveillance and walks away or whatnot. So I thought no more of it. I never heard that any of your people went missing. If Amiri was still among the living, I would have our Mr. Grayling in Tehran debrief him for all he knows. As it is, I'm afraid all I can do at the moment is offer you my sympathies. But if there is anything that we can do to assist in finding your officer, you have only to ask."

"Ewan, you just did," Kathy assured him.

It had taken Barron's assistant less than fifteen minutes to set up the video conference. It crossed seven time zones across three continents and sixty-three hundred miles.

Kyra recounted her encounter with Ebtekar for the group. "Do you believe him?" Barron asked.

"I don't know," Kyra admitted. She was squeezing her fist so hard that her knuckles hurt, her best attempt to stop the shaking in her hand.

Barron nodded. "Good answer," he said. "Whether the president chooses to believe his story or not will hang on whether the techs say Ebtekar's footage is genuine or not."

"Forget the president, the better question is whether the Israelis will believe him," Jon asserted.

"Ebtekar said that if Mossad hit Iran again, they would retaliate, and I do believe that," Kyra added. "He said that he convinced the supreme leader to give him time, but it sounds like the clock's run out on him. He won't give up the RTGs. I told him that might be enough to get Mossad to back off, but he said that his own people would throw him in Evin Prison if he tried."

"Too big a concession. Jon, Kathy, what do you have?" Barron asked.

"Sir Ewan says he was the man who connected Fallon and Amiri," Kathy reported. "He knew that the meeting between Amiri and Todd never took place, but he never heard that any of our people went missing."

"That's because it would've been Fallon's job to report it and ask the Brits for help finding her." Barron muttered some quiet curse that the encryption muffled. "Well, that's something," he said. "At least

I can fire him now. I'd have Rhodes arrest him, but the *Post* would probably catch wind of it and then we'd have journos sniffing around. Are you and Kathy ready to come home?"

"I think we'd like to stay in London a bit," Jon said. "Our last trip was cut a bit short."

"Whenever you're ready," he advised them. "Kyra, send me a copy of that drive. I have to take it to the president. Pass a copy to the Brits, too. It might smooth things over a bit with Amiri gone. Then get on a plane to Tel Aviv. Assuming the president agrees, I'll clear the road for you to meet with Gavi Ronen."

"Yes, sir."

CHAPTER THIRTEEN

Ben Gurion International Airport
Tel Aviv, Israel

There were no direct flights from Tehran to Tel Aviv for all of the obvious reasons. She'd had to fly to Europe and then take a second flight southeastward to reach the Jewish state, a roundabout itinerary that left her more jet-lagged than she could ever remember being. It was fortunate, she thought, that the Israelis had a healthy number of coffeehouses. She would need to find one and soon.

Kyra made it through Immigration and Customs without trouble, not that she had expected any. Gavi Ronen knew she was coming, courtesy of a call from Barron, and she hoped that the *ramsad* would have called the airport and told them to remove any hurdles. She would be happy just to get out of the airport without an interrogation. The Israelis usually were friendly enough to Americans passing through. The number of religious pilgrims coming to see Christian sites any given year was considerable, as were the tourist dollars they spent during their stay. But when the *Shin Bet*, the internal security service, did pull someone aside for scrutiny, the trip turned sour in a hurry. *Shin Bet* interrogations were mind games that used tactics perfected over decades to weed out the terrorists and extremists trying to infiltrate this little country. The Israelis had gotten very, very good at spotting such people and tearing their cover stories apart.

The passport control officer ran the usual security check and raised his eyebrows when he entered Kyra's name into the system.

What information appeared on the man's screen she couldn't see, but he let her proceed after a few minutes on the phone, speaking Hebrew, of which Kyra understood not a single word. She had only carry-on baggage, which she took to Customs Control, but there was nothing to declare and she went through the green lane, which moved smartly along. Past that last checkpoint, she had made her way toward the airport exit.

She had guessed correctly that Ronen would send someone to meet her. The driver holding the card with her name said nothing to her when she announced herself and did not offer to carry her bag. He was no taller than she was and not heavily muscled, but his demeanor and bearing implied that he was not a mere functionary.

His car was an armored SUV, with a bulletproof divider between him and the back. They rode in silence, twenty-five minutes west, then north. Kyra stared at the Israeli city, content to say nothing to her chauffeur. Tel Aviv was almost nothing like Tehran. The buildings were densely packed but cleaner, most not as tall, and there was no Islamic influence in the architecture anywhere that she could see.

The driver took the exit off the Ayalon Highway, which dumped them onto an eastbound freeway, and she could see the Mediterranean perhaps four kilometers ahead. Tel Aviv was a coastal city, with all of the rain and salt air that came from living by the sea. She had never been here before but she could feel the personality of the place like few cities she'd ever known.

Tel Aviv felt alive to her. There was so much history in this region, she knew, so much of civilization had developed so close to this place. The Egyptians and Phoenicians, the Carthaginians, Greeks, and Romans, later the Ottomans and the Muslims—they had all traveled to this place. Some had ruled it, all had left their mark. Her own country was so young compared with this. Israel was so ancient and so modern all at once, and it amazed her how clearly she could feel it.

No wonder they fight so hard for their country, Kyra realized. *No wonder the Muslims want it back.*

The driver led her to a small room, almost unfurnished except for a table and two office chairs inside. He directed her to one and she obeyed, after which he left her, never having told her so much as his own name. She waited for an hour before the door opened again. Kyra looked up and saw a man walk in, midsixties, shorter than she was by almost half a foot, moderately overweight. He wore a pair of thick glasses decades out of fashion, and kept his white hair shaved close enough to be almost invisible. He was not handsome by any standard. She thought most people might actually try to avoid looking at such a homely man, which he probably considered an asset given his job.

"Miss Stryker?"

"Yes," she confirmed.

"My name is Gavi Ronen," the man said. "I am the director of Mossad. It is a pleasure to meet you." He offered his hand.

Kyra stood and offered her hand in return, unsure if Ronen really meant what he said. The Israeli *ramsad* was a professional intelligence officer after all, and had been in the business far longer than she had. She knew he had ambushed Jon in London a few days before. Doubtless, none of the tourists who had passed him in the British Museum had imagined that this short, nearsighted man had signed the death warrants for the Iranians shot down on a British street by a Mossad kill team. How many people Ronen had killed himself before he had become the Mossad director was anyone's guess, but she knew that in ordering his men to assassinate Israel's enemies, he was only asking them to do what he had done himself, perhaps many times.

"Thank you, sir," Kyra replied.

"I understand you attended the University of Virginia?"

"I did," Kyra replied, trying to keep the suspicion out of her voice. She wondered how much Ronen knew about her and whether the mole back home had passed him information.

"I went to Columbia, for my graduate training," Ronen said. "Your field experience comes from dealing with the Russians and the Chinese, not the Middle East."

"Yes," Kyra admitted.

"But you were responsible in part for uncovering Iran's illegal nuclear facility in Venezuela a few years ago. That was a great service to us, I assure you."

"I'm not at liberty to discuss Agency operations," she countered. "Other than the immediate one."

"I'm sure." Ronen nodded, and then the Israeli's mood changed, his charm replaced in an instant by a cold focus that caught Kyra entirely off guard. "Then why are you here?"

Kyra reached into her bag and pulled out the thumb drive. "I was on Kish Island, meeting with Asqar Amiri, when your team assassinated him. He had information on one of our officers who went missing. Adina Salem was there. Once she found out I was American, she decided not to kill me—for which I'm grateful, by the way."

Ronen nodded at her, a silent expression of approval, but said nothing to stop her. "I went to Tehran after to meet with the British, but I was detained by Iranian intelligence," Kyra continued. "They took me to Evin Prison, where I had a meeting with someone I believe you know. His name was Eshaq Ebtekar."

"The head of their intelligence service? The VAJA? No, I have never met Eshaq Ebtekar."

"He says that he knew you before the Revolution. That you met for the last time in Honarmandan Park the evening that the US embassy was taken over."

Her words shook the *ramsad*, she saw. The Israeli had kept his face still as she spoke the name, but her mention of the park and the revolution had knocked him off balance, a sure sign, she thought, that Ebtekar had told her the truth. She waited for him to speak.

"What did he tell you?"

"He said that Tehran didn't order the bombing of Haifa. That it was done by the supreme leader's brother to strengthen his family's wealth and political power. He asked me to give you this as evidence." She held out the drive.

Ronen watched the video three times on the laptop before he spoke. "The supreme leader's own kin."

Kyra nodded. "Ebtekar took me to the cell where he was being tortured. I refused to look in, but I heard what was going on."

"I assume that Ebtekar wants me to order my people to stand down."

"Yes," Kyra confirmed. "He also asked me to pass you a message. He said that if you'll stop, 'perhaps we will not have to wait until the next life for peace.' He said you would know what that means."

"I do," Ronen said, a hint of depression in his voice. "I regret that I cannot accommodate him."

"Why not? Iran hasn't hit you back for all of these assassinations—" she started.

"That doesn't matter. We have expected their retaliation from the beginning. That they haven't yet taken steps is just an unexpected blessing," Ronen said. "The fact is that someone used a radiological device against us. Salem reported your information about the RTGs. They are still out there, and as long as they remain unaccounted for, Iran could hit us again. We must remove that threat."

"Ebtekar doesn't want a war," she said. "Israel has the right to defend itself, but if you don't stop, you're going to start one."

"Miss Stryker, you are trying to preserve a peace that does not exist," Ronen assured the woman. "The Arab states attacked Israel the day after Ben Gurion declared us a state, and we have been at war with them ever since. Just because these enemies might not shoot at us on any given day means nothing, and the world refuses to do what is necessary to keep nuclear materials out of their hands."

"Our countries have enjoyed seventy years of friendship," Kyra replied. "We are *not* selling Israel out."

"I do not believe you are selling out my country, but that does not mean your president is not making a mistake, for which my country will bear the consequences," Ronen sighed and reclined his chair as far as it would go. "I am sorry."

"Sir," Kyra said, "Ebtekar asked me for a specific favor. He said that he included directions on that thumb drive for contacting him, and that if you couldn't or wouldn't call off the attacks, he had one other thing he could offer to convince you."

"And he did not tell you what it was." It was not a question.

"No, sir."

Ronen nodded. "Very well," he said. The man sounded tired. "Thank you for bringing this to me, Miss Stryker. I am indebted to you. I will have my man drive you to your embassy so you can make your report. Please feel free to enjoy our country for as long as you wish. I will ensure that you encounter no difficulties at the airport whenever you decide to return home."

"Thank you, sir."

Ronen stared at the thumb drive. "It is my honor."

The woman had been gone from his office almost an hour when Ronen finally opened the lone text file on the thumb drive. He and Ebtekar had not shared words for four decades, and seeing his old friend's message was like hearing from a dead man.

In the name of God, the most Compassionate, the most Merciful,

Gavi,

    I regret we have not been able to talk since that night in the park when the Revolution began and we watched the students dance on the embassy walls. The story of my life since that time has been a winding course that I wish I could describe to you. Allah's hand has been in it every moment. Given that we are both positioned now to stop a war, I believe his hand must have guided your course also. I know that it would not have been safe for us to reach out, but regrets care little for such realities. It is not safe even now, but I fear that the dangers rising beneath us carry more risk yet.

I pray to Allah that after watching these videos, you will believe my country gave no order to attack Haifa. The supreme leader and his followers will never stop calling for Israel's destruction, but I promise you that they did not take this step. I ask you, with all the honor I can claim, to call your people home. I have kept the promises that I made that night in the park and am trying to keep them now.

Still, you may decide that you cannot desist based on my word alone. If the evidence does not convince you of Israel's safety, then send word by the directions included. It will work one time and one time only. Then watch for my signal and please consider my words again.

Hasan

Ronen read through the comms protocol that Ebtekar had included. It was a simple process. He turned in his chair to the unclassified computer on the desk behind him, brought up an e-mail client, and began to type.

Hasan,

Your message is received. I, too, regret the long silence between us . . .

He was not a fast typist and it took him five minutes to enter his thoughts into the machine. Then he rechecked the comms protocol.

A public encryption key was included and he used it to secure the e-mail behind a wall of mathematics that supercomputers could not crack in all the years remaining in the life of the universe. Then he sent the message along to the address Ebtekar had included, an account with a nonsense name at one of the world's largest online e-mail providers. Then he sat back in his chair and reached for the bottle of brandy on the desk by the monitor.

What will you do now, Hasan? I cannot wait long.

Headquarters of the Ministry of Intelligence and Security (MOIS)
Tehran, Iran

Ebtekar preferred to arrive at work before his subordinates, a habit that had terrified his secretaries. He had had to assure them that he did not require them to precede his arrival in the morning and, in fact, preferred that they did not. He liked the quiet of the morning and having time to himself before he had to listen to others.

He raised up the blinds on his window to let the morning sunlight in and looked out at Tehran as his computer came online. It was not a beautiful city to his eyes. He had seen too much of the world to have any illusions about that. It had changed since the revolution, but he realized now that the changes had been too gradual for him to perceive as they'd occurred. Still, for all its faults and ugliness, it was home.

He pulled a disposable smartphone from his pocket. It asked for his fingerprint, which he provided, and the mobile device presented him with a desktop of icons laid out in a grid. There was only one that was important. He launched the secure e-mail app, as he had every morning for the last several days. The in-box had been empty each time, until now—a single message waiting for him. He touched it with his finger and the phone reminded him that the text was encrypted. He entered another set of credentials, unlocking the private encryption key that paired with the public one he had included on the thumb drive he had given to the American woman.

The handheld computer worked for several seconds, performing mathematical computations that he could not begin to fathom. Then the block of gibberish text was replaced by clear sentences written by a man he'd not seen since his youth.

Hasan,

Your message is received. I, too, regret the long silence between us, though the events of the years have forced it on us. It will always be so, I think. We can always pray for miracles, but we must live as though they will never come.

You are correct that I cannot call my people home on your word alone. Though the material used to make the Haifa bomb may have been in the hands of criminals then, I have no doubt it is in the hands of your leaders now; and I fear they may choose to use it again and blame the very criminals you now have in your custody. As long as those devices exist, my country will not be safe; and until it is safe from them, we must push on, and duty will not allow me to rest my country's safety on the word of any one man, no matter his name. But you have promised a signal that my country is safe in your hands. I will wait on it and then reconsider.

That you have survived and led a long life brings me joy I cannot express. To know that there is one good man, perhaps the last good man in Tehran, does give me hope that we may yet see peace in this life.

Gavi

Ebtekar stared at the message, reread it, then read it again. He knew he had to delete it, for the sake of security, but it pained him to do so. To finally receive a message from Gavi after four decades had moved him more than he had imagined it would and he wished he could save it. But his discipline asserted itself and he wiped the message. He replaced the phone in his pocket, where it would stay until he arrived home that evening, at which time he would toss it into the furnace in the basement.

Ebtekar turned to his other work until he heard the first of his assistants arrive in the outer office. He picked up the telephone. "Get me the travel office. I need to travel to Qom in the morning."

I had hoped you would decide otherwise, Gavi, but I knew that you likely could not. I could not in your place, he thought. *One last operation. I hope you are watching.*

CHAPTER FOURTEEN

35,000 feet above the Atlantic

The British Airways Airbus A380 was the quietest plane Kyra had ever known. It was a monstrous thing, double decks the full length of the fuselage, four engines below the wings, and the business-class seats offered enough luxury that she imagined the first-class lounge must be fit for a king. The flight home technically wasn't long enough to qualify for anything better than coach, so Barron must have waived regulations or told someone to look the other way when booking her seat. Perhaps she'd earned it, but she thought that just walking out of Evin Prison had been reward enough. Unlike Sam Todd, she was going home.

The interview in London with Sir Ewan and his people had been unpleasant. Kathy and Jon had been in the room for moral support, and the spymaster and his immediate subordinates had been perfectly polite in that cultured way that all British seemed to master . . . but she was sure that underneath, there was a suspicion that this American girl had somehow gotten their asset killed. Kyra had answered every question they'd put to her, hiding nothing and offering her recollections in excruciating detail, but she doubted that the interviewers were truly satisfied. She could not judge them for that. The situation reversed, she or Clark Barron would have picked apart whatever British agent had sat before them without mercy or hesitation.

She had traveled with Jon and Kathy to Heathrow in one of London's famed black cabs and parted ways there. None of them had been free to discuss the reasons for their coming and going and so there had been little to talk about.

She looked out the window starboard side and watched the Atlantic shoreline pass under the aircraft. The pilot announced that they would be landing at Dulles only a few minutes later than the 2:00 p.m. scheduled arrival. The caffeine pills would help with the jet lag and her town house in Leesburg was only twenty minutes from the airport. Barron had ordered her to go home and Kyra could take a day to rest if she wanted it. She was inclined to obey. She didn't know what she could do back at headquarters.

She didn't sleep on the flight. There was still a mole, or a pack of them, at Langley. Fallon was still the leading candidate for that. He'd certainly gotten Sam Todd killed and a man willing to cover up something like that for his own benefit suggested he was willing to break any other rules. Still, the puzzle had embedded itself in her mind and refused to let her go. Why would Fallon help Mossad?

Money? It was the most likely answer but also the easiest for Rhodes and his FBI team to track down, and they'd found nothing.

Revenge? For what? Who had wronged Fallon? No one that she could see. His career had stalled after Todd's disappearance. Was that enough to drive a man to commit treason? Even if it was, it didn't explain why he would choose Mossad as his partner in that particular crime.

Ideology? The man was a narcissist. He had no religious ties to Israel, and his loyalties, as far as she could detect, were to himself alone and perhaps a few of his close friends, and she wondered how far that stretched in a scrum like Fallon was in now.

Ego? She could believe that, but most of the spies in the game for that reason started early in their careers and Fallon was far along. Had he been engaging in treason all along and only now had made his mistakes? It was possible, she supposed, but this line of inquiry only led her back to the first question. Why help Mossad? It seemed an unlikely choice. Perhaps the answer was more psychologically complex than she could fathom, but it felt wrong to her. And why would others join in if the whole point of the exercise was to gratify one man's ego. If there was a pack of moles at play, surely they were in this for something more than Fallon's personal pleasure, and all of the other reasons reared up again with all of their complications. The pieces refused to come together neatly in her mind in any way that she could arrange them.

She saw another plane in the distance flying in the opposite direction, a long contrail stretching out behind it. She pulled out her cell phone, connected it to the Airbus's Wi-Fi network, launched a flight-tracker app, and pointed it at the aircraft. The phone ingested the data and reported that the transport in the distance was a United flight, had just taken off from Dulles, and was bound for London, the city she had just left.

She shut off her phone and stared at the eastbound plane. *Going the other way,* she thought.

Is the mole helping Mossad?

Or is Mossad helping the mole?

Her thoughts tumbled around in her mind faster, the bits of data piecing themselves together again, moving and turning in different ways.

The mole had picked the Banshee Reeks site. Why? For the reason she'd thought? Just so Fallon could have an easy cover for action? Maybe, but Fallon had access to some of the leaked intel that had been recovered in the package, which guaranteed he would be the logical suspect if the intel was recovered.

No, not if, she realized. *When.*

Money, ego, ideology, revenge? She had let herself become trapped by that model, seventy years of counterintelligence cases telling her what the boundaries were, what the motivations of a mole had to be. Now, perhaps, there might be a new reason to add to the list.

It took her another minute to rearrange the pieces in her mind, to turn them over and fit them together in different ways. They came together and the solution to it all became painfully clear.

The Airbus touched down ten minutes later. It took a half hour to evacuate the massive plane and Kyra rushed through Dulles, pulling her carry-on behind her, and then almost breaking out into an open run when she got outside. Her truck was in the parking deck to the west, a half-mile walk from the drop-off zone. She threw her case in the back, clambered in, and made her way down and out onto the airport road as fast as she could manage. It took another five minutes to get onto the Dulles access road. Langley was twenty miles to the east. Kyra opened up on the accelerator.

Qom, Iran
78 miles southwest of Tehran

The tractor trailer was older than the guards who waved it through the checkpoint, paint stripped in lines from its body by a thousand scrapes, other bits eaten away in small bits by rust that had started in on the metal underneath. The battered machine spewed black smog as the driver shifted gears with a leathery hand, and it rolled forward, crawling toward the old factory entrance. The trailer it pulled behind was heavy, more weight than he could remember hauling in years. The man behind the wheel had been ordered not to look inside, which had been no temptation anyway. He had stopped caring long ago about what he was hauling on any given day, and once he realized that he would be carrying this particular load to a military facility, he knew that ignorance was a better course anyway.

The sentries grimaced and held their breath until the breeze cleared the black fog from the air. Guarding a rusting old warehouse, their duty was now made worse by the fact that they now got to breathe pollution, and they muttered curses at whoever had approved entry for the moving smokestack.

That man was in the car behind, an armored black Mercedes S600. Mahmoud Akhundi had not wanted the vehicle. Too ostentatious, too *obvious*, he'd told the president. He had not wanted this job either, securing the RTGs for Iran's future use, but he'd had no more choice about that than he had about the car and the security guards. Men doing work like this needed to move about quietly and a vehicle fit for the supreme leader himself could draw the attention of armed drones in the sky, not to mention spies on the sidewalks. The president had ignored both protests. Mossad was on a rampage, the head of the nuclear program had been gunned down on a public street, and so the president refused to let him decline the security. The murder of the director of Iran's nuclear program had enraged the mullahs, but the supreme leader was playing the calm philosopher, refusing to lambaste Israel in public at the behest of the MOIS director. *Silence is the beginning of all security,* Ebtekar had told him.

As though silence could make the Israelis forget about Haifa, Akhundi thought. *Or make them believe that we have only peaceful intentions.* The only people who still believed that were the same breed of useful pacifist idiots whom Saddam Hussein had once used as stage props as he tried to stop the US from coming for him. The Israelis were not idiots and they were most definitely not pacifists. How many of his country's nuclear sites had they bombed over the years? Akhundi tried to remember. *Khormabad in 2010. Bidganeh in 2011, Isfahan, the same month. Fordo in 2001, Parchin the year after.* How many scientists had the Mossad killed over the years? He knew the names. Some of them had been friends. He had seduced one man's wife and Mossad had murdered the cuckold a week later, saving Akhundi from an unpleasant argument. He was sorry the man was gone, though less so about the timing of his demise.

The cargo ramp had been installed inside the building to keep the American satellites from seeing the construction. It was long and winding, built to let trucks like that one make its way deep underground by traveling down in a wide spiral. The cargo truck would need ten minutes of one long, slow, and steady turn to reach the lowest level and Akhundi had no desire to crawl behind it. There was a more comfortable way down at his disposal.

Akhundi unlocked the seat belt before the car stopped and he opened his own door before his driver or any of his armed escorts could do it for him. The security force said nothing, just stepped quickly to take up their positions around him as he walked. One of the guards offered him a hardhat, red with a blue stripe around the circumference. He put it on without argument.

"Not that way, sir." The leader of his security escort pointed him a different way.

"We are not going down by the elevator?" He pointed to the complex adjacent to the warehouse. It was an industrial office park, no longer new but not old enough for the facade to have started crumbling as much as it appeared to have done. Perhaps it was better not to fix the place up. The security force, cameras, and fences kept it clean of graffiti and enough wild cats roamed the perimeter to keep the rodents out; but a facility kept too clean and repaired in this part of the city would have drawn notice. And the main building was only two stories but had an elevator cabin on the roof. That had been a design mistake. Some American intelligence analyst staring at a satellite photo might ask why a two-story building needed an elevator, and it would not take long to conclude that the elevator was not for travel up, but down—six stories in this case.

"Orders from the minister. The perimeter is secure, but we don't want to risk you going outside. The investigation team on Kish recovered evidence from the warehouse of snipers. So, the stairs, if you would, sir."

Akhundi frowned but didn't argue the point. They walked to the stairwell, the bodyguards checking it first. Two men took the lead, the rest following Akhundi inside. The first sublevel was all pipes and pumps, the industrial systems needed to heat, cool, and pump water throughout the facility. Placing the infrastructure on that level also masked the heat signatures from below from satellites and planes and drones and whatever else the West sent over Iran every day. The second sublevel was the central control room, where visitors would soon be able to watch the production of uranium fuel rods below through tall glass panels on sublevel three.

The fourth sublevel was three stories high, and housed the only facility of its kind in the Islamic world, a separation factory where scientists would extract plutonium from the used fuel rods brought from the heavy-water reactor at Arak. They would only be able to extract ten kilograms of plutonium each year from the waste, twelve in a very good year, but Akhundi was a patient man. Western surveillance had turned nuclear proliferation programs into the work of decades.

The fifth sublevel was home to the metallurgy department and the most advanced machine shop in Iran, though the equipment was now sitting idle. Amiri—Allah protect his soul—had had to procure all of the equipment at Akhundi's request because the Europeans had not been allowed to sell any of it to his companies directly. *Sanctions, so sorry*, was the answer Akhundi had heard for years. But the Europeans' strict adherence to the law was only skin deep. They'd even sold the equipment at a discount in return for prompt payment.

Akhundi looked at the three large crates in the middle of the room. The middle crate was open and empty. It had not been his decision to crack open the first radioisotope thermoelectric generator and extract the strontium inside. He was still trying to determine who had given that order. The supreme leader and the president had both denied any involvement. Assuming they were being truthful, that left very few possibilities, none of whom Akhundi was anxious to confront. Those were men so powerful that his own political connections would offer him precious little protection.

The sixth sublevel was the loading dock.

The crew chief and several of his workers were milling around the area, waiting for the truck's arrival. He saw one man standing alone on the dock. The workers seemed to be avoiding him, whether out of fear or some other reason, he couldn't tell. He approached the man, who sensed his arrival and turned.

"*Salâm,* Mahmoud. How are you?" Ebtekar asked.

"I'm doing very well, sir. I was not told you would be here."

"I felt it necessary to come and see things for myself after recent events. Are the RTGs here?"

"They are," Akhundi confirmed.

"And the rest of this new cargo?"

"Off-the-books parts for one of the new reactors at Bushehr."

"Ah," Ebtekar replied. "I will be finished with my own inspection here once the truck is unloaded, and I will be returning to Tehran within an hour afterward. You will notify me at my office when the RTGs have been secured at the new site."

"Yes, sir."

They stood in silence until the tractor trailer finally arrived. It had taken fifteen minutes to make the trip down the spiral ramp. The driver had taken his time, not for the sake of the truck, which could have scraped every concrete barrier on the spiral and looked none the worse for it. He had seen the security and assumed that, whatever he was hauling, the buyer wanted it to arrive intact.

Shipshape and Bristol fashion, Akhundi thought, repeating an old phrase he'd heard during his student years in London. He appreciated the driver's caution. Not all men were so careful.

The truck rolled to a stop smoother than Akhundi had imagined and the cargo crew broke up their loose formation and swarmed around the back. The driver stayed in the cab, another order he'd been given before starting this assignment.

They disconnected the trailer in less than a minute and the crew chief ordered the truck driver to swing wide and make his way back up the ramp. The gears crunched, the truck moved again, spewing its smog, and there was no breeze here to clear it out. Akhundi smelled it and wondered whether the cloud wasn't more poisonous than anything the truck driver had just delivered.

The truck rolled up the ramp out of Akhundi's line of sight, and only then did the crew open the trailer. The crew chief climbed inside and disappeared for several minutes, the beam of light from his torch all that Akhundi could see.

"Any problems?" Akhundi asked as the chief finally clambered out.

"I am not certain, sir."

"What is it? Is something broken? Stolen?" Akhundi asked, his voice rising. It was not uncommon for smaller pieces of equipment to go missing, but to have this happen before the intelligence director was embarrassing. It was all smuggled in to begin with, so it was very easy for any of these workers to steal something to sell to one of the smugglers passing through Kish for sale on a black market in some other country. He would have to order the Quds Force to retrace the entire shipment and start interrogations—

"No, sir, that is not the problem," the crew chief corrected him. "The opposite, in fact. We were expecting a total of seventeen. The shipment that arrived this morning carried one crate more than expected, but all of them were part of the larger manifest, so we thought it had simply been shipped out early because space was available. But now, with the number we just received, we have an extra."

"An extra crate?" Akhundi twisted his head and looked around the cargo dock. There were dozens of wooden and metal boxes stacked everywhere. "Which one?"

"I don't know," the crew chief admitted. He had never been diligent in tracking the paperwork and now his carelessness had finally caught up with him. "We'll have to unload these and then compare everything against the manifests."

"It will not appear on the manifests," Ebtekar announced.

"Sir?" Akhundi asked.

"The extra crate is here on my order," Ebtekar said. "I will explain everything to you shortly. But preparing the RTGs is your first priority. Get to it."

"Yes, sir."

"I will meet you upstairs. Report to me when the RTGs are ready for transport."

"Yes, sir."

"*Khoda hafez,* gentlemen."

"Good-bye, sir. I will see you shortly."

Ebtekar took the elevator up. Akhundi went upstairs to the central control room and spent two minutes talking with the facility director to ensure that there would be no serious delays. He was tired of all this maneuvering, if he was honest with himself. His influence over these men, his power to give orders, derived entirely from the fact that he was the supreme leader's lackey, and he hated that fact. All of the trappings of his position were a charade. No one respected him, not even the man to whom he answered. They kept him because he was useful and gave them plausible deniability. Once those facts were no longer true, he was sure that his fall from grace would be impressive, if not fatal.

The phone on the wall rang. The facility director answered it, spoke quietly to the party on the other end, then hung up. "They are loading the RTGs now. They will be ready to go in thirty minutes."

"Very good."

Ebtekar walked out the front door and checked his watch again. His driver pulled up in the Mercedes S600 and the director climbed in. The car pulled away from the building and through the front security gate.

Six stories below the surface in the loading dock, the extra shipping crate, a metal box labeled in Farsi script, sat behind a stack of wooden containers surrounded by dozens of other pieces of equipment. The dockworkers had tried to open it when they'd first pulled it off the truck, but the key provided hadn't matched the lock, there had been no bolt cutters on hand, and the driver who'd delivered the package had already departed, so they could not ask whether he'd given them the wrong one. That driver was a regular, so they had simply decided to ask him about it when he returned the next day. They would have settled on a very different course if he had told them how he had gladly taken a several-hundred-thousand-*toman* as a bribe from a beautiful woman he'd met at his usual bar to deliver the crate. How she had known he made deliveries to this site he didn't know, but his lust and her money had convinced him not to ask the question. She had told him that it was computer equipment that one of her smuggler associates was going to resell. He hadn't cared whether she was telling the truth or not. She hadn't been impressed with his crude attempts to flirt, so he had settled for her money and some leering glances. If he did the job well, there could also be more in the future, and maybe other chances to seek more than monetary payment from her for his services.

The detonator inside was connected to both a timer and a radio receiver wired to the crate itself, making the entire box an antenna. The timer had counted down from twelve hours, giving Mossad time enough to deactivate the system if there was any reason to do so.

The detonator fired a millisecond after the timer reached zero.

The explosion turned the metal crate into an oversize grenade, two thousand kilopascals of pressure shredding the sides of the box and every other crate around it into countless pieces of shrapnel that cut the workers into bloody ribbons. The blast wave hit them two milliseconds later, smashing their bones to powder, their organs to jelly, and the heat vaporizing nearly all of what remained of their bodies before gravity itself had time to pull their mangled corpses to the floor.

The nearest load-bearing pillar was less than ten meters away, and the blast wave shattered it and every other pillar within twice that distance before deflecting up and smashing into the ceiling. The entire building shook for an instant, and the fifth-level floor above the cargo dock fell away, dropping men and machines into the burning storm below. The fourth level held its ground for a moment as the support beams and pillars stressed and twisted, crumpling as the unbalanced weight of the entire building pushed down on them. The third level dropped onto the fourth, finally causing it to crumble. The separation factory hurtled down, nuclear waste and extracted plutonium spilling out of their vessels into the fire, radioactive particulates rushing skyward on the rising air. The second level crashed down, the first a second later, men now having had time to scream as they saw their deaths below them for a few moments before they landed.

The guards around the warehouse outside had felt the rumble before they heard it, wondering for an instant whether Qom hadn't suffered one of the temblors that rattled the windows at random times. Then the concrete under their feet fell away, the entire street level above emptying into the ground as fire and smoke rose up through the cracks faster than the street fell into the earth.

The crater was a city block square and growing as it took everything aboveground into its widening mouth and vomited smoke toward the blue sky.

Ebtekar felt the car shake. The driver pressed the brake and the car came to a gradual stop.

The people would think it had been an earthquake at first. Iran suffered them sometimes, sixes and sevens on the Richter scale. One had hit Bam in 2003 and killed more than thirty thousand. Another had killed fifty thousand in Manjil in 1990. The mullahs lived in fear that one would hit Tehran and destroy the entire city, Allah's judgment for their hypocrisies.

Ebtekar pushed the car door open and stepped out, then stared at the scene behind him.

The facility was gone, replaced by a small volcano in the earth, flames and smoke reaching for the clouds.

The RTGs were buried now, crushed at the bottom of the hole that had eaten the entire building he had just left, buried under tons of earth, metal, and the bodies of dead men.

Ebtekar looked up to the sky, where the US satellites were orbiting. He checked his watch. *On schedule. They will share the pictures with you, Gavi,* Ebtekar thought, hoping his distant Israeli friend might hear him. *It is your choice now.*

CIA Operations Center

"Anything on your side?"

"No," Hadfield told his FBI counterpart.

"You know, I worked as a sheriff's-office dispatcher for a year when I was trying to get into the Bureau," the FBI officer admitted. "New guy on the totem pole, so I got the night shift, five nights a week. Small county in West Virginia. So small that all the sheriff's deputies went home after midnight. You know what's on the television in rural West Virginia at three o'clock in the morning? Infomercials, Country Music Television, and *Baywatch* reruns. That's it."

"I'd be doing as much for my country watching any of those as I am processing these reports," Hadfield groused. "There's not a— wait . . ." The message on his screen was one that he'd seen maybe once before. He clicked the link and stared at the window that opened. Then he sent the image to the monitor array on the front wall.

All heads in the room looked up at the live satellite image that had replaced the news feeds. A pillar of smoke was rising out of a crater surrounded by cargo warehouses and flatbed trucks. "Where is this?" the senior watch officer asked.

Hadfield checked the alert. "Qom, Iran. Suspected nuclear site."

The senior watch officer reached for his secure phone and dialed. "Director Barron, this is the Ops Center. Sorry to wake you, sir. There's been an incident."

US Embassy
Tel Aviv

Ronen stood in one of the reception halls on the embassy's main floor, a US marine standing behind him at parade rest, hands behind his back. He'd spent the afternoon in a meeting with the American ambassador and the station chief. After reviewing the material they'd given him, he'd asked for a few moments of personal privilege, which the Americans had kindly granted. The State Department was hosting an art exhibit this year, portraiture on loan from the British government, and the *ramsad* had asked for permission to view the artwork on his way out of the building. Gentleman that he was, the ambassador had approved the request, with the caveat that an escort accompany him and he restrict his movements to the public areas. The marine had kept a respectable distance, but that would change quickly if Ronen tried to venture anywhere away from the exhibition. *The way we treat our allies*, Ronen told himself, then laughed at the absurdity of the observation. Given the operations he had approved in recent weeks, he had no right to complain about how his country's allies were treating him.

The request to come to the embassy had been a surprise. Such invitations were rare and he had thought that he might find himself subjected to a demarche, but the ambassador and the CIA station chief had both been courteous. They had not bothered to waste his time with trivial matters, which he appreciated. The station chief had given him an envelope, which he had opened to find satellite photos of a burning warehouse. Ronen had given no orders to destroy it and the Americans had not done the deed. Five pages of NSA intercepts, translated into English and Hebrew for his convenience, let him review a conversation between the director of the Ministry of Intelligence and Security and Iran's president. The director, Eshaq Ebtekar, had been present, had barely escaped the facility moments before its destruction in fact, and had made the call over an unsecured cell phone, no doubt forgetting in the shock of the moment that it was an unencrypted connection. He confirmed that almost fifty men were believed dead in the rubble, including one of his own senior deputies. The RTGs were buried under the pile, their condition unknown but likely destroyed. Ebtekar had recommended that they not try to exhume the devices. The smoke rising from the hole showed no sign it carried radioactive particles, but that alone did not prove the RTGs were intact. If they were breached, they could yet pollute the sky or the groundwater with strontium. Better, Ebtekar thought, that they fill the site with concrete, to ensure that any radioactive material stayed where it was. If the president disagreed and ordered an excavation, it would take months to clean up the site, and every shift in the wreckage would threaten to turn the RTGs into dirty bombs that would contaminate all of Qom. Iran would then know what Israel had felt after Haifa.

Ronen stared at Hysing's *Portrait of an Unknown Man* for almost five minutes, looking but not seeing.

Ebtekar took a long drag on his cigarette, never looking away from the students dancing on the embassy walls. "I don't know where Mossad will send you after this . . . but wherever you go, always keep your eyes here on Tehran. Khomenei and those who come after him want to see Israel pushed into the sea, but they have seen you defeat the Arab armies and how you deal with terrorists. That will leave them only one option. Do not ever let them lay hands on it."

Ronen digested the man's words while Ebtekar finished his cigarette. What was the term he had heard the Americans use? The Islamic Bomb. "That would be the most difficult mission Mossad ever takes," he said, his voice depressed. "And the most vicious."

The *ramsad* shifted his feet as the memory played through his mind. It had remained sharp and clear despite the years, and he could remember the look on Ebtekar's face as the Iranian told him what the future held.

"I know," Ebtekar had said. "That is why men like you should lead it. It is as your boss, Meir Dagan, has often said: 'The dirtiest actions should be carried out by the most honest men.' You are the most honest man I know. I do not think you and I will ever see each other again after tonight. To survive, I will have to become one of them and I will have to do some very ugly things. I will have to hurt your country. As the years wind on, please trust that I will take no pleasure in it, no matter what you may ever hear me say. I do not care for Israel, but you are my friend. And I will do what I can to stop my people from getting their hands on the bomb, because I know what they would do with it. Trust me that I will do what I can to prevent war between our people."

Ebtekar had removed the RTGs from the field, and he had destroyed a nuclear facility and killed his own men to make the point for an audience of one person.

Ronen turned to the escort. "I'm ready to leave. You may show me out."

The marine held out an arm, directing the Israeli to the door. Ronen stopped at the front desk and retrieved his cell phone, then walked outside.

. . .

Mossad's campus was five kilometers north of the embassy, less than an hour's walk. It was not especially safe for the *ramsad* to travel on foot, even in his own country, but Ronen decided he needed to breathe the sea air, to clear his mind as he thought. Several members of his security team walked with him in a respectful circle, two ahead, two behind, one to each side. He said nothing as he marched north at a steady pace. His mind was miles and years away as he thought about the last words he and Hasan, now Eshaq Ebtekar, had ever spoken.

"I will miss your company," Ronen had said.

"Bedrood, my friend."

"Tzeth'a leshalom, Hasan."

"I think peace will have to wait for the next life."

He looked up at the traffic sign—Einstein Street. He saw the classroom buildings of Tel Aviv University rising just a block to the east. There were so many students there, young people whose safety and futures depended on the decisions he had to make, and this one more important than any other in his life.

Ebtekar was in the same position, he knew. So many young Iranian men and women who hoped they would never have to actually fight an open war, no matter what their leaders in Tehran said. Did Ebtekar feel the weight of that? Ronen thought a man would have to be a monster not to be aware of it.

The *ramsad* breathed in deep. He had not imagined on that night that either he or Ebtekar would be their countries' chief spies four decades later. *What were the chances of that?* he asked himself. Two young officers, once friends, now serving countries that were enemies, unable to talk to each other for half a lifetime. But they each knew who the other was now, how high he had risen, and what his duties demanded.

Ebtekar had shown that he still remembered their last conversation that night when revolution had taken his country. Could a man remember such words forty years after if they meant nothing to him?

The *ramsad* made his choice.

Ronen pulled his cell phone from his coat and dialed a number, never breaking his stride, and held the unit to his ear. The call connected. "All teams are to stand down and return home immediately," he said.

He ended the call and replaced the phone in his pocket. *I will trust you, Hasan. I pray you will keep your promise.*

Maybe peace would have to wait for the next life, he thought, but if they could have it in this one, that was the place it should start.

An Eastern Beach on Kish Island

Salem watched as the men lifted two forms wrapped in canvas and laid them in the boats, one in each—their dead from the warehouse. Two other men were helped in, the walking wounded who had taken rounds in a shoulder and a knee, the latter man drugged heavily to keep him from screaming in agony with each step. Whether either man would serve Mossad in the field again remained to be seen, but they would receive Israel's highest honors when they got home. The awards would be secret, of course, but no one joined Mossad for fame.

Salem turned away from the scene and looked back at the island lights while the rest of the team finished packing the gear into the two rubber dinghies. There was nothing left for them to do in this place, no one left to target. She doubted she would ever see Kish Island again. That did not bother her. She'd never had any desire to see this place before she'd come and had not enjoyed a moment of its pleasures while she'd been here.

She pulled a satellite phone from her pack and dialed a number. It rang only once before the man on the other end took the call.

"Report," Ronen ordered.

"As you ordered, our evacuation is under way," Salem told him. "Two dead, two wounded but stable."

"You've done us all a great service," Ronen told her. "Please have the entire unit report to me when you arrive home. I would like to offer my thanks to everyone in person. Also, tell them that I will visit the families of your fallen to share our gratitude and sorrow with them."

"*Toda*, sir," she said.

"*Al lo da-var*," Ronen replied. "*Tzeteh' Leshalom.*" *Return in peace.*

The call disconnected. Salem replaced the phone in her pack and slung it over her shoulder.

"We're ready," one of the men announced.

She marched across the wet sand and crawled into one of the small boats as two men pushed them out into the shallows and then heaved themselves aboard. The drivers fired up the motors and the dinghies surged forward through the low waves and turned south, running for the cargo lanes of the Persian Gulf. The Israeli navy had stationed the Dolphin-class submarine INS *Rahav* five kilometers south of Kish days ago; it had sat on the bottom a mere eighty-six meters below the surface. The gulf was shallow and the sailors had certainly heard cargo ships and Iranian military vessels passing only a few dozen meters overhead, but they were brave men, no less than her own team. The *Rahav* would surface on schedule, the Mossad officers would board with their equipment, and they would settle in for a cramped ride home, which would take a few weeks. Ronen would debrief her and the rest of the officers, and then she would go back to Haifa content that she had repaid the injury done to her home.

But an eye for an eye would never give Israel the security Salem wanted her country to have so much. It was too small a nation to just trade blows when it was outnumbered so heavily, and to hit their enemies harder than their enemies hit them would just escalate the violence until Israel was destroyed or Tel Aviv used nuclear weapons, which likely would produce the same result. What was left? *Fear, only*, Gavi Ronen said. Israel had to make her enemies afraid to act, and that meant striking at the very people who gave the orders to attack and those who carried them out. The people who would pull the trigger must know for a certainty that to strike Israel was to pronounce a death sentence upon their own heads. *Is that terrorism?* Salem wondered. Perhaps, but she thought there was a difference. If Israel's enemies buried their guns tomorrow, there would be peace. If Israel put away her guns tomorrow, there would be slaughter in the streets of Jerusalem and Tel Aviv, and there was the difference.

The cold spray of the gulf wet her face. She did not bother to wipe it off.

She would return to the field and fight again. Salem thought she would probably die on an operation like this one, as two of her team had, but it would be a good death. And if there were enough in the world like Shiloh, helping her and Mossad identify the men who needed to be made to fear for their lives, then Israel would survive.

CHAPTER FIFTEEN

CIA Red Cell

The vault door opened and Fuller came in, staring down at papers in a file. Rhodes looked up from the classified terminal on his desk. "You have something?"

"Just some contact information from the bank where Hadfield deposits his alimony." He offered the file to the senior agent. Rhodes took it and stared at the front page. Then he slammed it shut and ran for the door, the papers clutched tight in his hand.

CIA Director's Office

Rhodes entered the office after the assistant outside finally gave him permission, his frustration bordering on anger. He held up the file that Fuller had delivered to him minutes before. "Sir, I just—" He stopped short, seeing Kyra on the couch.

"Welcome back," he said, no warmth in his voice. "What did you find out?"

"Who the mole is," she told him.

"So did I," Rhodes said.

"You show me yours, I'll show you mine."

"You first," Rhodes replied. He took a seat on the couch next to her. Barron came out from behind his desk and seated himself in one of the chairs by the young CIA officer. "I'm listening."

"If you look at the access lists of the breached compartments, there's someone on each one who served under William Fallon," Kyra explained. "We've been thinking that meant the people were funneling the intel to Fallon and he was passing it to Mossad."

"That's the theory," Barron replied. "But we can't prove it."

"We can't, but the mole can. The mole knows who they are and wants to take them out," Kyra offered. "He has a copy of the reports that Todd sent to Fallon. I don't know how or where he got them, but he left one at Banshee Reeks. We recover it, and it puts us on Todd's trail, and then we connect the others by association."

"Okay, I follow that," Rhodes said.

"That theory only holds up if you arrest Mossad at Banshee Reeks trying to recover the intel," Kyra said. "It depends on the intel being recovered, and that doesn't happen unless the Bureau is already watching the Mossad officer tasked with retrieving it."

"Adina Salem," Rhodes said, thinking out loud.

"Correct. And how did the Bureau know to follow Salem?"

"Because Hadfield identified her after she pitched him."

"Yes and no," Kyra corrected him. "Hadfield identified her, but Salem never pitched him at all."

He hadn't heard from Sam in months. He'd left messages, but she'd never returned any of them. He'd thought she just didn't want to talk, that she'd wanted to disappear into her work. She'd gone back to the Directorate of Operations, and they'd sent her to Iraq, or so he'd heard from the few friends of hers that he knew. He'd made a few inquiries, but no one could tell him anything.

"Unless you're family, you have no need to know." And he wasn't.

Frustrated, he settled on a course that he knew would anger her, but he supposed she was angry enough that another minor sin would hardly matter. He remembered the passwords that Sam recycled for her online accounts. It was poor cybersecurity tradecraft to use the same ones repeatedly, but it was so hard to remember more than a few that she thought it safer to use a handful she'd memorized than to use a long list of stronger passwords that she would have had to write down.

He guessed the password to her online Dropbox account. Most of the files were old, dating back to their time together. But there was a new folder there, the files more recent, all encrypted. That didn't worry him. Sam would have used the same passwords to protect those as well.

One was a database file. He decrypted it. The filename was nothing he recognized.

```
Amiri.db.
```

He opened the file.

"He knew who she was because he'd already met her," Kyra declared. "Salem was his *handler*. We took him at his word that he'd met Salem because the mole told her that he might be vulnerable to a pitch. That was backward. He pitched his services to *her*. That's how he identified her from the FBI's book."

He'd only needed two hours to read through the entire database. Then he'd closed his laptop, walked to his car, and driven east to the Tyson's Corner mall. Once inside, he found a quiet corner in the two-story Barnes & Noble and sat down in an easy chair, trying to control the wild thoughts tearing through his mind.

Sam had been working the streets in Baghdad, talking to informants, trying to set up human networks, making dead drops and brush passes as she gathered intelligence. All of her reports had been sent through encrypted e-mail over the Internet directly to William Fallon. She had kept encrypted copies in the cloud, never on her own machine, in case the authorities or anyone else ever decided to detain her and search the drive.

Fallon's e-mails to Sam were full of exclamations of approval, flattering the young woman, telling her how valuable the information was that she was gathering. But other e-mails that Fallon was sending, e-mails in which Sam's name didn't appear on the distribution list, said otherwise. Fallon wanted more information, he wanted it faster, and he was frustrated by the rules that were slowing her down.

Then Fallon told her to meet with an Iranian nuclear proliferator in Basra, in the Iraqi south just across the border from Iran. Sam had asked for the man's vetting file. Fallon had told her that he couldn't send it over these channels, but to trust that he'd checked that box.

He had thought about turning the database over to the Office of Security, but the rumor mill had quashed that idea. "Sam Todd? Yeah, investigation's closed down, I heard. The Seventh Floor just wants this to go away. They think she's dead already and they don't want Congress to give 'em a rectal exam over it."

Hadfield had no problem believing that the Agency's senior management would cover it all up. They were the same people who kept promoting William Fallon, after all, ready to help each other climb the ladder.

He copied the database to a thumb drive and then deleted it from Sam's Dropbox in the cloud.

They assigned him to work in the Ops Center. Another bureaucratic box needed to be checked off and his managers couldn't find anyone willing to take the job. Finally, someone decided that Hadfield should do it. "What else is he doing?" He had protested, but they had promised that they would remember Hadfield's willingness to take a scut assignment. It was another lie.

They gave him the night shift, of course. Sleep deprivation arrived within days, as his fitful slumber in the daylight hours left him exhausted and the depression grew worse. He began having thoughts that death would be better than life. Caffeine pills and Red Bull kept his body going, but he had no mission, no purpose to keep his mind and soul going.

The USB drive sat on his small makeshift desk in his basement apartment. Eleven months after he had found it, he read the e-mails through again, and something moved inside him. The anger inside him spread through him like the leukemia had done in Aric. The cancer had ripped his son out of his arms a little bit every day as he watched, and he had not been able to do a single thing about it. Sam had left him because of it, and now she had been ripped away from him in an instant because an ambitious manager had been too arrogant to follow long-held rules. He had the evidence, so he had the power to make it right. He had his mission. He just had to find the path.

He copied the database onto another drive and mailed it to the Washington Post with an anonymous letter explaining what had happened. He waited three months, reading the paper religiously, hoping to see some sign that a journalist was doing something. There was nothing.

Hadfield dismissed the possibility of sending the e-mails to Wikileaks. He had no desire to play any part in Julian Assange's narcissistic campaign to damage the United States and stroke his own ego.

It all tore at his soul. Samantha Elizabeth Todd Hadfield was gone. She'd divorced him and even returned to using her maiden name, as though trying to erase every vestige of their life together to ease her own pain. The Agency bureaucracy had processed her requests, separating her affairs from his, pulling them apart in the electronic records as completely as if they'd never been married. Now the man who had led her to her likely death—a man who cared so little for anyone that he'd forgotten one of his subordinates had been trying to save a child from cancer—had been promoted, onward and upward, more responsibility, more people under his command, all vulnerable to whatever rule-breaking scheme Fallon developed to secure his next promotion.

Even the drugs were not holding the depression off now. Hadfield had a side arm at home, hidden in a lockbox. Peace was a bullet away.

He thought about bringing that same weapon to work and using it on Fallon, but he thrust that idea out of his mind. He was no killer. He wanted justice for Sam . . . or was it vengeance against Fallon? He wasn't sure anymore. Could he have both? Were they one and the same?

He felt like his mind was being torn in half, his conscience bludgeoned into insensibility by relentless anger and the monotony of his pointless life. He began to double his daily consumption of Zoloft with a dose of Xanax to top off the cocktail. Still the depression pressed in on the edges of his mind, like a madman staring into a house through a window at night.

Then a ship exploded in the dockyards of Haifa.

CIA Director's Office

"You people have been defending him from the get-go," Rhodes snapped. "I thought he was guilty from the start."

"But not for any good reason. We wanted to make sure that you weren't ignoring better suspects because you'd latched on to one person and developed tunnel vision," Barron told the younger man.

"Well, nice theory, but it's not probable cause for an arrest," Rhodes admitted. "We've had surveillance on Hadfield since he first reported the pitch. He hasn't done anything incriminating. He never went near Banshee Reeks before that dead drop."

"You're assuming that he would make the drop close to the time Salem was going to recover it," Kyra corrected him. "He could have placed the intel weeks before he ever reported that he'd been pitched."

"If that's true, there could be other dead drops already out there," Rhodes replied. "He almost never leaves home. He could be signaling the drops from his apartment over the Internet, and we never see him go anywhere."

• • •

Hadfield had driven home that morning, his mind nagging at him. In his apartment, he pulled out the small drive that held Sam's e-mails from the space behind the open rafter in the ceiling where he was keeping it. He plugged it into the laptop, ran a search against its contents—and there it was. Sam's report that talked about Amiri buying RTGs from the Russians for Iran. Another simple search, this one on the Internet, confirmed that some Russian RTGs used strontium 90 as their power source.

He knew how the Iranians had built their dirty bomb.

Did the Agency know? Hadfield went to work that night and searched the archives for any report, any hint that the CIA knew Amiri had struck a deal with the Russians. There was nothing.

Hadfield knew. Fallon surely knew, but he wouldn't tell. If he did, the director would ask where he had gotten that bit of intelligence and Fallon would not want to answer the question. So he would stay silent to protect himself while tens of thousands of Israelis fled their homes and Mossad lashed out in Israel's defense. And, eventually, Iran would build a second dirty bomb and a third . . .

That could not stand. Fallon could not be allowed to cover his sins while the Middle East plunged into yet another round of bloodletting and violence—

And then Hadfield was able to see his path as clearly as he could read a map.

It took a few days for him to find the vault where Fallon worked. He stayed late, went to that office very late, after dinner. One person was still working there, some young woman. He sat in the secretary's chair, pretending to work for a half hour until she finally logged off and checked the vault to see whether she needed to lock up or could leave that task for some other late-night denizen. Seeing him, she hesitated, not knowing the stranger sitting at the secretary's desk. "I'm new here," he told her. "They don't have a desk for me yet, so I'm hot-desking around until they find one. I'll lock up."

It was past dark. Tired and wanting to leave, she accepted the explanation that she was primed to believe. "Sure."

The door closed behind her and the vault was quiet. Then he marched through the vault, checking every cubicle and office. They were empty and he was alone.

Fallon had left papers on his desk. Hadfield assumed that a man so disdainful of every other security practice would be no better about securing his own papers, and the analyst was not disappointed. He went through the file folders on Fallon's desk and found several with cover sheets that identified them as compartmented reports. Handwritten notes confirmed that several had come from Staunton and Ramseur and others, Fallon's former subordinates who were willing to ignore security rules for their old friend and patron. Fallon shouldn't have had most of them and all of them should have been locked in the file cabinet in the corner. Hadfield photocopied their contents and replaced the originals. The copies he folded and stuffed into an envelope, then stuffed that into a manila folder and sealed the whole with tape. Then he stopped and laughed at himself. He had just followed the standard protocol for protecting classified information to be carried out of the building when he intended to give it up to a foreign service.

CIA Director's Office

"Did you get a warrant to tap his phone and his computer?" Barron asked.

"Yes," Rhodes confirmed. "But he just watches movies and posts to Facebook."

"I suggest you take another look at his Facebook posts," Kyra said.

"You think he made another dead drop?" Rhodes asked.

"Maybe. Hadfield set Salem up for arrest, but it wasn't a given that you would pick her up that night, or if you did, that you would connect the stolen intel to Fallon. So Hadfield would have needed to keep passing names to Mossad until we could triangulate enough breached compartments to suspect Fallon. And Mossad took out Amiri and Rouhani after you grabbed Salem, so either she went through the package right there at Banshee Reeks before she came out or Hadfield set up another dead drop. Maybe both."

"The package was open when we retrieved it," Rhodes admitted. "Either way, Hadfield gets indicted for treason and life in prison."

"I don't think the treason is just the means to his end. What he really wants is for you to arrest Fallon."

"If he wanted to take down Fallon, why didn't he just hand over Todd's reports to your people?" Rhodes demanded, looking at Barron. "Far easier and a lot less criminal."

"I don't know," Kyra admitted. "Feel free to ask him when he's in custody."

"As I said, I've got no probable cause to arrest him. It's a nice theory, simple and clean, but it's still a conspiracy theory of one, and breaking a conspiracy is tough business unless someone confesses. Fallon won't talk, Mossad's not going to talk, and Hadfield sure won't talk."

"He might be more willing to come clean than you think," Kyra offered.

"Why?"

"Because I don't believe he was helping Mossad for money or revenge or any of the other usual reasons people commit treason. He's trying to get justice for Sam Todd."

"What is she to him?" Barron asked.

Rhodes offered his file to the CIA director. "What is this?" Barron asked, opening the folder.

"Bank records," Rhodes explained. "Specifically, the account into which Hadfield has been paying alimony to his ex-wife, Elizabeth Hadfield. *Samantha* Elizabeth Hadfield."

He loaded the drop for an Israeli handler he didn't know yet and then went home. Once the investigation began, if the Bureau decided to watch him for some reason, they would never see him load a dead drop or set a signal.

The letter came next. He had taken much of the language from the letter that Robert Hanssen had first written to the KGB decades before and then stared at the laptop for an hour. Such enormous damage done by such a small act. It was surreal, he thought, how an act as simple as sending a letter could be a crime as serious as treason. Once he dropped it in the box, there would be no calling it back.

That would be the real moment he committed treason. He could undo it all right now if he wished. He could drive out to the sites, recover the papers, and destroy them. No one would know he had ever taken them.

And no one would ever know that William Fallon had sent Samantha Todd to Iraq to disappear forever.

```
Personal Information
Samantha Elizabeth Todd

GS and Step:          14-2
Time in Grade:        Suspended (see Current
                      Employee Data)
Entry on Duty (EOD):  14 Jan 2002
Military Service:     none


Awards and Commendations
12 Exceptional Performance Awards


Current Employee Data
Career Service:       Directorate of Operations
                      (DO)
```

```
Occupational Title:   Case Officer
Current Status:       Missing since 1 June 2017
```

Education

```
BS Business, 1999, Virginia Polytechnic
Institute
```

Kyra and Rhodes stared at the two personnel files on the desk. The one on the left was Hadfield's, the one on the right was Samantha Todd's.

"Where's the personal information?" Rhodes demanded.

"Back page," Kyra told him. She turned the pages in both files back to the front. "There." She pointed at the relevant sections in both files. They were identical.

Personal Information

```
Marital Status:       Divorced
Children:             Aric Michael (deceased)
```

Hadfield had watched his own son die, but he had at least been able to hold Aric's tiny hand the moment the toddler had gone limp. Sam's pain had been as sharp as his, but he'd always hoped that she might come back after she healed.

And then William Fallon had sent the mother of his boy off to die and covered it up.

Hadfield mailed the parcel the next day and did not bother to look back at the mailbox. It carried his letter and one of the compartmented reports.

He had entered Langley that morning by the Old Headquarters Building entrance. He had walked to the Agency seal on the floor, then stopped. He had turned left. The Agency's motto was there, chiseled in marble.

And ye shall know the truth, and the truth shall make you free—
John 8:32

Matthew Hadfield had found the truth. William Fallon would not sacrifice another person to his ambition. And all those who might have become victims of Samantha Todd Hadfield's killer would be free.

It had taken Barron's approval to release the medical and other sealed files for both Hadfield and Todd. Kyra held up a note from a doctor at the INOVA Fairfax Women and Children's Hospital.

Aric Hadfield has been diagnosed with acute myelogenous leukemia (AML). The recommended protocol will require five rounds of chemotherapy of one month each. Average life expectancy of AML patients across all age groups is 40 percent at five years post-diagnosis . . .

"So Aric, Hadfield's son . . . Samantha Todd was his *mother*," Kyra concluded.

"She must've gone back to using her maiden name after the divorce," Rhodes observed. "And he always told us her name was Elizabeth . . . never mentioned 'Samantha' once. He had to know we'd find that out eventually, and sooner rather than later." He smacked the file against the table. "Why do you people list the personal information in the *back* of the file?"

Neither officer spoke for a minute. Kyra finally broke the silence. "Maybe her boy's death explains why she went back out into the field. Then she disappeared and Hadfield had lost both of the people he loved most in short order."

"And thanks to Fallon, he could focus all of his anger on one person," Rhodes added. "But why would he wait years to target Fallon?" Rhodes asked.

"I don't know," Kyra admitted.

"We still need evidence. All of this is still just theory."

Kyra thought about that for a moment. "Maybe Hadfield will give it to us."

Fallon frowned. "What're you thinking?"

CIA Operations Center

"I need to talk to you," Kyra said, her voice low. It was bad form to speak in a normal tone here unless some disaster was in the making.

Hadfield looked up, surprised to see the woman over his shoulder. He pointed at the door. She nodded. He stood and followed her out into the very small foyer created by the wall separating the entry ramp that led up into the room.

"The director asked me to let you know about the status of our investigation into Adina Salem, just so you can relax. You'll be seeing a cable on all of this pretty soon, but he wanted you to hear it first. You remember when Special Agent Rhodes asked you about William Fallon?"

"Yeah. Still don't know who that is."

"I know," Kyra assured him. "When the Bureau grabbed Salem, one of the intel reports she was carrying gave us a lead on the Haifa bomb, but it was written by a case officer who went missing in Iraq a few years ago, near the Iranian border. Fallon was her boss, so Rhodes thought he might be our mole. That's why he was trying to see if you might have been connected with Fallon. Anyway, I went to Iran . . . Kish Island, to run down the lead and see what I could find out about our missing officer. I found her and the source of the dirty bomb. Director Barron wanted you to know that it was your lead on Salem that led us to it. He thought you might take some pride in that."

"Where did the dirty bomb come from?" Hadfield asked.

"Some missing Russian RTGs, sold to Iran by some soldiers looking to boost their pay. A lot of that's gone on since the Cold War ended."

"What about the missing officer?"

"An organized crime group from Iran took her. She died in Evin Prison a few years ago. I don't know exactly when," she said. She thought there was no harm in telling him that much. "The Iranian government buried her on the grounds of our old embassy. It was Fallon's fault, all of it. He broke rules and she paid for it."

"Is anything going to happen to him?"

"Nothing soon. The Bureau's still watching him, and if the director moves against him it could blow the investigation. Even if he could, the Department of Justice would be the agency that prosecutes him, and they'll never move on him for Todd if they think they've got an espionage indictment coming down the road. So my guess is that he gets a pass on Samantha Todd. Maybe they'll add that charge to the indictment if they arrest him for passing intel to Mossad, but even if that happens, it'll be years. You know how slow the Bureau is on counterintelligence cases."

Hadfield stared at her, no expression on his face. "Okay," he said. "Was there anything else?"

"No, except that I don't think you'll have to worry about Rhodes bothering you anymore." Hadfield answered her nothing, just nodded. "Have a good morning," Kyra said.

"Yeah, you too." He held the door open for her. Kyra walked out into the hallway and the man closed the Ops Center door behind.

Kyra walked into her office. Rhodes was already there, sitting in the guest chair. "I talked to him. I violated need-to-know six ways from Sunday, but I talked to him."

"He didn't say anything incriminating, I assume?"

"No. And that wasn't the point anyway," she replied. "Let's see what he does next."

• • •

He did nothing extraordinary for a week. Hadfield left home every night to go to headquarters and returned midmorning the following day to eat and sleep before rising after dark to clean up and leave again. He worked the weekend, took Monday and Tuesday off, and then started his week again. He watched movies on his laptop, talked to no one on his cell phone, and posted Facebook messages that the Bureau scrutinized for any hidden meanings. There were theories but nothing anyone could prove.

Hadfield emerged from his house at the usual hour. The rain was heavy, but he didn't bother with an umbrella. His car was parked on the street, leaving him to walk down the inclined driveway, which was slick with rainwater. He climbed into his car, started the engine, turned around in the cul-de-sac, and drove out to the main road.

"He's moving," Fuller said into his radio.

The analyst drove to the first major intersection and then deviated from his usual course, taking a left instead of a right. "That's different," Fuller observed.

"Stay on him," Rhodes ordered.

Hadfield drove west instead of east toward headquarters. "He's not going to work," one of the junior agents observed.

"Then where's he going?" Rhodes asked.

Kyra set her iPad down on the counter, a map on the screen. She watched the blue dot move for several minutes, then zoomed out on the map, moved it around with her finger. "He could be going to Banshee Reeks."

Rhodes stared at the map. The Woods Road that led to the nature preserve was coming up. Hadfield turned left onto it. "Fuller, go lights out." The second in command hefted his radio and began giving orders. The van turned onto the road behind the analyst, following his car at a distance.

He stopped at the entrance to the park. "Now we're talking," Fuller said. He slowed the van to a stop. The dark and the rain had cut the visibility to less than a hundred yards and they could not see their target. He almost certainly could not see them.

Then, for a moment, he appeared in the headlights of his own vehicle, walking to the gate with a tool in his hand. He vanished for less than a minute, then reappeared, climbing back into his car, which pulled forward.

"Give him some space," Rhodes ordered. "Maybe we can catch him making a drop."

Kyra shook her head. "No, this is something else," she said. "He'd have to be an idiot to use a compromised drop site twice . . . and even if he is that stupid, Mossad isn't."

"You think he's here to meet Fallon?" Fuller asked.

"Can't think of another reason." Rhodes picked up the radio. "All units, stand by." He nodded at Fuller. "Let's see what he *is* doing." The van crept forward.

They reached the entrance. The gate was open, the chain cut. Hadfield's taillights had disappeared in the dark. "We've been down this road before," Fuller noted. "It's the only way in and out, unless he wants to try Salem's run across the field. He wouldn't get far. This rain's probably turned it into a mud pit."

Rhodes nodded again and the van started into the woods. He eased the vehicle forward, barely faster than they could have run on foot.

"The drop site was just up there," Rhodes told Kyra after several minutes. He pointed at a small brick building. "That was the outbuilding we saw on the drone cam. Salem grabbed the package from somewhere behind."

"There's his car," Fuller said, slowing the vehicle. The car was barely visible in the dark, catching only the faintest light visible in the downpour.

"Is he in it?" Rhodes asked. He turned to the technician in the back.

The man stared at his monitor. "Infrared says no."

"Is he in the trees?" Rhodes moved toward the back and stared at the screen. The technician shook his head. "Where did he go?"

Kyra stared off into the dark and then down at the map on the iPad in her lap. "He's not here to meet Fallon," she told Rhodes. "That's not why he's here at all."

"Then why is he here?"

"He's going to Fallon's house." She grabbed the handle to the door, pushed it open, and began to run into the woods.

"Wait!" Rhodes yelled. He turned to Fuller. "Go!"

Fuller put the van in reverse and mashed the accelerator. The van sped backward. He cranked the wheel hard over and the vehicle turned. The rear tires slid off the asphalt road onto the grass. Fuller slammed the shifter down and pushed hard on the gas pedal again. The wheels spun on the wet foliage. The man cursed, stopped, then tried again. The van sat still.

Rhodes grabbed the radio. "All units, converge on Fallon's residence." He grabbed the technician by the jacket. "Outside, with me. Time to push."

Hadfield emerged from the woods into the subdivision and reached the sidewalk. He felt inside his waistband for the Glock 17. The magazine carried a full load of 9mm rounds, though he would only need the first one. He'd gone off the drug the day before to erode that barrier, but he still had more of it in his system than he'd expected.

He hefted the gun. There was a round in the chamber. The Glock felt very heavy in his hand, like he could hardly lift it. It should have been easy, shouldn't it? Just place the weapon to his head or in his mouth, pull the trigger, and then the world would go dark.

Someone would find him in the morning, maybe Fallon, maybe

one of his neighbors. The police would search his body and find the envelope, with the note, the marriage certificate, and the thumb drive holding Samantha Todd's archive. Then they would have to act. The Bureau would finally arrest Fallon and Hadfield would be beyond their reach.

Fallon's house was just down the hill at the corner.

Kyra ran along the edge of the woods as fast as she dared on the wet ground, her course set for the lights of the subdivision ahead. She slipped, landed on her hands, pushed herself up and kept running. The closest streetlamp was maybe a hundred yards away now.

She reached the development and found the sidewalk. She looked around, found the nearest crossroads and ran for it, pulling a small Taclight from her pocket. She read the street names, then closed her eyes and stared at the map in her mind that she'd copied into her thoughts from the iPad. Then she turned and began to run again.

Hadfield stood in front of the house. Fallon's home was enormous, the kind of mass-produced suburban mansion that Hadfield knew he could never afford now. The lights were on inside and he could see into the building. He could see the fine furniture that Fallon owned, the enormous hardwood dining table in one room, the bookshelves filled with leather volumes meant to be admired by visitors, not read by their owner.

The rage welled up inside him, as fierce as it had that first day when he had gone back to work . . . when he'd learned how completely everyone had forgotten about him and Sam and Aric.

He hefted the Glock again.

Kyra reached the next crossroads, read the names, compared them to the image in her mind, then turned left and ran, praying she was remembering the map right.

Fallon set the beer bottle on the nightstand, his fourth in the last hour, and changed the channel for the tenth time in as many seconds. Two hundred fifty channels and at least that many Blu-ray discs on the shelf and nothing appealed to him, courtesy of the alcohol and boredom. He cursed Barron's name privately again. He thought about calling Mackie Staunton or Sally Ramseur to ask what they could tell him, but decided against it. Even with four beers in his system, he could still tell a good impulse from a bad one. The FBI was probably tapping his phones—

The knock on the front door was sharp and loud. Fallon looked up from the television to the door, then to the window. He saw the rain coming down in waves through the streetlights.

He got up and walked down the winding staircase to the front door. He unlocked the deadbolt and began to open—

The door slammed inward, the wood smashing his nose, cracking the bone and knocking him to the floor. His vision blurred now, he looked up and saw only the barrel of a Glock pointed at his eyes.

Hadfield held the pistol at Fallon's face and stared at him for long seconds. His hands were steady. Two bullets then, one for Fallon, one for himself.

He closed his eyes, took a deep breath, held it, then released it. It was just a matter of will now—

"Who are you?" Fallon asked, open fear in his voice. Hadfield opened his eyes and looked down at the man.

"What do you care?"

"Who are you?" he asked again.

"You killed Sam."

Fallon recoiled. "No! I didn't mean for her—for that—"

"Shut up," Hadfield ordered, his voice quiet. "Just shut up."

Fallon's mind raced, searching for some bit of information that might save him. "Are you . . ." He couldn't remember the name. "Are you Sam's husband?"

Fallon pushed the gun forward, his finger tightening on the trigger. "I was—"

"Matt!" He turned his head until he could see the open door.

Kyra Stryker stood there, in the rain.

He stared at the woman. How could she be here? He'd only decided an hour before—

He understood. "Rhodes is with you," he said.

"He—" she started.

Rhodes appeared on the porch out of the dark, his own service weapon drawn and raised. "Put the weapon down!"

Kyra stepped between him and Hadfield. "Rhodes, don't—"

"Move!" Rhodes yelled. "Put the weapon down!" he repeated.

Kyra raised a hand toward him. "Wait," she said quietly. "Wait." She turned back to Hadfield. "We know about you and Sam . . . who she was to you. I'm so sorry about Aric."

Hadfield said nothing for a long time. Finally, he broke the silence, still looking down at Fallon. "*He* killed her."

"We know about Fallon, too," Kyra told him. "You have proof of what he did, don't you? That he sent her out on an unauthorized op?"

Hadfield saw three more men appear from the darkness behind Rhodes, weapons raised, all pointed at him through the doorway. "It doesn't matter. Nothing matters to them."

"Your life matters," she countered. "You've just been hurt in ways we don't understand. But you're a good man."

"I was. I'm not."

"You are. You have a chance to prove it to yourself, right now."

Hadfield considered that. "They won't do anything to him—"

"You can't run. If you don't put your gun down, they'll kill. It's the only way for you to live . . . and I want you to live," Kyra explained, her voice quiet.

"Do you?"

Kyra nodded. "Please."

Hadfield stared at her . . . and then she saw him begin to shake. His arm went weak and fell to his side, the Glock pointing at the floor. He held out his other hand, a small thumb drive in his palm. Kyra raised her hands, stepped forward slowly, and put her hand on the gun. He didn't resist her. She took the weapon and the memory stick from him and stepped back and offered them to Rhodes, who took them from her hand.

Hadfield's body shuddered, and then he came apart. He fell onto his knees and for the first time since his son had died, Matthew Hadfield cried. Kyra knelt down, reached out, and held the man as the long-caged agony of years came out all at once.

CHAPTER SIXTEEN

William G. Truesdale Adult Detention Center
Alexandria, Virginia

The list of terrorists and traitors that had been detained here before trial in the US District Court was a long one. The FBI preferred to keep those charged with crimes against national security close to home. Having grown up in the shadow of Jefferson's Monticello and Madison's Montpelier, Kyra usually appreciated good architecture, but the style of building here was of a disturbing kind.

It reminded her of Evin Prison, she realized. It was far smaller and much cleaner, more sterile, almost antiseptic, but it was a prison just the same. There was a common spirit between the two places, an atmosphere devoid of hope.

And yet Hadfield exuded none of that. The man sat in his wooden chair, calm, his hands folded on the table. The room was bright, the light artificial and harsh. There was no other furniture but Kyra's own chair, and no windows. She had been surprised for a moment that there was no two-way mirror, but she supposed that the video camera in the corner fulfilled that requirement these days. The sheriff's office that ran the facility would be taping their session, of course, and the Bureau would review it all later to see what it could use in court. The Department of Justice prosecutor had wanted to do the interrogation himself, but Hadfield had made a conversation with Kyra a prerequisite for his cooperation. The DOJ lawyer had resisted, even threatened him, and Hadfield had countered with a threat to go through with a trial and then grant the interview to someone else after he was settled in whatever prison the Department of Corrections chose for him. The government didn't want that. The case involved classified information and dead agents and official misbehavior, so the prosecutor had finally given in to the demand. Still, he had stuffed a list of questions into Kyra's hand on her way into the room.

She didn't bother unfolding the paper after sitting down. "Thank you for talking to me," she said.

"My lawyer said I shouldn't," Hadfield told her.

"Then why—"

"They offered me a deal," Hadfield said, cutting her off. "Cooperate and they won't put me in Supermax. I'm going to take it."

Kyra tossed that answer around in her head for a minute. "You won't have any leverage at sentencing if you tell me everything."

"They'll make sure I'm in prison until I'm dead no matter what I do. The only question is which prison I end up in," Hadfield told her. He shrugged. "The Agency will want to interview me eventually anyway . . . one of those counterintelligence studies to see what they could've done to prevent me from committing treason."

"So what could they have done?" Kyra asked.

Hadfield looked down at the table. He smiled, a dark grin that Kyra found morose. "Tried to save Sam, for starters. They don't care about right and wrong up there on the Seventh Floor," he said.

"They didn't know that the man leading the search had a conflict of interest in her being found. There are good people up there, on the Seventh Floor. I know several of them. But we have our share of sociopaths, the same as every other agency." She stared at him. "You're not one of them. You're a good man."

"You don't have kids."

"No."

"Are you religious?" he asked.

"Episcopalian, in theory."

He sighed. "Sitting in that hospital, month after month . . . we saw other people's kids die. Little girls and boys eaten up by cancer. But we convinced ourselves that it wasn't going to happen to our boy. He was special, he was going to make it. Then he didn't. Watching your child die like that . . . it cleans up your priorities. You know what really matters? Life. That's it. Every single person on this planet is alive, and that makes them infinitely valuable, and when they're dead, we can't get them back." The man finally looked up. "You saw my personnel file."

Kyra nodded. "I did."

"Do you know how many times anyone called me after Aric went into the hospital, to ask how he was doing? How I was doing or my family? Not once. I never heard from anyone at the Agency. My first day back, I walked into my chief's office. You know what he said? 'Oh, where have you been?'" Hadfield looked up at the camera in the corner, silent, running the memories through his mind. "They completely forgot about me . . . about Sam and our son. Sam tried to deal with all of it by cutting me out of her life and disappearing back onto the street. Me? They stuck me in a storage closet, like they didn't want to see me so they wouldn't have to be reminded of how they dropped us when Aric got sick."

Kyra kept her face still, but she could taste the disgust rising in her chest. Hadfield had already served a prison sentence of a kind.

"So I had time on my hands to think in there." He was talking to the wall now. "They don't care about us . . . managers, any of 'em, all the way up to the Seventh Floor. They don't care about us or the people in the field or our assets. They don't even care about defending the country really. Doesn't matter if they don't get the job done, as long as they don't screw something up. They just care about protecting their little empires so they can move up to take over another one that's a little bigger than the last one. You have to leave for a while because your kid gets cancer, and they just forget about you because you're not doing anything to make them look good. You get sent on some mission and go missing, well, they'll just cover that up, never mind actually trying to save you." Hadfield shifted in his chair and finally looked at Kyra again.

Kyra stared at him, amazed, her mind trying to sort through the implications of his admission. "You never cared about Israel."

"I care the same as everyone else," Hadfield said. "But I would've talked to some other foreign intel agency if it would've done the job."

"That's cold."

"I know," the man said, surprising Kyra. "I didn't see another way. Maybe it was the wrong thing for the right reason, but the Agency wasn't going to do the right thing for the right reason. Tell me if you think I'm wrong."

She wasn't sure that he was. Kyra let the silence settle for almost a minute. "You knew the Bureau was going to find you eventually," she protested.

"Yeah, probably," he agreed. "But you know what kept going through my mind? That, at some point, Sam must've realized she wasn't going to see home again. She wasn't going to see her family again. Do you know what that feels like, when you finally give up hope?"

"No," Kyra admitted.

Hadfield nodded, approving of her honest answer. "I do. I got a taste of it when the doctors told me Aric was going to die. They knew a week before it happened." Hadfield shook his head. "But Sam? One person, unique in all the universe, and they let her die, all alone. I sat there wondering how long she held on before she gave up hope." He looked down. "Someone had to make it right."

Kyra considered that for a moment, pushed herself away from the table, and stood up. "I'll be in the courtroom tomorrow, if you want me there."

"That would be very nice, thank you," Hadfield said. "Would you tell Sam's family what happened to her?"

"That decision hasn't been made, but I think they will be told,"

Kyra offered. "I know Director Barron. He's a good man. I think he'll approve it."

"Will you do something for me?"

"If I can."

"Tell Sam's family what I did for her."

"I don't know if I can do that," Kyra replied.

"Whatever details you can share," Hadfield pleaded. "Let them know that I loved her."

Kyra pressed her lips together and considered the request. "I'll find a way," she promised.

Mossad Headquarters
Tel Aviv, Israel

"You have done our country the highest service," Ronen announced. Salem and her team stood in his office at formal attention. "Two of your team gave their lives. Two others are in the hospital and do not stand with you today. We will honor them all very soon. But all of Israel thanks you."

"Thank you, sir," the senior *Ayin* replied.

"Have you anything to ask me?" Ronen offered. "In this life, we often must act on orders without knowing why. I think you have earned the right now to ask for the reasons behind your mission."

No one spoke for several seconds. Finally, the *Ayin* broke the silence. "We do not need to ask that."

"Very good," Ronen replied. "Our thanks to you all. I ask you all to join me at the hospital tomorrow when I go to meet with your injured teammates."

"We will be there," the *Ayin* confirmed.

Ronen nodded and the team began to file out of the room. "Salem, a moment," he said.

She stopped and waited for the rest of her teammates to leave the room. "Sir," she said.

"What do you think of this team?"

She waited a moment to answer. "I have not been with them long enough to speak with authority, sir . . . but I will be very surprised if there is a better unit."

"That is a good answer," Ronen told her. "Loyalty and humility are both traits we value here. Would you like to stay with that unit?"

"If they will have me," Salem agreed.

"I will talk to them tomorrow."

"Sir, about your offer earlier . . . may I ask a question?"

"Yes," Ronen assured the woman.

"The explosion at Qom that buried the RTGs . . . was that one of our teams?"

"Teams? No. It was one man," Ronen told her.

"I was not aware that we had any officers acting alone in Iran," Salem said, confused.

Ronen smiled. "He was someone who stayed behind there, a long time ago. So long that I had thought he had forgotten us."

"If he ever wants to come home, I would like to volunteer for the operation to bring him out," Salem offered. "It would be a privilege to perform that service for such a man."

Ronen nodded. "He will never ask that, I am sure. But we will have need of other services from you, Salem."

"At your convenience, *ramsad*," Salem said.

Appomattox, Virginia

It had taken the convoy over three hours to drive this far from Langley. The director's SUV, armored and flanked by two others filled with security officers carrying heavy arms, rolled west on Route 360, having left Richmond more than an hour before. Kyra knew they were following the path that Robert E. Lee and his Army of Northern Virginia had marched during their last week before Grant had finally caught them. They had passed Five Forks, then Burkeville, Saylor's Creek, High Bridge, and Farmville, all sites Kyra had read about many times in the Civil War books that filled the bookshelves in her apartment up north, but she had never come to see them. She would have to correct that now. History was not meant to stay only on the printed page.

The surrender site was only a few miles ahead, a lonely little village, on the way to nowhere. This had been tobacco country once, farms worked by slaves who outnumbered their masters. The slavery was long gone, but change still came slowly to this part of Virginia. Most of the countryside was filled with cornfields, dead stalks marking the harvest just finished, and enormous pine forests that looked almost the same as when General Lee and his troops, clad in butternut rags and dying of exhaustion and lack of food, had passed through.

Kyra could imagine why Samantha Todd's mother had settled here after her daughter had gone missing. The CIA officer had grown up less than thirty miles away and she knew what the people were like here. They would be friendly, helpful when Sarah Todd needed help, but no one would pry into her life. When someone finally did figure out who she was, the locals would give her a respectful distance, never asking her to talk about what happened more than she wanted. When she did finally open up, she would encounter nothing but Southern compassion, endless hospitality, and more people sharing her disgust for Washington than she could have imagined. The opinion that the locals held of the federal government hadn't improved much since Lee's surrender.

Kyra smiled. She wondered how many Yankee tourists even noticed that the cannons on display in front of the local courthouses in Virginia still always pointed north.

Kathy and Jon were sitting in the seat behind her, holding hands, saying nothing. Jon had always been comfortable keeping company only with his thoughts, which trait he seemed to have passed to his wife, who was looking out the windows at the farms and small businesses along the roadside.

Barron was sitting next to Kyra in the seat behind the driver. He would be the Agency director for a few weeks longer, and she wondered who would replace him. *Not William Fallon*, she thought. Matthew Hadfield was a traitor, but he had done his Agency a service. *He got what he wanted*, she thought. It just cost him what little he had left.

"You look disturbed," Barron said, and she turned toward him. She had thought he was reviewing papers. Lost in her thoughts, she hadn't noticed him put them away.

"Thinking about Matt Hadfield," Kyra said.

"What about him?"

"He was a traitor, but he wasn't wrong." Kyra looked over at the man. "When we recruit foreign assets, we're always hoping we get that one who does it because he sees his government is corrupt or dangerous and wants to fix it. It hurts when we're the corrupt ones."

Barron nodded. "Yeah, it does. You read the history of the Agency and heaven knows some of our people have gone off the reservation over the years. And it'll happen again."

"How do we stop it?"

"You can't," Kathy said. Kyra turned toward the backseat. "People forget that honor is earned by the way we do things as much as by the things we try to do. You remember Edward Snowden?"

"Yes."

"When I was the director, a reporter asked me one time whether I considered Snowden a patriot or a traitor. Of course, she expected me to say that he was a traitor. So she was surprised when I told her that he could be both."

Kyra furrowed her brow. "How is that possible?"

"Assuming that Snowden was telling the truth about his motives, his goal of exposing systems that were violating civil liberties wasn't a bad one. The intelligence community has a responsibility to obey the law. So in that sense, he was a patriot. He saw something wrong and he thought someone should act," Kathy said. "Where he went wrong was in how he chose to act. He grabbed a mountain of classified information, fled the country, and began spewing it across the Internet. He decided that his cause was just, so anything he did to achieve it was also just. He decided the ends justified the means. He ended up endangering a lot of people and compromising a lot of programs that weren't violating anyone's liberties." Kathy sighed. "So he's a traitor. Maybe his goal was righteous, but his actions in pursuit of it did an astonishing amount of damage. Was the damage he caused worth reaching his goal? That's the question, and that's why he needs to come home and stand trial. He can argue yes, we can argue no, and let a judge decide who's right."

Barron nodded. "Hadfield was in the same position. The Agency is better off without people like Fallon, but Hadfield helped Mossad wage a covert war on Iran. They killed Iranian scientists, terrorized an ally, murdered a man who was helping the Brits keep an eye on Iran's nuclear program—"

"I think Gavi Ronen would say that Israel is better off for it," Jon observed.

"It might be," Kathy admitted. "But Hadfield's loyalty isn't supposed to be to Israel. It's supposed to be to the United States. So the only time he gets to decide whether the US should be helping Mossad is when he votes in November. If he doesn't like that, he's free to give up his citizenship and emigrate."

"Don't you think what he did is partly the Agency's fault?" Kyra asked. "The way his managers treated him after his son died? I can't blame him for deciding that no one cared, and once he reached that conclusion, it wasn't much of a jump for him to decide that the Agency had left Sam Todd to rot on purpose. I can't help but think that he wouldn't have followed that path if someone had tried to connect with him after his son died."

"I think that's probably right," Barron agreed. "No question, a lot of people failed him. No doubt, he needed some PTSD counseling that he didn't get, but in the end, he took the same oath everyone else did, and that oath doesn't make exceptions for when our leaders treat us badly or even when we have emotional problems. We're all responsible for our own decisions, no matter what happens to us personally. If we think we've come to a place where we can't keep the oath, it's our duty to walk away. Hadfield didn't. The rest of his story might mean he deserves a lighter sentence than someone who committed treason for money, and he'll get counseling and meds in prison. But in the end, he made the wrong choice and he needs to answer for it."

The SUV turned off the main road onto a winding driveway, unpaved, the solid rubber tires kicking up loose rocks. Through the trees, Kyra could see a house, colonial design, remarkably modern for this rural county. "And now," Barron said, "we get to answer to Mrs. Todd." He turned to the other passengers in the vehicle. "Thanks for coming."

"Thank you for asking me to come," Kathy told her successor. "I wish we'd been able to do this years ago."

"It wouldn't be fair to do it without you," Barron replied.

Sarah Todd stepped out of the front door onto her porch and stood watching the convoy of black vehicles rumble down her driveway. She was an old woman, her hair entirely white now, looking far older than the woman Kyra had seen in the newspaper. Standing behind her were two others, a man and a woman, both of them her children.

"They have to know why we're here," Kyra said.

Barron nodded. "Yeah. But there's still something about having someone come and deliver the news in person. It's terrible and won-derful at the same time. It hurts to let go."

"This isn't the first time you've done this," Kyra realized. She looked back at Jon's wife. Kathy said nothing, but the look on her face was one of complete understanding. *Not her first time either.*

"No, it's not," Barron confirmed. "Probably my last."

The cars rolled to a stop. Barron didn't wait for the security escort to open his door. He pushed his way out, then helped Kathy from the SUV. Jon followed, resting his weight on his cane as he found his footing. Kathy took his hand in hers and they began to walk toward the porch as Kyra dismounted and followed behind them.

"Mrs. Sarah Todd?" Barron asked.

"Yes."

"My name is Clark Barron. I'm the director of the Central Intelligence Agency. This is Kathryn Cooke, my predecessor."

"I know who you are, Mr. Barron. And we've met, haven't we, Miss Cooke?"

"Yes, we have," Kathy agreed.

"You're here to talk to me about Samantha," the old woman said. It wasn't a question.

"Yes, ma'am, we are." Barron gestured toward the analysts in the group. "This is Jonathan Burke and Kyra Stryker, two of our officers. They took on your daughter's case recently and they found out what happened to her."

Jon nodded at Kyra, who stepped toward the woman on the porch. "Ma'am, I—"

"Is my girl alive, Miss Stryker?"

Kyra felt her eyes begin to well up.

Sarah Todd saw it and knew the answer. Tears slid down her cheeks. "Where is she?"

"I can't tell you where she is or how she died, Mrs. Todd. All of those details are still classified. I would tell you if I could," Kyra said, wiping away her own tears. "But I can tell you that there's someone watching over her and he's promised to make sure she comes home, eventually."

"And you trust this man?"

"I believe I do, yes."

"Can you tell me how you found her?" Mrs. Todd asked.

Kyra looked over to Barron, who nodded at her. They'd gone over it all in his office back at Langley before they left. "That's also classified, but . . . someone committed treason to make sure your daughter wouldn't be forgotten," Kyra told her. "I can't tell you who or what they did, but I can tell you that someone cared about Sam. He never gave up on her."

"It was Matt, wasn't it? Matt always loved her. He would've done anything for Sam." Sarah Todd wiped her face off with her sleeve, then looked up and stared past the group at cars passing behind them on the highway. "Please come in, Miss Stryker. Tell me what you can."

Kyra looked back at the group behind her. Barron nodded at her to go. Kathy and Jon stood behind him, holding hands. Jon was smiling at her, a rare thing for him. Kathy was fighting not to cry.

Kyra turned back and walked up the steps into the old house.

ACKNOWLEDGMENTS

I must always begin by giving thanks to my dear wife, without whose unfailing patience and support I could not begin to write the first page; who worked on the completed and cleared draft as hard as any professional editor; and who endured with me the many hard years that were the foundation of much of this story. Janna, I love you more than any written words could tell.

Yet again, I must express my gratitude to the staff of the CIA Publications Review Board (PRB) and others who reviewed the manuscript as required. This one was, by far, the most difficult and time consuming of all my books to get through the clearance process for reasons that cannot be stated here. The PRB staff—you know who you are—were professional to a fault, and I appreciate their willingness to suggest ways I could maintain the integrity of the story as far as was possible while protecting national interests.

Thanks to Jason Yarn, my literary agent, for lifting many of the business burdens off my back. We've managed to get four books out now. I hope we get to publish many more together. Also, my gratitude to Lauren Spiegel, my editor; Jessie Chasan-Taber (I hope you had a happy and soft landing); Rebecca Strobel; Shida Carr; and the many others at Simon & Schuster who work so hard to make sure that every book is as good as possible and stronger than the last.

I must also give thanks to Trina Cummings, my young volunteer editor who saved me from a number of embarrassing errors and grammatical gaffes. I'm grateful for your hard work. Are you up for another one?

Finally, to the doctors and, most especially, the nurses of INOVA Fairfax Children's Hospital and Children's National Hospital in Washington, DC, and the Ronald McDonald House of Fairfax, Virginia. For two years, you gave our family hope and comfort when both were in very short supply, and virtually the only happy memories we have from that time all include you. You have our eternal gratitude and love.